ONE KISS LED TO ANOTHER

ONE KISS LED TO ANOTHER

Harris Dulany

HarperCollins*Publishers*

HarperCollins books may be purchased for educational, business, or sales promotional use. For information, please write: Special Markets Department, HarperCollins Publishers, Inc., 10 East 53rd Street, New York, NY 10022.

FIRST EDITION

Designed by George J. McKeon

Library of Congress Cataloging-in-Publication Data
Dulany, Harris, 1940–
    One kiss led to another / Harris Dulany. — 1st ed.
      p. cm.
    ISBN 0-06-017737-3
    1. Private investigators—New Jersey—Fiction. I. Title.
PS3554.U42054   1994
813'.54—dc20   93-41419

94 95 96 97 98 ❖/RRD 10 9 8 7 6 5 4 3 2 1

In loving memory of Betty Leeds,

who enjoyed a good mystery

The author wishes to thank Ed Breslin for his help and encouragement, and Deputy Inspector Joseph Dunne of the New York City Police Department and Dr. David S. Cohen, attending physician in neurosurgery at Kings County Hospital in Brooklyn, for technical advice.

1

Somehow, you'd think I'd enjoy this, interviewing young whores. Actually, that's redundant—young whores. There's no such thing as an old whore—only old ex-whores.

Anyway, I was interviewing whores on Pacific Avenue in Atlantic City. It was 10:30 on a Thursday night, and Pacific was just starting to hum, quickening its pace as the business night began.

If you've ever been to Atlantic City you've been on Pacific Avenue. It's the narrow street that parallels the Boardwalk, the congested one you drive along dodging jitney buses and tourists wondering where to park and what casino to start in first. You get a nice look at the backs of some of the casinos and their parking garages and at the beginning of the dinginess that is Atlantic City away from the glitter of the casinos.

I'm six-foot-two, clean-shaven and have sandy brown hair with a little gray at the temple that I pretend will go away. Because of these looks the whores think I'm a vice cop and start out guarded and unfriendly. They come around after I convince them I'm not a cop, but then swing right into annoyance when they figure out I'm not a customer either. It's a tough job being a whore. In addition to the recreations and humiliations you get hired to perform, you have to be on the lookout for vice cops and psychos, cheapskates and brutes. In many ways it's like being a detective.

It was a nice night for a stroll. The early May weather was almost summerlike with a westerly breeze bringing in the left-over warm air from the South Jersey farmlands. Now and then

I could hear the surf thud against the pilings under the Boardwalk a block to the East.

The whores weren't too hard to spot. They wore the tightest, shortest skirts, the lowest tops and the most face paint. Some strolled; others stood on corners and waved at the traffic on Pacific.

I had already talked to two of them I didn't know, both visiting talent from Washington. A serial killer was slicing up prostitutes in the D.C. area, so most of the whores from our nation's capital were on the road in cities along the Bos-Wash Corridor.

The two I'd talked to hadn't been any help in my search for Bonnie Arnold. I was carrying a high school graduation picture her grandfather had express mailed to me, but I was fairly sure the freckle-faced cheerleader with wiry blonde hair had changed her appearance if, in fact, she was turning tricks on Pacific Avenue.

I was standing on the corner of Missouri Avenue waiting for the light to change and watching the stretch limos pull into the Caesar's garage when I spotted a local whore named Phyllis coming toward me. On the street she called herself Charmaine. When she spotted me she had just parted a crowd of college boys on the sidewalk like they were the Red Sea. They were blushing and trying to recover by howling after her and pushing each other.

"Hello, Connie," she said. "You looking for a party?"

That's my name. Connie. Short for Cornelius. Cornelius Leeds. I prefer Con. But I get Connie most of the time. Con Leeds gets said so quickly it doesn't sound like a whole name to people.

You could see why she left the college boys gasping for air. She was wearing a simple black cocktail dress that gave her the appearance of elegance. A single strand of phony pearls completed the impression. But it stopped there. The rest was the attention-getter.

The dress was in two pieces exposing a good foot of midriff. The skirt, a tight sheath, wasn't much more than a foot long from waist to hem. After that it was all leg, tan and bare and ready for action and elongated by a pair of four-inch stiletto heels. A short halter top barely contained her.

The outfit was completed by a pure white wig, thousands of lacquered strands of hair wandering around above her head like frozen snakes. With huge red pouty lips and wide circles of purple eye shadow she was pure street theater.

She frowned until I flashed a smile and asked: "How's the kid, Phyllis?"

"Just fine, Connie," she smiled back.

Phyllis lived in a two-bedroom rancher on four acres in Galloway Township where she owned a mare, a gelding and a small barn. I'd been there once. To a barbecue. As far as her neighbors knew she worked in the gaming industry, which she certainly did. At home, she had mousy brown hair that she kept short and wore Levis and work shirts all the time, even to church.

"Have you ever seen this one?" I asked, hauling Bonnie Arnold's picture out of my jacket pocket.

She took the picture from me and studied it carefully. Horns honked, and men hooted at her from passing cars.

"I don't think so," she said. "But they change when they go on the street."

"I know," I said, letting my eyes travel sarcastically up and down the length of her.

She swung her small purse at my arm.

"Stop it," she hissed shyly.

We were standing in front of the driveway entrance to Trump Plaza. There were two hansom cabs in there attached to concrete statues of horses. The original plan called for real horse-drawn cabs but there was nowhere to go except into the slums in the Inlet. Concrete horses don't make a mess in the street either.

"She had a slight lisp and smoked a lot of pot the last time her relatives saw her," I said. "Short, well-built, so I'm told. I never had a look at anything but this picture."

"I'm sorry I can't help you, Connie. Why don't you ask the Baron?" The Baron was a pimp; gold teeth, long white car, the whole nine yards. "I heard he had two new girls last week. From Pennsylvania. They were working the lounges."

"I didn't think I'd have to go all the way on this one," I

said. "It was a nice night for a walk. Four or five discreet inquiries. You girls always know about the competition. Especially if it's new and young."

"Don't be cruel."

"She's either out there or she's not. Besides, I don't want to owe the son-of-a-bitch a favor."

"I'm sorry I can't help, Connie."

I handed her my business card with my home number written on it. "Call me if you hear anything. Or if you start giving it away."

"I never give it away, honey, but for a hundred bucks, I'll do anything you want."

"If I give you a hundred bucks, will you paint my house?"

She smiled tiredly. The joke was almost as old as her profession.

"If she's here, the Baron will know about it." She turned and sashayed off, parting a crowd of tourist couples who already had sunburns even though it was only May.

I crossed the street and went into Trump Plaza. I'm not a gambler. I love Atlantic City but casinos give me a headache. Too busy. The lights and decor make me jumpy. But you don't find pimps with gold teeth in the Irish gin mills on Atlantic Avenue.

The lounge was almost empty. I took a seat at the bar. The bartender ignored me while he flirted with one of the floor waitresses who was filling her tray with complimentary drinks for the table players.

The bartender's name was Eddie Mac-something. Local kid, liked to talk sports. I hadn't been in here in a couple of months, but when he recognized me he brought the tequila bottle with him.

I put my hand over the shot glass he placed on the bar.

"Just a short beer, Eddie. I'm working."

"It's on me, Con. I need to ask you something."

I took my hand away. He poured the tequila. I drank it and waved away the dish of limes he offered. He put a small complimentary-sized glass of draft beer in front of me, the kind they bring around to the slot players. I drank it. He put another one in front of me. I hauled out Bonnie's picture and put it on the bar.

"Ever see her?" I asked.

"Don't think so. But they hardly ever look like their high school yearbook picture when they come in here."

"You mean you don't look like you did at Atlantic City High?"

"Holy Spirit," he corrected.

"Football 1,2,3,4. Baseball 1,2,3,Captain 4," I quoted from an imaginary yearbook.

"Bad knees 5," he continued. "U.S. Navy 6,7,8. Wife, kids, bills 9,10,11 etc."

"You never had it so good," I said, draining the second beer. He drew a third. I put a twenty on the bar but he didn't even look at it.

"I think my wife's screwing around when I'm on nights," he said. "Can you check it out?"

"I don't do matrimonials unless I'm starving," I said. "Especially not for friends."

"Can you recommend somebody?"

"Eddie, do yourself a favor. Call in sick some night and hide in the bushes. Save yourself two or three bills."

"Winston Barbay has some new girls."

"Is that the Baron?"

"Same guy. Gold teeth, island accent."

"I heard about those girls. Will he be in here tonight?"

"Most definitely. Or at least one of his girls will be."

I put Bonnie's picture away and produced another business card with my home number.

"You think you could get him to call me?" I stood up without making a move to pick up the twenty. Grandfather Arnold's expense money.

"Sure, he'll call," Eddie said. The waitress was coming back, and he made the twenty disappear before she got there. You don't get anything for nothing in Atlantic City.

On my way out I bought ten silver dollars and put them in the slots one at a time. The machines were in endless flashing rows and about half of them were in use. Most of the bus-tour types had gone home, and the nighttime players were still arriving. Fire bells went off here and there for the big winners. A fat woman worked two machines next to me and grunted each time she pulled down a lever. I could hear a black man cursing behind me.

I won three dollars but put them back in too. The whole thing took less than five minutes. The slot machine room was so big it took me several minutes just to walk across it to the exit.

I was beginning to feel slimy. I found my car on Atlantic Avenue and started for the Expressway, but I couldn't remember whether I had any beer at home so I took the White Horse Pike off the island and bought six Corona long-necks near Route 9 in Absecon. The night was dark and starry, clear with no moon yet. There was still a light on in a house here and there. It was chilly, but I left the windows down so I could smell the pines after Egg Harbor City. The north end of Atlantic County, the end that pushes into the Pine Barrens, is another world. Coming into the Pines is like going up a mountain. The air is clear and cool. The tall pitch pines loom in the headlights, solid and spacious. From the bridge over Egg Harbor Lake I could see a mist on the black surface of the water.

The dog banged around the screen door with its tail when I got home. I live in a two-bedroom cottage on the Mullica River that I bought two years ago when I retired after working as a cop in New York City for twenty years. I opened a Corona and fed the dog. When she was finished eating we sat outside and watched the river while the moon came up. I have a dock and a twenty-two-foot Sea Ray Pachanga with a 454-cubic-inch Magnum engine. It'll do seventy miles an hour and could get me to Atlantic City in a half hour. If I wanted to go. Across the river is Wharton State Forest. Ninety-six thousand acres of it. There are lots of cedars in with the pines over there.

A fish jumped and landed flat on the water. I couldn't see it but the ripples reached me in a short while. The tide was running in. A duck squawked at some intrusion in the darkness. The dog barked one short bark, and I hissed her quiet. I could hear the faint whine of tires from a solitary car on County Route 542 in the forest across the river. And then it was quiet. The quiet of the pines. You could only sense the river moving. The day's heat was rising into the clear dry air. I drained the beer and felt a chill, so I went inside. It was cold enough to build a fire or turn on the furnace, but I didn't do either. The sheets were cold on my bare legs but I was out as soon as I pulled the comforter up over my shoulders.

The windows were gray when the phone dragged me up out of the depths of my sleep. I fought to go back but it kept ringing.

No one answered right away when I picked it up. The birds were making a racket in the dark trees outside. I said hello three times and was reaching for the line plug when a deep voice said: "Leeds?"

"Yeah. Who's this? Baron?"

"The girls come home and say you're on the Avenue asking about a woman named Arnold."

"Bonnie Arnold," I said. "She's seventeen. She's from New York. Private-school type. Pot smoker."

The room was getting lighter.

"Is she in trouble, man?"

"Does she work for you?" I was supposed to ask the questions.

"No."

"Do you know her?"

"I don't want to talk on the phone, you dig? Can you meet me?"

"When?"

"Now. Half an hour."

"I don't want to drive back to the Island for something I can get tomorrow."

"It is tomorrow, Leeder-Man. You can buy me breakfast."

"It can wait." I didn't know whether to call him Baron or Barbay or Winston. Although we weren't acquainted, we had been operating on each other's fringes for some time. Atlantic City is just a small town with a big electric bill. I only wanted to crawl back into my warm bed. Bonnie was one of a million teenage runaways. She could wait until morning. After you found them they didn't want to go home anyway. And as far as I could tell, Bonnie's relatives didn't even want her back.

"Where are you?" he asked.

"Cedar Bank."

"Where the fuck is that?"

"Near Egg Harbor."

"But that's not far. I used to work some girls out of a motel out there on the Black Horse Pike."

"That's Egg Harbor Township. I'm near Egg Harbor City."

"Where the fuck is that?"

"On the White Horse Pike. Near Hammonton."

"Where the fuck is that?"

"Halfway between Atlantic City and Philadelphia."

"I always wondered what was out there."

"I'll give you a tour some day."

"You better come. She might be in some trouble."

He named a diner in Pleasantville, and while I was pulling on my pants, I decided to put Grandfather Arnold's charges into overtime. I also strapped a little .25 semiautomatic on my ankle since it was the wee hours of the morning, and I didn't know much about Mr. Barbay.

It was almost full daylight, but the sun hadn't topped the horizon when I pulled into a diner parking lot that was filled with vehicles, half of them pick-up trucks. There were a few bloodshot night types left inside but it was mostly flannel shirts eating fried meat and eggs before work. The Baron was alone, tucked into a corner booth sipping a cup of tea. If I didn't know better, I'd say he looked fresh enough to be just starting his day. Except that most people don't start their day in black leather pants and red velour with enough gold chains to back a small business.

"Hello, Leeds," he said. "Nice of you to come." He had my business card beside his cup for reference.

"Con is fine," I said.

"Okay, Connie. Connie the curious dick. Curiosity killed the cat, you know, Connie."

"And satisfaction brought him back."

I ordered eggs and bacon and drank a cup of coffee before they arrived. He had half a cantaloupe and another cup of tea.

"You have a local name," he said at one point, fingering

the card. "How come I'm just starting to notice you?" His Jamaican accent was fading fast.

"I've only been here two years," I said. "My father grew up here."

"There's Leedses from Leeds Point to Leedsville. The mayor of Atlantic City used to be a Leeds. Even the Jersey Devil was named Leeds."

"I was raised in Brooklyn."

"I heard that you were a cop there." It was a statement of fact rather than a question.

"You heard right."

"I'm a local boy too. I grew up in the Inlet."

"I thought you were Jamaican."

"It's an impression I like to give that's good for business."

He smiled and I worked on my eggs in silence. The sun had come up and was warming the side of my face through the windows.

"You haven't been around long but you have a good reputation," he said. "People say you know how the world works. I wanted to see who was looking for Bonnie."

"Do you know where she is?"

"No, but I'm going to trust you with some information."

What an honor. A pimp trusts me. I nodded, mopped my plate with a piece of toast and waited. Questions make a guy like the Baron nervous. I wasn't a cop anymore and I didn't have his yellow sheet in front of me, but I knew for certain he'd done big time somewhere. To a con like him information was hard-earned currency. To be spent wisely.

"I know what you're thinking," he said, smiling a wise-crack smile. "You're sure I got that little girl stashed somewhere and that I'm peddling her ass to the high-rollers at a grand a night, no rough stuff please. And that at best I'm going to give you a price to take back to your client, her rich father—"

"Grandfather."

"Her rich grandfather or, at worst, try to discourage your search with some random violence."

"Something like that," I said.

If he had backup with him, I couldn't spot it. The waitress came to the table and topped up my coffee. He waited until she left and then leaned forward and put his elbows on the table to show me he was getting to the important part.

"But it's not like that. She doesn't work for me. She's a personal friend."

Yeah, right, I thought. And I'm Herbert Hoover. It was time for me to ask a question. He had paused to let me know that.

"How's that?" I put to him. Astute and articulate. Sometimes I amaze myself.

"I'm a drug addict."

No shit.

"Recovering drug addict and alcoholic. I haven't had a drink or a drug in eight years. She started coming to our meetings back in February. I got to know her pretty good."

"Meetings?" I asked. "AA?"

"NA. Narcotics. She was coming up on her ninety days clean. Doing real good. One of my girls is her sponsor. But nobody's seen her or heard from her in a week."

"Your girls are addicts too?"

"Recovering addicts. Two of them. The other three don't use drugs or have a problem with alcohol."

Healthy New-Age hookers. They probably all strapped on portable CD players in the morning and jogged on the Boardwalk in pastel spandex.

"She had a boy with her when she first started coming around. Had a scruffy red beard. I forget his name."

"Billy."

"That's him. But he kept using, so she moved out on him."

The Baron's story tied in with my information. Bonnie Arnold had left New York with her boyfriend, Billy Cameron, in January. Billy had returned with his tail between his legs three weeks ago and been shipped to a drug rehab near his old summer camp in the Midwest. Father Cameron had provided Grandfather Arnold with the Atlantic City lead. Grandfather Arnold had called a tennis partner who was a retired deputy police commissioner who had called my old precinct captain who gave him my name for private work in the Atlantic City area. I'm New Jersey–licensed but I'm not in the phone book.

They gave me the address of a furnished apartment in the Chelsea Heights section but she was gone when I checked it out the day before.

The Baron said: "But something's wrong. She's mixed up in I don't know what." He was moving it now so I just sat back and let him rattle. "She took up with this guy in the program. And she changed. She wasn't drugging but she was under his spell, you dig? I make a nice living pleasing women and helping them with the difficult choices of life."

"Manipulating them."

"Nasty word." His look feigned disapproval, almost a smirk. "Anyway, I know a spell when I see one. Pretty soon she quit her waitress job and stopped coming around to meetings. Nobody seen him these days either."

"You said one of your girls was her teacher."

"Sponsor. Don't worry about her. I'm telling you everything she knows."

Translation: I won't let you talk to her. Don't try.

He looked at me levelly and continued: "Bonnie cleaned out of her room three days ago. No forwarding address or phone number."

"I was there yesterday. What do you know about the guy?"

"Italian stallion. Name of Roland Starza. Good-looking. Young. Drives a bus. Mola Land Cruises. Brings the old folks down from New York City with their social security checks."

"You do good work," I said. I meant it. "There shouldn't be too many Rolands at Mola Land Cruises. I owe you one."

"You bring Bonnie back so we can help her stay straight, you don't owe me nothing. But, hey, Connie-Man. Be careful, honey. Cat's connected." He bent his nose to one side with his index finger.

"Aren't you connected?" I asked. "You work hookers in Atlantic City and live to tell about it."

"Shit," he said, making two syllables out of the word. "Do

I look like a motherfucking Italian to you? They just sell me the license. Same as the state do for the casinos."

"Expensive license," I said, motioning to the waitress for our check.

"It keeps me moving," he said, smiling large enough to show a lot of gold.

2

Because I had worked late into the evening and then been roused before dawn, I had spent most of the drive to the diner promising myself I would return to my river cottage for some delicious snoozing and then sneak into work early in the afternoon. I had an insurance fraud case that needed some phone work, and I wanted to narrow the trail of Roland, the bus driver, with some calls to New York. But after breakfast with the Baron and three cups of coffee, I dutifully pointed the car down the Pike toward Absecon Island.

The day was clear and spring warm. The rush-hour traffic headed toward Atlantic City into a low, blinding sun that reduced speeds. I flapped my sun visors down and snapped on the radio into the whistling finale of "Rockin' Robin."

The DJ cut in over the diminishing tweets: "The greatest oldies of all time. Oldies Twelve-ten. WOGL. Philadelphia."

The next song was an up-tempo mannered version of "Let the Good Times Roll." I waited for a moment, but it was too peppy and nervous. I liked the original version, slow and insinuating and, like a lot of blues songs, about making love. This one—perhaps an attempt at an aerobic version—was just neurotic.

I flipped to WCBS all-news in New York and learned that two lanes of the in-bound G.W. Bridge were blocked by a jack-knifed tractor-trailer, but that information didn't seem useful and there was too much buzzy static, so I punched in the FM, found WSLT, one-oh-six-point-three in Ocean City, and was suddenly in the middle of a clear, sweet Mozart symphony. The two in-bound lanes of the Black Horse Pike weren't blocked by anything, and we moved smoothly into the sun's glare.

The casino-hotels and condo towers appeared in a line on the horizon ahead of me like chunky Godzillas marching ashore to attack the marshland between me and the island. A billboard advertised Las Vegas by the Sea—Tropworld. Both sides of the Pike were lined with car dealerships and cheap motels, including the Pair-O-Dice Pool Motel ("Yes, we are much less—casino coupons and parking available") where an irate cheating husband had taken a shot at me last summer on the last matrimonial case I will ever take.

The Mozart ended and the announcer reminded me that it was Friday morning. Benjamin Arnold, Bonnie's grandfather, my client, was arriving today from New York, and I was meeting him and his wife at their hotel at six for drinks and a verbal report.

Well, the good news, sir, is that your granddaughter's not a prostitute. The bad news is I haven't been able to find her, and her friends can't find her either.

It didn't bother me that I didn't have a lot of information for him yet. What itched where I couldn't scratch was that he had suggested it would be nice if I could give him a little tour of the casinos so he would know his way around over the weekend. Now I'm not licensed as a tour guide and don't ever hope to be, but I had wanted his job so I said sure, I'd show him around, and now I was wondering if he'd hand me the retainer check before or after I took him into the slot acreage at the Taj Mahal.

That retainer check would pay May's rent on my office. Not that I was struggling for it. I have a pension based on twenty years with the New York City Police Department and no mortgage on my cottage. My ex-wife is remarried, I don't have any expensive habits, and two months ago I made the final payment on my Honda Accord. Financially I'm all set. It's just that I like my little detective business to pay its own way. If it doesn't at least break even and I have to put personal money into the overhead, then I have to start calling it a hobby.

My office is in Margate, down the island from Atlantic City, so I swung right as soon as the causeway touched the island at Bader Air Field. I had already been in this Chelsea Heights section of Atlantic City hoping to find Bonnie Arnold at her furnished apartment. I detoured two blocks to drive by the house, but her windows were still shadeless and looked as empty as they had yesterday when I had talked to her landlady.

When I got to the office my watch said 7:50. I'd never been there that early. Across Ventnor Avenue at Parti-Pak Deli the parking lot was filled with trucks and vans delivering bread and newspapers and milk.

My office is above a boutique near Washington Avenue, the social hub of this sleepy residential community a couple of miles down the island from Atlantic City. I crossed Ventnor, noting a profusion of hot pink and purple azaleas that had sprung into bloom in the yards that stretched to the left and right parallel to the ocean two blocks away. There wasn't any traffic except a few bicyclers in sweatsuits. The air was cold here on the island and so clear it hurt my eyes.

I brought back the *Atlantic City Press,* the *New York Times* and a container of coffee. A locked glass door beside the boutique led to the stairway to the office. A typed label Scotch-taped above the bell said: "C.M. Leeds, Investigations." I made a mental note to use my free time this morning to order a presentable-looking plastic replacement.

I could hear the phone ringing as I climbed the stairs. It had stopped and by the time I got the upstairs door unlocked, a woman's voice was leaving a message on the answering machine. When I snatched the receiver from its cradle, feedback howled and screeched from the machine until I punched the power button off.

The voice belonged to Grace Somers, a blackjack dealer I had showed the picture of Bonnie to on my rounds last night.

"Been up all night?" she asked. Her tone was teasing, but I could tell she considered it a possibility. We were just starting to get to know each other. I had met her a week earlier when I played at her table. I'm not much of a gambler but my work brings me into the casinos frequently and I usually have time to kill. If you work in Venice, chances are you're going to wind up riding in a gondola now and then. We had made a date last night to have dinner on Monday, her next day off.

"I always get here early," I said. "So I can jog on the Boardwalk."

"There isn't any boardwalk in Margate."

"I swim down to the one in Ventnor."

She laughed. I liked her laugh.

"And what are you doing up at this hour?" I asked. I knew. Her shift had ended at four A.M. She'd grabbed a couple hours sleep and then cooked breakfast for her seven-year-old before he caught the school bus. So many good-looking single moms; so little time.

"I'm getting ready for my five-hour nap," she said. "I was going to leave a message. I already left one at your home number."

"Are you breaking our date?"

"No way. If you don't show, I'll come looking for you. I just want to tell you that you weren't the only person asking about that girl last night."

I had a sinking feeling about my office rent. Maybe Grandfather Arnold had hired someone else.

"Who else was there?" I asked.

"A woman. She asked my pit boss, and he pointed her out to me. He's the one you should have asked. I never look at the players. Unless I think they're cheating. I watch my cards."

"Your pit boss isn't as cute as you are," I said.

"Flattery will get you everywhere," she said.

"What did she look like?"

"Not bad looking. Lots of blonde hair. Glasses. Older though."

"How old?"

"In her forties, I'd say. But moved like she was in good shape. Athletic."

"How was she dressed?" Witnesses usually started with the clothes. Grace had a good eye for the right details. I wondered if she'd like a day job.

"Straight gray skirt. Stockings. Plain white blouse. Dressed like a secretary, if you know what I mean. Modest, efficient."

"Tall? Short?"

"Taller than average, I guess. Nice build too. Not overly top-heavy. Nice legs."

"You notice things like that?"

"Just checking the competition."

"Did she have a picture too?"

"Yes, a Polaroid. I didn't see it. Rick said it had a couple of people in it."

"Rick who?"

"Rick Watson, my pit boss."

"Can you give me his number?"

"I'd better have him call you."

"I'll be here all morning. After that tell him to try my home number. Did she leave a name or a phone number?"

"No. She just said that your girl . . . I forget her name—"

"Bonnie."

"That Bonnie liked to play blackjack, and she was trying to find out if she was in town."

"She's too young to get into the casinos."

"A little make-up and nobody asks."

"A seventeen-year-old blackjack expert?"

"I've seen stranger things. Go in the lounges and ask the hookers how old they are."

I gave her my beeper number and told her to call me if she or Rick saw the woman again tonight. I also told her I would try to get Grandfather Arnold to her table tonight if he turned out to be a decent tipper.

There were no messages on the machine. I had phone calls to make but it was way too early. I was working on an insurance case involving the burglary of a summer house in Longport. The company was sure that the guy had robbed himself, and so was I. By a stroke of needle-in-the-haystack luck I had located two of his cameras in a pawn shop in Camden. The guy who pawned them fit the owner's description. I had a list of pawns in Philadelphia and Camden that I wanted to call before I drove up there, but none of them were open yet. Only the pawn shops of Atlantic City are open at eight in the morning.

I had a lot more enthusiasm for that case than I did for my

runaway teenager. Runaways seemed old-fashioned, like bell-bottoms. I worked in a precinct in the East Village on my first assignment in the early seventies, and I saw enough of them. But now they smoked crack cocaine, and it took them out of this world a lot faster than the pot and acid that the old hippies did.

New York information had a Mola Land Cruises on Court Street in Brooklyn. You had to be quick with the New York operators. Before I could con the street number out of him, he flipped on the voice synthesizer and let it give me the telephone number.

I got another machine when I called the number. It told me that a live person would be available to talk to me at ten o'clock. I hung up without leaving my name.

I read the *Press* and then the *Times*. I was doing the *Times* crossword puzzle, which was very difficult because it was Friday, when Thelma Herzog showed up with another container of coffee at 9:30. I was pretty wired with caffeine by then, but Thelma is my landlady and the owner of the boutique downstairs, so I didn't refuse the coffee.

My office is the front part of what used to be Thelma's apartment. I have one large room from which I can see the shimmer of the ocean over the deli roof on Ventnor Avenue and behind the motels and condos on Atlantic Avenue. I have a powder room too; that is, a sink, a toilet and a mirror. The office is furnished with a desk, a filing cabinet, three heavy-duty plastic client chairs in black, a two-cushion convertible sofa in gray, a charcoal rug and a ficus plant. The women from the boutique water the ficus when I don't, and the people who clean the boutique also clean my office once a month, including a detailed wipe-down of the vertical miniblinds Thelma left behind.

"What brings you out so early?" she asked, coming around behind the desk so she could kibitz my very incomplete puzzle.

"Busy, busy, busy," I said.

She snorted sarcastically.

Thelma is a leathery tan widow in—she says—her early sixties. She has a whiskey voice, smokes too much and looks like a combination of Lauren Bacall and Lillian Hellman; not as good-looking as Bacall, not as homely as Hellman. When her husband dropped dead at a craps table in the old Tropicana fifteen years ago, she sold their house in Ventnor and put that money with his life insurance benefits to buy this building and move in upstairs and stock a sportswear shop downstairs.

She now has seven boutiques, three of them at the shore, and the other four in malls between here and Philadelphia. She also has a five-bedroom house on the beach in Longport and likes me because I'm from New York, which she calls the greatest Jewish city in the world. I like her because she doesn't bug me about the rent. I think she'd give me the place for a dollar a year as long as I kept her up to date on my interesting cases.

"What's new?" she asked, still poring over the puzzle.

"Teenage runaway," I told her.

"Sounds interesting. Ewer."

"What?"

"Ewer. Four-letter word for pitcher. Seven across."

I penciled it in, and she lit a cigarette. She smokes Pall Mall.

"Give me some details," she said. "Juicy ones."

"Socialite. Reformed drug addict. Parents don't want her back. Grandfather hired me but I haven't met him yet. Or seen any scratch."

"Is he rich?"

"I'll find out tonight."

"Is his wife still alive?"

"Thelma honey, I'm a detective, not a marriage broker."

"So who wants to get married? A woman considers men, judges them, all the time. She tries them on like clothes to see how she'll look. It's a habit that's hard to break. And there's always room for improvement."

"The search for the perfect man?"

"He doesn't exist."

"How about me?"

"You're pretty close. Except you don't make enough money, and, you and me together, everyone would think I'm your mother, including you."

"Every man needs a mother."

"Mmmm." She lowered her attention to the puzzle again. "You need a horse. A big white one. And an Indian sidekick."

We both sipped coffee and puzzled over the crossword for a while. She took my pencil and erased one of my few answers and put in something else. I had lost interest. I knew I wasn't going to finish it anyway.

"Do you think you'll find her?" she asked.

"If she's in the area, yes."

"Do you think she's dead?"

"I don't have enough information for any guesses like that." Smoke from her cigarette had filled the room.

"That bad, eh?"

I showed her Bonnie's picture.

"Pretty," she said. "What kind of drugs does she use?"

"What?"

"Drugs. You said she was a drug addict."

"Reformed drug addict."

"What did she use?"

It was a good question. And one I realized I didn't have the answer to.

"Her grandfather said she smoked a lot of pot."

"That's not a drug addict. Did she shoot heroin or cocaine or smoke crack or snort cocaine or take pills?"

I knew where she was going with this. Find out what she used; find some people who use the same thing, then maybe you'll find her.

"How do you know so much about drugs?" I asked.

"From the eleven o'clock news." She penciled in another word and added: "I should have been a detective."

"I always said that."

"But you can't make any money at it unless you're corrupt."

"I always said that too."

"It's just a lot of fun."

"I never said that."

She sank her Pall Mall butt in her coffee container and left, taking the *Times*, puzzle and all. For the next hour I called pawnshops in the Philadelphia-Camden area until I began to realize I was wasting my time. In a lot of ways I'm still learning I'm no longer a cop. A call from a private investigator doesn't get the same respect a call from a local cop would. The owners all knew that I wouldn't send a couple of uniforms over there to ticket cars outside their stores every day for the next two months if they didn't cooperate. I'd have to go up tomorrow and "shop" some more. That's how I had found the cameras.

I put my list aside and turned my attention to two young women in shorts walking up Washington Avenue toward the beach. It was warming up outside, and limbs that hadn't been seen since last fall were being uncovered in distracting quantity.

The phone rang. My ear was still hot from the hour I had been on it. The caller identified himself as Rick Watson. I was tired, and it took me a moment to catch up with him.

"I work with Grace Somers," he added when I didn't respond.

"Oh, thanks for calling."

"What do you want?"

He was annoyed that I hadn't recognized his name. I tried to remember what the men in the pit had looked like last night. Suits with blank faces. With his attitude I was pretty sure he was short.

"A woman showed you a picture last night. A Polaroid."

"You're a private detective?"

"Didn't Grace tell you?"

"Yes. Will the police be involved in this?"

"No."

"My gaming license is very important to me. It's my life. I don't want it in my file here that the police came to ask me questions."

"You can count on me, Mr. Watson. As far as I'm concerned you don't even exist."

"What can I tell you?"

"Grace said there were several people in the picture. Besides the young blonde woman, can you describe the others?"

"I don't know. They were bikers, I guess."

"What did they look like?"

"They looked like bikers. You know. Beards, tattoos, leather jackets. They all look alike to me."

"How many were there?"

"Two, plus her."

"They both had beards?"

"Well, actually the shorter one didn't, now that I come to think of it."

"And he was wearing leather and was tattooed?"

"No, he was kind of normal. If you compare him to the other one, I mean."

"Looks?"

"Handsome, but a greaser."

"You mean black hair?" I realized I was leading him, but left alone he was a hostile zero.

"Lots of it and sideburns. A greaser. You know what I mean. South Philly hood." Maybe that was our Roland.

"And the other one? The one that wasn't normal?"

"Older. Heavier, I guess."

"How was he not normal?"

"Just a look. You know, a crazy look in his eye. He looked like he'd do anything, anything at all, and not think twice about it."

"Where were they?"

"How do I know?"

"Indoors or out?"

"Out."

"Can you remember the background?"

"No."

"Were there trees?"

"Sure."

"What kind of trees?"

"How should I know? I don't know one tree from the next."

"Leaves or needles?"

"What? Oh, I see what you mean. Pine trees maybe. I'm pretty sure they were pines."

"Anything else? Any vehicles or buildings?"

"Not that I can remember. No, just pines. Oh, and a bridge."

"A bridge?"

"Yes."

"A bridge over what?"

"A little river. With sand banks."

"How big was the bridge?"

"Oh, real small. Real small. I guess a car could go across it, but I wouldn't want to be driving. The road was just two ruts in the sand."

After I hung up, I wondered what kind of relationship Grace had with him. Did they date? He was a petulant little prick, and she was probably a foot taller than he was. Was I jealous? I hadn't even been out with her yet. I decided I was just tired and irritable.

I unstrapped the .25 and its holster and put them in my desk drawer and massaged my ankle. I thought about pulling out the convertible couch-bed and napping. If I had been at home the day would have been shot.

The first year I was down here full-time, I put an ad in the yellow pages and worked out of the cottage. But I couldn't stand all the sad stories from the people who called. Jilted lovers and lost dogs and cheating spouses and business partners with their hand in the till. So I finally switched to an unlisted number and rented this office. Legitimate customers could never find the cottage anyway. But I knew the crooks would. And after twenty years of police work, there were plenty of crooks whose memory might be jogged by an ad in the phone book at Las-Vegas-by-the-Sea.

A woman named Loretta answered this time when I dialed Mola Buses in Brooklyn. The name Roland Starza puzzled her for a moment.

"Oh, you must mean Rocky," she said finally. "He's on his way to Atlantic City. He left at nine."

I glanced at my watch. It was a little after eleven.

"Where does he drop them?" I asked.

"Who?"

"The people on the bus?"

"This trip?"

"Yes."

"The Taj."

The Taj Mahal was all the way at the other end of the island.

I thanked her, hung up and strapped the .25 back on my ankle. I didn't think I was going to find him, but if I hung around the office any more, I was either going to die from coffee poisoning or fall asleep and fracture my skull on the desk.

3

I took Atlantic Avenue up the island. There were a few buses coming down Albany Avenue from the Black Horse Pike headed for the Boardwalk casinos at this end of town. I stayed with Atlantic to miss the congestion at each casino along Pacific, and soon there were more buses turning in both directions from the expressway that entered the island behind the old bus station. For the decades before gambling this solid brick terminal had been Ellis Island to the summer refugees from sweltering, humid inland places who had come to lie on the sand and tumble in the cool waves. The locals called these day immigrants "shoobies" to mock their shoebox lunches, and the word remains a term of disrespect for nonislanders to this day.

The fatigue inside my skull was growing into a full-blown adult-sized headache. Multiplied by the diesel fumes I inhaled as I dodged up Atlantic, a major thumper bloomed behind my eyeballs. The Honda's air-conditioning, which hadn't functioned since last September, only blew hot air in my face, and the sun heated the car quickly with the windows up.

There were buses coming down Atlantic now from the upper end of the island where they came in on the White Horse Pike. I was only interested in the ones heading toward the northern end of the island, and those had diminished to two, a green one from Leprechaun Lines and a brown one from Domenico Tours.

At Virginia Avenue the three of us turned right toward the Taj Mahal. The buses continued across Pacific and down the

white-walled drive toward the garish sultan's towers. I couldn't
see any other buses down there so I cut left a block up Pacific
and turned down Maryland Avenue toward the private bus
depot behind the casino.

There was a kid with a crew cut down there wearing a
blue uniform and a day-glow orange and yellow flak jacket.
He was prepared to direct traffic whenever there was any, but
for now he stood to the left of the roadway on an island of
empty bus terminal stalls, glass partitions and crowd-control
rails. Driverless buses from A & R Trails and Bell Transport
sat in two of the stalls. On the right, green gondolas filled with
garbage sat on rails in recesses under the towering white walls
of the L-shaped hotel. Although I knew the ocean was only a
few hundred feet away, the air was warm and still in this cul-
de-sac canyon.

I slowed to a halt on the zebra stripes of the crosswalk. As
the flak jacket approached the car, I rolled the window down
and seriously considered asking him if he had any aspirin.

"Good morning, sir," he smiled. "There ain't no car parking down here. This here is only for buses."

He didn't look like a kid when he reached my window. He
was in his early thirties, had acne on his forehead and wore a
wedding ring. I saw him in a hot, dusty trailer park on the
mainland, too many daughters in hand-me-down bathing suits
playing in a hose sprinkler on a brown patch of lawn.

"I'm looking for a driver," I said. "Mola Land Cruises.
From New York. Have you seen them?"

"I don't give 'em much mind," he said. He put his hands
on the roof of the car and leaned in the window close enough
for me to smell his chewed out spearmint gum. "As long as
they don't block things up here. There's a lot of buses come
through here."

"Where do they go?"

"Who? The buses?"

"The buses. The drivers."

"They go rest up for the return trip."

"When's that?"

He turned to greet a black-and-red uniformed Trump security guard who was crossing in front of the Honda, and I could

see more acne on the back of his neck. The guard scrutinized me through the windshield. But for the Grace of God and my City of New York pension, that could be me, I thought. I shuddered. When my little traffic manager turned back to me again he looked surprised to see me. I began to wonder about the capacity of his brain displacement.

"When do they pick up their passengers?" I repeated.

He stared at me for a beat, collecting himself and then said: "Late in the afternoon. Between five and seven. There's a lot more buses coming in then too."

"And where do the drivers go?"

"Did you say Mola?"

Maybe he needed fresh batteries.

"That's right. Mola Land Cruises."

"They were just here, I think. About twenty minutes ago."

I stepped on the clutch and eased the gear shift into first. "Where do the drivers go?" I asked again.

"The bus drivers?"

"Yes." I had the sincere urge to leave the car and shake him until his teeth rattled.

"Try Andersen's," he said. "That's where they talk about."

"On the Pike?" I eased off the clutch pedal a tad, and the car made a hint at moving forward. He took his hands off the roof and stepped back.

"Albany Avenue."

"Same thing." I gassed it and pulled forward and made a U-turn. When I came back past him I waved and shouted: "Thanks." He had another surprised look on his face. I felt a little guilty about being short with him. My head pounded like someone was trying to split it open with the dull edge of a meat cleaver, and for a brief moment I again considered giving up on Roland and starting my weekend early.

Andersen's Bus World is in the marshes just off the island on a landfill beside the Black Horse Pike. I had passed it on the way in that morning as I had passed it each of the hundreds of times I had come or gone that way.

What you could see from the Pike were several brown two-story buildings and a large one-story garage painted green. The parking lot had to be two or three acres. It was about half-filled with charter buses painted in a rainbow of designs. A small sign high on a pole beside the Pike said: ANDERSEN'S BUS WORLD—$18 FOR 24 HOURS.

I had always thought the place was a parking facility and repair garage for the hundreds of buses that came and went from the casinos each day. I had only vaguely considered what the drivers did for seven or eight hours while their passengers worked at donating their pension checks to the gaming industry. Walked on the Boardwalk? Bought lacquered clamshell ashtrays with "Atlantic City" painted on them? Wagered their day's wages in a short hour at the roulette table? It had never occurred to me that Andersen's might be a motel too. It also never occurred to me that there would be security to get past, but there he was, an elderly black man in a gray uniform sitting in a little gatehouse with a toll bar, collecting vouchers and checking in the several buses that were lined up ahead of me on the driveway into the complex.

"What can I do for you?" he asked when I got to the gatehouse.

"I'm meeting a driver here named Roland Starza from Mola Buses." I handed him my voucher. It was green and had a picture of Andrew Jackson on it. I was continually amazed at how people in Atlantic City could make twenty dollar bills disappear. He folded it with one hand without crumpling it and then palmed it so that it looked like it vanished up the sleeve of his gray shirt. The toll bar went up.

"I don't know him. Ask the drivers. Somebody'll know him. Or check at the office."

He waved vaguely toward the buildings, his attention already on the bus growling behind me. I pulled slowly into the complex and started reading buses.

It didn't take me long to find what I was looking for. The lot sat above a vast expanse of marshland that was cut by the causeways to the island, wandering waterways, a railway line and strings of telephone wires and poles. On the back edge of the lot in a line of buses parked above the shimmering waters of a swollen high tide sat a red, white and green Mola Land Cruises luxury bus.

I got out of the Honda and tried the bus door but it was

locked. Just inside was a large-screen TV and VCR rig facing the empty passenger seats. I walked around the bus and felt the engine housing. It was still hot even though a chill breeze blew across this elevated site. A shift in wind had brought clouds in off the ocean and the salt water shone silvery-gray on the flooded plains and islands of brown grass below me.

When I came out from between buses I startled two drivers walking by. Both wore blue uniforms with name patches above the breast pocket. Gus and John. John wore glasses.

"Excuse me," I said. "Do you know where I can find the driver of this bus?"

Gus took a step back and craned his neck to read the name on the side of the bus.

"You looking for the card game?" he asked.

"Yes," I lied, hoping the game would lead me to Roland.

"Well, there hasn't been a game for two weeks. Ever since Rocky left."

"I heard he was back."

"If he is, I don't know about it." He looked at the other driver who shrugged, palms up, in agreement.

"Do you know where the game used to be?"

"Over there. His company keeps that room," he said, pointing at the two-story building. We could only see the upper floor above the rows of buses. "In the back on the first floor, that corner." He motioned to his right.

I thanked them and got in the Honda.

At the corner room Roland Starza jerked the door open on the first knock. Or at least I assumed he was Roland Starza. He fit the description. Short, good-looking, lots of slick black hair. And he was tan, very tan, verging on black. He was wearing green bus-driver pants but had taken his shirt off and showed a line of bathing suit white at his belt. A heavy gold rope chain around his neck held a large gold cornu.

By his surprise I knew he was expecting someone else when he opened the door so readily. He tried to slam it shut in my face, but I threw my shoulder into it. He clipped me with an off-balance hook that stung my eye, but I moved at him and pushed him with two hands so that he had to back-pedal to keep his balance. He sprawled on one of the double beds, bounced once and went over on his stomach, clawing open the night-table drawer. I stomped it shut on his hand and managed to get the .25 off my ankle while I had it up there. He screamed in pain, and I dropped my left knee on his brown back and jammed the barrel of the gun into his ear hard enough to make it bleed.

"Who the fuck are you?" he wheezed under the pressure of my knee.

"I'm the misery that'll put two holes in your head with one bullet if you don't get your hand out of that drawer. Slowly!"

He took his hand away. I transferred the .25 to my left hand and found a 9mm semiautomatic in the drawer. I slipped it into my jacket pocket.

I fought a terrible urge to pistol-whip him. He had rapped me with a good shot, and my right eye felt tender and puffy to the touch. I think I might have taken a couple of whacks at him if my own head didn't hurt so much.

Instead I backed away, keeping his middle covered with the .25.

"Are you a cop?" he asked, rubbing his hand and sitting up slowly. Blood trickled onto his jaw from the top of his ear.

"You'll wish I was a cop if you try another move like that," I growled.

"If it looks like a cop, waddles like a cop and quacks like a cop," he sneered, "then it must be a cop."

"You're not in charge here, Roland. In case you hadn't noticed."

"You're a cop. Or a private dick. I can smell you guys. And you won't do shit because you broke in here without a warrant."

"Let me read you your rights," I said. I slapped the gun barrel backhand across his face, opening his cheek and giving him a streak of blood that matched his ear.

"You have the right to remain silent, Roland," I said.

"I don't like to be called Roland. My name is Rocky," he said, fingering the cheek. I made a feint to whack him again, and he flinched.

"Your name is dickhead," I said. "Or whatever else I choose to call you, dickhead."

I appreciated his identifying himself. I didn't want to be pulping the face of just any old bus driver with an attitude. My headache seemed a little better now that I was giving him one.

"What do you want?" He looked at me uncertainly and then dropped his gaze to the floor.

He was deflating quickly. The arrogance had come and gone. He had been surprised and frightened by me at the door, and the fear was returning to his face now.

I knew I wasn't exactly inspiring his confidence, but I had a job to do and questions to ask, and I wanted to get on with it. He was probably right. It was my fault that this simple missing-person case had turned into a contact sport. Except I was sure that he would have used his gun on me if he had reached it.

"I don't have any of it," he said suddenly. "Doc's got it all."

"Any of what?" I asked. We were breaking new ground. I could hear the buses rumbling outside, and I eased back to shut the open door without taking my eyes off him.

"Who the fuck are you?"

Attitude again.

"My name is Leeds. I'm a P.I. I'm looking for Bonnie Arnold."

There was blurred movement behind me as I reached for the open door. Roland's startled glance shot over my shoulder.

And somebody clobbered me on the back of my aching head.

The blow was hard enough to chip my teeth and drop me to my knees, but it didn't quite put me out.

I remember looking at Roland curiously to see if he was going to kick me. Instead he pushed me sideways and bolted past me. The push caused the second blow to miss my head and land instead on the high bone at the point of my left shoulder. That one showed me a few stars and a pain that felt as if a railroad spike had been sledgehammered into my shoulder. I crumpled to the floor and heard the door slam shut behind me. The rumble I had heard in the parking lot turned into the roar of a motorcycle engine.

I pushed myself upright using the edge of the bed for support and realized I still had my gun in my hand.

I wobbled to the door, cracked it open cautiously and took one step outside, just far enough to see Roland's brown back headed up the Pike away from Atlantic City on the rear end of an antique but powerful Harley-Davidson Police Special. Roland blocked my view of the driver, all except the pointed spike of his Prussian Army helmet. They were too far away to see a plate number.

I staggered back into the room and shut the door and sat on the edge of the bed. No one seemed to have noticed our quick little fracas. No alarm had gone up out in the parking lot; no drivers were rushing to the room to defend their colleague. I wondered if the place would have stayed as calm if I had emptied my little ankle gun at Rocky's fleeing back.

I tucked the gun back in its resting place on my ankle and lightly touched the top of my shoulder. It hurt like hell but I didn't have any problem moving it. My headache didn't seem any worse although I had a tender lump on the back of my skull, and my hand came away sticky with blood when I touched it.

I stood up wearily and shuffled into the bathroom. Although there was no other visible damage from the sap attack, Roland himself had given me an ugly purple shiner with his lucky punch at the door. It seemed to grow even as I watched it in the medicine cabinet mirror, swelling with bad blood and rapidly closing my right eye.

Supposedly, in an earlier, simpler time, you could buy a leech or two from your corner drugstore to suck the dead blood out and make you presentable in case you had a social engagement. I did have a social engagement at eight with Benjamin Arnold but, given the choice, I'd keep the black eye. You only had those choices in the good old days; the same good old days when drugstores sold cocaine and morphine over the counter.

I washed the blood from my hair under the cold water spigot and stood blotting the last of it with several wadded-up towels. Roland's shaving kit sat on the edge of the sink. It contained the usual shaving and tooth-care accouterments, a three-pack of condoms and the sweetest thing I had seen all day, a small travel-size bottle of aspirin. I popped three and swallowed them with a handful of water from the sink spigot.

I thought I should toss the room but there wasn't much to toss. The dresser was empty and there was nothing under the bed, the mattress or the rug. Roland had obviously just arrived. In his hasty departure he had left behind the green shirt to his uniform, a sleeveless undershirt and a small plastic flight bag with the name of a Brooklyn travel agency printed on the side. The only thing in the bag was a black ribbed sweater.

I almost missed the passport pocket on the side of the bag. In it was his voucher for the room and a Polaroid snapshot of a burly grinning biker with his arms around two young women. Although it was probably winter or early spring, the biker wore a black leather vest over a black T-shirt. Both his arms were heavily tattooed. Neither woman looked nearly as happy as he did. They both wore denim jeans, flannel shirts and windbreakers. The taller, strawberry blonde had her hair pulled back in a red bandana. The shorter one, on the left, clutched a small day pack by its shoulder straps. It was Bonnie Arnold.

I sat on the edge of the bed and thought about the description of the picture Grace's pit boss had been shown last night. There were trees in the background of this picture too, mostly pines, and what looked like the edge of a road, but no river and no bridge. A heavy wave of fatigue swept over me, and I fought an urge to sink back on the bed and rest until it went away. The pounding in my head pulsed to the rock and roll beat of my heart, and my shoulder throbbed like the rhythm bass.

I slid the picture into the breast pocket of my jacket and dug Roland's gun out of my side pocket and slid the chamber open. There was a hollow-point bullet in there. I pulled the clip and put the bullet in it and slipped the full clip into my left pocket and the empty gun into my right. I wondered what Roland had done first when he entered the room: taken off his shirt or filled the chamber and stashed the gun in the Gideon Bible drawer. Be prepared; that's the boy scouts' marching song.

He hadn't seemed very interested in retrieving his weapon when he fled. Although I had been more or less helpless in my kneeling position, I must have looked like I could still put a couple of rounds into his testosterone supply.

So now I had a dirty gun if I chose to keep it. In twenty years of police work a dirty gun was one of the occupational temptations I had not succumbed to. I had worked with a lot of guys who had carried them and at least one who had used his and then discarded it.

I needed to stand up, and I felt better when I did. The door slip-locked behind me, and I was able to duck into the Honda without being seen. Driving to the security shack, I had to wait for the guard to raise the gate. I didn't turn my head toward him, hoping he wouldn't notice my puffy purple eye. Out of the corner of my good left eye, I could see him wave to me. I flapped my arm in his direction and headed up the pike toward home.

I took my usual dodgy route of pike, expressway, and Garden State Parkway, exiting into the rest stop at Mile 41, past the Roy Rogers Restaurant and down the hill to Jimmy Leeds (an ancestor) Road in congested rural Galloway Township. The cold ocean breeze didn't reach all the way to County Route 561, and by the time I was on my way toward Egg Harbor City the sun shone brightly on the farm fields, blueberry patches and woods of blackjack oak and pitch pine.

Mountain pink phlox spilled over garden walls, and dogwoods blazed white and pink in the farmyards. Wild wisteria climbed up into a huge leafless white oak and hung hundreds of drooping bunches of flowers that looked like lavender grapes. Because there was only scant spring leaf cover, you could still see deep into the woods, into shades of light green and chartreuse splashed here and there with the blood red of budding maples.

At the intersection of Philadelphia Avenue on the outskirts of Egg Harbor even the flashing yellow of the traffic light seemed intense and cartoonlike.

I pulled the Honda off the road beside the cyclone fence that enclosed the Egg Harbor Yacht factory and inspected my face again in the rearview mirror. My right eye was completely closed, and I could only see my left pupil, but it confirmed my suspicion. It was widely dilated. I was speeding. High as a kite on crank. I should have known better than to borrow pills from an aspirin bottle that belonged to a drug-addicted long-haul bus driver.

I pulled the Honda cautiously back onto sunny, empty 561. As I shifted smoothly through the gears, I realized the upside of my predicament—my headache and fatigue were totally gone.

4

Somebody once told me that you never get a second chance at a first impression. That always seemed like a fairly lame proposition to me. Irrefutable, yes, but lame too in implication at least. Make a good first impression, and they'll always remember you that way. But make a bad one, and you'll never improve it. It's the first premise that is fallacious. You can erode a good first impression with a lousy second and third and ninety-ninth. Pretty soon they've downgraded the first one with hindsight to prove to themselves that they knew all along that you were a no-good.

I knew Benjamin Arnold had formed a good impression of me over the telephone. He had hired me. I was a decorated police veteran, and I came highly recommended by an old buddy of mine. Plus, I was the only P.I. he knew anything about in the whole state of New Jersey. And now it was time for him to get a look at me. That's why I had my best suit on. And a soft matte shine on my conservative shoes. And a subdued businessman-special tie. And a Springfield government-model .45 semiautomatic with a slightly shortened barrel to better fit under my aching shoulder in my well-worn leather holster. I didn't expect to need the gun. It's just that I think new clients like to see it; to catch a glimpse of its squared-away authority tucked in there next to your ribs when your coat falls open. It gave an allusion of protection and professionalism. And maybe a distraction too.

I certainly needed all the distractions I could muster. I was thankful no one could see into my brain, because it was still skidding and fishtailing around corners and sliding across thoughts and ideas like stocking feet on a well-waxed floor. But it was the eyes that I couldn't hide.

I had left for the shore a little early and had stopped at the CVS pharmacy cum supermarket near the Dorset Avenue Bridge in Ventnor and bought a pair of tinted sunglasses, the kind that darkened in sunlight, with very intellectual tortoise-shell rims. Even in the dim early evening light their slight tint masked the dilation and obscured the obscene violent puff of the shiner. I had tried on the dark variety, but for evening wear they were too pimp, too drug-dealer. I decided that I looked very FBI with the tinted variety and a suit and tie. Or at worst like a VIP bodyguard.

I had fussed away the afternoon at Cedar Bank riding out the drug. Whatever it was that I had taken, probably some kind of amphetamine, it had not been enough to blitz me; just give me a buzz sort of like a chubby housewife who takes a couple of extra diet pills to lighten up a rainy afternoon.

Of course the delicious nap I had been anticipating since my sunrise meeting with the Baron had been out of the question. I hadn't even tried. I had called Thelma and explained my predicament, and she had suggested chamomile tea as an antidote. I drove to Hammonton and bought some in an Italian grocery, and when I had steeped and drunk the bitter brew, it seemed to take the ragged edges off my anxiety and give me the illusion that I could do something about my condition.

I got a lot of fussy little cleaning jobs done around the cottage, moving from task to task with my head cocked to be able to view things with my good eye. I amused myself while I worked by thinking about the nasty things I was going to do and say to Roland the next time we met. I didn't think he'd be back for his bus even if it meant stranding fifty senior citizens in Atlantic City. I decided not to stake it out anyway. In mid-afternoon I had called the bus company again in Brooklyn, and the woman I had talked to that morning had confirmed this. Rocky had abruptly left their employ. A replacement driver was on the way.

I leafed through my notebook and found her name. Loretta. "Loretta, this is Con Leeds again from Atlantic City.

Did Rocky leave any forwarding address or phone numbers down here?"

She put me on hold for a minute and then came back on and read me the number I already had for Andersen's Bus World.

"He had some nerve," Loretta said. Her voice quavered with emotion. Perhaps a tear fell into her Rolodex. "He just got back from vacation."

"Where was he going?"

"He wouldn't tell me."

"Any idea where he might be headed now?"

"No."

"Did he own a motorcycle?"

"Of course not." Her voice began to rise. "And he can rot in hell for all I care. He's a no-good, conceited son of a bitch. And if you find him, you can tell him I said so."

The line went dead.

Some broken hearts never mend . . .

I adjusted my tinted glasses and straightened my preppie tie in one of the shining copper panels of the elevator on the way up to Benjamin Arnold's penthouse suite. I was sharing the ride with a breathtaking blonde in her mid-twenties who had looked me over boldly when I pressed the PH button on the elevator panel.

The drug had been giving me the stares all afternoon, and I was staring at her now. She wore an expensive dark blue sheath dress whose simple elegance showed an ample figure. She was all class. Mornings as a hospital volunteer, afternoons at tennis, evenings at the roulette table. She was returning my stare.

We broke the stare when the elevator slowed for her at the seventh floor. As the doors slid open she thrust a business card at me and stepped out into the hallway, fixing a bemused smile on me as the doors closed. The card read: "Elegant Escorts—a sophisticated and discreet professional service for all occasions." And, in the corner, her name, Darlene. I buried it in the sand of the vestibule ashtray when I got to the penthouse.

There were only two doors in the vestibule. PH I and PH II. I realized my program for the evening didn't contain that information, but being a methodical detective, I decided to start at the top and work my way through the list. I rang PH I. The lady or the tiger? I heard the click of high heels that sounded nothing like a tiger approaching behind the door. There was a moment's pause while she checked me out through the peephole. I resisted the urge to flash a toothy smile and preen my hair.

The tall brunette who answered the door was definitely not a tiger. At least not here in the polished chrome vestibule. Like the hooker on the elevator she wore a simple dress, this one a dark green. Unlike the elevator girl, her expensive clothes did not exaggerate her figure, although somehow I knew it was there. She had emeralds on her ears and a fat gold bauble on one wrist and a Rolex on the other. She looked to be in her early thirties. Very well-kept early thirties.

"Hello, Mr. Leeds," she said, extending a pale long-fingered hand. "I'm Cynthia Arnold."

"Con Leeds," I said. She glanced discreetly at my swollen eye, just a glance, and stepped back to usher me into the mirrors and marble of the foyer. Behind her was a large living room with fat pieces of white leather furniture, lots of it, set on chocolate wall-to-wall so thick it looked as if it needed a gardener. The back wall was all glass, and fifteen stories below I could just see the dark horizon line of the churning Atlantic in the last of the evening twilight.

"What an interesting name," she said. "Is Con a nickname?" She was teasing me, flirting.

"It's short for Cornelius," I said. "A centurion who was the first Roman to convert to Christianity. I haven't used it since my birth certificate."

"How interesting," she said, a faintly bemused smile on her face. She glanced toward my rib cage, but I hadn't let my coat fall open yet, so she couldn't see my gun. Then she glanced at my crotch and then back up at my eyes and turned and let me follow her into the living room. She had wonderful long legs but not much of a behind. You can forgive that in a tall woman. She probably played a lot of tennis but was definitely not a hospital volunteer.

There was a long blond oak bar that you couldn't see from the foyer in the living room. It was backed by a wall of mirrors and lit by high-hat spots set in the ceiling. A tall, rugged-looking man with white hair stood behind it pouring Canadian Club into a cocktail shaker.

"Ben Arnold," he said. His handshake was hard, his hands large. "Cornelius was sent to arrest St. Peter and wound up a saint himself. He was also the first convert to be exempt from circumcision, if I'm not mistaken."

"Only way he would make the deal," I said.

He was a handsome man but looked to be more than twice Cynthia's age. For a moment I wondered if she might be his daughter, Bonnie's aunt, or even her sister. She dispelled all that by reaching across the bar and touching his arm as he was about to tip a bottle of Cinzano Red into the shaker.

"Not too much vermouth, dear," she said.

Ben Arnold stared at my eyes. I could tell right away that he was less tactful than his wife, and I knew that the dim room had lightened the tint in my glasses.

"You're a mess," he said levelly.

I wondered if I was fired.

"One of your granddaughter's playmates plays rough. I had to take a gun away from him." It was time to let my coat fall open.

I returned his stare and slid the Polaroid out of the inside breast pocket of my jacket. He noticed my gun. I flipped the picture on the bar beside the cocktail shaker. He lowered the Cinzano bottle and studied the picture without moving for a long moment. Then he looked back into my eyes and asked: "Do you care for Manhattans, Mr. Leeds?"

"Love one," I said. "Two cherries." Actually, I cared for anything wet. I'd had a dry mouth all afternoon from the speed and had finished a two-liter bottle of Diet Coke while I putzed around the cottage.

"I'm afraid I don't have any cherries," he said, splashing vermouth into the shaker.

"Darn," I said.

While he stirred and poured our drinks he continued to study the picture.

"Do you know those other people?" I asked.

"No," he said, turning the picture around for his wife, who stood next to me at the bar. "Where did you get it?"

I described my encounter with Roland. I considered leaving out the part about swiping the pills, but I wanted to find out what they knew about Bonnie's drug habits, so I used that part of the story to segue into Thelma's question.

"Your granddaughter belonged to a Narcotics Anonymous group down here. That's like AA for people on dope instead of booze."

"I'm familiar with the program, Mr. Leeds."

"Please. Call me Con."

He stared at me for a beat. I could tell he didn't like me. I was being abrasive. I get like that. But he wanted my information. Badly.

"Were you aware of her drug use?"

"Last October Bonnie was in a twenty-eight-day outpatient program at the Payne Whitney Clinic in New York Hospital. I was in daily contact with her physician there and several of her counselors."

"Then you know what she used."

"What?"

"What kind of drugs she took."

"I don't see the relevance—"

"I need to know what kind of drugs she preferred."

"That is not an issue in locating her."

"Look. Ben. The seamy side of Atlantic City is not the kind of place you'd want to be. But it's what I do. I get paid for sorting it out for people; knowing where to look for things that are lost. Like granddaughters."

I glanced at Cynthia Arnold, who met my eyes nervously as if to warn me to back off.

"The crackheads here, just like in New York or Houston or Walla Walla, hang together. The same goes for the heroin addicts and the glue sniffers. If you could provide me with a little direction, I wouldn't have to wade through all of them inquiring about Bonnie."

He took a sip of his Manhattan and glared at me. He was either going to fire me, agree with me, or bust me in the mouth.

"She's clean," he said angrily.

"Maybe she was clean the last time you saw her. When was that? Six months ago. And she might be clean now. When, and if, I find her. But she won't be clean just because you say so. She's vanished from her last address like the earth swallowed her up, and a guy named Rocky closed my eye today and tried to pull a gun on me, while a friend of his banged on my head with something that felt like a lead pipe. I'd say Bonnie has a good shot at being in some serious trouble, and you stand there withholding information I need to help me find her. I can't work like that. You owe me five hundred for the week and forty dollars for two snitches. The picture is yours. I'll fax a written report to you on Monday. I'm out of here."

I drained the Manhattan in one huge gulp, but when I put the glass down, Cynthia Arnold covered my arm with her hand and squeezed hard enough to hurt me. Strong women turn me on.

"Please, Ben," she pleaded. "He's only trying to do his job."

"Look at his eyes," he said. "He's high too."

I started to tug my arm free but she tightened her grip. I didn't want to get into a wrestling match with her.

"He told you about the pills he took that he thought were aspirin," she said, her teeth clamped together, her voice lowered almost to a growl.

Her anger took the puff right out of him. I could almost hear the hiss of air from him, and he seemed to shrink behind the bar.

"Pot," he said.

She relaxed her grip on my arm.

"Marijuana?" I asked.

"Yes."

"You told me that on the phone. You don't need four weeks in Payne Whitney for chronic pot-smoking. What else?"

"Occasional recreational cocaine use."

"Recreational? I love it. 'Do you want to go bowling or blow some coke?'"

Cynthia tightened her grip sharply. I stifled the urge to grunt.

"Did she inject any drugs? Heroin? Even the coke?"

"She had tried it, intramuscular only, but using needles made her nauseous, so she stayed away from them."

"She told you this?"

"Her doctor did."

"Wasn't the program confidential?"

"She's a minor. I hired him."

"Are you her legal guardian?"

"No. My son is. But he's incapable of caring for her." He paused and shot an inquiring look at his young wife. He seemed to be controlling some powerful emotion.

Cynthia smiled softly at him and relaxed her grip on my arm. She continued for him: "Bonnie's father lives with another man upstate on the Hudson. He's been in and out of a dozen alcohol rehabs but won't stop drinking. He tested positive for HIV several years ago, and now has full-blown AIDS. Bonnie's mother was an alcoholic too. She died during a seizure in a detox unit in Long Island College Hospital five years ago. Ben has provided most or all of Bonnie's care, including private school tuition, since then."

She stopped and looked at Ben Arnold, who nodded to her and said to me: "Well, now you have all our dirty laundry, Mr. Leeds."

"Did she live with you?"

They both started to answer at once, but she bit hers off, deferring to him.

"Yes," he said. "But our house in Brooklyn Heights is quite large. She had her own separate apartment."

"Ah, the good life." I paused and then asked: "What else?"

"What do you mean?"

"What else did she take?"

"Pills," Cynthia blurted out. Ben Arnold twitched but didn't say anything. "Diet pills. Valium. Quaaludes when they

still made them. Pills were her drug of choice. We're still finding hiding places in her apartment. Places even she had forgotten."

"She was a pill-head," I said. I was tired of tact.

Ben Arnold had finished his Manhattan. Now he put the
glass on the bar with a thump. "That's the term her counselors
used too," he said. "I didn't like it then and I don't like it
now."

"Was the program exclusively for pill-heads?"

"The program was for abusers of prescription drugs. Yes."
He looked at me levelly. "I think you are a very abrasive
man."

"It's one of my better qualities. Try to remember I'm here
professionally, not socially. In other words: I'm working."

"Always the tough cop."

"You should see me with the criminals."

"Is it necessary to treat me like a criminal?"

"I'm not. You're getting the hostile witness routine."
I smiled.

He laughed abruptly and turned to empty the watery dregs
from the cocktail shaker into the small sink behind him. Cynthia Arnold smiled at me and puckered her mouth into a quick
airborne kiss. It wasn't a sexy come-on kiss, but more like one
of "good-little-boy approval," meant for my forehead. I wondered if she would ever glance at my crotch again.

"Bonnie was overmedicated as a child," Ben Arnold said.
He added ice to the shaker from a bucket on the bar, starting a
fresh batch of Manhattans while he talked. "Her parents kept
a thousand-capsule jar of ampicillin in their refrigerator and
fed it to her for every sniffle. They said she was hyperactive
and used phenobarbital and Ritalin on her like baby-sitters
while they went out barhopping." He finished concocting the
Manhattans with a dash of bitters, stirred them thoroughly
and poured them out into three glasses. "The whole damned
society is overmedicated," he grumbled as he put the shaker
down on the bar.

"I'll drink to that," I said, raising my glass.

"You have an odd sense of humor, Mr. Leeds."

"Your feathers ruffle too easily, Mr. Arnold."

We smiled at each other, and I knew we had established the distance at which we could communicate.

He took an envelope from the inside breast pocket of his jacket and handed it across the bar to me. It wasn't sealed, and a quick peek inside showed me a check made out to me for twenty-five hundred dollars. May's rent was paid. And June and July too.

"That's a two-week retainer for your services on an exclusive basis plus five hundred as an advance against expenses."

I get a thousand a week if you want my undivided attention. A hundred a day, and your problem shares my time with the insurance companies and attorneys that keep me in breakfast cereal and beer. We had discussed my rate over the telephone. "Thank you," I said, slipping the envelope into my own breast pocket next to the .45.

"You come highly recommended. They said your work was excellent, especially at the street level. They told me you'd be abrasive. They were right. I opted for the exclusive arrangement because I think there's some urgency in the matter. I'll expect you to work on this full-time."

"I have some leads to run down on an insurance matter tomorrow morning, and then I can table that, and I'm all yours." I didn't tell him I had tickets for Sunday's Phils-Mets game at Veterans Stadium.

"I'll expect a telephone report at least every other day. Preferably between four and five in the afternoon."

I ignored that.

"Does the name Doc mean anything to you?" I asked.

"No. Should it?"

"I don't think so. Roland blurted it out when he thought I was someone else."

"We haven't had any contact with Bonnie since she left in January," he said. "We don't know anything about her life down here. Or her acquaintances. Up until three weeks ago we didn't know where she was. Or even if she was alive."

"She's alive all right. She was at a Narcotics Anonymous meeting on Arctic Avenue last Friday night. And she was clean."

"Thank God," he said. "What time is that meeting?

Today's Friday. Can we go there again? Maybe she'll show up."

"Relax. Let me be the detective. If she shows up at any NA function between here and Philadelphia, I'll know about it immediately."

I pulled my jacket back and let him see the beeper on my belt. My beeper is an important tool of my trade. I use it a lot more than my gun. I told him about my conversation with the Baron, leaving out his occupation. While I talked, Cynthia left the room and brought me back a fat accordion file filled with Bonnie's letters, phone bills, pictures, address book and even their own charge and credit card bills marked in red with the purchases Bonnie had made over the last eighteen months.

"You do good work," I said to him after I had pawed through it.

"Cyn did it," he said, tipping his Manhattan in her direction.

"I always wanted to be a detective," she said, smiling. "I think I got everything you asked Ben for over the phone."

I retrieved the picture of Bonnie in the threesome from the bar and dropped it into one of the accordion slots.

"You do good work too," I said. I noticed that my tongue missed the D in good this time. Imperceptible. But I could tell the Manhattans had found the fatigue that was lurking behind the speed. If I was going to keep my good first impression, it would not be by slurring and stumbling through a casino tour.

When he offered to pour the dregs of the Manhattans into my glass I covered it with the palm of my hand. He drank them himself, and we left for our tour with my speed-zapped, Manhattan-soaked mind sorting through excuses to leave them as soon as possible.

I parked them in an oyster bar on the Boardwalk level of their hotel and lugged the accordion file to the parking garage and stowed it in the trunk of the Honda. The walk was a long, laborious ordeal. My body was finally breaking the chemical down, and my legs felt thick and clumsy as I trudged along the concrete surface in the fluorescent parking glare. Speed, as I understand it, is a stimulant to the central nervous system and the heart, and now my poor abused ticker was returning to its normal state and was telling my body and brain to either put it to bed for the night or give it some more speed.

When I rejoined them in the oyster bar, Ben and Cynthia were working on two dozen Blue Points and a bottle of Dom Perignon. Normally I love oysters, but tonight I had no interest in the slimy gray creatures. With the appetite suppressant in my system, even peaches and cream would have stuck in my throat. But the champagne went down very nicely, thank you. And it was a mistake. I was halfway through a third glass when the room began to spin. Well, not spin exactly, just tilt a little.

Cynthia Arnold noticed it first. She was napkining oyster slime from the corner of her gorgeous red mouth when she looked at me and said: "You're white as a ghost." She had a look of genuine concern on her face. "Are you all right?"

"No," I said. "I'm about out of gas."

Ben Arnold looked at me with mild disapproval.

"Overmedicated, I'm afraid," I told him.

I think I asked them to excuse me for the night, and I think I navigated the short course out of the restaurant in a mostly straight line. I'm not sure. But I do know that I patted my jacket when I reached the lobby, and that I still had my retainer check and my gun.

I stood under the portico outside for a long time, breathing deeply and letting the cold, humid salt air clear what it could of the cobwebs and odd carbon chains in my head. After a while the doorman, who was dressed in black tails, asked me if he could have a parking attendant bring my car.

"Cab," I said. It was all I could muster.

"What was that, sir?"

"Cab," I said with a little more volume. I realized I didn't want to speak too loudly because my headache was coming back.

"Good choice, sir," he said. A wise guy. I didn't care. I just wanted some sleep. He raised his hand and a cab shot out of the darkness. I didn't tip him, and he slammed the cab door behind me.

I told the cabby to take me to Margate. He told me to tell

him if I felt like I was going to be sick and he'd pull over. Hard-working, half-poisoned detectives with black eyes get no respect. I felt my face and patted my pockets. I couldn't find the sunglasses and couldn't remember taking them off. But I still had my retainer check and the gun.

5

I spent the night on the convertible sofa in my office. It wasn't the first night I had slept there. When I'm on the island late and have an early morning appointment, I bed down there. Normally it's a planned visit, and I make arrangements to have a neighbor walk and feed my dog, but this visit was more spontaneous, and I hadn't done that.

It had taken a while for my mind to slow its frantic pace after I climbed under the covers. My legs jumped and my heart thumped and my brain just would not quit. Thelma hadn't been expecting me and had turned the heat off. I shivered in the cold spring darkness as I lay there thinking about Ben Arnold and his alcoholic son and drug-addicted granddaughter. What would he do when I brought her back? Lecture her about pill-taking, pot-smoking and moral turpitude? I could see it was going to be as difficult to convince her to go home as it would be to find her. And I was far from optimistic about finding her. The best I could hope for was that Bonnie wasn't involved in whatever had put that startled look on Roland Starza's face when I caught up with him. She had come here and taken a few small steps toward beginning a new life. Now I had been hired to rescue her from that and return her to her role as shuttlecock in the family badminton game. Well, that would be up to her, when and if I found her. I couldn't hog-tie her and run her up to New York. I hoped I had made that clear with the Arnolds. I could locate her if she was still in the Atlantic City area and, hopefully, put them in touch with her. But something was moving her around and driving her off course, and my instinct told me that something was about to make me earn every dollar of the fee that I had carefully stashed in the office desk drawer before I even pulled the sofa bed out.

I don't remember anything that resembled restful sleep that night. I was under the covers by eleven, but the office is in a neighborhood of bars and clubs that cater to a kind of super-annuated college crowd, and there is street noise and cars roaring around until the wee hours on the weekends even before the summer months begin. Mostly, I lay there going over the events of the day and melting an hour away here and there in a state of semiconsciousness. After the laughter and fights stopped and the streets got still I could hear the faint surging rhythms of the sea behind the silence. When the windows started to show gray light I relaxed and slept and woke sweating in the hot morning sunlight that covered the bed.

Thelma heard me moving around and brought me a pint container of coffee from the deli. She was gearing up for a busy Saturday and only stayed long enough to tell me I looked like hell and I should get more purpose in my life. I explained to her, as I have done so many times, that I am a confirmed Episcopalian and that her Jewish Mother routine does not work on me. I hauled Ben Arnold's check out and showed it to her and told her that I had worked late into the night at my profession, an enterprise that had included a purposeful day of getting poisoned and lead-piped by two bikers.

While I finished the coffee I called a cab and played back the only message on my machine, which was from the Baron inquiring if I had any new information on Bonnie. I had the cabby take me to the drive-in window of my bank on Atlantic Avenue so I could deposit Ben Arnold's check. The morning was sunny and dry, the sunlight filled with the strength of the summer but tempered yet by a chill spring wind. Bikers, joggers and walkers in various combinations of sweatsuits, windbreakers and shorts were headed for the beach and the boardwalk all along the avenue as we drove toward Atlantic City.

My car was on a level in the garage that was for transient gamblers and not for hotel guests, so there were only three other cars on the floor. The attendant gave me a big knowing smile when I pulled up to his booth as if to say he knew that I'd at least had some luck with the ladies last night. It made me feel good even if I hadn't, which is what he intended anyway.

The day was positively balmy back in the pines as it often is at this time of year. It was a little before eleven when I got home. The air was still and warm, and bees buzzed the white dogwood that stood in the field behind the cottage. I took the dog for a good run and threw a stick half a dozen times for her to retrieve from the cold river. Thelma's comments about getting more purpose in my life had rankled me a bit. I was surrounded with purpose. The dog loved me and depended on me, the cottage needed maintenance, the grass needed its first cut of the year and there were perch and catfish in the river that needed to be caught. Why did I have to explain to my landlady why I had a black eye and spent the night on the couch in my office? I built a little pine fire in the fireplace to take the chill off the living room and then fed the dog. I hung up my suit carefully and took a shower, and when I had dressed I sat at the dining table with the accordion folder Cynthia Arnold had given me.

There were a few formal high school pictures of Bonnie in the folder, some snapshots with friends at parties and in a park, their healthy young faces filled with self-conscious hilarity and braces. I tucked them back in the folder with the address book and the charge bills, intending to give them more careful study when I had time. I wanted to spend the afternoon in Philly drawing lines through the names of a half-dozen pawn shops I hadn't visited on my insurance fraud canvass and then get back to the Arnold business full-steam on Monday. But Saturday was flitting away, and I was beginning to feel a little pressed because I was behind schedule. That's what happens when you take a big fee; they expect you to do things, to jump through hoops, and I was used to moving at my own pace.

I saw the South Jersey 609 area code almost as soon as I pulled out the stack of New York Telephone bills. There were eighteen months of long distance records from the Arnold apartment with an occasional 609 scattered through them. Then in November and December of last year South Jersey numbers came up repeatedly. Several of them I recognized as Atlantic City exchanges. A quick check of my phone book revealed that another frequent one was in Ventnor. I tucked the whole batch of bills back into the folder and began to gather myself for the drive to Philly. I started to feel like I was earning my two grand just knowing I could track these numbers on Monday.

I spent the afternoon working the pawn shops in Center City and around Philadelphia's larger hospitals, shopping for jewelry, cameras and video equipment. I was finished with my list by eight o'clock, but I didn't find another thing I could trace to my insurance thief. Instead of the disappointment I usually felt when I came up with a blank, I was relieved that I didn't have to file any reports or go any further with it for a while and could concentrate on finding Bonnie Arnold full-time. I treated myself to a pair of very dry Tanqueray Martinis and the best prime ribs I've had in a long time at an Italian joint I knew on the Jersey side of the bridge, and by eleven I was under the cold covers reading Raymond Chandler and feeling my body relax in shuddering waves.

I woke up with the paperback open on my chest, smelling the pines, in the cool clear light of a spring Sunday morning. If I had been frazzled and impatient on my drive to Philadelphia less than twenty-four hours before, I was almost euphoric this time. By ten o'clock I had put a full diner breakfast under my belt, bought three Sunday papers and was headed up an almost deserted White Horse Pike toward the green artificial grass expanse of Veteran's Stadium. Sunshine, spring and baseball. What more could I ask for on my day off? I pulled into the nearly empty parking lot well away from the stadium where I could read my papers undisturbed as the lot started to fill. When I finished the papers I went inside and watched the Phils and Mets take batting practice. Eventually fifty thousand other people filed in to keep me company, enough of them New Yorkers to keep the Phillies fans yelling to drown them out. The Mets won, and the shadows began to cover the sunshine, and the air took on a chill. I was glad the Mets won, not because I'm partial to New York teams but because I don't like the Phils. I'm an A's fan, but the Athletics haven't played in

Philadelphia since 1954, the year they wandered west to Kansas City and later to Oakland, where they now reside. Nobody in my family ever liked the Phils. My father was an A's fan and my grandmother and probably my great grandparents too. That's how I got this name, Cornelius McGillicuddy Leeds, after the gentleman who owned and managed the Athletics for more than fifty years, the last man to wear a suit and a straw hat in the dugout, a man who had the good sense to change his name to Connie Mack.

The traffic fades away quickly coming south out of Philly on a Sunday evening. Most of the ballpark crush diverts into the suburbs along the Delaware, and within twenty minutes of reaching the Jersey side of the bridge I was on the Atlantic City Expressway in a smooth flow of headlights plunging into the vast expanse of pine forest that sits between the city and the seashore. The late afternoon chill had turned frosty, and I rode with the windows up and the heater on, carefully sorting out the cars around me in the limited visibility of a twilight aggravated by a turquoise and peach-red sunset. I exited the Expressway at Hammonton and by the time I reached my driveway in Cedar Bank the only colors outside the illumination of my headlights were the black of the pines and the fading gray of the cold spring sky.

It is almost a thousand feet from the road to my cottage, and the bumpy dirt drive bends through a thicket of cedar and pitch pine so that you can't see the cottage or the river until you are almost to my door. As I turned in the drive I could hear a flock of Canada geese making a noisy descent to the water, and when I rolled my window down to get a bearing on where they were, I smelled the pungent odor of cedar smoke borne on the chill breeze coming from the direction of the cottage. I killed my headlights and engine and let the Honda roll to a stop and clicked off the overhead light switch so that the light wouldn't go on when I opened the door. I took the flashlight from the glove compartment, but as soon as I opened the car door I knew there was someone at my cottage. In addition to the cedar smoke that I could see above the pines, the driving thump of the bass on my stereo speakers came to me through the trees.

I have a fairly elaborate security system in the cottage, but it's all internal. There are no shrieking sirens or bells, just small red lights in the living room, master bedroom and kitchen, and when I activate the switch, a simple click at five-second intervals, both triggered by sound and motion sensors in the woods, on the dock and the driveway. The sensors are sophisticated enough to know the difference between a man and a raccoon. Retired cops, ex-cops and on-the-job cops everywhere are excellent customers of the security equipment industry. We have learned not to think about the men who lie on their prison bunks working through their time by planning elaborate mayhem on the people they think put them there. Very few of them ever do anything about it, and my system helps me minimize my concern about the one who might.

I gave myself a minute until my eyes could pick out the puddles on the gray line of road ahead of me, and then I started silently for the cottage with the high-impact flashlight as my only weapon. I hadn't worn a gun to the baseball game because it added to the discomfort of three or four hours crowded into a small hard seat, and I never leave one in the car. That just gives the opposition an opportunity to gain more firepower by stealing it.

There were three guns in the cottage, my .25 and .45 and Rocky's 9mm, all of them locked in a floor safe that is well-concealed in my bedroom. I hoped they hadn't been located and that the dog, my roaming security device, had not been harmed.

A white Lincoln Town Car sat by the kitchen door, and every light in the house seemed to be on. The music came from one of my Blues tapes, the cut Jimmy Reed's "Ain't That Lovin' You, Baby." There didn't seem to be anyone in the yard or the car, and when I got close enough a movement through one of the windows showed a thin black woman in blue jeans and a green silk blouse dancing slowly by herself. I crouched behind the car and watched her for a moment. At first I thought she was singing along with the full blast of the speakers, but then I realized that she was talking above the music to someone I couldn't see. I duck-walked to a position between the car and the window and raised myself enough to see a black man crouched in front of the fireplace holding one of my long-handled, hinged fish grills into the fire. When he turned to answer the dancer, I saw that it was the Baron. The dog was there too, sitting happily by the fire alternately watching the dancing woman and the cooking meat. I stood up and walked silently up on the porch. After a moment I opened the front door and stuck my head inside without saying anything. Neither the Baron nor the dancer noticed me, but the dog ran toward me wiggling her rump. There was a young blond woman with a freckled fading suntan setting the table in the dining area. She wore a man's flannel shirt that was too big for her and jeans that were too small. Her eyes followed the dog's movement and then found me. Her mouth opened but made no sound as her arm froze holding a fork in mid-descent to the table. I recognized her immediately. It was Bonnie Arnold.

Her eyes darted toward Barbay, who was still crouched on the hearth, and then fearfully back to me. The dancer noticed me when I stepped all the way into the room. She stopped her rhythmic movement and shouted: "Winston!" over the beat of the music.

He craned his neck and looked back at me and then stood and turned with the fish grill in his hand. Between the two hinged wire screens were six hot dogs. I put the flashlight on the mail table and moved to the stereo rack and flipped the volume dial on the amplifier from nine to two.

"My man," Barbay shouted, too loud now in the quiet room.

"*Mi casa, su casa,*" I said, taking the hand he offered as I unzipped my windbreaker.

"How many hot dogs can you eat?" he asked.

"Two," I found myself saying.

"We brought beans too," he said. "We're having a country cookout. Just think of us as urban kids visiting the farm on the Fresh Air Fund. This is Irene." The woman came over and shook my hand.

"My pleasure," I said.

She had calm, bright eyes that met mine and seemed to ask a question. I liked her without knowing why. Barbay handed her the grill.

"Two more for our host," he said to her without a trace of the Island accent. "And this is the much-sought Miss Bonnie Arnold." He swept his arm in her direction. She had put the fork down but otherwise hadn't moved from her position at the table. Her eyes darted toward the front door and then back to me. I stopped an urge to move the two steps necessary to cut her off if she bolted, because I was afraid I'd spook her. Both Barbay and Irene watched her, motionless, and I knew they were fighting the same impulse.

"I recognized you from your pictures," I said. "You're even prettier in person."

The eyes darted toward the door and then rested on my chest and a blush crossed her tan face. The mouth started to screw into a cynical smirk but somehow wound up in a tired smile, and I knew we wouldn't be chasing her through the woods, at least not at this moment. She took a step toward me and thrust out her hand, an exact copy of the greeting Irene had just offered me.

"This is the fabulous detective and champion of justice retired, the Con-Man Leeds," Barbay said. The tension had passed. Bonnie turned and began placing flatware on the table again, and Irene disappeared into the kitchen, presumably to add hot dogs to the grill.

I jerked my head toward the door, and Barbay, with a big phony smile on his face, followed me outside. Although it was only early May, the last few days had been warm, and there were already a few moths and other night creatures circling the light above the door. One of them bounced off the top of Barbay's head as he stepped outside, and he batted wildly at it and ran down the porch steps into the yard above the dock.

"Man, I hate bugs," he hissed, embarrassed.

He wasn't the first city person to visit me who faced fierce urban dangers on a daily basis and then turned to jelly at the blundering flight of a June bug. I was angry that he had broken into my house, but he looked so silly and vulnerable now, flinching and swatting at imaginary insects that I had to turn my head and smile into the darkness.

"How did you find me?" I asked.

"Friend in the phone company," he said. "I left you three

messages, man, starting at about noon. Check your machine if you don't believe me. Then I called my friend, and she told me where your number lived so we drove out. That Bonnie child is too hot for A.C. She came to Irene this morning and Irene brought her to me. Irene is her NA sponsor I told you about. I know I could disappear her for days up in the Inlet even with her white face, but she has nervous feet and wants to put A.C. in her rearview, you dig, so we got her on the road and then I told her about you, that you were working for her family and that you lived in the pines and she said she'd talk to you and I started calling you on the car phone and you never started answering and it got late and I called my friend and she found the address of your unlisted phone. I'm sorry about the B and E, man. It got real cold sitting in your driveway and I couldn't take her back. I was careful coming in and didn't break nothing. I did B and Es for a living for a while when I was younger and it was easier to get up on the roofs."

"And the dog? You're afraid of bugs but not dogs?"

"'Tis easy for a countryman from Jamaica," he said, sliding into the lilting Island accent. "De dawg he look in m'eye an' he see a fren'. An' he look in m'hand an' he see a hot dog." He dropped the accent abruptly and asked: "Speaking of eyes, what happened to you?" He squinted to see my face better in the light from the porch. The swelling was gone from my eye but I still had a black pouch beneath it and an orange bruise on the outer rim of the socket.

"I found Rocky on Friday," I said. "He had another guy with him, and I couldn't hold him."

"That's who she must be running from," he said. "She won't say though. She's zipped up tighter than a clam. Even with Irene."

"Is Irene a prostitute?"

"Irene is my wife."

"You said—"

"Irene is the mother of my five children."

"You said Bonnie's sponsor was one of your girls."

"What I say is often an illusion to mask an unprofitable reality."

"Okay, Winston, let's cut the bullshit." He took a half-step backwards. I was annoyed and it must have showed. "Maybe you had this little filly stashed. Maybe you didn't." He opened his mouth to protest but I wouldn't stop. "I took a gun away from Rocky after I had breakfast with you on Friday, and I have to believe he had every intention of using it. And then a friend of his tried to empty my brains on the pavement, and if I thought you were masking an unprofitable reality by not giving me the girl when I first asked for her, I'd be very, very angry."

"I swear to you I was looking for her too."

"And now you found her, or she found you, so you tell me. And you're just making her a present to me."

"Take her home, man. She's too hot to be around here."

"If you know something you're not telling me, and someone comes at me again, I'm coming right after your ass, Mr. Barbay."

"Don't you threaten me, Mr. Detective. I'm just trying to help her. Thursday night you were huffin' and puffin' up and down Pacific Avenue scaring the working girls and generally being bad for business. And then Friday night you were staggering around on the Boardwalk and people saw you, and I know you saw the man and got paid because your checkbook, which was lying right out there on your desk for any fool to see—"

"It was locked in my house!"

". . . for any fool to see that it got heavier by two and a half large and here it is only Sunday and I already solved your case for you and I don't want none of that money which I surely would if I was holding her like you say. So there she is free, gratis, my compliments and get her the hell out of here."

"What's all the shouting about?" Irene stood with the door half open. "Dinner's ready," she said and ducked back inside.

"I want a drink first," I said.

"Not now," the Baron said. "We're going to an AA meeting in Hammonton as soon as we eat."

"So what?"

"You're going with us."

"No way."

"Bonnie needs to go to a meeting. She hasn't been to one for over a week."

"But you said AA. I thought you said she went to the Narcotics one."

"This will do. She abused alcohol too. And the nearest NA tonight is in Atlantic City. And she shouldn't be there. They won't find her here, but you're going along just in case. I presume you have a gun either on you or in that floor safe in your bedroom."

"What were you doing in there? Did you read my diary too?"

"I couldn't find it."

"I'm not going to a goddamned AA meeting on a Sunday night in a church basement."

"How do you know where it is?"

"Hammonton is a small town."

"This is your case, man. You got paid good to find her. Well, you found her. And in that church basement is where she's going to be at 8:30 tonight. If she decides to get lost again and you're not around, it seems to me you're not doing your job."

"You're very persuasive," I said. "I see why your girls do such a good job for you."

A flock of geese started a raucous honking almost directly above us, trying to find the river in the darkness. Another flock already on the river immediately answered back.

"What's that?" Baron asked, alarmed.

"Tree leopards," I said. "They're changing their spots."

He bounded up the porch steps and then turned and looked back at me.

"I mean I know that it's fucking geese, man," he said. "But it's still scary out here."

Inside, I went to the kitchen and poured a rocks glass full of tequila, put an ice cube in it and cut a wedge of lime to squeeze over it. When I carried it across the living room, all three of them watched me silently until I shut the bedroom door behind myself. I could hear them giggling and whispering while I dialed Ben Arnold's number in New York on my bedroom extension. I got his answering machine but didn't leave a message, because I was afraid he might rush down here while we were out, and I knew a confrontation would make her bolt. I took the .25 from the floor safe and sat on the edge of the bed to strap it on my ankle. I stayed there until I finished my tequila.

They had eaten, and the table was cleared when I came out. Two hot dogs in buns sat on a plate for me. I put mustard on one and ate it and gave the other one to the dog. There were still two Coronas in the refrigerator from Thursday night, and I washed the hot dog down with about half of one while they waited impatiently for me. I pulled the Honda down the drive, and we all went in the Lincoln. Baron wouldn't let me bring the rest of the Corona in his car, so I left it on the porch. I sat in the back with Bonnie, but she was silent for the twenty-minute ride to Hammonton.

6

We were a few minutes late, and the meeting had already started when we got there. About two dozen people sat around three cafeteria tables pushed together end to end. Overhead fluorescents provided bright white light from the low ceiling, and a huge coffee pot gurgled on a table in one corner. We sat in a row of empty folding chairs against the back wall.

They were taking turns reading from a small blue book that was passed around the table. They all looked fairly normal to me. A lot of them had those calm, bright eyes I had admired on Irene. I had vaguely expected old men in raincoats who smoked and coughed a lot. True, the men outnumbered the women about two to one, but they were a diverse lot; from blue collar to white, from housewife to heavy metal and from very elderly to a little blonde who looked much younger even than Bonnie. The Baron and Irene were the only nonwhites, and seemed to know some of them.

A tough-looking guy in his fifties ran the meeting. He said that his name was Bernie and that he was an alcoholic. His face, particularly his nose, had a few dents, like a retired boxer. When they had finished reading, he began to call on people.

Bonnie put her hand up right away and said: "Hi, I'm Bonnie and I'm cross-addicted." She had a very slight lisp so that it came out "croth-addicted."

She said she had been a good student who had skipped a grade and graduated high school a year ago at the age of six-

teen. She had come to the shore for the summer with her high
school boyfriend and they had roomed with a bunch of people
who did drugs. She said she had primarily smoked pot and
drank before that but had started taking a lot of pills last summer because they were readily available, especially metham-
phetamines. She had gone to college in New England in the fall
but had only lasted a month before she went home to New
York and entered a rehab. When she came out in early November she had continued to smoke pot because she didn't think it
would hurt her. In January she and the boyfriend had moved
back to the shore, but he started doing hard drugs and pills
again, and she began to take him to NA meetings. But he was
hopeless, she said, and she locked him out and refused to see
him but kept going to the meetings in Atlantic City where she
met her sponsor. Here she gestured to Irene. On February seventh she smoked her last joint and now she had ninety-three
days clean and sober. When she said that, they all applauded.
She said she had missed her ninety-day celebration in Atlantic
City but that she had not had a drink or a drug even though
she had been in a messy and abusive relationship that had actually started in the rooms of NA during her first month in the
program. She said she was afraid to stay in Atlantic City and
afraid to go home to New York, and then she broke down and
cried, and Irene put her arm around her while she sobbed.

   I got a good look at her too for the first time, transported
as she was by the telling of her tale and unaware of my
scrutiny. She was a beautiful child. I was close enough to her
to see a soft golden down on her tan face and limbs that
seemed to make her glow. Her wiry blonde hair curled tightly
and fell in long ringlets around a finely featured face. She had
ice blue eyes that smiled even when her mouth didn't, and
when they filled with tears they showed fear and outrage,
being still too young to show much sadness. The overall
impression was childlike. Except for the body. That part of her
had become a woman, an object of sexual desire. And the first
unscrupulous man had taken a whack at her and sent her reel-
ing. And Irene and the Baron were there to support her, along
with the people in this room, and to keep her from using herself up with drugs and alcohol.

Bernie, the chairman, called on me next. I was still watching Bonnie and it surprised me. I wanted to protest that I was just there working and to please ignore me, but I said: "My name is Cornelius and I'm just visiting." Cornelius?

They all murmured in unison, and it took me a moment to realize they were saying "Welcome."

While the next speaker talked, I got up and had a cup of their coffee because my mouth was dry. What I really wanted was the rest of that Corona sitting on my front porch. A guy named Marty said he was an alcoholic and a compulsive gambler. He talked about stumbling around drunk in the casinos and how they wouldn't throw him out as long as they knew he still had the money to gamble. He used to take amphetamines and cocaine to straighten himself out so he could get more credit. And then because he was straightened out, he could drink more and then take more speed and coke and then drink more, and so on and so on. It made me think of my own stumbles on Friday night. Baron glanced at me a few times while the man talked. That annoyed me, but I let it slide. I knew I was different from these people. Someone had poisoned me on Friday afternoon. These people, when they were out there, had poisoned themselves.

On the drive home, Irene told Bonnie she had to stay at my cottage for a few days.

"Are you staying too?" she asked.

"No," Irene said.

"I'll stay at your house then," Bonnie pleaded.

"You can't," Irene said, and we were all silent for the remainder of the trip.

At the cottage Baron left the Lincoln running and went inside with me while Irene and Bonnie talked in the car.

"She'll do what Irene tells her," he said, shutting the front door behind himself while I took a long pull on the Corona I had retrieved from the porch. It was very cold and didn't seem at all flat.

"Then Irene should tell her to get on a bus and go back to her grandfather," I said. Another pull finished the beer. It seemed flatter on the second try.

"Irene can't make choices for her."

I crouched and put the empty Corona bottle on the hearth and began balling newspaper sheets and stuffing them into the cold fireplace. I knew what he meant. I couldn't make choices for her either. Even if I forced her to go to New York with me, she wouldn't stay a minute if she thought she was being threatened or harmed. They had a bunch of slogans in frames on the wall of the AA meeting. The one that caught my attention was "Live and Let Live."

"New York is the rock," Baron was saying. "And Atlantic City is the hard place. Maybe New York is the best for her. Somebody there, her grandfather I guess, cared enough to get her the medical attention she needed. The worst thing for her would be to do another geographic. She doesn't know yet that wherever she goes, she takes Bonnie with her. And if she bolts into another new landscape, there will always be another Rocky there too. And another and another. Until she's used to being used."

"You should know," I said. I tossed kindling and three small pine logs on the newspaper and lit it.

"I'll ignore that," he said, frowning. We both stood watching the fire flare up.

When the kindling began to crackle, he said: "She's not ready to fly yet. But she will be if she can just stick to her program and be nurtured. The people in the program in New York will help her. But she has to connect right away."

"Any thoughts on how to get her there?"

"I did what I could, man. That's all I expect to do every day. I brought her to the professional finder here, and now he's going to do his best."

"In other words, you're leaving her here with me."

"Something like that."

"Any ideas about who might come knocking on my door looking for her?"

"You heard her at the meeting, man. She leaving a messy and abusive relationship. Now you know as much as I do."

"Does Irene know anything about it?"

"I got to go, Leeder-Man. And she can't go with me. It's in God's hands now. And yours."

"Why don't we all sit down and—"

The front door opened. Bonnie came in with a small suitcase that she put down by the door. The fire was roaring and snapping now, and she moved to it and stood warming herself with her arms extended toward the flames.

"Irene's waiting," she said to Baron. She turned slowly toward him and they hugged. It was a fierce emotional hug. I could hear a little grunt from her from the pressure of his arms. When they broke off, Baron hugged me, catching me by surprise. I had the fireplace poker in my right hand and could only pat him awkwardly on the back with my left hand.

"Use the phone," he said over his shoulder to her as he left. He shut the door carefully behind him. Neither Bonnie nor I moved. We could hear the door of the Lincoln open and shut. A moment later the headlight beams flashed across the living room windows and the sound of tires on the dirt drive receded and was gone.

Bonnie and I stood silently for a moment and then our eyes met. I expected to see tears but there were none. She looked at me curiously and then stepped toward me and hugged me. Her hard young breasts surged against my stomach. The only sound was the popping and snapping of the pine logs. I patted her on the back with my left hand.

When she stepped back, she said: "Where's your TV? We couldn't find it."

"I don't own one," I answered, moving to the front door. I crooked my finger, beckoning her to follow me.

"What do you do at night?" she asked, somewhat astonished.

"Here?"

"Yes, here."

We stepped out on the porch.

"Put your arms out," I said.

She did, and I stacked oak logs on them from the iron ring that sat by the door. I took a few myself and held the door for her. We dumped our logs on the hearth, and I squatted and poked the pine fire with one and then stacked three on it.

"I spend a lot of time cutting, splitting and stacking wood," I said, standing.

"No, I mean at night." She brushed a few oak slivers from her sleeve and the front of her flannel shirt.

"At night I burn the wood. And read. And listen to music. And sleep."

"What about sports? Men like to watch sports on TV and drink cans of beer."

"Well, for one thing, I prefer my beer in bottles. And for another, sports are better on the radio. Especially baseball. When I'm listening to a game, I can walk around, do the dishes, write reports."

"Don't you get lonely?"

"You mean without TV?"

"Yes, I guess."

"No. I go out. I have people over for dinner."

Flames grew as the oak logs caught, less crackle and pop than the pine but hotter and longer-burning.

"We're not supposed to get lonely," she said. "Hungry, angry, lonely and tired. H.A.L.T. They told us that in the rehab. Even TV makes me lonely sometimes. Especially sit-coms. The canned laughter. I imagine a whole audience full of skeletons, laughing."

The vision chilled me for some reason. On more than one occasion I had seen exhumed bodies.

"I have friends," I said. "Dates. I have a date tomorrow night."

"Is she coming over here? Will I have to stay in my room?" She smiled, teasing me. "Is she going to spend the night?" she added.

"It's our first date."

"So? I've slept with guys on the first date. I've even slept with guys before our first date." She laughed.

"You won't have to worry about it," I said. "You won't be here. You're going home tomorrow."

"Where's that?" she said, smirking.

"To your grandfather's house."

"You haven't called him, have you?" She suddenly looked alarmed.

"No."

"Can you wait until morning?"

"Sure."

"And can we talk about it first?"

"Fair enough."

"Thank you."

"What are you running from?" I asked.

"Nothing," she said too quickly. She searched my face, trying to determine if that answer would satisfy me. Then she added: "Men."

"Rocky?"

Fright and then anger showed briefly in her eyes, and then she turned away from the fire. We stood silently long enough for me to understand that she would not answer the question. When she turned back to me, she was smiling. "What do we do now?" she asked.

It wasn't an open invitation. I don't know exactly what it was. Maybe a simple statement that said: If we have sex, it's okay. Make no mistake; it was there. What bothered me the most was that I recognized it. Recognized it and acknowledged it, even if unwillingly, by the tug I felt beneath my belt. She was almost a baby, seventeen years old. And even younger emotionally. Drugs and alcohol had seen to that. She smiled, waiting for my answer.

"I'm going to read. And drink a beer," I said. "And when I'm sleepy, go to bed. If the beer part bothers you, I can read and drink it in the bedroom."

"And what am I supposed to do?" she asked.

I gestured to the bookshelves that lined the walls to the right of the fireplace and along the east side of the living room. "Pick out a book," I said. "There's over a thousand here and in the bedroom."

"I can't read. My attention span is all shot. It's not unusual at my stage of recovery."

"There are plenty of photography books and books of paintings," I said. "They're on the lower shelves."

"I suppose I could walk the fuck out of here too," she said, flaring up. She tightened her lips and folded her arms over her breasts in anger. End of invitation.

"You could," I said. "But it's cold out there, and clear enough to bring a frost. Just the kind of night the Jersey Devil loves."

"That's cheap," she said. "Do you think you can scare me into not leaving?"

"I don't know," I said. "But I know my devils. The Jersey Devil was a Leeds. One of my ancestors. The thirteenth child of Mrs. Leeds of Leeds Point. That's right down the road from here."

"Stop it," she said, her eyes darting around the room. Just then what was left of the pine collapsed in the fireplace, and two of the blazing oak logs thudded out onto the hearth in a shower of sparks and a cloud of pungent smoke. She screamed and threw her arms around me and literally clung to my neck while I squatted, donned the fire-proof gloves and restacked the logs.

She let go when I stood up, and I carried her suitcase into the guest bedroom. She followed me into the room and right back out again. When I went to the kitchen to get the last Corona, she walked halfway across the living room to keep me in her sight. She said she didn't mind the beer, so I sat at the dining table and opened my Raymond Chandler. She stood opposite me.

"Do something," I said.

"I'd like to take a shower," she said.

"So take a shower."

"I'm afraid."

"Afraid of what?"

"Did you ever see *Psycho?*"

"Of course. But don't worry. He won't get past me."

"Who?"

"Norman Bates."

"Oh," she said. "But I always think of it as a woman. She'll stab you in the head like she did to Martin Balsam. He was a detective too."

Eventually she took her shower. With the door ajar. So she could hear me being stabbed. She padded without self-consciousness between the guest room and bath and back in men's Jockey briefs, her only concession to modesty covering her breasts with one arm. That was our generation gap. They didn't invent coed dorms until after I had graduated from college. She had a bikini-strap strip of white flesh across her back but the rest of her that I could see was well-tanned.

She emerged from her bedroom in jeans and a clean flannel shirt and carrying an armload of photography books and sat opposite me at the table.

"Where did you get the tan?" I asked.

"In the sun," she said.

Later that night I was awakened by the insistent click of my security alarm. From the living room window I could see her standing on the dock with the dog, illuminated by a half moon, wearing my denim jacket, looking out over the river. I didn't think she would bolt on foot, and I had the ignition key to the Honda in my pillowcase.

I went back to bed, and when she came in, she stopped and looked in when she passed my door. I could only see her silhouette in the darkness.

"It's very beautiful here," she said. I don't know how she knew I was awake. Maybe she didn't.

"I know," I answered. "Get to sleep."

"There are hundreds of geese on the river. You can't see them unless you're very still. Big ones and little ones moving around in the moonlight."

"The little ones are mallards," I said.

"Can't you sleep?" she asked.

"The audio alarm woke me when you were outside."

"I've never been anywhere so quiet in my life. I'd like to stay here for a while."

"When you're old enough we'll get married. But right now I'd like to go back to sleep."

"Fuck you," she said, moving out of the doorway toward her room.

In the morning I cooked us a big country breakfast of bacon and scrapple and eggs scrambled with canned green chiles. We tied the fifteen-foot canoe on the Honda and took it up to Batsto Lake and came down the lake and carried it around the dam at Batsto Village and spent two hours coming down the narrow Batsto River through the wilderness of the Pine Barrens. Two hours without seeing another person or dwelling, but thirty or forty box turtles and snappers and diamondback terrapins basking on fallen logs and sand banks in the warm morning sun and then splashing into the clear cedar-stained water as we slid silently by them. Bonnie delighted in each sighting like the child she was, pointing excitedly and hissing me quiet if I was talking, and then laughing and clapping when they flopped into the water.

We beached the canoe and sat for a few minutes on a high sand bank in the warm midday sun. When we started again the river widened almost immediately, and we skimmed across a field of lily pads and then joined the Mullica at Forks Landing. Houses and docks of the river communities of Pleasant Mills and then Cedar Bank appeared on the right bank, while the pitch pines and tall cedars of the state forest continued on the left.

The Pine Barrens are to the Bos-Wash Corridor what Central Park is to New York City. Over one million acres of wilderness sit within easy access of thirty million metropolitan souls. Part of the western border of the Pines is a corridor of rail lines and north-south highways that carries the largest traffic volume in the world. But nobody was home today. Bonnie and I had a three-hour stretch on two of the prettiest rivers in America all to ourselves and the turtles. We were almost to my dock before she recognized the cottage.

"It looks so different from the water," she said, not moving from her seat in the bow. I tied up and picked up the paddles and flotation cushions and turned toward the house.

"We have to go now, don't we?" she asked.

"Well, you can't live in a canoe," I said. "When it rains, it fills up and sinks."

"You're going to call my grandfather now, aren't you?"

"Yes."

"Do you have to?"

"Yes. He hired me to find you. He also has a lot of police departments in two states looking for you. If they find you before I let your grandfather know I have you, they might say I acted irresponsibly, if you know what I mean."

"I wish you would. Act irresponsibly," she said. She stood up, and I took her hand to help her step up to the dock, my eyes carefully avoiding hers.

"I'm not going back until I'm ready," she said firmly.

"Fair enough," I said. I dropped the cushions on the porch and propped the paddles against the cottage wall and held the front door for her. "But I want you to talk with him."

"Do I have to?"

I didn't bother to answer.

Ben Arnold's secretary answered, and after I identified myself, she put me on hold for a long time. She came back on the line finally and said: "Mr. Arnold says he told you to call between four and five."

"I know that. I was there when he told me. Tell him I have his granddaughter."

She put me on hold again, and I hung up. Bonnie looked astonished and then giggled.

"Did you hang up on her?" she asked.

"Of course. He'll call back. Let's go get the car."

"How do we do that? In the motorboat?"

"No, we'd never get across those lily pads. We'll hitch-hike."

She broke into that radiant, impish smile I was getting used to. She had a throaty little baritone laugh to go with it that made whatever amused her a conspiracy between the two of us. She was a brat, but a beautiful brat, and it was pure pleasure to be with her. As long as I didn't have to be her parent. Or her lover.

We were just starting up my driveway when the phone rang. I have a bell outside so I can hear it from the dock.

"That's probably my grandfather," she said.

"The hell with him."

"Ooo," she said, grinning again. "I'm going to tell him what you said."

"The hell with you too."

She punched me hard on the upper arm and ran ahead up the road laughing.

The first car that came along picked us up. It was a neighbor, a man my age whom I vaguely knew. He had chickens, and I bought eggs from him occasionally. He rode us all the way to a path just below the dam on 542. Bonnie sat up front, and he drove with distraction, his eyes wandering over her tan freckled face and upper body more than they were on the road.

From 542 we had a two-mile hike up a sunny sand road that wound through the pines to where we had left the car beside the lake. It was one o'clock by the time we got back to the cottage, and we both agreed that we were very hungry despite the large breakfast. The phone was ringing when we got out of the car, and I wondered if it had ever stopped.

I could hear Ben Arnold's voice finishing a message as I unlocked the front door. There were six messages on the machine, all from him. When I played them back, I hit the fast-forward each time I recognized his voice, which got more angry and exasperated with each message. I wondered how a man who had such a hard time getting out of the way of himself had ever made so much money.

I called with Bonnie watching me anxiously. He yelled and blustered, and I was finally able to convince him that this wasn't a police matter and that I couldn't handcuff her to a radiator until he got there. At his insistence I put her on the line, giving her the palms down sign to warn her not to escalate the argument. To my surprise she didn't. She didn't have to. He was putty in her hands. I could almost hear him shift registers from bluster to apologetic whine. She was a little control artist, a natural at it, and by her reactions to what he was saying I could tell she was getting what she wanted.

"Okay, Grandpop," she said, winding up. "I love you and thank you for your concern. And I'm looking forward to seeing you soon. I can't wait until Friday. Here's Mr. Leeds."

She handed me the phone. I clamped my hand over the transmitter and sputtered angrily:

"Friday. Jesus Christ, girl. Who said you could stay until Friday?"

"He says he already paid you for the whole week," she smiled.

"Not to baby-sit."

"Oh please, Connie."

It was apparent no one had ever said no to her before, and I also knew that I wasn't going to be the first, at least not on this matter.

I took the phone from her and said: "Listen, Ben."

"Hello, Mr. Leeds. Good job," he said. He had no intention of listening. "You were absolutely right," he continued. "I can't compel her to return. Or tell her where to live. She's agreed to meet with Cynthia and me on Friday in Atlantic City. We'll be at the same hotel. I realize you've done what I hired you to do. But if you could just look after her until then or until she decides to come back. On a bodyguard basis. Keep that gentleman away who blackened your eye."

Rocky. I'd keep him away all right. Away at the bottom of the bay, wired to a cinder block, a puncture hole in each of his internal balloons.

"And, Mr. Leeds?"

"Yes."

"Keep the five hundred expenses advance too as a bonus. You've earned it."

When I hung up I was no longer annoyed. I felt sorry for her. Nobody wanted her. Sure Ben Arnold was willing to pay thousands to locate her. But that was out of pride and an antiquated sense of justice. He just didn't want anyone else to have her.

I grumbled and fed her canned vegetable soup for lunch. If I was going to run a camp this week, I decided it would be more boot camp than sleep-away. After lunch I took her outside and equipped her with a lawn rake, a machete and a pair of suede work gloves and got her going on the spring clean-up I had been putting off since early March. She went at it enthusiastically, and while she cut brush and raked pine needles and winter rot and detritus, I worked on a longhand draft of my insurance company report. I joined her at around three, and we worked steadily until after five. She looked sweaty and exhausted as we were putting the tools in the shed.

"You'll sleep good tonight," I said.

"Are you still going out?" she asked.

"Yes."

"Where are you going?"

"Dinner. A casino show. Aretha Franklin. My date is a dealer. She has ticket connections."

"Can I go along?"

"Of course not."

"What am I going to do?"

"I don't know. Read. Sleep. Watch the radio."

"Why are you always so sarcastic? I'm afraid."

"Afraid of what?"

"To be here alone."

"The dog will protect you."

"Can I have a gun?"

"No."

"Why not?"

"Guns are dangerous. Why would you need one?"

"I'd feel better."

"Have you ever fired a gun?"

"No."

She took a shower, and I sat on the porch with tequila over rocks and watched the tide run out in the twilight. A doe stepped out of the forest and grazed on the opposite bank. It was cooling rapidly again, and when I finished my drink I built her a fire in the fireplace.

I showered and when I reappeared in a sport coat and tie, she was heating frozen french fries in the oven and searing two more of the Baron's hot dogs. I fed Suzie her dog food, but she was more interested in Bonnie's cooking. Bonnie made one more attempt to avoid staying in the cottage, asking me to drop her at the movie complex at Shore Mall. She said she would watch movies until my date was finished and I could pick her up. I said no and blew her a kiss as I went out the door. She gave me a forlorn look and took a bite of her hot dog.

I had a good time with Grace Somers, and I could have stayed out a lot longer. I apologized for cutting the evening short, and we agreed to see each other again as soon as Bonnie was gone. I had the urge to kiss her good night in her driveway, but her seven-year-old son came to the window and stared at us, so I didn't try. On the drive home I felt a twinge of guilt about my description of my house guest. I had given Grace the impression that Bonnie was a bratty teenager, which she certainly was. It's just that I left out the good parts, so that from my description I'm sure Grace saw a pig-tailed thirteen-year-old with braces and acne. It seemed better that way.

Instead of the voluptuous near-woman with a dazzling smile and flawless skin that she was.

As I approached my own driveway I began to doubt the wisdom of leaving Bonnie alone for the four and one-half hours that I had been gone. More luck than work had been involved in finding her, but given her erratic history and in hindsight, it still seemed like a poor decision. I wasn't worried so much about Rocky finding her as I was about her own flight. And hadn't Irene, her AA sponsor, told me to call if there were any problems? Grace certainly would have understood. My behavior suddenly seemed unprofessional.

I was enumerating all these doubts as I wandered from room to room in the cottage trying to find my guest-client-prisoner. All the lights in the place were ablaze, as they had been the night before, except this time there was no loud music playing. Nor did the dog come wiggling and thumping its tail in the doorway. The dog was not there. Nor was Bonnie. The carpet was turned back in the master bedroom, exposing the floor safe, but the safe had not been opened.

Nothing seemed out of place except the carpet. The ashes in the hearth were barely warm, indicating that the fire had been out at least an hour. Bonnie's small suitcase was still in the guest room, her underwear still in the dresser drawer. I checked each room twice, and the second time through, I opened the safe and tucked the .25 in my pants pocket. On my way out the front door I noticed that my denim jacket was missing from the rack of wall pegs.

As I stepped out on the porch, Suzie came crashing out of the brush up the driveway and scared the hell out of me, enough to make me jerk the gun out of my pocket and level it at the woods. The brush moved again, and Bonnie stepped out barely illuminated by the porch light. She was wearing my denim jacket. I had the .25 aimed directly at her middle. I lowered it gingerly. She ran to the porch, and before I could say anything, darted inside.

I followed her cursing under my breath and imagining how I would explain to Ben Arnold that I had found her, protected her and then shot her. I stomped angrily after her and caught up with her in the living room where she had tucked herself into a corner of the couch.

"You have to stop acting goofy, girl," I shouted. "I damn near shot you."

She didn't respond. The sleeves of the jacket covered her hands, which were jammed between her legs. She looked up at me fearfully. Her face was ashen, and I wasn't sure she recognized me.

"What were you doing out there?"

Still she didn't respond, and I began to wonder if she was high.

"Hello, Bonnie. Earth to Bonnie," I said, bending closer to her face. "What were you doing in the woods?"

"Waiting," she said. Her eyes were pointed at my face but they were focused beyond me.

"Waiting for what?"

"Waiting . . . for you . . . to come home," she said haltingly.

"In the woods? Why did you leave the house?"

"I felt trapped in the house. I felt like someone was watching me." Her voice trembled, and I realized she was shivering. She had evidently been outside long enough to get chilled to the bone. I drew her gently up off the couch and wrapped my arms around her and held her until she stopped trembling.

When she finally shuddered and was still, I held her for a few moments longer, and then she drew back and looked up at me shyly and said: "I'm leaving."

"Why?"

"I called my grandfather. He's sending someone to pick me up in the morning."

"Why are you leaving?"

"I want to. I don't feel safe here."

That stung a little. I thought I was doing a good job. She seemed to need the most protection from herself anyway.

"Safe from what?" I asked.

She turned away without answering, hesitated after one step like she was going to say something and then went into the guest room and shut the door. I thought about building a new fire, but it was almost one o'clock and I wanted to get some sleep. The front door has a safety chain that I never use, but when I locked up I connected it. I don't know why. Maybe it was the look on her face. The answering machine was blinking in the bedroom, but when I played it, there was only Bonnie on it saying "hello" and then it cut to Ben Arnold's angry string of messages from the morning. The recording device is voice-deactivated, meaning if you pick it up late after it has started to record, the sound of your voice shuts it down. Bonnie had evidently answered the phone just at the end of my outgoing message. I went out and tapped on the guest room door.

"Who called?" I asked.

"No one," she said through the door.

"There was one unit on the machine."

"It was a wrong number."

She opened her door. She had taken off her jeans. The flannel shirt was unbuttoned, but she held it together with one hand.

"Let me have a gun. Please."

"No. It's not necessary. Any shooting in my house will be done by me."

"It's not funny, Con. I'm afraid."

"Afraid of what?"

"Can I sleep in your room?"

"No."

"No sex. I'll sleep on the rug."

"No."

She stepped back and slammed the door.

We didn't have much to say to each other in the morning. I made French toast but neither one of us was very hungry. The stretch limo arrived at ten. She had her bag packed. I walked her out and watched while the driver tried to turn the long car in my narrow driveway. When he got it headed up the drive, she stretched up on her toes and kissed me lightly on the lips. "Thanks," she said and pulled a pair of sunglasses from her shirt pocket and put them on. She sat in the limo, and I shut the door. I could barely see her behind the tinted glass. The driver put her suitcase in the trunk and slammed the lid. I waved even though I couldn't see if she was looking at me as they drove away.

7

I could feel an immediate vacuum at the cottage after Bonnie left. I didn't wait around to fill it. I gave Suzie a swim and a good run and then drove to Margate and spent the afternoon typing and mailing both the insurance company update and my final report to Ben Arnold. I didn't bother to call him. I didn't want to have to try to get past his secretary again. And maybe I was half afraid he'd ask for a rebate on the fee. As far as I was concerned it was an easy two and one-half grand, but I had earned it and I wanted to keep it. All of it.

Thelma Herzog and I finished the day together at Maloney's on Washington Avenue with margaritas and shrimp scampi. I entertained her with all the details of my latest successful case, and she picked up the check. When I got to the part about going to the AA meeting in Hammonton, she told me that her husband had quit drinking and was going to AA meetings for about six months before his death. She said she wondered sometimes if that was what had killed him.

That was Tuesday.

Bonnie Arnold was dead by Sunday morning.

A family of early churchgoers found her body slumped on a bench in Marcy Park in Brooklyn. I knew the place. It was a nasty little needle park beside a housing project in the Seventy-ninth Precinct. When Ben Arnold called me to tell me, he referred to the neighborhood as Clinton Hill. The New York papers called it Bedford-Stuyvesant. The New York papers were right.

Of the two papers that covered the story, the *Daily News*

had the most facts. The autopsy showed the cause of death as an overdose of fentanyl, a synthetic tranquilizer that they said could be twenty-five to one hundred times as potent as heroin. The drug had killed twelve people over a weekend earlier in the year, most of them in the South Bronx. Improperly cut, the article said, a large dose overwhelms the opiate receptors in the brain causing suffocation. In plain English, Bonnie had gotten so high, she forgot to breathe.

The *Post* played it for laughs. They gave it a front-page headline: STUDENT-ARTIST OVERDOSES. And they went into a lot of background on Ben Arnold's investment banking firm, his messy divorce from Bonnie's grandmother who had remarried a rock musician who was fifteen years her junior in 1979. They said Bonnie's father had been fired from the family firm some years back and now lived in "same-sex conjugality" in upstate Kingston. They didn't mention his AIDS, but I'm sure that wasn't out of discretion, but only because they didn't know about it. On the inside jump they ran a picture of the family's twenty-five-room mansion overlooking New York Harbor in Brooklyn Heights. The picture under the front-page headline was a blow-up of the yearbook mug shot I had been showing around the casino lounges the previous week. It looked absolutely nothing like the young woman who had canoed down the Batsto with me the previous Monday.

The *Times* didn't cover the story, and *Newsday* wasn't available at the tobacco shop in Hammonton. I bought the papers on my way to New York Monday morning and read them in the Vincentown Diner on Route 206. I didn't realize I wasn't hungry until I had the menu in my hand. I drank a cup of coffee and headed north in a cold spring rain. The *Post*'s need to caricature the victims of violent or unusual death rankled me. If an archaeologist in the thirty-fifth century had nothing but New York tabloids to reconstruct our history with, he would paint a picture of a New York City strewn with the bodies of cheerleaders, honor students, aspiring actresses and altar boys. Bonnie qualified to become a student-artist because she had registered for a summer school design course at Pratt Institute, about eight blocks from where her body was found.

She had registered for the noncredit course on Thursday morning, and as far as Ben Arnold knew, it was the first time she had ever been on the campus at Pratt. She expected to get her high school diploma in the fall, Ben told me, and wanted to attend Pratt or the Fashion Institute of Technology in Manhattan afterward. She was very positive when she returned from her sojourn in South Jersey, he said. Although he was worried when she didn't return home or call Thursday night, she had mentioned that she might be staying at a girlfriend's house whose name he had forgotten. The next night, Friday, he had called the police, and on Saturday morning he had called me to ask me to reactivate my search in the Atlantic City area.

My search had involved one phone call to the Baron. Irene answered the phone and told me he was sleeping. She had not heard from Bonnie since Tuesday night when Bonnie had called on her first night back in New York. She assured me that they would let me know immediately if Bonnie turned up anywhere in Atlantic County, drunk or sober, using or clean.

The next phone call I got from Ben Arnold woke me around midnight Sunday night. He said he was sorry he hadn't called sooner, and he gave me the bad news. He had been with the police, the district attorney's office and the medical examiner for most of the day, and he had simply forgotten to call. He was very gracious, and I told him I would drive up immediately. He thanked me but said it wouldn't be necessary, at least not in any official capacity. He told me about the overdose but couldn't remember the name of the drug. They had found the needle she had used under the park bench with traces of the same drug in it that was in her bloodstream. The pathologist who had done the autopsy counted twelve recent track marks in the veins of her left arm and hand. In addition to the drug that killed her there was residual heroin in her blood.

The Baron was silent for a long time when I told him. I could hear his breathing over the phone. After a while I said his name quietly.

"Just a minute, man. I'm praying," he said. There was another long pause and then he finally said: "Bullshit."

When I told him about the track marks and the heroin and

the hypodermic needle he said it again. "Bullshit. That poor child didn't do that to herself. That's that fuckin' Rocky Raccoon, man. I knew he was no good the minute I laid eyes on him, all smooth and full of shit for the ladies. He even had Irene goin' for a while. I told her he was no good for Bonnie. But you can't change nothing but yourself. Except I'll tell you one thing, Con-man: if that motherfucking cocksucker ever come on this island again, the only way he leave it is in a rubber bag. Jails, institutions or death, man, and I been in two out of three, I'll do it with my bare hands. I'll rip the veins and arteries out of his sorry neck. I'll . . . " He began to sob and Irene took the phone.

As I said, I left the next morning, Monday, in a cold spring rain. When I'm out of town Suzie goes to stay on a river farm in Lower Bank that is run by a couple of duck hunters named Mike and Mary Sooy. The Sooys only board dogs that they like, and they only like dogs that get along with their pack of Labrador retrievers. Suzie is always very excited to get there and very reluctant to come home.

The second half of the two-hour trip to New York is mostly New Jersey Turnpike, and on Monday morning the inbound New Jersey Turnpike is mostly trucks. Normally I keep up with the seventy-mile-an-hour traffic flow, but that morning I drove absently, my foot often easing up on the accelerator unconsciously until a horn blast or flashing headlights in my rearview mirror warned me to speed up or pull to the right. I finally got into the far right lane and stayed there, washed intermittently by the spray from the eighteen-wheelers as they blew by me and welcoming each momentary windshield blur that isolated me from my reluctant journey.

I had a nagging guilt that there was something I could have done to prevent Bonnie's death. I went over and over the events of the thirty-six hours I had spent with her. If there was anything I could have done I couldn't think of it. My job had been to find her, and I did. I couldn't chaperone her. She had returned home and slipped off her support wagon and into the abyss.

But guilt wasn't the only thing nagging at me on that gloomy drive north. Had she actually slipped or was she pushed into death? Everything was wrong with the way she died. It didn't fit the way she had lived. People did unbelievable things to themselves. I had seen a lot of it and been told of a lot more by other cops. But I had spent two nights and a day with her, and I had talked at length with people who loved her and wanted the best for her. And because of that I couldn't lump her in with all the destroyed people, dead or alive, who I had come across in twenty years of police work. She had had something they didn't have. She had hope.

She wasn't a needle person. When she was using drugs she took pills, smoked pot and drank. She had skin-popped once or twice by her own admission, and it had repulsed her. She had never tried to find a vein in her life. And then suddenly she had done it a dozen times in three days. It didn't make any sense. The heroin would have made her sick, and she would have called Irene.

Maybe the Baron was right. Maybe Rocky had done her in. Or at least been there when she died. Maybe he supplied the dope. And showed her how to tie up her arm to make the vein bulge. Maybe he'd been doping with her, expanding the high, running farther and farther toward the edge until they got to the fentanyl. And panicked when she overdosed. And left her to die. It occurred to me, as I settled into stop-and-go traffic on the Staten Island Expressway, that I would like to talk to Rocky again. Soon.

With that in mind, in Brooklyn, I exited the Gowanus Expressway before the trench at Hamilton Avenue and swung up Union Street to Court and parked at a meter beside the Longshoreman's Medical Center. I consulted my notebook and found the phone number for Mola Land Cruises but no street address. I was out of the car and fishing in my pocket for quarters for the meter when I saw the poster. It was a good snapshot likeness of Bonnie, probably taken over the winter. It was grainy from being blown up and copied onto a letter-sized sheet of paper. She was smiling and looking off to the right, and her curly hair was a little longer than when I had known her, but she would have been easy to recognize from the picture. "Have you seen this woman?" it said. "Last seen Thursday near Pratt Institute." Then came the date, Bonnie's height and weight, hair and eye coloring and Ben Arnold's office number in Manhattan. For some reason I felt embarrassed for her, and I pulled the poster down. The paper was soggy from the rain and came away easily, leaving two horizontal strips of masking tape attached to the metal pole. I balled it up and tossed it into the wire litter basket on the corner. There was another one on the next pole and several more on the next block. I didn't disturb them.

The rain had dissipated into a drizzle that was still thick enough to soak my hair by the time I ducked into a luncheonette two blocks from the car. I had to wait a few minutes for the pay phone on the wall behind me to be free. When it was I dialed Mola Land Cruises. I got a recording of my friend Loretta's voice telling me that they would be right back. The counter and tables were starting to fill up with the lunch crowd. I ordered a club sandwich and a cup of coffee, and the second time I tried the number, Loretta was there and gave me the address, which was only two blocks away. I paid my bill and went back out into the drizzle curious to see what the voice on the phone looked like.

The neighborhood I was in is called Carroll Gardens. It has a handful of good family Italian restaurants and is a great place to shop for homemade pork sausage, fresh mozzarella and pasta. The longshoremen who had dominated the neighborhood before cargo containers replaced them were dying off and selling their neat brick and brownstone row houses to the yuppies and Wall Street types who couldn't yet afford Brooklyn Heights, a mile to the north.

Twenty years ago when my ex-wife, Mary Ellen, and I bought an old brownstone near here, this neighborhood still considered itself part of Red Hook. I guess it was the real estate brokers who named the place Carroll Gardens. True, there is a Carroll Park, a square block of playground, basketball and bocci courts named after some forgotten politician. But for me this place would always be The Hook.

Mola Land Cruises had their track shoes on. One desk, one chair, one phone, one sign leaning up against the inside of the front window. Ready to run. These little charter outfits and travel agencies that specialize in Atlantic City junkets are scattered all over the eastern United States and are the lifeblood of the casino industry. They bring in 50,000 players a day and add one billion dollars a year to the casino coffers. But the New Jersey State regulators are very nervous about organized crime. Anyone with even the vaguest mob ties can't own, operate or even be a janitor in a casino, and that includes running charter trips. But telling the private bus industry in New York to divest itself of its ties to organized crime is like telling the dairy industry to divest itself of cows. So most of the time the casinos look the other way about who is ferrying in the gamblers. Until someone squawks. Then the owners of outfits like Mola put the leaning window sign under their arm and move to a new location. Until the next complaint.

When I stepped in the office there was a woman walking toward me from a partially closed door at the far end of the otherwise empty room. I could hear a toilet completing its flush behind the door. She was tall and in her late twenties and had ringlets of black hair that fell over her shoulders. She was very pretty and very pregnant.

"You must be Loretta," I said. There was no wedding ring on her left hand.

"How do you know my name?"

"I just talked to you on the phone."

"I didn't tell you my name."

"I've talked to you before."

"Are you from Casino Control?"

"No."

"A cop?"

"Used to be."

"Jersey?"

"No. Here. NYPD. I live in Jersey now, but I'm not a cop anymore."

"Then what do you want?" She stood by her desk, impatient for me to leave.

"I talked to you on the phone two weeks ago. My name is Leeds. I'm a private investigator from Atlantic City."

"At the risk of repeating myself, what do you want?"

"First, let me tell you what I don't want."

She glared at me.

"What I don't want is attitude," I said.

Her mouth opened and shut but she didn't say anything. She turned and walked around the desk and sat down. When she looked up she was smiling.

"I'm sorry," she said. "I've had a rough morning. We're moving."

"I wanted to ask you about a guy named Rocky who used to drive here," I said.

"Now I remember you," she said. The sneer tried to come back but she couldn't manage it. She looked down at her desk and started fussing over some papers there. I let her fuss. When she looked up again, her eyes were watery.

"You better get in line," she said.

"For Rocky?" I asked.

"All sorts of people are looking for him," she said, her eyes flickering toward her stomach and then back up at me.

"Besides you and me," I said. "Who else?"

"Cops."

"City cops?"

"Yes. And state police. And Feds."

"What kind of Feds?"

"Mr. Russo said it was about drugs."

"DEA?"

"I guess."

"Who's Mr. Russo?"

"He's my boss. There were some businessmen from Philadelphia here too, if you know what I mean. They asked me to leave, and then they had a long meeting with Mr. Russo when all the furniture was still here. One of them was Rocky's uncle. I'm not sure I should be telling you all this. You're a detective?"

"Private detective. Do you have any idea where Rocky is?"

"I wish I did. I haven't heard anything about him since you asked me last week."

"Are you sure? It's different now. Somebody's dead."

"Is that why everybody's looking for him?"

"No. That must be for something else. I don't know anything about that."

"Who's dead?"

"A friend of Rocky's."

"A man or woman?"

"She's seventeen. Was."

"His girlfriend?"

"I don't know." I wasn't sure whether I was telling a lie or not. "Did you know her?" I asked.

"Who?"

"His girlfriend."

"I'm not even sure he had one. But something was different about him. And he stayed down in Atlantic City a lot more. And then when he came back from Florida I knew he'd been with a woman."

"How did you know that?"

"He wasn't . . . you know . . . as attentive."

"When was he in Florida?"

"He just came back."

She had more to tell, so I just stared at her and waited. The year I made detective, I had a sergeant who used to say that there are times when a person will tell you more if you don't ask a question than if you do. You have to know when to stand still and keep your mouth shut. This was one of those times.

"Then he left again," she continued. "He told me he had made a big score and that we were going to be rich and to go ahead and have the baby and he would send for me when things cooled off." She was crying now, not sobbing, just letting a tiny stream of tears and mascara run down each cheek. "I don't know why I'm telling you all this. Mr. Russo'll kill me if he finds out. And then he took a load to Atlantic City."

"A load of what?"

"You know, a busload of gamblers. And he never came back. I didn't think he meant he would leave so soon. It took us three hours to find a substitute driver to bring them back. People were really pissed off. They're still coming in here to bitch. Mr. Russo thinks someone complained in Atlantic City, and they pulled our file. And maybe that's why they're being a pain in the neck, and why we have to move."

She found some tissue in her purse and started cleaning up her cheeks.

"Did Rocky say where he'd be?"

"Florida, I guess." She was out of tears, and anger was replacing them.

"Did he say when?"

"After I had the baby. I already told you. But it won't happen."

"Why not?"

"Because I'm not due for another six weeks. And if he doesn't show up between now and then, he can go piss up a rope, pardon my French. My mother didn't raise any fools, and certainly not one who would bundle up a newborn baby and go off alone to a strange place where I didn't know anybody to meet a drug-addict bus driver."

"What drugs was he addicted to?" Thelma's question.

"I don't know. I don't take drugs. Well, I have smoked pot with my sister a couple of times." She finished smearing her mascara around with the tissue and looked up at me. Her eyes were very large and very brown, and it was hard to mess them up, with or without make-up. "He sniffed some kind of powder."

"Cocaine?"

"No, I asked him that. He was always trying to get me to try it. He called it crank." The trucker's friend. What else did I expect from a bus driver. Roland the speed-freak.

"Did he ever use heroin?"

"No, he said heroin was for black people."

"What about needles? Did he ever shoot the stuff?"

"Not around me he didn't. He had a little leather case that looked like a pen and pencil set that I found once that had two needles in it. I told him to never use them around me."

"Do you know who he bought the stuff from or if he ever sold drugs to anyone? Or to any of his friends?"

"He didn't have friends. Just girlfriends," she said angrily. "And Doc."

"Who's Doc?"

"Doc was someone he used to call in Atlantic City. But he didn't want me to hear him talking. If we were at my house he would shut the kitchen door when he was on the phone to him."

I waited her out again. She was angry this time.

"Doc was the guy he made the big score with. I shouldn't be telling you this. I didn't even tell Mr. Russo this part. Rocky idolized Doc. It was always Doc did this and Doc said that. One time he came home with a cowboy hat that he said Doc gave him. But he never wore it."

She stopped but she looked like she might have a little more, so I said: "Anything else?"

"Yes. One time Rocky was doing, you know, sniffing crank. We were in bed. He liked to do it then. He was using my make-up mirror to put the lines on, and he said: 'Doc makes good shit.'"

"Are you sure he said makes? He probably meant he cuts it strong or he buys good stuff or something like that."

"I'm just telling you what he said."

"Did you ever see this Doc? Or hear his last name?"

"No. He was always in Jersey. Or Florida."

"Florida? He was in Florida too?"

"That's who Rocky went with the last time he went."

I thought of Bonnie then. And of that spring tan she had. Now I knew where she got it. I wondered if they had all been there at the same time. It seemed fairly likely that they had.

"Do you know where they were in Florida?"

"You mean what city?"

I nodded and she began to rummage through a desk drawer. She produced a postcard that showed a bikini-clad model with a large stuffed alligator biting her butt. Rocky's message was inane. The postmark was from Daytona Beach. Biker heaven.

"Was Doc a biker?" I asked.

"You mean a motorcycle type. Like in *The Wild One*?"

"Yes."

"I don't know. I doubt it though. I seem to remember Rocky telling me once that he was a lawyer, but I could be wrong."

"A lawyer?" I returned the postcard to her. I guess my astonishment showed. I couldn't imagine Rocky associating with anyone who could even read. "Are you sure?" I added.

"I don't know. I really don't know. Christ, you might not be a cop anymore but you still ask questions like one."

"I'm sorry," I said. "Old habits die hard."

Suddenly I couldn't think of any more questions. She was out of gas anyway. I stifled the urge to ask her out to dinner. I didn't think she had any more information to give. I was just anticipating a case of the lonelies when the sun went down. I get like that when people I'm fond of die on me.

She stood up from the desk and walked me to the door. She was almost as tall as I was. And very attractive even with the belly swell. Or maybe because of it. A lot of pregnant women are. Maybe my judgment was clouded by my fondness for single moms. After all, in another six weeks or so she would be one.

"They were here too," she said at the door.

"Who?" I asked.

"Motorcycle guys. They were from Philadelphia too. I didn't see them, but I could tell they scared Mr. Russo. He says they drive by now looking for Rocky, but I never see them. I sure hope you find him first."

"Why," I asked. I thought I knew the answer.

"Because you seem like a nice guy."

She was right. I was a nice guy. A sucker for habeas corpus and due process. As much as I wanted to turn his face inside out when I found him, there was a good chance I wouldn't.

"Since I'll probably never see you again," I said. "Can I ask you a very personal question?"

"Sure," she said, leaning against the edge of the half-open door.

"What's a nice girl like you see in a bastard like Rocky?" I thought I knew the answer to that one too.

She pondered the question for a moment. It didn't seem to upset her. "I don't know," she said finally. "I guess I think I can straighten him out, and then he'll be wonderful. Dumb, huh? But who else are you going to meet around here anyway? Plus, it keeps Mr. Russo off my ass. He's got four kids."

Out on Court Street the rain had stopped and the sun was trying to break through the clouds. There was a flower shop in the block where I parked my car. I stopped in and had the woman behind the counter send her a dozen long-stemmed roses. I signed the card Mr. Nice Guy.

8

Driving up Clinton Street in the glistening pink light of late afternoon, I couldn't help but think about what a nice place Brooklyn was. Thick-trunked sycamores rose above the ornate cornices of the brownstones, their swollen leaf buds forming a hazy green tunnel overhead. Children with schoolbooks and rucksacks grouped on corners as I passed, restrained by the matronly arms of blue-uniformed crossing guards. People I know in New Jersey laugh at me when I express my fondness for Brooklyn. But then again I know people in Brooklyn who laugh at me when I tell them how nice it is in New Jersey. I can drive two hours south of Brooklyn and be deep in pine-scented wilderness. A two-hour drive north of Brooklyn will put you somewhere in the middle of Yonkers with a lot of road ahead of you to get to Cape Cod, Vermont or even the Catskills.

Nineteenth-century Brooklyn had been a temperate paradise of woodlands and farms where wealthy New Yorkers went to escape the stench and pestilence of Manhattan Island. In a way they are still doing that, but eventually they brought the pestilence with them. Some of the wealthiest people in America live on the bluff above the East River known as Brooklyn Heights, and some of the poorest live less than a gunshot away in Bedford-Stuyvesant and in other neighborhoods called Bushwick, Brownsville and East New York.

The Arnolds lived on the bluff overlooking the East River. I own a house in partnership with my ex-wife, Mary Ellen, in the next neighborhood south, Cobble Hill. That's on the back slope of the bluff. We bought the house early in our marriage, and it grew in value by over one thousand percent during the seventies and eighties. By 1985 I was telling people that my house made more money every year than I did, which was true. When our marriage wore out, when Mary Ellen got tired of being a cop's wife, when her second belated attempt at carrying a child died on the bathroom floor, when I wandered away drinking too much and looking for love, or at least a warm body, in all the wrong places, the house seemed too profitable to sell. We made the four upper floors into two three-bedroom duplex apartments with working fireplaces to rent to young urban professionals who go off each morning in suits and sneakers to battle for the bucks amid the stench and pestilence of Manhattan Island. After real estate taxes, heat and maintenance, we split almost twenty thousand dollars profit a year. I send Mary Ellen a check each month and an accounting every six months to Norristown, north of Philly, where she and her husband own a house near her widowed mother. I don't cheat on the figures, although her husband thinks I do. She never cheated me.

For this management, I get the use of a small basement apartment whose bedroom windows look up to street level and whose bathroom consists of a stall shower and a toilet tucked in behind the furnace room. I brush my teeth over the sink in the kitchenette, and the bedroom doubles as the living room. What it lacks in elegance, it makes up for in convenience and economy.

It also has a phone, and I used it to call a Brooklyn homicide detective I knew named Jack Conlin. He wasn't in his office so I left a message, and before I had unpacked my bag, he called me back. I was surprised that he knew as much as he did about the case, but he told me that someone had made waves all the way down to his own lieutenant. I explained to him who Ben Arnold was. He told me he would find out who was in charge of the investigation and get back to me. He also said he thought it was being worked as an accidental overdose.

I had brought along a dark suit. I put it on, and since the car was legally parked, I walked up to Brooklyn Heights. It was late afternoon by then. The sky had cleared and the streets were drying up. The first suits were coming down Clinton Street on their way home from the subway stations in the Heights. As my steps brought me nearer to the Arnold house, I began to wonder what my reception there would be. Ben Arnold had already told me I wasn't needed professionally. There wasn't anything to investigate. Maybe I could answer some questions for the family, but I certainly wasn't looking for further employment. I could find Rocky for them, but to what end? If I located him and gave the information on his whereabouts to the Baron, I could probably work some second-hand revenge on him, but then who was I to be judge and jury? I didn't even know if he was involved. Bonnie had left my river cottage so suddenly, how did I know she didn't rush happily into the adventure that had killed her? Drugs kill thousands of teenagers a year in America. They are provided by people like Rocky, but the kids march willingly into the open pit that is their grave in search of kicks.

But that was just me thinking like a cop again. After twenty years on the job, it's not hard for me to understand where that thinking comes from. It's vestigial now and shrinking inside me, but every cop gets it after a while. It's a defense mechanism you need to survive. It keeps you from getting involved.

She is standing on my dock in the moonlight, her back to me, looking out over the river. "I'd like to stay here for a while," she says. She moves out of my bedroom doorway illuminated by the same moonlight falling through the cottage windows.

I was hurt and wanted someone to blame; wanted to catch them and make them pay. To hurt them. Rocky would do. A cop can't afford these emotions. He can't spend his whole day hurting people. Some cops get that way. But I'm not a cop anymore. I was simply a friend of the family, going to the Arnold house to pay my respects. Nothing more. It was the customary way of procrastinating one's grief.

I turned down Montague Street, the Main Street of Brooklyn Heights. Montague Street has always reminded me of Greenwich Village. Its four blocks run from the court house at Borough Hall down to the Promenade, a half-mile esplanade set along the edge of the bluff overlooking upper New York Harbor and lower Manhattan Island. The street is narrow and congested and lined with shops whose entrances are up cast-iron stairs or beneath them or on street level or on the converted parlor floors above them. There are boutiques, bars and bookstores, lots of real estate brokers and Korean greengrocers, a shoemaker and enough delicatessens, ethnic restaurants, bodegas and coffee shops to keep a case of heartburn going for a month without being in the same place twice. It is like the more innocent Greenwich Village of the early sixties when Mary Ellen and I could sit on the grass in Washington Square Park on a summer night drinking cans of Ballantine Ale and necking. The last time I had to cross Washington Square several years ago, I walked around. The grassy areas were sealed off with fences, and the walkways were choked with drug dealers and transvestites.

The sight of so many different eating establishments made me realize I was hungry. I bought a copy of the *Post* and ate a cheeseburger deluxe platter on the corner of Hicks Street in a place called the Promenade Restaurant, a place best described as a coffee shop with a liquor license. I hadn't been in the place in over two years, but the burger was still excellent, and the french fries were still the tasteless frozen variety. I washed the whole thing down with two Heinekens, and when I got back out on the street there were a lot more suits on their way home from work. My funeral clothes fit right in.

There were posters with Bonnie's picture on every light pole down the last long block of Montague Street. I turned right on Pierrepont Place past a vest-pocket park where small children and their nannies were being replaced by a crowd of after-school kids who smoked cigarettes and were too big for the swings and seesaws that overlooked the harbor and skyscrapers of lower Manhattan. After the park, Pierrepont Place does a little dogleg to the left and becomes Columbia Heights, a street of stately brownstones and small elegant apartment houses. The Arnold house was somewhere along this street but something turned me toward the Promenade and its expansive view. I knew I was putting off what lay ahead of me: meeting the rest of the grieving family and explaining my connection to Bonnie. Although I had been successful at the job I had been hired to do, finding her, I felt somehow responsible for her death. No one had invited me to the house. Ben Arnold had actually asked me to call him at his office when I got to New York and had discouraged me from coming except to pay a personal call.

As I walked along the Promenade with the late afternoon strollers I was less interested in the soaring view to my left than I was in speculating about which house and garden might belong to the Arnolds. The suits had changed into jeans and sweaters or jogging outfits, and, singly or in pairs, people strolled or sat on the benches that faced the river. Runners in shiny bright colors puffed by, and a black kid on a small bike weaved in and out pulling his vehicle up into joyous wheelies as he made his way down the grand view.

I recognized Cynthia Arnold immediately. She was standing on one of the cast-iron galleries that overlooked the long gardens stretched out behind the Columbia Heights houses. Her arms were folded tightly across her breasts and she was talking heatedly with a thin young man whose brown hair hung straight to his shoulders. He was wearing a dark suit that was obviously several sizes too large for him. Their conversation was strictly a one-way street. Cynthia scolded the man, and he looked dejectedly at the blue boating sneakers he was wearing. Although I was only about fifty feet from her, I didn't think she could pick me out of the crowd. I didn't want her to see me, but I wanted to know why she was so angry. I counted how far the house was from the park and turned and walked back out to the street.

A handsome woman in a tweed suit came to the double doors when I rang the bell at the top of the stoop. She was pale and gray-haired and looked to be in her mid-fifties, her face dominated by broad high cheekbones with thin slits for eyes and lips. When I told her I was a friend of the family, she took my card and ushered me into the front hallway and disappeared between the partially open double doors of the front parlor.

The ceiling on this floor had to be at least fifteen feet high, and the staircase in front of me started with a wide turn and followed the wall, narrowing and turning right as it disappeared into the upper reaches of the second floor. It was a grand staircase. Busby Berkeley could have easily put fifty girls on it. There was a mail table with claw and ball feet and a dappled brown marble top. I looked through the mail, but it was all junk.

The woman came back and pulled the parlor doors wider. She said her name was Mrs. Abraham and that she was the housekeeper. "Con Leeds," I said, extending my hand. She looked at it curiously for a moment and then shook it and stepped aside.

"The family is in the rear parlor," she said. "Mr. Arnold would like to see you."

She turned and I followed her through the double door into a magnificent formal parlor. Two windows stretched up from the floor almost to the high ceiling. Between them was a gilded and ornate pier mirror as tall as the windows. Another huge gilded mirror hung over a carved white marble fireplace whose cavity was tall enough to hold a standing jockey. A Chinese Oriental covered most of the floor, leaving the elaborate parquets around the edge bare. The furniture was mostly Edwardian or Victorian, although I'm no expert, and there were large Chinese vases and urns on stands and tables and a large lighted trophy case that looked like it held a collection of jeweled knives and daggers.

Mrs. Abraham led me through another pair of sliding doors with opaque etched-glass panels and through a formal dining room with mahogany wainscoting and dark red and gold fabric wall covering. The long table seated fourteen and this stand-up fireplace had a mantle of black marble with a wandering pink grain. There were no windows in this room and eight triple-candle sconces lighted the walls. In both rooms elaborate crystal chandeliers hung from ceilings whose plaster molding was a relief of intertwined grape with detailed leaves and bunches of grapes.

The double doors of the next archway had been drawn back into the walls, and the final room was flooded with golden light from the sunset that was materializing over the skyscrapers across the river.

Ben Arnold stood holding a rocks glass dark with whiskey and very little ice. The sunlight slanted over him through windows of many leaded panes, topped by stained glass. The furniture was large, dark and leather, and another Oriental covered more parquet and yet another large mirror hung over another stand-up fireplace, this one mantled in gray slate and bordered by blue and white tiles that depicted Dutch windmills and country scenes. The effect was very men's club, very old boy and very much Ben Arnold's lair. As he watched me approach, I felt the power of his wealth, something I had not felt when we met in Atlantic City.

Mrs. Abraham stepped aside as I crossed under the dining room archway, and I became aware of other people in the room. Cynthia Arnold was coming from the outside gallery, still talking to the young man with brown hair, and neither had noticed me. A familiar-looking woman in her twenties with strawberry blonde hair stood near Ben and had obviously been talking with him, and an emaciated man of perhaps fifty sat on one of the couches. He wore thick glasses and was trying to find me by craning his head in the direction of my footsteps. A white cane was propped against the couch arm. The skin of his face was puckered with the bluish-gray reptilian lesions of Kaposi's sarcoma. I was familiar with this advanced stage of AIDS. I had begun seeing it in the mid-eighties, particularly in the Village, as my cop career moved toward retirement. But you never get used to it, especially the full-blown variety.

Ben Arnold extended his hand, and I took it. "I'm very sorry about Bonnie," I said. We held eye contact long enough for me to see his sadness. His eyes didn't show it. They showed anger. But sadness was hidden behind that.

"Thank you, Mr. Leeds," he said formally.

"Con," I said.

"Of course." He turned slightly toward the woman and nodded.

"This is Julie Stockton. Con Leeds."

The woman was tall, and I could see that her hair could be red or blonde, depending on what she was wearing and what kind of light fell on it. She had an angular, intelligent face and was strikingly beautiful.

"Julie is . . . was a friend of Bonnie's."

"I'm sorry," I said, trying to place her face.

Ben took me by the elbow and led me to the couch. "This is my son, Ben Junior," he said. "Bonnie's father." The light was behind me, and I could tell Junior saw at least my shape because he extended a hand directly toward me. His eyes wobbled, doubled in size behind his thick glasses. I hesitated and then took the hand.

"I'm sorry," I said.

"You know Cynthia," Ben said, turning. She had come up behind us and was standing with the man with long brown hair. I shook her hand, but I was finished saying I was sorry.

"And this is Dan Pickering. Dan is Ben Junior's companion."

He stood slightly behind and to the side of Cynthia, and I didn't shake his hand. He didn't offer it. He wasn't as young as he looked from a distance. I could tell by his neck and the lines around his eyes that he was my age or maybe even a little older.

"So nice of you to come," Cynthia said. I could tell she was glad to see me. Real glad. As a cop you can get a lot of mileage out of eyes, and I was getting a very friendly message from hers, just like I did in Atlantic City. I bet she did that to all the guys.

We stood in a little group by the couch, and nobody could think of anything to say. Mrs. Abraham joined us and asked me if I wanted a drink. I wanted tequila on the rocks with a squeeze of lime, but it didn't seem appropriate in this elegant setting.

"Bourbon," I said. "Rocks. No branch."

"Excuse me," she said, the slightest bit of a withering glance flashing from her narrow eyes. Mary Ellen had those kind of mad Celtic eyes. I had learned to duck when I got that look.

"No water," I said.

Dan Pickering sat on the couch beside Ben Jr. and began a quiet conversation with him, and the rest of us drifted back toward the leaded windows and the showy tangerine sunset that was developing. A helicopter flew high over the river and then began settling at the Wall Street Heliport on the other side. Cars streamed up the East Side Drive and over the bridges. The number of strollers and joggers had increased on the Promenade out behind the garden. It was hard not to stare at Julie Stockton. She caught me doing it once, and I blushed and looked away. She was easy to look at for sure, but her face rang a bell with me and I was trying to remember where I'd seen her before.

When Mrs. Abraham had brought me my drink, Ben Arnold excused us and took my elbow and steered me into the dining room. He repeated what he had said to me on the telephone earlier in the day, that he was satisfied with the preliminary police findings and that my services would no longer be required. Mrs. Abraham brought in a tray of hors d'oeuvres, mostly little crab and melted cheese things on toast points. She glared at me when I took one. I do that to some people.

I repeated to Ben Arnold that I wasn't looking for work, but that there were some things about the death that didn't sit right with me. I told him I liked his granddaughter very much and thought she had turned the corner into a new and happy life. I told him about the AA meeting I'd been to with her and about her circle of support and the friends who loved her. I left out the details about her two closest friends being a black pimp and a retired prostitute. I told him her life had been filled with hope.

"Was that the first AA meeting you've ever been to, Mr. Leeds?" he asked. He wouldn't call me Con. It kept him in control.

"Yes," I said.

"Bonnie's mother was an alcoholic, as was my first wife. Addiction is an incurable disease. Bonnie was merely in remission from the disease. It's how the program works. If you follow it, hopefully it keeps you in remission and you can lead a normal productive life. Bonnie was not cured. She was merely beginning to feel good again as the alcohol and chemicals left her system. It's a very dangerous time for them. Bonnie had what they call a slip. It was fatal. I'm satisfied that's what happened."

"What about the person she was with?"

"The addict is responsible for his or her actions. They are

cautioned in the program to stay away from people, places and things that will lead them to a drink or a drug."

"There was a man named Roland Starza who may have been with her. Small-time hood. Drug addict. With a little luck the police could put him with Bonnie during her run and maybe come up with manslaughter or negligent homicide."

"Mr. Leeds, I think your experience will tell you that this would be a very thin if not impossible case to build and that the police would be very reluctant, even under any political pressure I might be able to exert, to work on this. It is also quite possible that continued police investigation could very well bring to light the problems this family has had for three generations with alcohol and drug addiction. You have already seen how the press dealt with Bonnie's public death. My son out there is an alcoholic. He is in recovery, although one would have to admit that it's a little late for him."

"Surely you don't mean to suggest his AIDS was caused by drinking?"

"His drinking led to indulgence. His indulgence led to the rest. He's never had to work a day in his life. My father took care of him. That's the way the Arnolds do it, right back to great-great-great grandfather Matthew, the poet, in England."

"What do you mean?"

"The Arnold money is inherited in every other generation. Ben Junior's money came from my father."

"And yours?" I asked, not sure I wasn't on confidential grounds.

"From my grandfather."

"Then your estate would have gone to Bonnie?"

"That's correct. Or rather half of it. The other half would go to my dear wife, Cynthia."

"And now? Will it go to Ben Junior?"

"No, he doesn't need it. And he'll be dead before I am. Now he has no heirs, so I imagine that little swish he lives with will get whatever he has left."

I was surprised by his intolerance. The denigrating words about Dan Pickering didn't seem in character. I could see that he was angry, and I wanted to bring the conversation back to my favorite subject.

"This man Starza is responsible for Bonnie's death. I'd like to go after him."

"Revenge is unprofitable and brings more of the same."

"I'd just like your approval to put a little shit in his blood as we used to say when I was a public servant."

"You don't have it. You are free to do whatever you think is right, but not with my sanction. If you get into any trouble I won't be able to help you, and if you cause us any adverse publicity or notice, I may even harm you." I wondered what the hell that meant.

"What is Mr. Leeds free to do, dear?" Cynthia Arnold had drifted into the dining room. We must have looked like we were arguing.

"Whatever he pleases," he said.

"That was not a common drug," I said, ignoring her. "There have been no other deaths from it in Brooklyn, whatever the name of it was."

"Fentanyl," Cynthia said.

I looked at her curiously.

"I used to be a nurse," she said. "That's where Ben and I met. When Ben Junior was my patient. Sublimaze is a brand name for it. They give it to women in labor as a tranquilizer."

Cynthia drew us back into the den. Perhaps she sensed my need for revenge, and was protecting her husband from participating in it. The sunset was fading into a dark pink beneath the gray sky of evening. Thousands of lights glowed in random angular patterns in the office buildings across the river. Mrs. Abraham snapped on several table and floor lamps, and the gloaming became evening.

Cynthia worked like a good sheepdog, herding me to Julie Stockton and cutting Ben out of the small pack for a private conversation. I pictured her as hostess of a large cocktail party, maneuvering, nipping at heels, controlling the action and direction of the affair. I didn't mind being pushed at Julie Stockton. I began to think of my own wolfish way to cut her out of the herd for the evening.

We admired the festive view for a while, although as the realist I like to think I am, I knew the office lights represented not festivity but rather tired office people working too late or nightshift people cleaning the lonely rooms.

"How do you know Bonnie?" I asked eventually, realizing as soon as I said it that I had spoken of Bonnie in the present tense.

"I met her when she moved to Atlantic City," she answered. "That's where I'm from." She turned her head away from the view and met my eyes.

"I live there too," I said.

Her look was intense and sad. Normally we would have been flirting, but neither one of us was up to it. She turned her body to face me, and I suddenly realized where I had seen her before. She was the girl with Bonnie in the picture I had found in Rocky's room. I had assumed she was a friend of Bonnie's from here in New York.

Dan Pickering came over and asked us if we would care to join him and Ben Jr. for dinner at Henry's End, a small restaurant not far from the house. Julie accepted, but I surprised myself and declined. As much as I wanted to be in the presence of a beautiful woman like Julie, I didn't want to be in a public place with Ben Jr. and my intolerance surprised me. Cynthia and Ben were going back to the funeral home where Bonnie was being waked, and I didn't want to do that either. A second bourbon and the circumstances were suddenly making me feel morose, and I needed to get away from all these people.

Julie jotted her telephone number down for me, and I told her I would call her when we both got back to South Jersey. Before I left, I asked Ben Arnold for the name of the medical examiner in charge of the autopsy on Bonnie, and he wrote it down for me: Dr. Murray Shapiro, Kings County Hospital.

Mrs. Abraham saw me out, and just when I expected more hostility, she smiled and handed me a card with her name and number on it. "Please call me tonight," she said. "I'm up until eleven o'clock. I have some ideas you might be interested in."

It was a mild spring night out on Columbia Heights. A few men and women were still coming home from work, hurrying into and out of the dappled lamplight that fell through the budding sycamores. I turned left and followed Columbia

Heights toward the Brooklyn Bridge. At Clark Street I turned right and headed up toward Henry with the vague idea of getting another burger or maybe a plate of spaghetti. The earlier cheeseburger was sort of a late lunch, and I thought I was getting hungry again or would before the evening was finished, and I knew there was no food in the apartment.

Clark Street Station, a bar and restaurant across from the West Side IRT entrance of the same name, looked appealing, and I went in there and sat at the bar with the last of the cocktail crowd. Jimmy Nichols, the bartender, and Eddie Dunne, the owner, both recognized and fussed over me. Eddie's brother, Joe, was a lieutenant in a precinct out in Queens and our paths had crossed a few times. Sitting at the bar, I realized I was very thirsty. Jimmy Nick kept the draft beer coming at me, and after a while I began to back them up with shooters of tequila. I kept seeing Ben Arnold Jr.'s thin scabrous face and his daughter's blonde curls, and the tequila made it go away. Sometime during the evening I discovered that Eddie had the Rolling Stones' "Wild Horses" on the jukebox, and sometime later I remember a guy asking me to stop playing it over and over, me asking him to button his lip and him leaving.

I was drinking morbidly and I never did eat. The place started to empty out after midnight, although the stools on either side of me had been empty for most of the evening. Eddie came over at one point and asked me if I was carrying a gun. I told him I wasn't and laughed at him. I wanted to tell him about Bonnie and her short unhappy life and her father with AIDS but I didn't. It wasn't something you told, particularly since I didn't consider the matter closed. I think I started asking people if they knew a guy named Rocky Starza, and that's about when Eddie asked me to leave. He offered to get me a car service, but I walked the mile to my house. I half hoped someone would jump me or cross me in some way or other so I could beat the hell out of them, but no one did. I must have torn down fifty posters of Bonnie, crisscrossing each street to get them all. So evenings die, in their green going.

9

I didn't have as much hangover as I thought I would the next morning, but because I expected one, I stayed in bed until almost nine o'clock. Except for a dull headache, I felt refreshed when I finally did get myself upright and walking around the apartment.

Mary Ellen was everywhere in the place. I couldn't remember the last time she had visited New York and stayed in the apartment. There was a visit two years before, shortly after I retired. She had come with her mother to shop and go to some Broadway shows, and had called me in Jersey to ask if she could use the place. I had come up the next weekend and realized that I had left a pack of condoms in the medicine cabinet and had found them hidden behind a box of Band-Aids. I was never sure who had hidden them, her or her mother, but I hoped it had been her mother. Perhaps she had been there since; I couldn't remember.

That morning I could smell her in the apartment, could smell the trace of a perfume she used to wear, perhaps something I had picked up by brushing against someone else in the bar, and it was not an unpleasant smell. There was a pair of rubber-bottomed L.L. Bean boots that she had left behind in a closet, and in a kitchen cabinet next to the coffee, a half-empty box of her Irish Breakfast tea bags. I wanted her there and I didn't. I was lonely and I wanted companionship, but I didn't want the bickering and disapproval that had grown between us during the final decade of our marriage.

I went out and bought the *Daily News* and a warm loaf of

Italian bread. The day was sunny, almost balmy. It was a little before nine o'clock and people still hurried to the uptown F train station at the end of my block. I was settled in with a second cup of coffee when the phone rang. It was Mrs. Abraham returning my call. Only then did I remember that I had called her late in the evening from the bar and left a message on her machine. She told me to call her Peg, and asked me what I knew about Bonnie's death. Her tone was much less formal than it had been when she was working, and I noticed now that she had a slight brogue. Or was it a burr? I told her only about the circumstances of the death, which she knew anyway, leaving out any mention of Rocky or the people Bonnie had known in South Jersey.

"What was she like during the days she was back before she died?" I asked.

"She seemed happy and directed," she said. "I sat with her and went over her course catalog right before she left for the registration at Pratt. She never came back."

I jammed the phone between my ear and shoulder and pawed with both hands through the notes in my case folder. I had forgotten the boyfriend's name.

"What about Billy Cameron?" I said when I had found it. "Was he around?"

"He calls several times a week. He's in an extended rehabilitation facility in Minnesota. As far as I know he doesn't know about the death yet."

I jotted the word *alibi* next to his name and realized I was treating the death as a homicide investigation as I had treated so many other deaths over the years.

I wrote *Peg Abraham* down on a clean sheet of paper and asked: "How long have you been working for the Arnolds?"

"Do you suspect foul play?" she countered.

"No," I said. "It was accidental. The police say so."

"Who are you?"

"Beg pardon?"

"Aren't you the police?"

"No, ma'am. I'm a private detective."

"Are you working for Mr. Arnold?"

"I was. I'm just a curious friend now."

"Did he hire you to investigate this? Is that why you're questioning me? Am I under suspicion of something?" She was suddenly very cold and formal.

"No, ma'am. I'm just going over some details that perhaps the police might have missed. I'll be at the station house this afternoon to talk to the investigating officer. I retired as an NYPD detective two years ago."

"I'm sorry," she said, her voice softening. "I came to work for Mr. and Mrs. Arnold seventeen years ago. I was Bonnie's nanny. I came from Scotland on an au pair contract, and Mr. Arnold helped me to get citizenship. There was a brief hiatus in my service during the two years of my marriage."

"What happened?"

"About what? The marriage?"

"Yes."

"We divorced. He drank."

I had a flash of leaving a midnight message on her answering machine with a belly full of tequila and Harp lager.

There was an awkward silence. I needed to fill it, so I asked: "Did you know Bonnie's mother?"

"I just told you I was first hired as Bonnie's nanny."

"Of course. I'm sorry. I'm a little slow this morning."

"You should be. You were drunk when you called me last night. My husband was about your age when he died of a stroke. He was drunk. Would you like to hear the message you left on my machine?"

"No." I couldn't think of anything else to say.

"I gave her that name."

"What name?"

"Bonnie. Her real name is Joanne."

"When did she die?"

"Who?"

"Bonnie's mother."

"When Bonnie was fourteen. She was an alcoholic. She died during detoxification."

"I know. Ben told me. What about Cynthia? Where does she fit into the family history?"

"Interesting you should put it that way. You must know something already."

"What do you mean?"

"She fits into the family history in many significant ways. She was Ben Junior's mistress when Bonnie's mother died."

"How do you know that?"

"She was Gwen's nurse here at home while Gwen, that's Bonnie's mother, was trying to recover."

"That doesn't qualify her as a mistress. Just for gossip."

"Mr. Leeds, I am the housekeeper. I am here most of the day. I saw them making love on more than one occasion."

"You spied on them?"

"I'm not ashamed to say I did."

"Where does Ben Senior fit into all this?"

"Mr. Arnold has always been a gentleman."

"What does that mean?"

"He courted Cynthia, proposed marriage to her and married her four years ago."

"Did he know about the affair?"

"No." She paused for a moment and then added: "It continued after their marriage."

"How could that be? Ben Junior is gay."

"Don't be naive, Mr. Leeds. Twenty years on the police force must leave you with few surprises."

I told her I would call her if I needed any further information. She invited me out to dinner that evening, and I think I would have liked to have gone, but I told her I was going back to New Jersey that afternoon. When I hung up I called Grace Somers, but I got her machine and didn't leave a message. I thought about AIDS and safe sex. Safe sex was no sex. What the hell was going on in this world?

Peg Abraham was right. Twenty years of police work had left me with an attitude that expected anything of people and was shocked by nothing. Cynthia had had an affair with a bisexual man who was now dying of AIDS and who was the father of her now-deceased step-granddaughter whose mother had been her patient. Wasn't there some sort of nurse's code of ethics? Some people should have their clothes sewn on them to keep them out of trouble, and she certainly was one of them. I wondered how much Ben Arnold knew. He didn't miss much.

Was there a good possibility that she carried the HIV virus and could give it to him? Probably not. Probably she had been tested and found negative. And how much did Bonnie know? Was it possible, however remotely, that Cynthia could have killed Bonnie for her half of Ben's money? She knew how to administer the drugs, but would have needed an accomplice to dump the child in Marcy Park. I wondered if she knew Rocky. That didn't seem likely. They were from two different worlds. I began to wonder about myself and my suspicions. All those years of watching seemingly decent people snuff each other added up. No one else seemed concerned about this death except as an accidental drug overdose. When I was a cop I would have been able to shut out this kind of obsessive think- ing. Now I had too much time on my hands. Too much time to pick and probe and work all the angles, even if they were imaginary. A lot of cops sought counseling when they retired to sort of slow down their life and get it back to normal. Although my body was willing to loaf in the Pine Barrens and take dinky insurance cases for a living, my mind was still on the job.

I called Kings County Hospital and asked for Dr. Shapiro. While they were ringing his extension, I thought about hang- ing up and getting in the Honda and driving away from this case.

"Of course I remember you," Dr. Shapiro said when I identified myself. "Angry. You were always angry when you were out here. Dead bodies seemed to make you angry. I didn't think you'd make twenty years to tell you the truth. But I make mistakes. I had a guy in here from the Seven-Eight last year. Used to eat tongue sandwiches while I autopsied his corpses. He was the kind of guy I thought would make it. Drank a half-gallon of Stolichnaya one night last December and took a dive from the tenth floor of his building."

"Vinnie Pelliteri," I said.

"Yes. Did you know him?"

"Not really. I heard about it. I was in the Seven-Eight a lot when I worked in Brooklyn."

"So what can I do for you, detective?"

"I'm retired, you know. I'm a P.I. now."

"I knew you were retired. I didn't know you were keeping your hand in."

"Insurance work mostly. I have enough work that I don't have to do matrimonial surveillance."

"Good for you."

"You autopsied an OD this week. Young Caucasian woman name of Arnold."

"Not you too?"

"What do you mean?"

"There's just a lot of interest in this case. I even got a call from Atlantic City. I understand her father has friends in high places."

"Grandfather."

"You work for him?"

"I was. She was missing. I located her. She died about a week after I brought her back."

"You suspect anything?"

"I don't know. I want to pick your brain."

"Come on over. I'll show you the photographs from the autopsy. I wish I still had her. They took her out yesterday."

"I know. I turned down an invitation to go to the wake last night."

"I don't really have much, but there are some inconsistencies with the track marks. Not enough for the police, but you'll be interested. She definitely wasn't alone when she was shooting the stuff. Come on over. I'll be in my office all afternoon. I'm on the third floor. I'll be in the cafeteria from twelve-thirty to one."

"I'll meet you in the cafeteria."

"You're actually going to come here to eat the food?"

"As long as I don't have to eat it in the same room with a corpse. I mean, look what happened to Vinnie Pelliteri. You have to be careful who you dine with."

10

Kings County Hospital is a huge medical, psychiatric and prison complex in the middle of one of the largest, most dangerous ghettos in America. Designed by Franz Kafka, built by the Marquis de Sade, it takes up acres and acres of slum blocks, some of it falling down with smashed out windows, some of it brand new and most of it dirty brick medieval castle. I found a parking spot on the Winthrop Street side near the psychiatric wing. Regretting that I was no longer a cop and couldn't park on the grounds, I put a PBA card on the dashboard in hopes that I wouldn't get a ticket. I couldn't tell what the parking regulations were because all the signs had been pulled down, but there were plenty of spots on the street. Nobody would leave their car here if they didn't have to.

It was only twenty after twelve when I found the cafeteria, but Dr. Shapiro was already there at a corner table eating a sandwich stuffed with what looked like corned beef. I wasn't in the mood for meat and found a limp tuna sandwich and two large cans of V-8 juice. I'm not sure whether the V-8 was good for my hangover or whether it was just to ease my guilty conscience and make me feel I was doing something healthy for myself for a change.

Dr. Shapiro was short with a black brush mustache and a flat-top crewcut. I had about half my tuna sandwich down when he opened the manila envelope he had with him and began to lay out pictures of Bonnie's corpse taken at the autopsy. I lost my appetite and started to hear the words to "St. James Infirmary Blues" ringing in my ears. "I went down to St. James Infirmary, just to see my baby there. She was laid out on a long white table, so cold, so clean, so bare." I couldn't remember if I had the words right. I gagged on my V-8. I didn't want to do this anymore. She was so thin and so vulnerable and horribly alone, her young breasts, small and exposed. There were close-ups of her arms and hands showing the track marks.

"Look at this bruise," Dr. Shapiro was saying.

I took out my handkerchief and wiped my eyes and mopped the sweat from my forehead. I looked at the bruise just below the inside crook of her elbow.

"The needle came out the back of the vein, and by the location of where it came out, unless the vein was distorted or stretched when her arm was tied up, the needle was put in almost parallel to her arm facing her, an impossible angle for self-injection."

"In other words, somebody shot her up and blew the shot."

"Yes. And whoever it was, if they did the other shots, they did an excellent job."

I thought about nurse Cynthia and about Rocky, who was also an expert with a needle.

"Did you tell the police about this?"

"Of course. It's in my autopsy report. It's mostly an educated guess though. I have an assistant who studied vascular surgery. Maybe he pushed it a little. He used a computer to enhance some of the puncture angles." He pulled a copy of the report from his manila envelope and handed it to me. "I made one for you," he said. "But it's really not enough for the police to try to build a case on."

"She had no history of heroin use as far as I can determine. This would be an enormous run for a first-time user, wouldn't it?"

"Well, Detective." A small cynical smile appeared on his lips. "It did kill her. Stranger things have happened."

"Heroin seems so old-fashioned, out of date. Wouldn't she be more likely to be smoking crack if she went up there?"

"How long have you been off the streets, Detective?"

"Two years."

"It's making a big comeback, heroin. And its synthetic cousins. It never really went away. Just diminished. But even the junkies look out for themselves once in a while. A lot of them stay away from crack now. They see how whacked-out you get in a big hurry. There's an increasing demand for heroin. And we're getting more overdose episodes in here each month."

"What do you know about this drug that killed her?"

"Fentanyl? Just what I read in the newspapers. They gave it to my wife when she was in labor with our son. It's a tranquilizer, and it's deadly stuff when it comes from a street lab. They don't seem to know how to control its potency."

He glanced at the second half of my tuna sandwich. I had no intention of finishing it, and I knew what he was thinking. I asked him if I could have one of the photographs, the one that detailed the bruise on her arm. He slid the report back in the envelope and gave me the whole set, saying it was a duplicate. I thanked him and left. I wasn't sure I wanted all of them, because I knew that morbid curiosity would make me pull them out again during some long night in the pines.

I called Jack Conlin at the Seventy-ninth Precinct from the lobby of the hospital. He wasn't in but whoever answered his phone said he'd be right back. My car was still in one piece, and it didn't have a ticket.

I drove past the station house on Tompkins Avenue and continued on down to Myrtle to have a fresh look at Marcy Park. It was more of an overgrown playground that took up a long block of Myrtle between Marcy and Nostrand. The afternoon was sunny, and the streets of Bedford-Stuyvesant and the park were full of people. A very fast full-court basketball game was in progress, and small boys chased each other around and over the benches. Mothers strolled with small children. It's always hard to spot the drug zombies during the daytime, but they were there, lounging in twos and threes here and there in the middle area of the park, raggedy men and women not interested in basketball or sunshine, ready to fade away when I stepped out of the car.

I have to make myself remember that I'm no longer a cop when I'm in situations like this one. First, I seemed to be the only white person in the area, and second, I look like a cop simply by the fact that I'm out of the car and am not a potential drug customer. Third, I'm not armed and I don't have any backup, nor do I have the authority of the law behind me. What I am mostly, especially if I don't keep moving, is a potential victim.

I walked to the chainlink fence past two heavy black women waiting at the bus stop on the corner of Nostrand and Myrtle. To my right was the middle area of benches where I guessed that Bonnie had died. The junkies had already evaporated, and the area was empty. I had been here before; had viewed a young black man face down beneath one of the benches, the exit wounds from three 9mm slugs torn through the flesh and shirt of his back. He lay in a large shiny puddle of congealed blood. His sneakers had been taken. He was the victim of a basketball dispute. No blood, no foul. He had drawn the ultimate technical. We were able to get lots of help on that one and picked up the shooter before sundown at his grandmother's house. Both boys were seventeen and had been best friends. You can imagine what enemies do to each other in this neighborhood.

What had Bonnie been here for? Nothing seemed to fit. If she'd had a black boyfriend, maybe the situation was plausible. But if you wanted heroin in Brooklyn, you didn't have to come all the way up here to get it, especially if you were a rich, well-dressed white girl.

The basketball game had stopped, and its sweating participants eyed me curiously. I wanted to sit on one of the benches, to see what Bonnie had seen before she died, but I didn't want to put the chainlink fence between myself and the street, so I got back in the Honda and drove up Tompkins Avenue to the station house.

Here was a place where I could park like a cop. My PBA card would be respected, and if I got a ticket, I could take it to Conlin, and he would get it voided. There was a spot not too far down Greene Avenue around the corner from the entrance to the building. Each cop's personal car was pulled diagonally up over the curb, and I was able to squeeze the Honda between two of these.

I knew the desk sergeant by sight but couldn't remember his name. He was busy talking to a young Hispanic couple and simply nodded when I went by. Conlin was in his squad room filling out a report when I got upstairs. He smiled at me and motioned me to a seat beside his desk. He was a worried-looking man in his early forties with a full head of gray hair. I could remember when the hair had been black. Unlike most cops he typed with dexterity and speed.

"Where did you learn to type like that?" I asked, truly amazed.

"I took a typing course in high school," he said. "So I could meet girls in the secretarial curriculum."

"Did it work?" I asked.

"Knocked one up. Now we have four kids and a mortgage."

He pulled the report from the typewriter. I don't think he was finished, but I could tell he wanted to talk to me. He pulled a pen from his shirt pocket and made a correction on the report and then looked up.

"Whatta you got?" he asked.

"Probably nothing you don't have."

"Impossible," he said. "I know you too long to know you're not being cute. Think a minute, Connie. You're working for the family."

"Was working for the family."

"Whatever. But you know the players. What do you know that we don't know? All we got is a good-looking young stiff and an autopsy report that says some of the holes in her arms maybe weren't made by her."

"Are you in charge of the investigation?"

"I could be." He paused to light two inches of cigar that he took from his ashtray. He didn't look like a cigar smoker, more like a three pack a day cigarette man. "Nobody really wants this one," he said, blowing out a cloud of blue smoke. "We got nothing. So . . . if I get something: Bah-bing, I'm in charge. I don't want to be but if I am, I get to go hang out with the good-looking, well-heeled women in Brooklyn Heights. I understand this one's got a knockout stepmother."

"Step-grandmother."

"Grandmother. Wow. I never did a grandmother. That'd be a new wrinkle." He laughed loudly. "Get it," he said. "New wrinkle. Grandmother."

"I got it," I said. "They're very nice wrinkles by the way. And the interesting part is, she used to be a nurse."

He sat forward in his chair. "Now that is interesting. You mean like a nurse who gives injections and can find a vein and draw blood. Interesting. Circumstantial, you have to admit. But interesting."

"Your victim also had a local boyfriend who shot speed and coke and owned his own set of hypodermics in a leather case."

"Ooo," he breathed, leaning back in the chair and blowing out another cloud of smoke. "I like that. You wouldn't happen to have a name on the boyfriend?"

"Roland Starza, aka Rocky. Drove Atlantic City buses for an outfit called Mola on Court Street downtown."

"Oh, that's excellent, Connie. I don't suppose you know where we could find this Roland aka Rocky?"

"If I knew where to find him, Jackie, he would be sitting next to me at your desk this very minute."

"I'm sure he would be, Connie. What else you got for me?"

"Nothing, Jackie. What do you have for me?"

He leaned forward. We were both smiling sarcastically. "I don't like to be called Jackie," he whispered.

"And I'm not crazy about Connie," I whispered back.

"Her I.D. was in her underwear," he said. "Driver's license and credit cards in there right next to the pubes."

"What's that mean?"

"I don't know," he said, grinding the tiny butt of the cigar in the ashtray. "Maybe she thought she might be ripped off. A fairly safe prediction for a white girl in a project park in Bed-Sty."

"You've got something else," I said. "I can tell by your shit-eating grin."

"Her shoelaces were tied backwards."

"Like Rockefeller's."

"The very same. Somebody dressed her."

"Then she might have died somewhere else."

"Except for her lividity. The autopsy shows that her blood settled in that sitting position on the bench."

"So somebody dressed her while she was still alive."

"Brilliant," he said. "Have you ever thought of a career in law enforcement?"

"What else?"

"That's it." He paused for a moment but he still had the grin on his face. "Why don't you ask me what I haven't got?"

"What do you mean?"

"I don't have any snitch reports. No sightings. Nobody, and I mean nobody, puts her in the neighborhood. Ever."

"How hard did you work at it?"

"Very hard. Twelve of us did it in two shifts, and then four of us canvassed for three days. The captain kept preempting the assignments, because her father kept calling. I understand he's well-hung politically."

"Grandfather."

"Okay, grandfather. Housing helped us in the projects. I promise you we covered the neighborhood. We leaned on the junkies and crackheads. You know what they're like. You squeeze 'em, they oink. Nothing. I'm telling you, Con, she wasn't here. Somebody dumped her here."

"So it's an ongoing investigation?"

"Not really. It's all dead ends. That's why I was hoping you had something. I guess we'll try to find this Rocky. But if he did it, or even just knows that his girlfriend bought it, he's not gonna be sitting in his apartment watching a ball game on TV waiting for us to pick him up. He's long gone, especially if he's our guy."

I told him about my encounter with Rocky at the bus drivers' motel. He looked thoughtful for a moment, and then asked: "Do you know if she had any black friends?"

I hesitated, not sure whether I should bring the Baron and Irene into it. They were 120 miles away in Atlantic City, and Baron had a record and they would use him up. Maybe Irene had a record too.

"Why?" I asked. I was stalling. I knew the answer.

"To connect her to the neighborhood," he said.

I told him about Baron and Irene then, painting them in a

positive way as people who wanted to help Bonnie overcome her alcoholism and drug addiction. To my relief he didn't seem interested and did not write their names down. He simply asked me to talk to them when I got back to Atlantic City to see if I could tie them to anyone or anything in Brooklyn, and if I did, to let him know.

"What do you want me to tell you, Con? She got some bad drugs. She's the sixth fentanyl death in the city this week. The stuff is easy to make, but it's impossible for these little apartment labs to control the quality. They make a batch like you'd make fudge in your kitchen. They make a bit, try a bit. They don't have a cage full of rats to inject it into first. We got cops on the streets with loudspeakers trying to warn the junkies off the stuff. A lot of them are after it as a special thrill. They're coming in from out of town just to try the stuff."

"How many of them died in Brooklyn?"

"She's the first one."

"I just saw an A.M.E. at Kings County named Shapiro. You know him?"

"Of course."

"He says heroin's back."

"Well, it never really went away. But he's right. It's making a comeback. Kids on the street, they see how quick crack turns you into an asshole. They want to get to be assholes slower, so they do heroin. You know what the big tip-off is?"

"No. But I have a feeling you're going to tell me."

"The throw-up."

"What?"

"You know. Vomit. The rice and red stuff splattered on the sidewalk. You see a lot more of it now. Take a walk around this wonderful neighborhood some Sunday morning. It's all over the place again."

"Please. I just had lunch."

"You got to watch where you're stepping. Like the poodle shit in Brooklyn Heights. Seriously though. You were twenty years on the job. You must've had a junkie throw up in your squad car once in a while."

"Never. They were too scared."

He leaned back and laughed hard. A detective at a desk across the room looked up at us curiously.

"She was a private school kid," I said. "Sailboats. Summers in Maine. She just doesn't fit the inner-city, hard-drug scene."

"I know you worked some tough neighborhoods, Con. You must know that white kids come here all the time. In fact, that's about the only reason they come here. To cop drugs. She was a junkie, Con. You know you can't trust a junkie."

"She was a pill-head. She didn't like needles."

"They all say that. Until the first time they try it. I've seen altar boys pick a vein open with a straight pin so they could push an eyedropper full of junk into it. Junk is a great leveler, Con. Who knows where she got the stuff. Maybe she brought it with her from New Jersey. But she took it, or her boyfriend gave it to her. She died, that I can guarantee you. She may not have got the drugs in this precinct, but she was certainly dead in this precinct. It's an old story, Con. And you know it. You knew her down in Atlantic City. You don't know what she was into here."

He leaned away from me and slid open a desk drawer and extracted a file folder and handed it to me. Inside was a pile of glossy eight-by-ten photographs. The top one showed Bonnie's body seated on a park bench. I closed the folder.

"You don't seem very curious," he said.

"I've got the naked ones from the autopsy in the car. They're not very pleasant. Can I keep these?"

"I guess so. I got another set. If I need 'em, I'll call you."

We stood up and shook hands. He held my hand for a moment too long to force me to make eye contact with him. I knew the trick.

"You didn't tangle with this little filly, did you, Con?"

"No," I answered flatly. "What makes you ask?"

"You seem emotional, involved."

"You get like that when you retire," I said.

"Jesus Christ, Con. She was an I.V. drug user. You didn't fuck her, did you?"

"Knock it off, Jack," I said. We left the squad room and walked past the front desk.

"What does it mean that you couldn't place her in the neighborhood?" I asked.

"I don't know. Maybe the boyfriend gave her the hit. And when she croaked on him, he dumped her."

"Why would he dump her carefully on a bench behind a fence in a park where it was dangerous for him to be and just as carefully tie her shoes and leave her needle behind where it could be found and put her I.D. in her panties so she wouldn't get lost in the morgue?"

We had reached the glass front doors. We had to step aside to let the constant flow of people pass. Two patrolmen brought in a small well-dressed black man with his hands cuffed behind his back. His head was bleeding and he was cursing the patrolmen.

"You read too much into the situation, Con. It's your only case. You need to lighten up. Get a hobby. Take up fishing. These kids come here all the time. She was a new student at Pratt. Maybe she wandered over here with her boyfriend. Sure the dealers don't know her. She buys the stuff from someone who bought it from a dealer. The stuff was killing people in Harlem not too long ago. It killed eighteen people in Pittsburgh last year. There's all kinds of shit being made out there now. We bust up these labs all the time. They give the shit they make brand names. Mongrel. Goodfella. This stuff was called Tango and Cash."

"But still, you couldn't place her here. Your men couldn't find anyone who saw her."

"Take that with a grain of salt, Con. Maybe somebody dumped her here, or maybe she was here and the people who saw her don't want to say anything. Nobody ever knows a dead body in this neighborhood. You know that."

He walked me out to the sidewalk. The late afternoon sun was summer-strong and warm on my face.

"We'll try to find the boyfriend. That's about the best we can do. Maybe he can fill in the gaps. But, if I had to end it right now, I'd say they pumped up together, first with heroin and then with the stronger stuff, she bought the farm and he dumped her."

He looked at me to see if I approved of his scenario.

"Maybe," I said.

"If you get any information on this Rocky in South Jersey give me a call."

We shook hands again. He turned and bumped into two women in patrol uniforms who were hurrying out of the station house. "Excuse me, ladies," he said and was gone, back into the chaos inside.

I walked to the corner and turned on Greene Avenue feeling vulnerable in this neighborhood. My car was about halfway up the block. When I reached it I saw that the small rear window on the passenger side had been smashed. Large crumbs of greenish safety glass covered the back seat, but I could see that the radio and tape deck were still intact.

I tossed the folder of photographs on the seat and got in the car and checked the glove compartment. It was empty, and the maps and insurance cards and receipts and other detritus that had been its contents were scattered on the floor under the dashboard. I couldn't find the manila envelope with the autopsy pictures in it, and that both pleased me and pissed me off. I was glad that I didn't have to look at them again but annoyed that someone else, some unknown street person, would also get a crack at invading Bonnie's final privacy. There was a little change drawer to the left of the steering wheel and that was empty too. I tried to recall what it had contained and seemed to remember three 35-cent Garden State Parkway tokens. I had a fifty- or sixty-dollar window-replacement job for a dollar-five burglary. I slammed the door angrily and walked back to the station house. Inside, I told the desk sergeant whose name I now remembered was Carberry that I didn't want to make a formal report, but that I wanted them to know about it so they could prevent it happening in the future. He was a tall man in his late forties with short curly red hair and a pot belly.

"I know," he said sadly. "We got an uneasy truce here. We lean on 'em and that gets 'em to leave the cars alone that have current shields in 'em. But we can't get 'em to stop breaking into the visitors' vehicles."

I left again, deciding I would get it fixed in Jersey. It was a warm spring day with no rain in sight. I could tape some plastic over it when I got to the cottage and have it fixed tomorrow in Hammonton.

I drove by Marcy Park again, but there was nothing more to see. The same junkies sat on the same benches or stood toward the back of the park, their shoulders hunched over, exchanging money or drugs. The same quick basketball game floated up and down the small court at the Marcy Avenue end of the park. More black women waited at the bus stop.

I drove down Dekalb Avenue and over Hanson Place past the Brooklyn Academy of Music and crossed Flatbush Avenue into Boerum Hill. It was a relief to get out of the ghetto. It was an immense and relentless place and had started taking hungry bites out of me the minute I left something unprotected. I was glad to be able to leave it behind. I had been able to leave my anger there too, and when I got to the house, I felt only impatience to leave the city.

I packed quickly and left, but on my way out the door, I noticed that the answering machine was blinking. There was a message from one of the tenants upstairs who had seen me come into the house. He had a leaky faucet. There was also a message from Loretta. She had talked to someone who thought they knew where Rocky was. I called the tenant and left the phone number of our handyman, a number I knew he already had. While I was dialing Loretta, I wondered how we had ever accomplished anything before these machines had been invented. It was a silly thought, of course. We talked to each other. And things got done just the same. We wrote notes, stopped each other in the street and made dates and appointments.

I got the Mola Land Cruises machine too with Loretta's voice on the recording. Because she was pregnant, she made a lot of trips to the bathroom, but I couldn't wait. I hung up without leaving a message and locked up my apartment and left.

Just across the Goethals Bridge on the twelve-lane New Jersey Turnpike, the late afternoon sun hung blood red in smog and haze over the petroleum and chemical storage tanks of Elizabeth.

Ninety minutes later I was on New Jersey 206 in the darkness of a misty spring evening with stunted pitch pines, cranberry bogs and orderly rows of blueberry bushes zipping by in the peripheral light from my headlights. I bought a ham and cheese hero at a Wawa convenience store and ate it on my dock when I got home. Inside I drank a Corona and tried to read, but I kept thinking about Rocky and where I might start to look for him the next day. I switched on the Mets game from New York, but there was too much static that night so I flipped to the Phillies-Cubs and listened halfheartedly as I nursed another beer. I wanted to talk with Loretta, but I didn't have a home number for her. I called Grace Somers twice and got her machine both times. The second time was at the end of the baseball game, and I told the machine to tell her I was going to bed and would call tomorrow.

11

It began to rain early Wednesday morning, first a few tentative drops, then a steady downpour, pocking the silver surface of the river with a moving pattern of dots and ripples. I was out on the porch with my second cup of coffee when I felt the wind shift and start to blow from the southeast. It was a little after eight o'clock and the rain started about ten minutes later. Soon it was coming down in sheets, obscuring the cedars on the far bank and driving in under the porch roof so that I had to go inside. By the time I had finished stacking the breakfast dishes in the dishwasher it had slowed down and then almost stopped. The weather vane on the gazebo at the far end of the dock showed that the wind had shifted again and now blew out of the west, and the rain had settled into a steady drizzle that I knew would last all day. I called the Sooys to tell them I would pick Suzie up late in the afternoon. Mary told me not to hurry, that Suzie had been romping with her dogs and swimming and having a wonderful time.

Before I left for Margate I reached into the back of the Honda, wetting one knee on the saturated seat, and taped a piece of clear plastic over the broken rear vent window. While I was doing that I discovered the manila folder of autopsy pictures partially hidden under the driver's seat. I was almost disappointed to have them back. I put the crime scene pictures from the park with them and slipped them into the fat accordion folder that sat on the seat beside me. It was the folder of Bonnie memorabilia that Cynthia Arnold had given me two weeks earlier. I intended to spend the rainy morning sorting the stuff out and hoping for a lead to Rocky's whereabouts. As I drove I noticed that a trickle of rain water still found its way inside the plastic and ran down the door panel fabric, vanishing behind the edge of the seat. The noisy slap of the windshield wipers gave me a lonely feeling in the gray morning silence, and I automatically punched in the cassette that protruded from the dashboard tape deck.

"I . . . want you back again." Mick Jagger's slow sensual rhythms annoyed me. "Tell me . . . you're coming back to me. Tell me . . . " I popped the tape and the Philadelphia news came on the radio, traffic reports from the Schuylkill Expressway. Somehow they were comforting, real. I had played the song over and over on the return trip from New York yesterday, but now it seemed just a depressing indulgence like waking next to the girl you went home with from a bar late at night. My cop friends used to call those late-night liaisons coyote dates, meaning that if you woke the next morning with one of them sleeping on your arm, you would choose to chew the arm off rather than wake her. I concentrated on the financial news. The stock market had closed mixed yesterday and would open in less than an hour. Interesting.

A half-hour later I was at my desk in Margate with the sports section spread in front of me. The A's were running away with the American League West and Mark McGwire was on a pace to break Roger Maris's home-run record. Ah, the promises of spring. Rain washed in sheets down my windows, obscuring my rooftop view of the ocean. The fat accordion file of Bonnie's credit card charges, phone bills, address books and other material sat on the client chair beside the desk, distracting me. I knew I had to go through it, but I didn't want to deal with my memories of Bonnie, at least not directly. I didn't want to look at pictures of her or sales slips documenting things she had bought for herself and never used. I could hear Thelma opening the store downstairs.

I found the number for Mola Land Cruises in Brooklyn and dialed it. Loretta answered on the second ring. She was very happy to hear from me.

"Those roses were the nicest thing anyone has done for me in a long time," she said. "They're absolutely beautiful and they smell divine. I'm looking at them right now. Thank you."

"You're nice," I said. "People should do nice things for you."

"My mother came in yesterday afternoon and saw them and wanted to know if you were someone I could marry. Honest to God. She's very Old World. I told her I didn't think so. But anyway, why don't you come over here and take me to lunch?"

"I'm in South Jersey," I said.

"That's too bad. How about the next time you're here."

"Love to," I said. I wasn't sure I meant it, but it didn't hurt to let her know I would anyway. It wouldn't be an unpleasant meal. She was a very pretty lady even if she was a hood's girl.

"I'm going to hold you to it," she laughed.

"Fine," I said. "Look, Loretta. I need some information. Anything you can think of. The girl that was killed. The one that was hanging around with Rocky. I think he might be responsible for her death." I knew this might clam her up for good, laying it out like this, but I had nothing to lose. Perhaps she gave me everything she had the day before. I had no way of knowing.

"I was hired to protect her," I continued. "She was just a kid. Seventeen. With everything to live for. I was fond of her. Like she was my own daughter. Do you understand?"

"I think so," she said quietly. "You hurt. I can hear it in your voice."

"I know you want to protect Rocky because you're carrying his kid. But I need to find him. If you can think of anything you haven't told me. Anything at all. He's the only lead I have. Maybe he's not responsible. But maybe he can lead me to the person who is and then clear himself."

"How did she die?"

"Overdose."

"Speed?"

"No, heroin. And something else like it."

"Rocky doesn't take heroin."

"You told me that yesterday. So maybe he's not responsible. Someone shot her up with heroin. But I need to know where he is. You left a message that you might know. I need to ask him some questions."

"He's in Jersey," she said.

"How do you know that?"

"He called me from there."

"When?"

"Last week."

"What makes you think he's still there?"

"I want to go to a more private phone," she said.

"Is someone there with you?"

"No, but they tap us all the time."

"Who does?"

"Mostly Casino Control."

"They're Jersey. How can they tap you in New York?"

"They do it through the Feds. They keep trying to prove that we're connected to organized crime. And we're just a little bus charter business."

"And are you?"

"What?"

"Connected to organized crime?"

"Well, I don't know how organized it is." She laughed. There were footsteps on the stairs and Thelma Herzog came into my office carrying two coffees and the *New York Times* folded back to the crossword puzzle. I put my hand over the mouthpiece and said: "I got one up a tree here, Thelma. You can stay and listen if you want, but it might be a while."

"I'll be back," she said. "I have things I want to do." She put one of the containers in front of me and left.

"I'm going to my sister's," Loretta said when I got back on the phone. "She just lives down the block. I'll call you back in two minutes." I gave her my number and she hung up. The coffee was too hot to drink and before it became cool enough, the phone rang and it was Loretta again. Her voice sounded tinny, and I knew she must be on a cheap phone.

"You sound far away," I said.

"Korean phone," she said.

"What's going on?" I asked. One of my sophisticated interrogation techniques.

"There was a big drug deal," she said in a low voice.

"Why are you whispering?"

"The baby-sitter is in the living room."

"Tell me about it."

"Rocky never said too much, but I got a lot from talking to Mr. Russo."

"Why didn't you tell me this yesterday?"

"I didn't know who you were. I didn't trust you. Rocky has people looking for him who want to kill him."

"How do you know I don't?"

"Instinct. And I have to trust someone. Rocky might need help."

Say it with flowers. My roses had worked better than a wallet full of twenty-dollar bills.

"How did this deal go down?"

"As near as I can tell, this man Doc that I told you about yesterday was in charge. He makes drugs or gets them from someone who does. I'm not sure."

"What kind of drugs?"

"Rocky calls it crank. I told you already. That's speed, right?"

"Where does he make it?"

"I don't know. Down there in Jersey somewhere."

"You don't know where?"

"No."

"Where do they sell it?"

"Philadelphia mostly and up here in New York now. They were just getting it set up here with people to sell it to."

"What happened?"

"I think they stole the drugs and stole the money on one of the deals. That was the big score that Rocky talked about. They waited for an extra big one to come along. I think what happened from what Mr. Russo said is that they made two deals, one in Philadelphia and one in New York. Then they stole the money from the buyers in Philadelphia and sold the drugs to the people in New York. So there's businessmen from Philly looking for them, plus the bikers are after them too."

"Bikers?"

"That's who makes the drugs. They owe them for the drugs."

"Doesn't sound too healthy."

"Boy, that's an understatement. I don't know what's going to happen to Rocky."

I had a pretty good idea. The little piece of him that I wanted was nothing compared to what other people wanted to do to the boy. It's not often that you get justice in this world but I had it right there in the palm of my hand. If I wanted harm to come to Rocky, all I had to do was wait and I knew as sure as the sun rises in the east that harm would come.

"Will you look for him?" she asked. I didn't really comprehend what she was saying. Of course I would look for him. I wanted him first because there wouldn't be much left if I got to him second.

"On a professional basis," she added.

I was afraid that's what she meant.

"You want to hire me to find Rocky?" I asked.

"Yes. I'll pay whatever your fee is. Don't worry about the money. My family is good for it."

"I couldn't do it," I said. "It seems like a conflict to me. I'm employed by the Arnold family. Or rather, was employed."

"But you're not employed by them now. They found her. She's dead."

That fact still took my breath away, and I had to pause for a moment.

"I intend to look for Rocky," I said finally. "When I find him I'll let you know. But you don't have to pay me. I'm going to look anyway."

"Please don't hurt him when you find him."

"I can't promise you that."

"Okay, you can hurt him. Just don't kill him. Think of my kid."

"I'll try my best," I said and hung up.

I stood and walked around my desk and stared at the heavy accordion folder that sat on the client chair. Then I walked to the window and looked out at the gray rain and the distant white-capped surf beyond the tops of the houses and stores. The rain made me think of my leaking car, and I turned immediately toward the door intent on getting it to an autoglass shop, glad to have an excuse to leave the office. But as I was reaching for my jacket on the coat tree by the door the phone rang. For a brief moment I thought about letting the machine pick it up, but I went back and answered it and was pleased to hear Grace Somers at the other end of the line. She had packed her kids off on the school bus and was returning my messages from the night before.

I confirmed that she had the evening off and we made a date to have dinner together. I agreed to pick her up at seven and we chatted briefly about the rain. When she said she was going to spend the day cleaning and grocery shopping, I thought that I would like to do that too. I wanted to do some pleasant routine things; anything that would keep me away from the accordion folder next to my desk. I decided that getting the car window fixed would be pleasant enough.

I was reaching for my jacket on the coat rack again when I heard someone on the stairs. I pulled the door open, and Thelma came in carrying more coffee. The container she had brought to me earlier was still sitting near my phone. The *Times* section that contained the crossword puzzle was folded under her arm, and the part that I could see looked about half done. There was no longer any need to go searching for a pleasant routine thing to do. It had arrived.

Without even greeting her, I turned and walked back to the desk where I lifted the accordion folder off the client chair to clear a seat for her. As I was bending to put it on the carpet, she asked: "What's that?"

It occurred to me to lie to her and tell her it was just boring insurance fraud papers. That way we could do the crossword puzzle and she would not want to nose through the material, and I could avoid looking at the stuff for a little longer. But that was a lie, and through the course of twenty years of interviewing liars on an almost daily basis, I'd come to the conclusion that it's easier to tell the truth. That way you don't have to remember so much.

"It's background on my teenage runaway," I said. "And autopsy and crime scene photos." I realized as soon as I said it that the last thing Thelma knew about the case was that I had delivered Bonnie safely to her grandfather in Brooklyn.

She looked shocked, covering her open mouth very briefly with her hand.

"STUDENT-ARTIST OVERDOSES," she said, bending to pick up the folder. "I saw it on the front of the *New York Post* at Parti-Pak but I didn't connect it with your girl." The folded *Times* slipped out from under her arm and landed in a tent shape on the carpet but she ignored it. "You've got a good one here," she said, standing the folder up on my desk and untying the ribbon that held it. "What was her name again?"

"Bonnie," I said, sitting quickly behind the desk because she looked as if she might take the seat herself. She spread the folder and found the manila envelope with the photographs in it immediately. Plopping down in the client chair, she began to leaf through them.

"Who do you think killed her?" she asked.

"It's what they call a victimless crime," I said. "She was shooting heroin and took a substitute and it killed her."

"Victimless," she snorted. "What a crock. Whoever gave it or sold it to her should be stoned to death. The concept that drug addicts aren't victims of a crime is absurd. Who do you think killed her?"

"What makes you think that I think someone killed her?"

"You have this file and you're a detective and this file is sitting here next to your desk waiting for you to go through it. You brought police pictures back from New York. And you liked the girl and want to believe that she wouldn't do that to herself."

"Well, there is some speculation that someone gave her one or two of the shots."

"See that. You do think someone killed her."

"Junkies shoot each other up all the time," I said. "It's not unusual. Like the line from the Bob Dylan song: 'I don't have the strength to get up and take another shot.'"

"I never liked him," she said. "Even if he is Jewish. No voice. Weird lyrics. Too much drugs."

"You were just too old for the sixties," I said. "You had to be there." We had had this discussion before. More than once.

"I wasn't too old," she said. "The people who created the

sixties and indulged in them were just too young to know any better."

"His name is Rocky. Rocky Starza."

"That's the guy who gave you the black eye."

"You have a good memory."

"And why do you think he killed her?"

"He screwed up on the drugs he gave her. The police aren't really interested. It's manslaughter two at best."

"And you don't believe it."

"How do you know that?"

"I know how you think. You told me last week that she was a recovering pill-head. Now all of a sudden she's running wild on heroin. It doesn't fit."

"I'm always amazed at how much you know about drugs, Thelma."

"You didn't invent them, you know. When I was a kid they put cocaine in the Coca-Cola."

"You're not that old."

"Is that a compliment?"

"This Rocky didn't like heroin either. And I found out this morning that he had just made a lot of money on a drug deal."

"And Bonnie knew the details."

"Possibly. And he had screwed and stolen from some nasty people who are now looking for him."

"And she knew where to find him."

"She was definitely a threat. He had a partner too who might not have liked her having too much information."

Thelma had put the large police photos down on the desk and was pawing through the folder again. This time she came out with the snapshots Cynthia had given me. She looked at each one briefly until she came to the Polaroid I had lifted from Rocky's room at the bus drivers' motel.

"Who's this?" she asked.

"That's Bonnie. The other girl's name is Julie Stockton. I don't know who the guy is." It occurred to me that I had showed that picture to Ben Arnold the night I first met him in Atlantic City. He had told me he didn't know Julie then. So had Cynthia Arnold. Were they lying or had they just met her during the funeral? Somewhere in my wallet or my suitcase I had her phone number, and I intended to call her. She would know who the biker type in the picture was. And if Ben and Cynthia had been lying.

"He looks familiar," Thelma said.

"You can't possibly know a whole lot of bikers," I said. "But then with you I am constantly amazed."

"I know him from somewhere else," she said, scrutinizing the picture. "Can I make a copy of this?"

Her request was strictly rhetorical. She was up and through the doorway and headed downstairs to the copy machine in her office before I could answer. Thelma's quickness constantly amazed me. She was more nimble than any old lady I knew and lighter on her feet than most young ones. She had been a dancer in the old days of Atlantic City. A Philadelphia showgirl, she liked to say, who wanted to be a New York City ballerina.

I emptied the remains of both cups of cold coffee in my toilet and sat at my desk again and drank some coffee from the fresh container. The manila envelope of autopsy photos sat on the blotter in front of me. It would have been easier for me to touch if it had been six feet of timber rattler. It was an effort for me even to push the folder to the back of the desk.

The phone rang as Thelma came back into the room. She tossed the Polaroid and two black-and-white photocopies on my desk as I answered it.

"I know who this is," she said, pointing to the photograph. I silenced her by putting my index finger up to my pursed lips. The caller was the Baron.

"I just tried you at home," he said. "I'm glad to see you are hard at work." He was using the Jamaican accent. I wondered if he'd forgotten that I knew about his humble Inlet beginnings.

"What can I do for you?"

"I have a new client for you. A very influential and wealthy man."

"And who might that be?"

"Mr. Winston Barbay at your service," he said.

"And does Mr. Winston Barbay want to pay me? Or is this pro bono community service-type work?"

"Mr. Winston Barbay will pay you handsomely."

"And the job . . . Let me guess? Contract killing? Never one of my specialties. Multiple bone-breaking? I'm not good at that either. I usually get my own broken instead."

"I just want you to find the motherfucker," he said, no trace of any island in his voice now, unless it was Rikers. "I'll take care of what happens to him. You won't have to worry about that. You can name your price." For once Thelma didn't seem interested in one of my telephone conversations. Instead she looked like the cat that ate the canary. When she caught my eye, she pointed to the picture again and then to the side of her forehead to indicate how smart she was to figure things out.

"Look Baron," I said. "I'm in the middle of something . . . "

When Thelma understood that I was trying to get rid of him, she waved me off, indicating that I should talk to him. Like a third-base coach. Go for it; try to score.

"What's up?" I asked him, savoring the irony of the day. I had been asked to rescue Rocky by Loretta. And to help murder him by the Baron. And both on a professional basis. I, myself, only wanted to pound him until he begged for mercy, which was somewhere in the middle. And not very professional at all. And Thelma . . . Well, Thelma thought the whole thing was pretty damned entertaining.

"She wasn't there," Baron said to my prompting.

"Who?" I looked at Thelma. She smiled.

"Bonnie. Who else?"

"Wasn't where?"

"Bedford-Stuyvesant, fool. She was not hanging around Marcy Park or anywhere else in Bed-Sty."

"How do you know that?"

"I called around, man."

"What does that mean?"

"It means that that Rocky fuck dumped her there after she ODed. That's what it means."

"Did somebody see her being dumped?"

"No, but how else she gonna get there? She wasn't hanging around. She was never on that scene."

"How do you know that?"

"Come on, Con-man. A white chick. A beautiful, blonde white chick coppin' skag in Bed-Sty. There's a big space and a lot of shit goin' down between Bedford and Stuyvesant avenues, but it ain't that big. There are homeys that know everything that goes on in that park, man. Every fucking thing. They were born there and they'll die there, you dig? And I know people who know these homeys, so I made some phone calls, been making them, a lot of them, and believe me when I tell you, Connie, man; she was never there. Somebody would have seen her. You don't just come and shoot up and nod out and die. You hang out a little. You buy the stuff. You cook it. Maybe you socialize with the other junkies. None of that happened. Do you understand?"

"How come you know so much about Marcy Park?" I asked. "Have you been there?"

"Naw, I ain't been to New York in ten years, Connie. And I never went to Brooklyn when I did come up there. I used to get in enough trouble in Harlem. But a needle park is a needle park, man. I been in plenty of them. The rusty playground equipment. The broke down benches. Maybe a half-assed basketball game. And a junkie is a junkie is a junkie, Ernest. That's where I been. Wasted days and wasted nights. Seen a lot of people using. And a lot of people dying. And never seen one like that little Bonnie child. It didn't happen, man. None of it."

I didn't want to tell him that Jack Conlin had told me the same thing, that the cops couldn't turn up anybody who could place her in the neighborhood either.

"How did she get there then?" I asked.

"Somebody dumped her there."

"So if your homeys see every fucking thing that goes on in that park, then why didn't they see somebody dump her?"

Thelma frowned at my language.

"Good question. I'm workin' on it," Baron said.

"Why don't you call me when you have the answer. And look, Winston, you didn't ask for my advice, but you're going to get it. If you keep telling people that you want to kill Rocky, and then he has a simple accidental death like walking in front of a speeding cement truck, you might have to pay for it anyway."

"I'll keep that in mind, officer. Cuff me. I'll go happy."
The phone clicked dead.

"Raymond Stockton," Thelma said.

I looked at her blankly because I was still thinking about
the Baron and how to prevent the mayhem he had planned if
he found Rocky before I did. If I could keep the Baron from
killing Rocky and Loretta from marrying him, I would have
saved two clients, even though I wouldn't take a dime from
either one of them and certainly wouldn't tell them I considered them clients, or that to hire my services all you had to do
was ask for them. And have a worthy cause.

Thelma flipped the Polaroid around and put it on the blotter facing me and tapped it emphatically.

"Raymond Stockton," she said, indicating the bearded
biker. "That's who that is. Raymond Stockton."

I tried to focus my attention on the picture. "The biker?" I
asked. "That's Julie's last name. How do you know a biker?"

"Who's Julie?" Thelma asked.

"Julie Stockton," I said. "The other girl in the picture."

"Relationship?"

"I don't know. Sister? Or maybe it's just a coincidence."

"I doubt it. Maybe it's his daughter?"

I scrutinized the picture. The beard made it hard to tell the
man's age. "Or his wife," I said.

"No. It's got to be a daughter or a niece. He's older than
he looks," Thelma said. I had the sudden eerie feeling that she
could read my mind. It was not the first time I had that feeling
with Thelma. Especially when she was excited about something and concentrating on it.

"How old?"

"Mid to late forties."

"How do you know him?"

"We were on the county board of the United Fund for a
year."

"Recently?"

"No. This was eight or nine years ago."

"They have bikers running the charities in Atlantic
County? There aren't enough upstanding citizens to do the
job?"

"He's an attorney. Well, he was. I haven't heard much about him lately."

That rang a bell. "Doc," I said.

"What?" Thelma asked. "Doc who?"

"Hold on a sec," I told her. I pulled the accordion file to me and began to rummage through it. One section was a mess of notes that I had been throwing into it, many of them seriously wrinkled from riding in my pocket for a day or two. As I had several times in the past week, I made a mental note to straighten it all out and type everything onto clean uniform sheets of paper.

I found what I was looking for, the notes I had made in the car after my face-to-face with Loretta in Brooklyn. On the second sheet I had written: "Doc—a lawyer. Rocky friend."

"Rocky had a friend named Doc who was an attorney," I said, scanning both pages of my notes. "He was from Atlantic City, or rather from somewhere in this area, according to Loretta."

"Who's Loretta?"

"Rocky's pregnant New York squeeze."

"Lucky her."

"And they were partners in a recent drug score. Rocky and Doc, I mean. Not Loretta. A big one." I explained to her about the rip off of the bikers and the Philadelphia mobsters as narrated to me by Loretta.

"I never heard anyone call him Doc," Thelma said. "You're making a big leap here by assuming Raymond Stockton is Doc."

"Why? Julie Stockton was a friend of Bonnie's. I met her at the Arnolds' in Brooklyn. If Raymond is her father or her uncle, then he probably knew Rocky."

"Makes no sense logically," she said. "There are a lot of bikers in Atlantic County and around the world. Your Doc might be somebody they both know. Or just a friend of Rocky's."

"I'll run it down," I said. "Detective work isn't always logical. Meanwhile, tell me about Raymond Stockton, the biker-lawyer."

"When I knew Raymond, he was a criminal attorney. And

a good one. A little odd but good. Wore a pony tail and expensive suits but didn't have that beard. And had begun to acquire a reputation for successfully defending drug dealers. And made a lot of money doing it. He was a city councilman in Linwood and very active in the community. A couple of years after our term on the United Fund board, he was forced to resign from the Linwood council after he admitted using marijuana at a party in his home. He claimed the charge was police revenge for the drug dealers he had gotten free on technicalities. There wasn't enough evidence for a criminal charge, and as far as I know he's still a lawyer. I seem to remember he stopped practicing altogether eventually, but I lost track of him. He had a real nice home in Linwood, so I was told, although I never went there. Wife, couple of kids. This girl must be one of the kids."

"That's easy enough to find out," I said, rummaging through the folder until I found the telephone number Julie had given me in Brooklyn.

"What are you going to do?" Thelma asked.

"Call Julie and ask her."

"Ask her what?"

"Who Raymond Stockton is. And what he is to her."

"I wouldn't do that."

"Why not?"

"If she is his daughter—and I'm almost sure she is—it'll tip him that you're on to him. And he'll be long gone like Rocky."

"I'm sure he's long gone already if he's our guy. You don't steal from a biker gang and the mob and then stick around to gloat over it."

"But she might know where he is. Even if she doesn't know what he did. You must be able to find a better, more subtle way to question her."

"Such as?"

"She's very pretty. Why don't you ask her to dinner?"

"Why? Well, for starters, she's at least fifteen years younger than me."

"That's good," she said, smiling a wicked little smile. "It'll make your blood course faster through your veins."

"And second, I'm on the threshold of a relationship," I said.

"You sound like my late husband, Shelly," she said. "He was always on the threshold of some young thing. He liked to rescue them from the evils of Atlantic City. Sort of like the cat rescuing the canary. And, like you, he always had undying loyalty to them . . . until the next one came along."

"Shelly had other women?" I asked.

"I was his only woman," she said. "Once in a while he had another girl. It made his blood course faster through his veins."

"I really like Grace," I said.

"Nobody said you had to sleep with this Julie." She looked thoughtful for a moment. "But you might have to if you're going to get her to give her father up."

"You make me blush," I said. "Your libido gets totally out of control now and again."

"Shelly used to say I had a lot of imagination in bed."

"Maybe you could give me some tips sometime," I said. "About what you like to do in bed."

"What I like to do in bed now is read," she said, looking wistfully out at the rain. "What happened to your window?"

"Where?" I asked, thinking she was talking about one of my office windows.

"In the car."

I told her.

"Are you going to get it fixed?" she asked. "Or get a sump pump installed? It seemed to be leaking in pretty badly when I parked behind you."

I stood up. "I'm going to get it fixed right now," I said.

"Can I take this folder downstairs?" she said. She picked up the accordion folder and began to tie the ribbon around it.

"What do you want it down there for?"

"I saw a bunch of long-distance phone bills in there. I'll get one of the girls to put them in the computer data base along with the dates they were made. And then we can sort them in numerical order and see which ones were most frequently called and if there is any pattern to the dates they were made."

"Isn't that a lot of trouble? You don't even know whose phone bills they are."

"I presume they came from the Arnolds. They must be important to your case or you wouldn't have them. And besides, I have no busy work for three salesgirls on a rainy Wednesday morning. Our summer stock is priced and on the racks, and I have to run up to Cherry Hill for a couple of hours. I'll be back by mid-afternoon. I'll meet you here after you get your window fixed."

"Computers. Data Base. We didn't have this kind of sophisticated crime lab detection when I was on the job," I said.

She started out the door with the folder under her arm.

"Thelma," I called. "What about these?" I held up the Polaroid and the two copies she had made.

"I have a copy downstairs," she said, turning again.

"And, please don't let your girls see the autopsy or crime scene pictures."

"Why not?"

"They're too gruesome."

"You're so old-fashioned. My girls will love this stuff."

12

Bonnie's body was seated in the middle of the park bench. It had to be in the middle or on either edge to be sitting upright because there were no back slats on the bench for her to lean against. They had all been broken away, probably used by the junkies for firewood during the winter, although two of the dark green slats had been left on the seat. Bonnie's back rested against one of the three thick concrete vertical slabs to which the slats had been bolted, and what you couldn't see in the photograph were the sharp bolts that had held the slats in place and how they cut into her back. Not that she cared about the discomfort.

Thelma slipped another picture, this one a close-up, to the top of the pile. In this one Bonnie's chin rested on her chest as if she had been reading and had fallen asleep. Except that there was no book on her lap. Her hands rested palms up on her thighs. The large bruise on the inside of her left elbow was clearly visible in this photo, and if you knew what to look for, so were the tiny track marks that followed the vein down the lower part of her arm.

We were in Thelma's private office. Her wall clock said it was five minutes after four. I had just returned from the auto-glass shop, and it was still raining. The little triangular window that had been smashed, about eighteen by twelve inches of safety glass, had cost eighty-five dollars installed.

It was still very difficult for me to look at the photographs, although Thelma couldn't seem to get enough of them. Some-how the pictures of Bonnie's body sitting in Marcy Park were harder for me to view than the clinical morgue photos of her lifeless naked flesh. Perhaps if I had kept her at the cottage until Friday as we had planned, I could have prevented the fatal chain of events that seemed to start with her course registration at Pratt on Thursday. But something had scared her away from the cottage; something that occurred when she had stayed alone the night I had my first date with Grace. Or if I had been at the park, maybe I could have done something for her there. But on the morgue slab she was hopeless and cold. I have no control over death. And very little over life.

I diverted my attention to the computer printout Thelma had given me. There were about thirty calls to the 609 South Jersey area code arranged in numerical order. None of them were repeated more than twice except a large clump in the middle made in November and December. They varied in length from one to seventy-three minutes, and all of them were to Julie Stockton's number. I had gone through these bills quickly before Bonnie's death, but had not paid much attention to the numbers or their frequency, even though I now counted fifteen to Julie.

Thelma had come to a close-up of the hypodermic needle lying under the bench.

"Were there fingerprints on this?" she asked, holding the picture up.

"I don't know. I never asked."

"And to think that the city of New York actually used to pay you to do police work."

"Can I call Brooklyn from here?"

"Sure," she said. She began to put the photographs back in the manila envelope.

I got the number for the Seventy-ninth Precinct from New York information. Thelma pulled out the family snapshots and spread them on her desk while I talked. Conlin was in the precinct somewhere but he wasn't at his desk. The guy who answered his phone let it drop with a clatter. I could hear him yelling for Conlin, probably out the squad room door. Conlin came on a moment later.

"You just caught me," he said. "I was about to go home. What's up?"

"Were there prints on that spike they found under the bench?"

"Nothing we could use."

I shook my head negatively for Thelma.

"Ask him if it was wiped," she whispered.

"Was it wiped?" I repeated.

"We couldn't tell."

"Could it have been?"

"Look, Con. You keep trying to make a case here. All I can do is repeat, we couldn't tell. You can jump to any conclusions you want to. If you want to take a look at it yourself, come on over tomorrow. I'll be here until four."

"I'm back in South Jersey already," I said.

"Like I told you yesterday, get a hobby. This one's a dead-end, Con. If anything turns up, you know I'll call you."

When I hung up, Thelma was scrutinizing her copy of the Polaroid of Bonnie and Julie and Raymond Stockton again.

"Don't you want to know about the prints?" I asked.

"They don't have any," she said. "I could hear him. I didn't think they would. I'd love to know where this was taken." She tapped the picture.

"In the woods," I said. My sarcasm drew a withering look from Thelma.

"You live in the woods," she said. "Do you recognize any of these trees?"

"Very funny," I said. "I'd recognize that pitch pine anywhere." I got another withering look. "What does it matter where it is?" I added.

"I don't mean to keep belittling your skills as a detective—"

"Yes, you do."

". . . but I thought you were from the old school. You know, run down every little lead, no matter how obscure, obtuse, minuscule or far out."

"What would I find there if I guessed the location?"

"How would you know until you got there?"

"And besides, the trail's got to be stone cold. See that box elder in the background?"

"What's a box elder?" she asked.

"It's a form of maple," I said. "It hasn't even budded out.

That means this picture was taken in early March at the latest."

"How does a retired detective from New York know so much about trees?"

"There happen to be a couple of box elders along the river near my cottage," I said. "They're like willows. They like to be near water."

"See, there's a deduction right there. Near water."

"Fantastic. We've narrowed the location down to the half-million acres of swamp, low-lying areas, streams and creeks in South Jersey."

"You're not trying," she said. "You don't care."

"Jack Conlin just told me to give up on this one. He said I should get a hobby. You heard him say it."

"So, are you going to?"

"What?"

"Give up."

"Oh, sure," I said. "All I've got here is a major drug deal pulled off by two guys who people all over the East Coast on both sides of the law are looking for. Plus a gorgeous little blonde who I was in the process of falling for, albeit in a Platonic way, who no doubt knew many details of this big deal and who was probably done in by one or both of these guys because of it. And another gorgeous large blonde, specifically one Julie Stockton, who may or may not have been fathered by one of the players in the deal and who may know more than she's told so far. Of course, nobody's asked her, which is probably why she hasn't told. Which would be my job, of course. To take her out, ply her with liquor, maybe even compromise her to get the information I need. In addition, she may be at some risk herself, just like the little blonde was, so as an added bonus I get to protect her from foul play, which as you know is my main purpose in life ... protecting gorgeous blondes, large and small, from foul play."

"Foul play? Do retired cops say 'foul play'?"

"Fair is foul, and foul is fair. And what happened to Bonnie Arnold was definitely not fair."

"I hate it when you're sarcastic."

"I learned it from you. And by the way, Thelma—"

"Yes."

"Knock off the crap about my detective skills. These insurance companies don't call me for their important pawnshop canvassing work because I'm some kind of slouchy gumshoe."

"I'm sorry. I didn't realize you were so sensitive."

"You know, it's easy for you to sit there in your comfortable chair and say: 'Ask him about the fingerprints,' or 'Go check out the riverbank.' But I actually have to hump it out there and do the work."

"How do you know it's a riverbank?"

"Did I say riverbank?"

"Yes. Riverbank."

"Well, I seem to remember that there was another Polaroid. Taken on a riverbank."

"Where is it?" She spread open the accordion folder and peered inside.

"I don't have it and I never saw it. A guy described it to me over the phone. I don't even know who the people in it were, except Bonnie. There were two guys who fit the descriptions of Rocky and your biker-buddy. So that's a long shot right there. But they were in the woods, piney woods, and they were on a riverbank with a small bridge in the background."

"Hey, all right," she shouted, startling me. "You've just reduced a half-million acres of wetlands where that box-type tree grows to a riverbank with a little bridge. What kind of road led up to the little bridge? Was it paved? Or dirt?"

"Sand, I guess," I said.

"What?"

"Those roads are all sand in the pines."

"I wouldn't know. I never was your woodsy type."

The door to the office opened and a young, Asian woman leaned inside. "Did you call me?" she asked Thelma.

"No, I was shouting at Mr. Leeds here."

The woman ducked out and pulled the door shut, and I said: "Didn't I tell you never to call me Mr. Leeds in front of your sales help, especially if she's pretty and Japanese."

"Chinese," Thelma corrected.

"Whatever. 'Mr. Leeds' makes me sound like somebody's grandfather."

She smiled sarcastically. "Are you going to check it out?"

"Check what out?" I stood up and looked toward the recently closed door.

"Not her. You're impossible. That New York cop was right. You do need a hobby."

I glanced up at the clock. It was almost four-thirty.

"I'm going home and get ready for my hobby right now," I said. "I have a dinner date tonight."

"The blackjack dealer?"

"Yes." I got up and walked to the door. "You keep the folder," I said. "I won't need it until tomorrow."

"Are you going to try to find out where the picture was taken?"

"I don't see what good it would do. The trail is cold, the footprints are washed away by months of rain, and the cigarette butts and sandwich wrappers, hopefully, have been picked up and carried out by more conscientious hikers or canoers."

"They could have been in a car."

"Not on those roads. Not without four-wheel drive."

"I like it. Your curiosity is stirring. You're thinking about it."

"Thelm, honey," I said. "When I go looking for needles, you have to understand that I first need to know where the haystack is."

"Get out of here."

"What's her name?"

"Who?"

"The Chinese girl."

"Bay-Ling."

"Is that her first or her last name? Or both?"

"Her first." A smile started across her face.

"What's her last?"

"Kravitz," she said, completing a wide grin. "She's married to my nephew."

13

By the time I got to the Sooys' farm the rain had stopped. Suzie was in the river with the Labradors. Mary Sooy and I toweled her off when she finally came out, but she still tracked mud and dampness onto the back seat of the Honda. I hoped Grace Somers didn't mind the smell of wet dog.

At the cottage I shaved and showered and sat on the porch with a tequila, rocks and lime and watched the late afternoon turn into early evening. A fat red sun slid briefly from under a bank of clouds and warmed my face and arms and turned the rain-swollen river a rich golden color. Before the sun sank behind the cedars on the far bank, it glistened on the new green leaves of the box elder beside the dock.

When I walked inside to put my glass in the sink before I left, something triggered a memory of the night Bonnie arrived and the Baron cooked hot dogs in my fireplace. Impulsively I looked up his number and dialed it. Baron himself picked it up with a curt: "Yo."

"It's Con," I said. "I want to talk to Irene."

"She ain't here, man," he answered. "She runs an NA meeting tonight up on Arctic Avenue. She'll be home around ten. What you want from her?" He spoke loudly over the din of children arguing and playing somewhere near him.

"I don't want to talk to her on the phone. I want to talk to her alone."

"About what?"

"About Bonnie."

"I already told you everything she knows about that child."

"Do you still want me to find Rocky?"

"Hell yes."

"Then here's what I want for doing that job. I want fifteen minutes of conversation with Irene. In my office or your house. Without you in the room."

There was a heavy thump in the background. "Hold on a minute," he said. He covered the phone, and I could hear his muffled shouts but not what he was saying.

"What do you think she knows?" he said when he came back on.

"Bonnie confided in her, right? She was Bonnie's AA person."

"Sponsor."

"Right. So maybe Bonnie told her things Irene hasn't thought of or doesn't want to tell you."

"Well, why would she tell you?"

"Because I'm a detective and not her husband."

"Man, you smell like a cop again tonight. I'll tell her to call you when she gets home." An infant suddenly shrieked into the phone and then began to sob steadily.

"I'll be out for the rest of the evening. Tell her to leave a message about what time is good to call her tomorrow."

"Yessir, officer." He hung up without saying good-bye.

I fed Suzie and left, locking the door behind me.

There isn't a whole hell of a lot to do on a Wednesday night in the Pine Barrens. There are a few nice places to go to dinner. Or you can go to one of those multitheater movie complexes and eat a tub of buttery popcorn. Or both. Or you can drive into Atlantic City and gamble or take in a show in one of the casinos, but that would have been a busman's holiday for Grace, and I didn't even suggest it.

We had decided to go to dinner and after she gave some last-minute instructions to the baby-sitter and kissed her son and daughter good-bye, we drove from her house in Mays Landing up the Black Horse Pike toward Philly to a restaurant I like right on the pike at Williamstown called Casa di Pasta. Being from Brooklyn, I fancy myself somewhat of an expert on

Italian cuisine. At least in South Jersey. And this place has exceptional sauces and dishes that I like. The restaurant is in an old house, the rooms are small and intimate and Nick, the owner, is always very attentive. He doesn't have a liquor license but I had the foresight to bring a bottle of Valpolicella, which Grace and I split while we ate far too much.

Although I'm not much of a gambler, I'm fascinated by the gaming industry, and having dinner with Grace provided a good opportunity to satisfy my curiosity about her job.

"I like dealing," was the way she put it. "But I hate the casinos."

"I don't like them much either," I agreed. We had decided not to have dessert and were sharing a pot of espresso. "The decor makes me nervous," I said. "Too garish, too much going on."

"It's supposed to be that way. Marketing research says that the busy atmosphere keeps everyone playing. You get used to it. What gets under my skin are the people."

"The ones you work with?"

"No, they're okay. It's the customers that bother me. They never seem to change. They're rude, especially the women. The men are rude too, but in a sexual way."

"I can imagine," I said sympathetically.

"No, not like you're thinking," she said. "It's not the propositions and the innuendo and double entendre. You get used to that. What I'm talking about is a kind of sexual superiority that makes a man think that since I'm a woman I couldn't possibly know how to play blackjack, so deal 'em up, baby, and I'll be glad to take advantage of you. I win a lot of money off jerks with that attitude."

Her hazel eyes flashed above her broad smile. They were eyes that changed colors like chameleons. Tonight they were bright green like her blouse. Her hair was dark red, almost brown in the restaurant light, and cut very short in the back and curved to a stylish flip along her jaw line. I liked her looks. Her divorce had been ugly from what little I knew about it, and she was raising two kids all on her own, but still she had those happy eyes.

It was early when we left, not quite ten o'clock. The night

was pleasantly warm, and dampness from the day-long rain hinted at the steamy summer nights ahead. We had the windows down in the Honda and soft pine-scented air washed over us as we cruised east along the Pike. We were headed toward her house in Mays Landing, but I was in no hurry because I didn't want the evening to end yet. And experience has taught me that it always does end when you get a single mom back to her nest.

"Would you like to take a moonlight cruise?" I asked.

"I don't see any moon," she said. She was right. The late-afternoon cloud cover had never lifted, and there was nothing visible in the night sky except a faint pinkish glow on the horizon ahead of us from Atlantic City, twenty-five miles away.

"It's too early and too pleasant to go home yet," I said.

"You're right," she said. "Where do you keep your boat?"

"At my cottage."

"Very nice. I keep forgetting you live on the water. Sure, let's go. I'd like to see where you live."

I turned north at the Weymouth Road, past Weymouth Furnace and across Makepeace Lake to the White Horse Pike and through the sleepy town of Elwood. Just outside Elwood on the Pleasant Mills Road we caught a doe in my car headlights. The road is very straight there, and from a distance out at the edge of my lights, she looked like a large dog.

"Oh, my goodness," Grace said, sitting forward in alarm as I eased up on the gas pedal. "Don't hit her."

"She'll move," I said.

I slowed to about twenty-five and we watched her, frozen in the glare of the lights. At the last moment she bolted and darted into the dark woods, disappearing with a huge final bound. A fawn that had been hidden behind some roadside brush scrambled across the road after her and I had to stand on the brakes to avoid hitting it. As it was, the little creature spun its spindly legs on the pavement and just cleared my fender close enough for me to see the individual hairs of its coat and the fading spots on its back.

The car skidded to a halt and stalled, and when I reached for the ignition key to start it again, I realized Grace had a tight grip on my right arm.

"I was sure you were going to hit it," she said.

"Me too," I said, turning toward her so I could see her face. We sat like that in silence for a moment inside the circle of illumination within the dark night. The only sounds were the tick of the cooling engine and, far off to the right, peeper frogs in some hidden swamp. I shifted my arm and she loosened her grip and slid her arm around my shoulder and I turned further toward her until my upper body faced hers and put my left arm over her shoulder so that my hand brushed the short hair on the back of her neck. With my eyes locked on hers I moved against her and kissed her.

It wasn't a very long kiss, but when our lips met, I shut my eyes. Her lips were firm and sensual and moved well, repositioning themselves over mine constantly. I felt vulnerable sitting out there in the middle of the dark road, and when I squinted an eye open I saw a single headlight top the rise about a mile behind us coming out of Elwood. She sensed my lack of concentration and we broke the kiss off and held each other for a moment longer.

"Hey," she said as we separated. "You promised me a boat ride."

"You kiss good," I said in my best Tarzan imitation.

"I get better," she said. "I'm out of practice."

I stifled the wise guy in me who wanted to say: "I can't wait," and kept quiet. I was out of practice too.

I started the engine, chasing the silence and the peeping of the frogs, and we drove into the hamlet of Cedar Bank holding hands across the gear box.

There's not a lot to Cedar Bank, especially after dark. The grocery store was dark and long closed. There's a canoe rental place, a volunteer fire station and a nineteenth-century Catholic cemetery. The church that was next to the cemetery has long since collapsed and been carted away, and the lot has turned back into pitch pine and briars on the high bank above the river.

There were still lights on in most of the houses along County Route 643, the town's main drag. Most of the river homes, like mine, aren't visible except when the road wanders near the water.

I had to let go of Grace's hand when I downshifted to turn into my drive, but I found it again after I'd pulled the shift into second gear and I held it all the way to the cottage. We kissed again after I got the car stopped and the headlights turned off. It was a black starless night without the car lights, and we bumped noses before we got our lips locked together. This kiss was much longer and more relaxed. When we finally got our arms situated around each other in the total darkness, we explored each other's mouths until I felt her breath quicken and realized mine was doing the same. Open or closed, my eyes saw absolutely nothing.

After we broke this kiss off, I turned the overhead light on and found the flashlight in the glove compartment. I got out of the car, but she didn't move. When I put the light on her, she said: "Don't look. I'm going to take my heels and my panty-hose off."

I pointed the light toward the dock and turned away from her. In the still night I could hear the sheer fabric sliding off her hips and down her legs. It was an exciting sound. When she shut the car door I turned the light to her again and saw that she was barefoot. I liked that. It was evident that she was comfortable here in the country and didn't mind putting her feet in the sand even in the black of night. Her legs were thin but looked strong, and, even without the lift from the heels, were very shapely. They were also extremely white in the beam from the flashlight.

"Where are we going?" she asked. I extended my hand and took hers and pointed the beam in the direction of my boat.

"Down there," I said.

With the flashlight I illuminated the short path to the dock. As soon as my foot fell on the first of the three wooden steps at the end of the path, I heard Suzie start an insistent whine in the cottage. She knew I was going out in the boat, and she wanted to go along. With Grace holding the light, I managed to get the rain cover unbuttoned and to climb aboard and get the engine started, but it was really too dark to enjoy being out on the river. The lights from the restaurant and marina downriver showed me the first few channel markers, but after that I had to use the spotlight to find each one. I took the boat past Crowley's Landing and the Cedar Bank Lagoons and anchored just off the channel opposite the marshy area before the Green Bank Bridge. I switched off the spotlight and we necked in the red and green illumination of the running lights while the boat swung downstream with the outgoing tide. A breeze had started and freshened and when we broke apart and lay against the back cushions of the seat, I could see that the cloud cover was starting to break up above us.

We were silent a while before she said: "It's going to be a beautiful day tomorrow."

"It's gorgeous now," I said.

"I had a really nice time," she said. "Especially now. It's so peaceful out here."

"That's exactly what Bonnie said when she stayed here." I regretted it the minute it popped out of my mouth. The last date I had with Grace was on one of the evenings Bonnie slept at the cottage. Grace had asked me about the case at dinner, and I had filled her in on Bonnie's fate and some of the leads I was working on.

"Poor thing," Grace whispered, her head resting against mine. "You really liked her, didn't you?"

"She seemed to have a future," I said. "Which is more than you can say about a lot of people in this world."

Grace turned and wrapped her arms around my shoulders and began to kiss my neck, and then worked her way up to my ear, sending shivers of pleasure through me. We necked some more, and when we were done, I hauled the anchor and headed upriver toward my dock.

"We'll have to do this again when we can see where we're going," I told her.

"Okay," she said. It was simple affirmation and I liked it.

A white glow showed around some of the breaks in the cloud cover, and I could see all the channel markers without the spotlight on the way back. I was squatting to secure the stern line to a dock cleat when a half moon broke from one cloud cover and scudded across an open space to another giving the illusion that it, and not the cloud cover, was moving rapidly across the sky. Grace looked up at it, and I was glad for the distraction because I was a little stiff when I stood up. She was ten years younger than me, and I didn't want her to notice the differences in our ages. Not yet anyway.

I put my hands on her shoulders and turned her toward me and kissed her lightly. Suzie began to bark steadily from the inside of the cottage. As we followed the beam of my flashlight up the path, I held Grace against me with my arm encircling her waist. Her body was firm but soft to the touch through the silk of her blouse.

"Would you like to come in?" I asked as we neared the cottage and Suzie's barking.

"Not tonight," she said. "My kids are up at six-thirty. I'll come in next time, when I can stay longer."

When we got to the Honda I opened the passenger door for her and said: "I'm going to let the dog out for a minute. Stay in the car or she'll get you all muddy. She loves to meet new people, but she's a little too enthusiastic."

As I rounded the corner of the porch I thought about how nice it was to have the time to put a relationship together. I liked this woman, but there was no rush, no deadlines. If it went anywhere at all, we would do it a piece at a time, a piece that we would make carefully and well and then stand back until the glue dried and we were ready to move on. I was thinking about love, and it was a very pleasant thought even with Suzie growling and barking herself hoarse inside the front door.

It was my own fault. I was too relaxed and should have recognized Suzie's warning. I didn't see either one of them or where they were hidden until my head exploded in a shower of stars and they had me clubbed half unconscious and down on the porch stairs with the cold steel barrel of a gun jammed against the base of my skull.

I could see the legs of another man in jeans now beside the steps.

"Don't move," the one on me said in a half whisper. "I love to fucking use this gun. Love it!" He sounded agitated and slightly out of control, and that made me want to listen to him.

"What is it, Con?" I heard Grace call. I could tell by the sound of her voice that she was out of the car.

"I'll get the girl," the second one said, darting away. His voice sounded familiar.

"Run," I shouted. "Run, Grace."

"Shut the fuck up," my man screamed. "I'll fucking shoot you."

He dropped down on me with both knees, blowing the air out of my lungs, and took the gun away from my head. I thought he would club me with the butt of it, but instead he fired a shot through the front door of the cottage, scorching the side of my face and totally canceling my hearing in my right ear. He had fired in the direction of the barking Suzie, but I had no way of knowing if he had hit her. Her barking stopped abruptly, but I wasn't sure my blasted ears could hear it anyway. And then he clubbed me with the butt of the gun, the blow smashing my upper lip against the wooden edge of the middle step. I could immediately taste blood, and I didn't think I would be kissing Grace for a long time to come. He grabbed a handful of my hair and jerked my head back so hard a bolt of pain shot through my neck. I realized he was shouting something at me but it sounded like I had balloons in my ears.

"Put your fucking hands behind your back." I heard him the second time because he shouted it right up against my left ear.

My hands were under my stomach where they had gone instinctively to brace my fall to the steps. He took his weight off my back so I could extract my hands but he didn't let go of my hair, and he jammed the gun barrel against my skull again. I could feel warm blood leaking through my hair and down the back of my neck. With my head pulled up like that I could see Grace come around the corner of the cottage in the new moonlight. The second man had his forearm encircling her neck in a choke hold and he held a snub-nosed .38 up against her temple. She didn't look at all scared; just pissed off. Until she saw me. Then her mouth dropped open in alarm. I could also feel blood pouring out of my mouth and dripping down off my chin.

"If you fucking move," my man said. "He ventilates her pretty brains. Now put your hands back here." He sounded far away, although I could feel the heat of his breath on my left ear, the same ear that Grace had been kissing ten minutes earlier.

In the dim moonlight I could see that the guy that held her wore a leather vest and a helmet with a clear plastic shield snapped down over his eyes. "Aw, and I didn't want to shoot her yet," he said in a phony whine as he approached us. "At least not until I fucked her. But if I do shoot her, I want to fuck her right away, because I don't like to fuck 'em after they get cold. That's for perverts." His voice sounded hollow under the eye shield but I recognized it this time when I saw it coming from his small frame. It was Rocky. Despite our situation, I was somehow pleased to see him; to know I would get another chance at him. Grace tried to struggle against his grip. But he had enormous strength for a small man, and he just raised his arm and lifted her off the ground by her neck until she was still. She gasped for breath when he let her down, and his hand strayed over one of her breasts.

"Leave her out of this," I said angrily, spraying blood in front of me. I had put my hands behind me, and I could feel the cold steel of a pair of handcuffs being laid against my wrists.

"You shut up, honey," my man said to me. He was having trouble with the handcuffs. They take some practice. I could tell he'd never cuffed anyone before.

When he finally got one of the bracelets on me, he put his lips close to my ear again and said: "You're the one I want to fuck, honey. Oh, I'm getting so turned on here." He stood up and jerked me to my feet by my hair. "But, business before pleasure," he said. He was still behind me where I couldn't see him, but I could tell he was big. I thought for a moment that it might be Doc, but I knew from the Polaroid that Doc wasn't much bigger than Rocky, and this guy was huge, at least six-four or maybe taller. His moment of vulnerability came and went when he brought me to my feet. He was off balance, and I had a rising momentum and could have given him a good shot in the nuts while I wasn't covered by the gun. But I was afraid they would shoot Grace . . . or worse . . . if I made it to the woods or dove in the river.

"Shine that light over here," he said angrily.

Rocky still had a lock on Grace's neck, but he solved the problem of what to do with her by pushing her brutally to the ground. "Stay still, bitch," he said and reached in his back pocket and came out with a flashlight. When he turned it on, I moved my head to try to see what the man behind me looked like, but he too wore a helmet and tinted face shield. When he felt me move, he jerked my hair violently again, and I lost my footing and dropped to one knee, pulling the free manacle from his hand. As he reached for it and jerked me to my feet again, the flashlight beam showed me his right hand and four jailhouse tattoos, one crude letter above each large knuckle: H-E-L-L. I wondered what the other hand said.

"The fucking thing's locked," he told Rocky. "Come over here."

They both fumbled for a moment behind me, and then I heard the second cuff click open. My free hand was jerked behind me again, and on an impulse, I pulled it away from his grip.

"You wise motherfucker," he said, grabbing the arm and pulling it back. He slipped the second cuff over my wrist and locked it and patted me down looking for a gun. Then Rocky stepped deliberately out in front of me and slammed his fist into my stomach. I doubled up, pulling my hair free, and stayed that way retching for a moment until he slammed the flashlight into the side of my head. I went down and stayed there, half-conscious and waiting for a kick that never came.

"Who's in charge now, dickhead?" he hissed.

"Don't worry about him, you asshole," the guy who had cuffed me said. "Get the girl."

"I got a score to settle with him," Rocky said. His voice was filled with rage as he hovered over me.

"Get the fucking girl," the biker screamed. He was out of control, speeding. Rocky moved away and the beam of the flashlight began to wander around, but it couldn't find Grace. She had vanished into the night. Carpe diem barefoot. I have a soft spot for courageous and quick-thinking women. Or perhaps it is an appreciation for anyone with a keen sense of self-preservation. Whatever, she was long gone, and the frantic flashlight beam bobbed into the woods and up the drive and under the Honda and to the dock. It glinted briefly off the chrome work of two Harley-Davidsons that were tucked into the briar patch behind my pile of pine wood on the other side of the cottage.

"You dumb son-of-a-bitch," Hell Knuckles shouted. "She's gone. I can't fucking believe it."

"It's your own fucking fault," Rocky sneered back. "You couldn't even get the fucking handcuffs on him, and you called me over."

"You shouldn't have let her go."

"Fuck you," he said. "It's his fault anyway. I owe him. He's dead." He knelt quickly beside me, and I felt the cold barrel of his .38 on my temple and heard the ratchet click as he cocked it. "You're wasted, Leeds," he breathed.

"Don't," the other one said with alarm. "Doc said no killing. Just give him a message."

There was a silence, a long one. I imagined them staring each other down. Frogs peeped far off in the cedar swamp across the river. I could feel Rocky's hand trembling with rage through the barrel of the gun pressing against my skull.

"Okay, Leeds," he said finally. "I'll have to wait until the next time I see you to kill you. The third time's a charm, baby." He stood up and I could see him tuck the .38 into his belt. I knew what was coming.

His first kick landed square on my left shoulder. He was wearing heavy biker's boots and he worked his way down my side with them, kicking me again and again and again until I could hear him begin to pant.

I passed out for a moment, and when I came to, Rocky had pulled me to my feet and was rushing me across the dock toward the river.

"No, no, he'll drown," I could hear his partner shout from up near the cottage.

I went down like a stone in the cold river. The water felt wonderful and refreshing after the beating I had taken. I immediately pretended to drown, flopping and coughing, although my feet were planted firmly on the sandy bottom at the edge of the channel. Even if I had landed in the channel, I could have bounced my way out, but as it was, I slowly bent my knees until my head went under, and then I pushed downstream until I needed a breath then tilted my mouth up and caught one and pushed downstream for another glide.

When I came up the second time, I heard the roar of the bikes high-tailing it up the drive away from the cottage. I fought my way up out of the water, slipping several times on the bank and then sprinting for the porch as best I could with my hands cuffed behind me. Grace was already on the porch, and I brushed past her and up the steps.

"Are you all right?" she shouted.

I stomped at the front door and managed to kick it open on the second try. Shouldering on the ceiling light switch, I backed up to the mail table and yanked the drawer open. Grace had followed me in and stood in front of me with a horrified look on her face. Suzie was in the kitchen, but when she saw it was us, she came out cringing and wagging her tail. She didn't seem to be harmed.

"In there," I shouted. "In the drawer. A handcuff key. It's skinny with no tag."

She found it, and I turned my back on her. Without a word, she inserted the key in one of the bracelets, and when I heard it chink open I jerked away and ran to the bedroom massaging my free wrist. I sat on the bed, dripping river water on the floor, and kicked the rug aside. When I had the combination run and the floor safe open, I knew instantly which gun I wanted. The dirty 9mm I had taken from Rocky. I wanted to slip it into my pants pocket but my pants were too wet. I stood up.

Grace pushed me down to a sitting position again.

"Where do you think you're going?" she said.

"The boat," I said. "I can catch them at the Green Bank Bridge."

I stood up again, and she pushed me down again. I was surprised at how easily I went. Rocky's gun seemed very heavy in my left hand. Grace put the key in the remaining cuff and unlocked it, and when the pair of them fell on the bed, I dropped the gun there too. I didn't want to pick it up. It was too heavy.

I tried to stand up again, but Grace wouldn't let me. I had to brush her aside though because I knew I was going to lose the rest of my Veal Picata. I bolted into the bathroom and when I was done throwing up, I looked in the medicine cabinet mirror to see what had horrified her. Blood and river water leaked out of my hair and over my ears and around my neck. The bleeding in my mouth had stopped, but there was still blood on my upper lip, which was so swollen that you couldn't see the lower one beneath it at all.

I realized I was having a hard time breathing and thought that maybe one of my ribs had gone through a lung or the stomping I got had collapsed one of them. I looked up at the mirror again and saw that Grace was standing behind me at the bathroom door holding the 9mm in one hand and the handcuff key in the other. I turned, and beyond her across the hall my bed looked extremely comfortable.

That thought, that it would be a very pleasant thing to do to lie down on that bed, was the last thing I remembered until I woke up in the back seat of the Honda bouncing over the potholes in my driveway. Grace was at the wheel. I didn't know how she got me into the car.

14

We wound up at Atlantic City—Mainland, a small but busy hospital complex near the parkway in Pomona. Grace figured I needed X-rays and I might not be able to get them until morning if she took me to sleepy little Kessler Memorial in Hammonton. Turned out she was right according to the technician who took the X-rays. The pictures showed two cracked ribs but not much else. X-rays don't show bruises. Or pain. Or anger. Rocky had worked me over good but the damage was minimal. The night resident in charge of the emergency room told me my lung was okay, probably just bruised.

It was about two A.M. when they finished. Grace stayed with me the whole time, which was considerate, except at the end when I tried to sign myself out and she sided with the head nurse and the resident about keeping me overnight. She had called her mother who went to stay with her kids. There was little they could do for my ribs. They didn't even tape them anymore. The doctor simply told me not to laugh too much. The night nurse and Grace thought that was hilarious, but it didn't amuse me. I could still feel Rocky's rage and the bullet he almost put in my brain. They gave me some antibiotics and a shot in the butt to put me to sleep, and in the morning Grace came back with her car and a change of clothes and took me to her house, where she had left the Honda. Outside of a fat lip, a lump on my head and a couple of large bruises on my left shoulder and upper arm, plus some very sore ribs, there wasn't much wrong with me. I say that not to brag or to be sarcastic, but to point out that it could have been much worse.

The job Rocky and Hell Knuckles did on me wasn't very professional in my humble opinion. I have seen a few professional beatings in my day, and believe me, these guys didn't even come close. And they got cuffs on me too. I remember a guy who was beaten by a loan shark's boys on President Street in south Brooklyn, an artful job that was meant as a message for his other clients and one that gave new meaning to the phrase: broke every bone in his body. And in his face too.

Grace drove very carefully from the hospital to her house in Mays Landing. We didn't say two words to each other during the entire twenty-minute ride.

"Thanks again," I said, easing myself out of her car when we pulled into the driveway. I started toward the Honda, but then came back with the intention of kissing her good-bye. She had gotten out of her car and was standing beside the open door. She had a very serious look on her face. I leaned toward her carefully for a kiss, not wanting to bump any other part of me that would cause pain. She didn't respond, so I backed off and looked at her curiously.

"I don't want to see you anymore," she said.

"Oh," was all I could say. I could tell she expected more from me, but I didn't feel very articulate just then.

We both stared at each other for a couple of beats, and then I said: "I'm sorry."

"So am I," she said.

We were silent for another long moment and then she said: "My father used to drink and beat up my brother. One time he broke his nose and he was unconscious so long we had to take him to the hospital. They made me lie to the doctor about what happened."

I was concentrating on my shoes. They were very scuffed from the night before.

"I'm sorry," I said again.

"I know," she said.

I looked up and stared at her for a moment. I was angry. Not at her, but at the job. Like when I was a cop.

"I used to tell my wife I was sorry," I said.

She broke our eye contact and tossed her head and folded her arms. She didn't want to hear about wives.

"Sorry I got shot in the stomach. Sorry I got my arm sliced half off by a berserk homeless man that I had to kill in the subway. Sorry my twenty-five-year-old partner with the infant son died in the crash of a patrol car I was driving."

She looked at me again and anger flashed in her eyes too.

"When that little one was kicking you, I knew he would kill you," she said. "I hated it. I never knew what terror was before that moment. It made me sick. I thought I was going to throw up. I knew they would kill you and then find me."

"Where were you?"

"Behind a tree. I'm still frightened. When I went back for your clothes this morning, I was afraid they would still be there. I can't believe how fast my heart is beating right now. I wet my pants. I took them off after they left. I'm sure you'll find them when you get home. I don't want them back. Throw them away. I'm sorry."

"Me too," I said. I turned and eased myself into the Honda.

It wasn't too difficult to drive the car. It would have been easier with an automatic because it hurt a little to shift, but everything that hurt was on my left side so it didn't interfere with making the car run. What hurt the most right then was my pride. I wanted to go back and argue with her. Tell her how much I enjoyed being with her, and how I knew she'd enjoyed being with me too. But I had to agree with her. I was unhealthy to be around, and she had just had one of the most horrifying experiences of her young life. And the chances of it happening again if she continued to see me were real good.

I took Route 50 out of Mays Landing but I didn't feel like going home. The morning was gorgeous, the beginning of a summerlike heat that would be shimmering and breathless by mid-afternoon. I turned east on the Black Horse Pike toward Atlantic City. It filled me with hope to know that Rocky was still around. I had been looking for the son of a bitch for two weeks and was certain he was long gone to Florida or Mexico or anywhere I couldn't begin to look for him. But now I had a chance at finding him again. And if I found him, I knew I could find Doc. I hadn't eaten much of the hospital breakfast but I did have two cups of their coffee. I had an alert and positive edge of anger that I knew was part caffeine and part what Winston Churchill meant when he said: "Nothing in life is so exhilarating as being shot at without result." Or in my case, stomped.

I hadn't been hungry in the hospital but I was famished now, so I stopped at the diner on Cardiff Circle and had some eggs and bacon and home fries and a big glass of orange juice. I was headed for Margate but I had no agenda except to go through my file again and call Julie Stockton and Irene Barbay and tell Thelma about the events of the evening and about locating Rocky, although he had actually located me. And about Doc's violent message and how it had screwed up a promising relationship. But as I was mopping up the last of my eggs and checking the counter copy of the *Atlantic City Press* to see if the A's were still in first place in the American League West, it occurred to me that I was near the editorial offices of that paper, so when I left the diner I swung down Washington Avenue to see if I could dig up anything on one Raymond Stockton, model citizen turned drug manufacturer and dealer.

The *Press* is a morning newspaper, so there wasn't a lot of action going on when I got there at 10:30. The offices are off-shore in a commercial area near the Black Horse Pike in Pleasantville. Like a lot of Atlantic City business and industry, the paper has moved off the island since the casinos came to town.

It was cool and dark inside the editorial offices. The receptionist was a top-heavy brunette with huge circle-frame glasses who looked to be in her late twenties. When I asked her about the library, she stood up and pointed over a rabbit warren of reporters' cubicles to a door on the far side of the city room. Standing, she had a nice pair of legs too. She turned quickly and caught me looking at them but didn't seem to mind at all. I gave her my card and she looked it over carefully and then looked me over carefully too. She said she would send someone in to help me as soon as she could. She couldn't help me personally, she said, although she'd like to, because she had to stay at her desk until her lunch hour at twelve-thirty. I glanced at my watch and she smiled at me.

Most of the desks in the cubicles were a mess from the night before. A few desk lamps were on but the overhead fluo-

rescents were off and the windowless room was in semidark-
ness. A thin man with gray hair sat peering at the screen of a
word processor in one of the cubicles to my left. A door to the
right led to the sports department, a large separate room that
was already well-lit even though its only occupant seemed to
be a young man with a scruffy beard who had his feet up on
one of the desks and was reading a paperback copy of *A
Farewell to Arms*. A phone was ringing in the office, but he
chose to ignore it.

The library was just a couple of rows of filing cabinets and
a bunch of cardboard bankers' boxes stacked against the gray
walls of an oblong room. There were three dented metal desks
and matching chairs that had to be reporters' hand-me-downs,
but there were no microfilm or microfiche machines, only a
small IBM compatible PC on one of the desks. The computer
was dark but I could see that it was wired into the wall, hopefully linked to a more sophisticated retrieval system than the
rows of filing cabinets and storage boxes. There was also a
pinwheel printer on top of a metal stand whose bottom shelf
held a stack of fan-folded paper, which was threaded into the
printer. On more than one occasion I had gathered information in the library of the *New York Times*. This was definitely
not the *Times,* although I had expected a little more.

I sat at one of the desks and waited. Eventually the telephone in the sports department stopped ringing, and a few
minutes later, the kid with the scruffy beard came in and asked
if he could help me. He introduced himself as Seth. Up close he
wasn't a kid. He looked to be in his mid-thirties, but from a
distance his slender build had made him look younger. He
wore chino pants and a brown and black plaid flannel shirt,
both of them quite wrinkled. He was pleasant enough, but
with an exaggerated lack of enthusiasm that was meant to
show me he preferred to be back in the sports department
reading Hemingway.

He was good though. I told him I was after material on
Raymond Stockton, and he seemed to recognize the name. He
came back with a bio file on Stockton right away and then
rummaged around in the cabinets and boxes and began to put
clippings on my desk that had words circled in the text for

their file names, words like *Linwood politics, drug charges, police arrest* and so on.

The clippings had dates stamped on them starting in the mid-eighties. The bio file he had handed me first began in the early seventies. In the back of the file there were clippings from ninety and ninety-one. As I jumped around in the file, I began to wonder if there might not be two Raymond Stocktons in Atlantic County.

The earliest mention of him was in a clipping from 1972. He was a twenty-eight-year-old prosecutor in the Atlantic County District Attorney's office, just a name in a paragraph of names of a team of county attorneys who had won the conviction of several Camden men for hijacking slot machines being delivered to Resorts Casino.

The next clipping was from 1974 when his name started to appear with regularity. By 1976, when he resigned from the county position to go into private practice, he had become the scourge of the Absecon Island underworld, busting up corruption and graft, drug dealing and drug using. He accompanied the State Police on drug raids and crashed brothels in the Inlet with Atlantic City's finest. In 1975, he was mentioned as a candidate for District Attorney. In a profile of possible candidates, the thirty-one-year-old county prosecutor lived in Linwood with his wife, Marcia, and their two children, Mark, eleven, and Juliana, nine.

His career in county politics didn't pan out, but his law practice took off, if in somewhat the opposite direction. In 1981 he was pictured on the front page of the *Press* shaking hands with a client, one Lorenzo "Johnny-Boy" Chirico of Philadelphia, for whom he had won acquittal from charges of being a major supplier of cocaine to the Atlantic City area. Although he was in his late thirties by then, the picture showed a boyish face and close-cropped hair. The next picture of him was in 1983, and the face was still boyish, but the hair was much longer and tied back into a tight ponytail. He'd done it again, this time in Jersey City, in the northern end of the state, won an acquittal for one Erasmo Gutierrez who had been charged with importing large amounts of cocaine from his native Colombia. There were some other well-publicized cases, and he won most of them. I didn't bother to read the details because I knew from Thelma that his victories more often than not came on technicalities like illegal searches and improper arrest procedures. The later articles referred to him with phrases like "brilliant attorney," "civil rights expert," "tireless and thorough defense counsel." I also knew from Thelma that, along with the fame that some of these case brought him, they were also providing him with a fortune in five- and six-figure fees. In 1984 he was elected to the Linwood city council, and in 1985 he was mentioned in a political column as a potential candidate for the state senate.

Raymond wasn't the only Stockton making news in the eighties. In June 1983, Juliana graduated as salutatorian of Mainland Regional High School. She would attend Princeton University in September, the article said. In 1985, Marcia Stockton sued for divorce. In 1986, Mark Stockton, twenty-two, an unemployed construction worker, was killed in a motorcycle accident on Shore Road in Somers Point. In 1987, Marcia Stockton was granted a divorce by a judge in Atlantic County Superior Court. In June 1987, Juliana Stockton was graduated with honors from Princeton University. She planned to work toward a Master's Degree in art history, studying in Japan until January and then completing her course of study at the University of California, Santa Barbara.

"You're a private detective?" The question startled me, and I looked up to see Seth standing beside my desk. He put another handful of clippings in front of me.

"I am," I said, smiling.

"A regular Philip Marlowe." He smiled back.

"I used to be a cop," I said.

"Atlantic City?"

"New York."

"I'm impressed. What brings you down here?"

"I live here."

"You work here too?"

"I do."

"That's all I could find on Stockton. It's a lot, though. With that much in the files we probably have an obituary on him. Do you want me to look it up?"

I nodded and pulled the new clippings across the desk. He flicked a switch on the computer that sat on the next desk, and a bead of light on the monitor quickly blew up into a gray pattern on the screen. Using the keyboard, he deftly brought a program up through several changes of screen and then entered what must have been a search formula and the name: Stockton, Raymond.

"How'd you know I was a detective?" I asked while we waited for the search to complete itself.

"Angie told me," he said, twitching his head in the direction of the reception area across the city room. I guess he had finally answered the insistent phone.

The screen in front of us blinked and asked: "Aka Doc?"

Bingo.

"Yes," I said without taking my eyes off the monitor.

He typed a Y and hit the return button, and double-spaced copy began to unfold in front of me.

"Do you want a printout?" he asked. "It's a dollar a page."

"Sure," I said. "Can you copy the clippings for me too?"

"All of them?"

"Yes."

"They're a quarter a page, regardless of what's on the page."

"Don't jam them up," I said. "I want to be able to sort them chronologically."

"Angie does them," he said. "I'll tell her." I understood from his tone that making Xerox copies was not part of his job. He punched a few more keys and the printer kicked on with a bump and a hum and then started rolling out the obituary of Raymond "Doc" Stockton. He gathered the clippings and the folder and went to give Angie her task.

The obituary was for the most part writer's notes and not a finished piece. Some of it was what Thelma had already told me. Stockton had resigned from politics, admitting that he was a marijuana user, and blaming the state police for forcing his resignation. More recently, he had acquired the name "Doc" and had represented a group of motorcyclists who had been arrested in a protest against mandatory helmet wearing. They had all been fined, and Stockton had been threatened with a contempt citation because of his behavior in court, although there was no indication of what that behavior had been. The event after that, the last one, was simply noted by the writer as: "Arrested—Driving Under the Influence, January 31, hearing postponed by a technicality."

I tore the two pages off the printer and reread them. I recognized the wording in some of the early events. It had been taken directly from the clippings I had just read from the seventies and eighties. Seth came back with a stack of pages from the copier and a bill for nine dollars even for the copying plus two dollars for the computer pages.

"Pay Angie on the way out," he said. He flashed me a wry smile, no doubt a comment on the note on the bottom of the bill that said: "Don't forget. I go to lunch at 12:30!!"

I looked at my watch. It was 12:20. When I stood up pain shot through my ribs. The constant ache had gone away while I was sitting, so I had forgotten about the pain and had moved too quickly. I winced, and Seth noticed.

"You okay?" he asked. I knew his concern was that I might not leave quickly enough for him to get back to Hemingway right away.

I nodded and picked up the stack of pages and made my way across the dim city room. I could feel sweat popping out on my forehead even though the room was air-conditioned. My shoulder began to throb before I got to the reception area. At Angie's desk, I put a ten and a one down with the bill. She stood up and stamped the bill paid and looked at me expectantly. She had her purse in her hand.

"I have another appointment," I said. "Write your phone number on the bill. I'll call you."

She obliged, and when she handed the bill back to me, she said: "You don't look so hot. What happened to your lip?"

"I got worked over by a motorcycle gang."

She rolled her eyes. I don't think she believed me. And I could tell she was sorry she gave me her number. She watched me fold it and put it in my pocket like she wanted it back. I must have looked a lot better on the way in.

The car was an oven from the midday sun. I opened both

front doors and stood outside for a minute to let the breeze
cool it. I realized I felt better when there wasn't anyone near
me who might bump me. I had a little bottle of Tylenol with
codeine samples that they had given me at the hospital in my
pocket, and I took two dry. I looked in the rearview and saw
that my face was a grayish white. I guess that was the message
from Doc, the pain. Stay away, there's plenty more where that
came from. It didn't scare me much, but it did piss me off. I
wanted to be having lunch with Grace. Just to sit and relax
and laugh and have a sandwich and a beer. Nothing more. But
I couldn't. Doc did that to me. He was different from Rocky.
Rocky was just a little street creep who needed a good beating,
preferably from me. But this lawyer-turned-biker needed something a lot better than that. As I swung my legs carefully into
the hot car, I had the urge to reach down and touch the .25 on
my ankle, but I knew it wasn't there. There was no doubt in
my mind that one of them had killed Bonnie and that the other
had assisted in some way or other. That was a certainty. What
I had not a clue about, was how to find either one of them.
But it was nice to know Rocky was still around. If he was
here, Doc couldn't be far behind. If they had skipped town to
Florida or Mexico or wherever, I had no way of tracing them.
They had supposedly made some serious bucks on their score,
so there would be no reason for either one of them to surface
for months or maybe even years. Yet something had brought
Rocky out of hiding for his visit to me. They must have
thought I was on to something. I wanted to know what it was.
If they were going to keep popping up, though, somebody
would find them. People with better resources than mine were
looking for them. If it was the law, no doubt I would hear
about it. And if it wasn't . . . well, you just had to believe that
what goes around comes around. I pointed the car toward
Cedar Bank rather than the shore. I needed to go home and get
my gun.

15

By the time I got to Cedar Bank, the painkiller had kicked in. My front door was closed but the bolt had splintered the frame where I had stomped it. There were two messages on my answering machine, the first from Irene Barbay returning my call the night before and the second from a Sergeant Mc-Kelvey of the Columbia Township Police Department. Suzie bounced around wagging her tail, happy to have me coming through the door instead of a bullet or a couple of hopped-up bikers.

While I was listening to the messages I opened the floor safe and strapped on my ankle gun. Rocky's 9mm was in there. Grace must have put it there and locked up the safe before she took me to the hospital. It would be a long time before I went without wearing a gun again. I had never worn one around the house, and it seemed strange to have it on. But then again, I had never been assaulted here either. Trouble comes when you least expect it. I know that from experience, but I hadn't worn a gun because I didn't want it to be in the way of the embraces I had hoped I might get from Grace.

When I was alone I did a kind of physical self-evaluation. Everything seemed to be functioning. I was sore and tired like I was back in high school and had been in a very rough football game.

My door frame didn't look as bad as it had on first inspection either. I decided I could patch it and screw the dead-bolt catch back without much trouble. Sergeant McKelvey had slipped his card under the door too. Detective Sergeant James

McKelvey, the card read. He had penned a note on the back to call him as soon as possible, but I wanted to fix the door before I did anything else. When I got started, however, I realized I couldn't exert enough pressure to set the screws without causing my ribs a lot of grief. I finally hammered the catch up on the frame with some flat-head roofing nails I found in my tool cabinet, but this simple task wore me out, and I laid down on the couch until I began to feel better. I would have napped, but I was hungry and I didn't have the energy to cook anything or even heat soup. I opened a can of tuna and ate that between two slices of white bread with a little mayonnaise and drank a big glass of orange juice.

I was putting my glass and plate in the sink when the phone rang. I let the machine pick it up because the food in my stomach was already putting me in the mood for a nap. I was just stretching all my aches and pains out deliciously on the couch when I heard Julie Stockton leaving her name and number. I eased my soreness up again but by the time I reached the phone, I had a dial tone in my hand. Suzie, who had been sticking to me like a shadow since I arrived home, trailed across the room with me, and, thinking my deliberate movements were some new game, jumped on me with her front paws sending a jolt of pain through my ribs. I shouted at her, and that hurt my ribs even more. I sat carefully in the chair beside the mail table and played Julie's message back and dialed the number she had left. On the fourth ring her message came on and I left my name. I pulled my wallet out and found the number she had given me in New York, but it was the same one. Suzie shadowed me back to the couch and laid down again when I did. This time I was able to cat-stretch my body out stiff as a board and then just let it melt into the cushions. Outside, beyond the trees that shaded the cottage, the afternoon was sunny and pleasantly warm. A soft spring breeze pushed the curtains gently away from the windows and brought in a cool scent of lilac and pine.

As it often did, the click of the alarm woke me without a memory of hearing it. From the couch I could see two of my flashing alarm lights, the one directly above the front door and the one in the kitchen next to the wall clock above the sink.

The wall clock said it was two-thirty. I sat up, gun in hand, pleased with my decision to nap with it on my ankle. Suzie bounded toward the door barking, and a moment later I heard car tires crunching the driveway gravel. My visitor was in a white patrol car with a red and white bubble bar on top, and as the car neared the house it showed a blue and gold six-pointed star on the door circled by the Columbia Township Police legend. I knew then that a nap wasn't in the cards for the afternoon. I put the gun back on my ankle and went outside.

Sergeant McKelvey was young and tall with broad shoulders that stretched out his khaki sport jacket. His hair was black and cut in a close flat-top. I could see the high point of his scalp in the middle of it from above him on the porch. He was wearing a blue shirt with a button-down collar and no tie. His black eyebrows were thick and grew perilously close to each other. He was carrying a clipboard, and he thrust out a hand as he came up the porch steps.

"Jim McKelvey," he said. His large hand enveloped mine. The surface of the palm seemed very hard.

"Con Leeds," I said. "I know your Chief Foglietta."

"He's mentioned you."

He said it in a neutral tone. A lot of cops don't like the private kind. I never cared one way or another.

"You were on the job in New York City?" he added. He framed it as a question, but the kind that didn't require an answer. I wondered if they said "on the job" in South Jersey or if he was just showing me he knew how we talked in the big city.

As a professional, I appreciated his persistence; as a napper, I was annoyed. I had planned to call him when I got up. I presumed he had received some kind of assault report from the hospital and was following up on it.

"I got your message, Sergeant," I said. "I'm not feeling so hot and I was resting. I went to work but I came home to take a nap."

"I was in the neighborhood," he said, letting me know he was not planning to offer me any sympathy. "I thought I'd stop by again and see if you were in. Save me a trip later on.

We had a report of a shot fired and I wanted to look around. Not a lot happens in this township, and when a weapon gets fired in anger, we like to go take a look."

"Well, I don't know if they were angry," I said. "Just doing their job, is more like it."

"Whatever," he said. "You were on my list. In fact, today you were the list."

"Slow day?"

"Most of them are."

"That's too bad."

"I like it that way."

He wasn't smiling. The peace had been disrupted in the little part of the world he was responsible for, and he wasn't sure if I had anything to do with it yet.

"You said you went to work," he asked. "Where's that?"

"Margate. That's where my office is."

"You don't work here?"

"State law says I have to have a legitimate place of business." Most cops know the law very well, especially when it pertains to one of their retirement industries. I was sure I wasn't telling him anything he didn't already know.

He also already knew there was a bullet hole in the lower half of the front door, and he crouched to examine it. He pulled the door shut and took a pen from his shirt pocket and stuck it through the hole.

"Mind if I go in the house?" he asked.

"Not at all," I said. "I'm going to make some coffee. Can I interest you in a cup?"

"Yes," he said without turning to me.

Inside, Suzie fussed around him, wagging her tail. I called her off, and he pushed the door shut and crouched again and put his pen in the splintered exit hole and then looked over his shoulder at the probable path of the bullet. The slug had gone into the top shelf of one of my bookcases. I knew it was up there but I hadn't gone after it because it would have involved standing on the rolling step stool and reaching up, and it hurt my ribs just to think about it.

"Marcel Proust. *Remembrance of Things Past*. Volume Two," I said.

"Huh?" he said. He stood up.

"Couldn't have hit a better book. I'm not going to live long enough to get through Volume One." I pointed to the top bookshelf.

"Up near the ceiling," I said. "I can see the hole from here. The beige book that's pushed all the way back."

He turned and saw the damaged book and then crossed the room and moved the step stool with his foot, stood on it and pulled the volume down and inspected it.

"Through and through," he said, an uncharacteristic smile touching one corner of his mouth. The phrase applied to a body wound, not a book.

He reached in and pulled out about two feet of books, his back muscles bulging under his sport coat. He looked at me expecting me to take them from him, but I shook my head no and simply said the word "ribs" and he understood and stepped down and put the books carefully on the floor.

"A little sore, are you?" he asked, smiling openly now.

"How did you know there was a shot fired?" I ignored his humor.

He had put his clipboard on the row of shelved books at waist level, and he consulted it to answer.

"A Grace Somers of Mays Landing gave us a statement at the hospital. She was with you, I guess."

"My date," I said. "Not a good way to end an otherwise great evening."

"You were unconscious at the time."

"Sleeping is a more appropriate word."

"It says unconscious here. The report was filed by the night patrolman."

"Whatever," I said, parroting his earlier phrase of dismissal. My sarcasm drew a brief, sharp look from him. "Let me put that coffee on," I said and went into the kitchen.

I turned the electric burner on under the water and was spooning grounds into a paper filter when he came around the corner, holding his palm out with a squashed slug in it.

"It was in the wall," he said. "Your door and the book must have slowed it down. Looks like a nine millimeter."

"I didn't see the gun," I said. I took the slug from him and rolled it in my fingers and gave it back. "It was up against the back of my head most of the time. The other guy had a .38 with a two-inch barrel."

"Were any other shots fired?" he asked, slipping the slug into his pocket.

"What does your report say?" I guess I was tired. I didn't mean to be irritable, but it came out that way. I knew Grace had answered that question already.

He glared at me for a moment and then said: "I'm sure you know the drill, Mr. Leeds."

"Con is fine."

"There's two ways we can do this, Con."

He meant the easy way or the hard way.

"Okay," I said. "There was only one shot."

"How many of them were there?" This time he looked at the clipboard that he held in his other hand.

"Two," I said.

"Did you know either one?"

"No."

"Why did he fire the shot?"

"To scare me."

"It wasn't fired at anyone?"

"No."

The kettle started a low hum, and I busied myself making coffee to shut him up for a while.

At the dining table, I gave him my version of the assault, prompted by his questions. When I described Hell Knuckles's tattoo, he wrote that down. It was the kind of thing a computer tie-in would pick up right away. I went into the bedroom and brought out the handcuffs and gave them to him and selected some details to tell him about Rocky and about Bonnie's death in Brooklyn. I didn't tell him about anything that might perk his interest though, like Bonnie's stay in the cottage or Doc or the tips I had been getting about drug manufacturing in the area. A lucrative activity like that last one had a way of reaching into the remotest places, and I didn't want to chance tipping anyone who might be involved, even the local cops.

"This kind of stuff is out of my league," he said. Now he

was just a good old country boy. "Sounds like this Rocky fellow wants you off his tail. The bikers probably came in from Philly. All I can do is swing by this way more often when I'm on patrol, and if I see anybody on bikes, I'll take a good look at them." He stood up to go. "You have a permit for that gun, of course."

He glanced down at my ankle. There was just the slightest bulge in my pants cuff.

"Yes. Do you want to see it?" If he was trying to piss me off, he was doing a good job.

"No. It's the twenty-five, right?"

"Yes."

He was letting me know he had checked my permits before he came over. Cops are a pain in the ass, but I would have done the same thing myself. I thought about the dirty 9mm sitting in my floor safe. I did my best not to smile as he went out the door.

16

got Irene Barbay on the second ring. It was almost four o'clock and the urge to nap had passed, helped on its way by the two cups of coffee I had drunk with Sergeant McKelvey. Irene said the Baron was out grocery shopping, but I told her that she was the one I wanted to talk to and that I was coming over and needed directions. She hesitated, but I told her the Baron said it was okay when I talked to him the night before and that she could wait for him to come home if she didn't believe me. She said he had told her about my request to talk to her privately last night but didn't know what she could add that I didn't already know. I told her to let me worry about that, just tell me how to get there.

I let Suzie out for a little while and put some fresh food and water down for her because I wasn't sure I wanted to come back that night. The place spooked me a bit even with the gun on my ankle.

The Barbay house was in a middle-class racially mixed neighborhood on the north end of Pleasantville near the Absecon border. The homes and lots were larger and older than the others nearby, built probably in the postwar prosperity of the late fifties. Fieldstone fireplaces ran up their sides, and the trees were full and mature and provided good shade. I wondered what the Baron told the neighbors he did for a living.

I pulled into a driveway that ended with a two-car garage and an expanse of concrete that had been widened to make a small full-court basketball area with two glass backboards on freestanding poles. Two large plastic big-wheel tricycles, and a small pink bicycle with training wheels, sat near the garage doors, which were closed. As I shut off the ignition, I saw one of the curtains near the brick vestibule fall back in place.

Irene opened the front door before I could ring the bell. She put a finger to her lips and whispered: "Baby's sleeping," and ushered me through a tastefully furnished living room and dining room into a sunny kitchen. A coffee pot gurgled on the white formica counter next to the sink. She poured us both a cup, and we sat at a table in a breakfast alcove facing a window that looked out over tall blooming lilac bushes and a well-kept lawn. She looked at me curiously, and I asked: "Do you know what I want?"

"Winston told me you wanted to talk about Bonnie. What happened to you?"

"I got bounced around by some bikers last night." I didn't mention that one of them was Rocky because I knew she'd tell the Baron and he'd get all worked up again. "There was a drug deal she might have known about," I added.

"I know," she said.

"You knew about that deal?"

"Yes. Didn't Winston tell you?"

"No."

"He was protecting Bonnie. Even after she was dead. That's the way he is."

"Why didn't you say something?"

"I didn't want to get the child in trouble."

"And now?"

"Looks like she managed to do that all by herself."

"I don't buy the accidental overdose script. I think someone killed her."

"Me too."

"Why?"

"You can ask all the doctors and social workers and drug counselors you want to, but you're talking to a heroin junkie here. I was hooked big-time for about four years. Winston got me into the program before it killed me, and I got myself straightened out."

Sunlight and shadow fell across her face. Her skin was

very black. She was a beautiful woman, thin and fine-featured with huge dark eyes and a close-cropped Afro. She didn't seem at all embarrassed about her past. I hadn't paid her that much attention the night I met her because I was too distracted by having Bonnie Arnold delivered to me.

"Bonnie wasn't into that stuff, believe me," she continued. "And you don't start out on a four-day run. Your first couple of tries make you sick as a pup."

"I know that."

"How do you know that?" she challenged. "You ever tried it?"

"No. I was a cop in New York in the late sixties and seventies. The great heroin plague was on. I took a night course at NYU in drug addiction and dealing with addicts. I paid attention."

"Somebody shot her up. It had to be Rocky. He knows how to shoot drugs. She knew too much about his deal. Winston is right. Rocky killed her. I have no doubt about it. Who else would have a motive? She wasn't involved in the deal, but Rocky was. She told him everything anyway. I kept my mouth shut because she had told him I knew about it. That worried me. Still does. Maybe he'll come looking for me. Winston wants him killed. Did you agree to do it?"

"That's not one of the things I do for a living."

"What?"

"Kill people. I already told him that."

"You better find Rocky before Winston does then. He'll do it himself, and then I'll be stuck with five kids while he does murder time."

"How did the drug deal go down?"

"I don't know really, except that Rocky ripped a lot of people off. That's probably why we haven't seen him lately."

"He's running?"

"Either he's running, or someone found him, and he'll never run again."

That was a good possibility, and I knew it.

"Did you ever hear of a friend of Rocky's named Doc?" I asked.

"Was he in the program?"

"I don't know."

"There was a guy who used to come around to NA meetings named Doc. I wonder if it's the same person?"

"His name is Raymond Stockton."

"He always said his name was Doc in the meetings."

This kind of response made me glad I was trained as a detective. I was taught that if you ask the same routine question enough times, you get a whole bunch of different answers, or what my first sergeant used to call focus angles.

"Recently?" I asked.

"No. Some time back. He stopped coming around. Thought he could handle it all by himself. As far as I know he's still out there using. Not a nice man."

"I think I can put him together with Rocky."

"Don't tell Winston that. He'll be after killing him too. And this man's a lawyer, and he had some bad friends too. And Winston might just find this one."

"What makes you think he won't find Rocky?"

"Rocky's got no roots. He's long gone. Nobody's gonna find him. Except his God."

"You don't know where he might be? Maybe he told Bonnie."

"Nope. He did tell her about a drug lab that moved around a lot. God, I hope you won't repeat any of this. I haven't even told Winston some of this stuff."

"What else do you know about Doc?"

"Him and Rocky were birds of a feather."

"What do you mean?"

"Selfish. Dishonest. Lady's men. Used to come around and pick up the newcomers, the scared little burnouts. Lived down the road here in Linwood. Lawyer. Politician, I think. Mayor, or something. Took a lot of acid and speed and bought a motorcycle and started hanging out with the bikers. At least that's the way he used to tell it. If he murdered my Bonnie . . ." Her voice trailed off.

"Did he have any kids?"

"Don't know. Didn't pay much attention to the man. He came on to me the first time he ever saw me. I cut him dead, and he never tried again. Kind of guy who wouldn't, no couldn't, be honest with himself. Thought he was better than the people in the rooms. They had character defects; he just took too many drugs, and he'd get over it, he thought. Nothing inside, no conscience. Capable of anything. He messed up a lot of lives. He was a racist too."

"What did he do?"

"Nothing a white person would notice. But if you're black, you figure it out."

"What do black people figure out?" the Baron said. He stood in the kitchen doorway, an imposing figure with a Pathmark bag of groceries in each arm. He was wearing jeans and a navy blue polo shirt with an alligator on it and penny loafers without socks. Behind him was a pretty girl of about eleven or twelve holding another bag. Her skin was very dark like her mother's, her hair in tight cornrows.

"That he was a racist," Irene said.

"Who?"

"Rocky." Her eyes caught mine to caution me. I knew she didn't want me to mention Raymond Stockton.

"That fool," the Baron said. He put his bags on the kitchen counter. The girl put her bag on the counter too and stared at me for a moment, and then, on a sign from Irene, left the room.

I didn't really want to see the Baron. Even if he was wearing penny loafers. I had been avoiding his phone calls, and I was suddenly very irritated. My ribs and my entire shoulder were starting to throb. The doctor at Mainland had given me a prescription for more painkillers, but I hadn't filled it yet and I wanted to. My interview was over. Irene had opened up, and if she thought of anything else she would now give it to me over the telephone.

I stood up.

"I've got to run," I said.

"You don't look so hot, Con-man. You moving like an old guy. Did you get the plate number of the truck that hit you?" He chuckled.

"Two bikers worked me over last night," I said. "Kicked my ribs in good."

"Sorry to hear that. Wasn't Rocky, was it?"

"No," I lied. "One of them had H-E-L-L tattooed across his knuckles. Two big white guys."

"No such thing as a black biker," Irene said.

"Not true," the Baron said. "I know plenty up in Philly. Ride with their own in a black club. But they affiliated with the Pagans I think the name is. That's a big club in Philly. I'll ask about the knuckles tattoo for you next time I see one of them. They come down to gamble, but the girls don't like them. Too rough."

"Ask them about a drug lab too. If I can find that, I might have a shot at Rocky. If they'll tell you."

"They'll tell me. They brothers first, and bikers second, you dig?"

From somewhere beyond the living room I heard a baby start to cry. Irene got up quickly and hurried out of the room.

"What you got for me?" he said when she was out of earshot.

"Nothing. Except that my aches and my pains tell me I'm going in the right direction."

"You talk to Irene?"

"Yes."

"So I did my part of the bargain?"

"Yes."

"Now it's your turn. You find that motherfucker for me, hear?"

"Yes."

"Did Irene know anything I didn't tell you?"

"No," I lied again. The Baron was the kind of guy you had to lie to. There were a lot of things he didn't want to hear.

"See. I told you not to bother. I told you everything she knows."

"I have to go. Tell Irene thanks for the coffee."

"No problem."

I drove across Shore Road through Pleasantville and Northfield parallel to the bay to Tilton Road and then turned east on the causeway to the Margate Bridge and the southern end of the island. I wanted to get my file back from Thelma and visit the pharmacy around the corner from my office to get my prescription filled. After a mile of causeway that crossed marsh and bay, the sunny May day downgraded to a chilly spring afternoon with a slight mist that wasn't thick enough to call fog. When it's warm on the mainland in the spring I often forget to bring a sweater or a jacket to the shore, and today was no exception.

The pharmacy was on the same block as my office. I parked in their lot and went inside and gave the druggist the prescription. My shirt sleeves were not enough against the afternoon chill, and I was cold and uncomfortable as soon as I got out of the car. The pharmacist told me he would have the painkiller ready in fifteen minutes. I walked the half-block to the office and had goose bumps by the time I got there. My street-level door was unlocked, and I knew something was wrong before I was halfway up the stairs. There was a draft on the stairwell, and I could hear the traffic noises from Ventnor Avenue very clearly. The office door stood wide open, and it was a mess inside. Someone had trashed the place.

Whoever did it had come over the roof of the single-story building next door and pried the molding away from the small side window in the powder room and lifted the whole frame out. When they were finished, they had exited down the stairs and out onto Ventnor Avenue. It was a professional job; too professional for my biker friends to have done it. The search had been very methodical. Each drawer in the file cabinet and in my desk had been emptied methodically, and the rug had been pulled up. A burglar will ordinarily just toss stuff as he goes through it, and if he's nervous and looking for a quick fix of cash or something he can sell within the next hour, he'll make the place look like a tornado touched down there. This one had laid the files out and then pushed them aside one or two at a time as if he had been looking through them. A lawyer would go through the files like that. Or an ex-lawyer. The typewriter and the answering machine had not been touched. I wondered if anyone in the boutique had heard anything, although I was certain a roof job like that would only be done at night.

I locked the place and went downstairs to the boutique. Bay-ling Kravitz was there with another young woman whom I had never seen before. This new one was tall and thin with auburn hair and a spray of freckles over her nose. She looked to be about sixteen, although lately a lot of women in their twenties were beginning to look like teenagers to me. She told me her name was Molly after I introduced myself as the upstairs neighbor. She had just finished her junior year at Penn and was working for Thelma for the summer. She had a great big smile and long legs, and I was tempted to ask her to dinner. But the fact that she might actually be nineteen, and technically still a teenager, stopped me. Bonnie had been seventeen. Women don't start to lose that youthful self-consciousness until about twenty-five, and I find that trait uncomfortable to be with for an evening. Sure, they're wonderful to look at across a dinner table, but they're quite often awkward and shy. And they tend to talk about things I know nothing about, especially when the subject gets around to current musical trends. You mention the Rolling Stones and they look at you like you're talking about elevator music. You just have to draw the line somewhere. Except that in South Jersey the attractive women seem to wind up with a kid or two by the time they get to the quarter-century mark.

Thelma was not there. They told me she was at her branch store in Ocean City. Bay-ling retrieved the file for me. She had opened the store at 9:30, and neither woman had heard any unusual noise upstairs since then. I was so sure the break-in was a personal matter that I decided not to report it to the Margate police. I told the women to have Thelma call me about having her handyman put the window frame back in and I left. I locked my street door and walked back to the pharmacy to pick up my prescription. I was putting the accordion file into my trunk when I saw Thelma drive by on Washington Avenue looking for a parking space so I walked back to the boutique. By the time I got inside I was trembling from the damp breeze that was blowing off the ocean. Bay-ling was with a customer, but Molly, who was standing by the front door, told me Thelma had already gone up to look at the damage. Molly gave me a giant smile that made me feel very old. I was afraid that if I took her to dinner, she might call me Pops. I turned and went outside and climbed the stairs to my office, my sore ribs making me go very slowly.

Thelma was crouched down with her back to the door looking at the folders that were scattered out in front of the filing cabinets.

"Do you want me to call the police?" I asked.

She jumped up, startled. She hadn't heard me come in.

"Christ, you scared me," she said. "I thought the burglar came back." She saw my fat lip for the first time.

"What happened to you?" she asked.

"I found Rocky," I said. "He came to the house with a message from Doc and a friend. I think he wanted to kill me. He would have but his friend stopped him."

"Was the friend Stockton?"

"No."

"When did this happen?"

"Last night."

"Do you think they came here too?"

"No way. Not those animals. This is a finesse job. It took a modicum of brains."

"Raymond?"

"Of course. But what the hell was he looking for?"

"Maybe he just wanted to see what you had. I think they're playing around the fringes because they're not sure of you. They did a large rip-off and had to do a murder to cover it up, and they want to see if you can cause them any grief."

"And if I can?"

"I think they'll kill you too."

"That's what I think too."

"But they haven't yet. So I think they think you're not much of a threat. That's why they just wanted to discourage you last night." She touched her chin thoughtfully and said: "That's why they didn't want to kill you. Right now, they've gotten away with murder. Nobody believes Bonnie was murdered except you and me and the Baron and maybe Bonnie's grandfather. Although right now Grandfather Arnold doesn't seem to want to make waves either. But if they kill you, they can't hide it or make it look like an accident. And you're a retired cop. So the whole screaming confraternity of law enforcement would come at them full tilt. If they think you have something, that you're a threat, first they'll look for an accidental death for you. I'd be real careful crossing streets if I were you." She laughed. Sometimes her gallows humor got on my nerves.

"Probably Rocky and his friend were supposed to do the same thing out at the cottage," I said. "You know, search it. But Rocky got into stoving my ribs, and my date got away, and they lost their nerve and ran like rabbits. I'll kill him the next time I see him. No conversation. No explanation. Bang, you're dead."

Thelma screwed her mouth into a cynical frown. "What's missing?" she asked.

"From what?"

"Here."

"I don't know. Doesn't look like anything. My case folder was down in your office. I lost my girlfriend though. That's the worst part."

"The blackjack dealer."

"Her name was Grace."

"Don't get sore. You know I have a hard time keeping track of your women."

"This one was different. Something lasting was happening."

"Have you met Molly?"

"Yes, I have. I could have a daughter Molly's age."

"What about the picture?"

"The Polaroid."

"Yes, where is it?"

"I don't know. Didn't you have it?"

"I brought it back. It was on your desk yesterday afternoon. And there was the computer arrangement of the phone numbers. He must have taken them."

"Or I put them in the folder."

"When? The folder was in my office. I hope it's still there."

"I got it from Bay-ling. I just put it in my car."

"Go see if the Polaroid is in it."

"You made copies, right?"

"Yes."

"I'll look when I get home. It's no big deal if you have a copy."

"I guess you're right. The phone numbers are in the computer too."

"Do you want me to call the police?"

"It's up to you."

"Can you get the window fixed? I'll pay for it."

"Of course. I already made the phone call. It'll be in this afternoon."

"I'm going home. I'm whipped. These ribs are wearing me out."

"What's wrong with your ribs?"

"Nothing a good night's sleep won't help. I spent the night in the hospital."

"And when you left yesterday afternoon, you thought you were going to spend the night with Grace. See, I remembered her name."

"Sometimes you're not very funny, Thelma."

"I'm not trying to be. It's life that gets funny."

I turned toward the door. "Will you lock up here?"

"Yes," she said. She was already bending over the folders again.

"Maybe I'll see you tomorrow," I said.

"Not tomorrow," she said. "I'll be in Cherry Hill all day. I'll see you Sunday."

"What's Sunday?"

"I'm bringing a picnic lunch out to your cottage."

"Thanks for letting me know."

"I'm doing that now."

"Do you want me to get anything?"

"Chill a bottle of white wine. Something dry. We're going bridge hunting."

"I'll be glad to go on a picnic with you. In fact, that sounds like fun. But I'll be damned if I'm going to wander around in the Pines looking for a bridge that we don't even have a picture of."

"I have a Xerox."

"Not of the bridge itself, we don't. Just of where you think the bridge should be."

"You sound so exasperated. Calm down. It'll be a nice day in the woods. I'd go by myself, but I get lost when I leave the island. I've lived here for sixty years. I mean forty-five. And I never go in the woods. I'm a city girl."

"There must be a dozen bridges, maybe more."

"Iron ones?"

"I don't know. Maybe less."

"Then we'll go to the ones we know. And we'll see what we see. And we'll have a nice picnic."

"Call me first."

In the drugstore parking lot I popped the trunk of the Honda and went through the accordion folder carefully. The picture was definitely not there anymore.

17

At the cottage there was a message to call Bill Harrison at Founder's Insurance. In case I missed him at the office, he left his home number in Moorestown too. Call no matter how late I got in, he said, it was urgent. If I didn't call, they would have to get someone else for the job. There were also two messages from Julie Stockton.

Julie Stockton answered on the second ring.

"Of course I remember you," she said. "I hoped I would run into you under happier circumstances down at the shore. And here you are. I didn't think it would be so soon."

"Would you like to have dinner?"

"I'd love to. But I can't tonight."

"I didn't really mean tonight. Sometime. Anytime, I guess."

"Are you free tomorrow night?"

"Yes," I said.

She gave me the address of a condo in Ventnor, and I told her I'd pick her up at seven. I called Bill Harrison and took a little heat for not returning his calls for the past week, but we made an appointment to meet in his office in Philadelphia the next day at ten. About the last thing I wanted to do was go looking for insurance cheats, but Founder's was one of my bread and butter accounts, and I didn't want to lose it. I wasn't making a penny chasing after Doc Stockton and Rocky.

I thawed a couple of meatballs in the microwave and cooked some spaghetti. There was a Phillies game on the radio but I only made it to the third inning. It was 9:30 when I gave the dog a walk around the yard and went to bed. I knew I would sleep soundly, so I turned the alarm up to maximum volume and put the .25 under the pillow next to me. Not that I expected any visitors. I just slept better with it there.

The job Harrison had for me was surveillance, and I spent Friday afternoon in the car with my Nikon, sweating and watching a factory entrance in Pennsauken for the owner. When he finally came out at 5:15, he was in a wheelchair just like he was supposed to be. I took a few long-range snapshots of him and left. I was expected to tail him to his home, but I was pretty sure he had spotted me. I didn't want to be late for Julie anyway.

It was Memorial Day weekend and there was a lot of traffic headed for the shore. I had to go home first to shower and change and then fight the traffic down the Expressway into Atlantic City. The day had been a warm one, and this time the island temperature was warm too with a bright red sunset over the marshes to my right and behind me. The air was still and dry when I got out of the car in Ventnor, and by the time I was in the elevator going up to Julie's condo my watch said 7:20. When I rang her bell, I heard her shout from somewhere back in the apartment that the door was open. I stepped into a small vestibule and shut the door behind myself. The apartment was on the eighth floor in a converted seaside hotel. Across the small living room I could see a balcony just big enough for two plastic chairs and beyond that the calm expanse of ocean in the gray twilight.

"I'll be out in about five minutes," she shouted from the bedroom. It reminded me of Mary Ellen. No matter how late I was—and when I was drinking with other cops after a shift that was sometimes two or three hours—she made me wait ten or fifteen minutes if we were going out.

There was a mail table in the vestibule with a gilt-frame mirror on the wall behind, and there was a pile of mail on the table that I went through out of force of habit. It was mostly junk mail, a few bills and some catalogs. The mail-table drawer held several ballpoint pens and a wallet-sized checkbook whose stubs detailed only routine utility, credit card and mortgage payments and a balance of a little under $400. The apartment was sparsely furnished like she had just moved in and was slowly collecting pieces. The hardwood floors were covered with throw rugs, and the couch and matching easy chair and glass coffee table looked new.

"Nice place," I shouted to remind her that I was here. "How long have you lived here?"

"I can't hear you," she shouted back. "Wait until I come out."

I had seen her at Bonnie's funeral at the beginning of the week, but somehow I had forgotten what a spectacular package she was. When she came out of the bedroom and strode across the living room, she took my breath away. At the Arnolds' she had worn a dark summer suit that revealed little of her figure, but the outfit she had on now left little to my imagination. She wore a short red skirt and a white sleeveless cotton jersey and little else except sandals. She was almost as tall as I was with full breasts whose nipples and aureoles stood outlined beneath her cotton top. Her waist was small, almost tiny, and her hair honey-colored in the fading light. But the feature that was special was her skin. It was flawless, a lightly tanned ivory. She shook my hand and then turned to check her appearance in the vestibule mirror, and when she did, I could see a line of bikini panties under the tight skirt. I cleared my throat and asked: "Where would you like to go for dinner? How about Atlantic City?"

"I hate Atlantic City," she said.

"How about offshore? I know a terrific Italian restaurant up the Black Horse Pike in Williamstown."

"I hate offshore too."

"I love a woman who knows what she wants," I said sarcastically, and she flashed me a dazzling smile full of large white teeth and bright red lipstick that matched her skirt.

"Do you like the Crab Pot?" she said.

"Love it," I said. "I thought maybe you'd want to get out of the neighborhood."

"I love to eat out on the deck there at night."

"The Crab Pot it is then," I said. The restaurant was in Margate near my office on the bay side of the island.

She took a white cotton sweater from the closet and draped it over her shoulders and we left. I walked slightly behind her to the elevator because I couldn't keep my eyes off her and I didn't want her to see me gawking.

The sun had set by the time we were seated on the Crab Pot deck above the boat slips and the bay. A line of fading aqua in the west ran between the night sky and the horizon. A soft breeze stirred the napkins under our drinks, mine a Margarita and hers a white wine spritzer. Julie's face and long graceful neck were pale in the flickering deck lights.

We both ordered lobster, and when we were well into our second drink, I asked her if she was related to Raymond Stockton, the Linwood attorney. She was bringing her glass up to her mouth, and she stopped in surprise at my question.

"Of course," she said. "I thought you knew him. He's my father."

Ask a simple question . . .

"Is his nickname Doc?" I was on a roll.

"I've heard that he calls himself that these days," she said and sipped her drink. "We haven't really been in touch in almost three years."

"You don't talk to each other?"

"Not if we can help it. He sends me a Christmas card with a hundred-dollar bill in it. That's about it."

"Any reason for the animosity?"

"I wouldn't call it animosity. His lifestyle has changed. And it's nothing I care to be a part of. He hangs out with bikers and other sleazy types and has become embroiled in a drug subculture that I think is dangerous and damaging to his health and mental stability. He was never really a stable person anyway."

Our lobsters came and my hesitant probing stopped for a while. At best, she was reluctant to discuss her father. She had a way of slipping through my questions so adroitly that several times I wasn't sure I had asked them.

When we had reduced our crustaceans to a huge pile of red shells and feathered innards and were rubbing lemons and damp hot towels on our hands, I ventured to ask: "Did you ever hear of a man from New York named Rocky?"

I watched her face carefully but it showed no reaction to the name.

"He was a friend of my father's, right?"

"Yes."

"A biker?"

"Sort of."

"Does he have a last name?"

"Starza."

"I think I met him once."

We ordered coffee. It was completely dark now except for a faint red glow in the west. I wasn't sure if it was the last of the sunset or the night lights of Philadelphia.

We chatted idly about the pleasant night and the merits of the lobsters, and then I asked: "You said earlier that your father was unstable. How did you mean that?"

A flash of annoyance crossed her face, but she answered with a studied patience. "He had been riding motorcycles and experimenting with drugs for a while before my brother was killed. But after that he went off the deep end. My mother had already left him."

"When was that? Your brother's death, I mean."

"In 1986."

"Your parents are divorced?" I knew the answer to that one. I wanted to see what her face looked like when I asked it.

"Yes," she answered. The face was set, getting annoyed.

"Where is your mother now?"

"Oregon. She's a high school teacher in Eugene." The irritated look came back across her face. She paused, and then asked: "Is this some kind of investigation you're doing? I thought we were just going to have dinner."

"Of course. I'm sorry. I get obsessed with Bonnie's death. I've pretty much tied this Rocky person to her, and some people I've talked to connect him to your father. I am definitely enjoying your company. I just can't turn off the detective stuff sometimes."

"That's okay. Bonnie is the nicest person I ever met. We were good friends, and her death was, still is, a shock to me. I wake up sometimes in the middle of the night sure that it didn't happen. That I dreamed it."

"How did you know each other?"

"See. There you go again."

"I'm sorry." I truly was. I just couldn't get it stopped. She was one of the most desirable women I ever sat across a meal from, and here I was pushing her to the wall with questions about her family and her best friend's death.

"Besides," she said. "You seem to know a lot about my father already."

"I looked up his public life at the *Atlantic City Press* morgue. I was just trying to get a feel for him as a person."

She didn't say anything for a moment, just stared at me. Her eyes seemed to go dead, to lose their light.

"As a person he was a real fuck," she said, her voice low and bitter. "He used people. I watched him eat my mother alive. And my brother. If there was any connection between him and Bonnie, I would have known. It wouldn't have happened."

"They both knew Rocky," I said. "And all three of them went to meetings. You know, AA and NA. I'd have to conclude that he at least knew who she was. It would have been difficult for a man to overlook her."

"This Rocky may have been a friend of my dad's, but the AA connection doesn't hold water. Dad hasn't been to an AA or NA meeting in a couple of years. He was drinking and using heavily the last I heard."

This jibed with Irene Barbay's information.

"How would you know?" I asked. "Do you go to meetings?"

"No. I don't know a whole lot about drugs, but I know what they can do to a person. And I keep tabs on Raymond. I like to know where he is so I don't ever bump into him." She used her father's first name as an expression of contempt, and she said it with a slight sneer. She was a gorgeous package, but this bitterness was ugly.

"Rocky and Bonnie were a thing. Did you know that?"

"I knew she was seeing someone from the program. I had encouraged her to go to NA in the first place. But I didn't think it was such a good idea to date someone else who went, and she wouldn't talk about him anyway. I used to call him

Mr. Secret. It's funny. I jumped to the conclusion that the guy was married, and that's why she kept him to herself. You think Rocky killed her, don't you?"

"He was responsible for her death, yes. Whether it was intentional or not, I don't know."

Her eyes had gone dead as if she could never smile again.

"Talking about your father really upsets you, doesn't it?" I asked.

"Yes," she said levelly. "He's embarrassing, swaggering around in his leather outfits, tattoos up and down his arms, talking about the First Amendment." She snorted a short contemptuous laugh.

"How about you?" I asked. "What's your bio? I'm tired of talking about your old man."

"I hope you mean that." She laughed again but this time it was with pleasure.

"I do mean it. What do you do for a living? Do you have any hobbies? Who's your favorite singer? Do you have any tattoos? What's your sign?" I rattled off my facetious list and she laughed again.

"I'm a dance therapist," she said. I knew I had seen some extraordinary muscles when I followed her to the elevator coming out of her apartment. "I work with mentally challenged and autistic children."

"In Atlantic City?"

"No. In Philadelphia. I'm also getting my doctorate at Temple."

"That must be a lot of commuting."

"It's not that bad. I have a comfortable car."

"What do you drive?"

"A Pathfinder four by four. With a tape deck and a big stereo system. It's a great road car. The Expressway is one of the most boring highways in America. I take the train a lot too. Especially when I have homework to do or a test to study for."

"Do you go up every day?"

"No. Just to work. I'm not taking any courses this summer."

We fell silent and stared into coffee cups that had been

refilled twice. The waitress came back with my credit card and a receipt for the check. I signed it and fought not to react to the pain that jolted my ribs when I stood up.

"What would you like to do?" I asked as we walked across the deck. It was completely dark now. "If you don't like Atlantic City and you don't like offshore, our options are somewhat limited."

"Do you like to dance?" she asked.

"You're a professional," I said.

"I mean rock and roll."

"Well, I used to. But it's been a while." My ribs wanted me to say no but I didn't.

"Let's go to Somers Point."

"That's offshore."

"Just barely," she said. The car was in a dirt parking lot across Amherst Avenue. It was lit only by the lights from the restaurant, so she looped her arm inside mine as we picked our way around a few small puddles and clumps of weeds. There was no moon yet but it was a clear night and there were stars. Somers Point is loaded with clubs because it sits next to the dry beach town of Ocean City. We went to three different joints, but there were lines to get into all three. We had over-looked the fact that it was Friday night of Memorial Day weekend. I think she would have waited in one of the lines, but she asked me if I wanted to brave it and I said no. There were droves of people milling around each one of these joints, and none of them looked any older than Julie. I was grateful I wouldn't have to bounce my sore ribs around a dance floor for a couple of hours. I wasn't sure I could have done it, but I had no doubt she wouldn't have had any trouble finding other dance partners.

As we drove along Shore Road, she said: "The moon will be rising soon. Would you like to watch it from my balcony?"

"Nice night for it," I said.

We came back to the island across the Longport Bridge. I wasn't paying attention and missed the split for Atlantic Avenue and wound up headed north on Ventnor. I pointed out my office when we passed it, and then just to make conversation I said: "I had a break-in night before last."

She waited for me to say more but I didn't.

"What did they steal?" she asked finally.

"Nothing that I can tell," I said. "I think it was your father."

"Raymond?" She seemed astonished. "What would he want?"

"There were valuables, but he didn't take any of them."

"How do you know it was him?"

"I don't." I didn't say any more. I had heard the bitter edge coming back into her voice.

I swung over to Atlantic Avenue, and we were almost to her building in Ventnor when she said: "I'm sorry he broke into your place." She paused. I pulled up to the red light at her corner and looked at her. She had that angry, stricken look on her face again.

"You don't have to apologize," I said.

"I'm not going to. I'm sorry for you, but I'm not responsible for his actions. I hate him." She turned and looked out her window away from me. The light changed and I turned toward the water and her building.

She had left the glass doors to her balcony open, and the apartment was cool from the night breeze blowing in off the ocean. We crossed the living room in darkness, spotting the coffee table and chairs by the hallway light before she shut the apartment door behind us.

Stepping out onto the small balcony and into the night, I had the sudden exhilarating feeling of moving into an immense space. You couldn't see any details of the beach eight stories below except light sand and the moving lines of surf beyond it. The casinos stretched out in a long colorful arc along the boardwalk to the left, and down beach smaller lights marked the waterfront homes in Margate and Longport. I sat in one of the plastic chairs, and Julie disappeared for a long moment and came back with two small snifters of very good cognac. Before she sat down she pointed toward a spot at about ten o'clock on the horizon and said: "Keep you eyes right about there."

That confused me for a moment until I remembered that

we had come up to the apartment to watch the moon rise. I had been watching the outline of her body against the bright casino buildings. She sat and we watched silently, and after maybe five or ten minutes, an orange glow started to grow so that you could see the actual line of the water out there where she had pointed. The moon itself, when it finally appeared, looked larger than I've ever seen it, even when it was only partially revealed. It was a half moon or a little less, and at first it appeared a dull orange, but as it rose above the water, it slowly took on the colorless glow that I was used to.

Julie took my empty snifter after a while and got us both another cognac. I had to stand up so she could squeeze by my chair, and I stayed that way until she came back. She stopped when she got close to me, and our eyes met in the moonlight. I put my hands on her shoulders and kissed her. She held the brandies very still and when the kiss was finished, put them on her chair and put her arms around my neck. We made love then clutching at each other and leaving a trail of clothes through the moonlit living room to the absolute darkness of her small bedroom. Later when she turned on the light and saw the bruises on my upper body, she gave a shocked, audible intake of breath. Toward morning she spent a long time inspecting the shades of purple and caramel along the left side of my rib cage and told me that if they were abstract paintings, they would be beautiful. My lip was still slightly swollen and the ribs ached, but neither diminished my desire for her. She talked about wanting me too, about how attracted she was to me at the Arnolds in Brooklyn, how she wanted me then and could see in my eyes that I wanted her, and how disappointed she was that I wouldn't go to dinner with her and Ben Jr. and Dan Pickering that evening.

We spent the Memorial Day weekend in bed, coming up for air occasionally to take short walks on the Ventnor Boardwalk. She was an extraordinary sexual partner for a woman her age; enthusiastic, energetic and as knowledgeable as a New Orleans madam. She knew when to go slowly, oh, so slowly, and when to go quickly. And she had all those strong and tactile dancer's muscles both outside and inside her body. That body plus her gorgeous face and her quiet erotic insistence kept me in a state of almost constant arousal until the sky began to gray beyond her balcony.

Early Saturday morning I called Mary Sooy and asked her to drive over to the cottage and pick up Suzie for a short stay. I could almost hear her leer over the phone when she agreed. Julie and I slept then, made love in the tangle of sheets and slept again. We got up at noon, stanched our hunger with piles of scrambled eggs and went down to the beach. She swam while I rolled up my slacks and waded in the cold surf. She was a strong swimmer, and when I commented on that fact, she told me she had worked several college summers as a lifeguard on the Margate beaches. When we came back upstairs, I wouldn't let her shower right away because I wanted to taste the salt on her.

I made a feeble attempt that afternoon to take some pictures of my insurance cheat at his weekend place in Ocean City. From the far end of his lagoon, screened by one of his neighbor's hydrangeas, I watched and snapped through the 1000mm lens as his son wheeled him down the dock to his fifty-foot deep-sea rigged Hatteras Sportfish and lifted him aboard. They headed out past me on an overnight voyage to Baltimore Canyon to fish marlin. My written briefing from the insurance company said that he made this run every Saturday afternoon in the summer when the weather was good. It didn't say what sort of fraud he had pulled, but it said he had been observed walking, and the company lawyers needed pictures of him standing without support or walking. It also said the boat had cost him half a million dollars, mostly financed by the insurance settlement. He was either legitimately paralyzed, very cautious or very good at spotting insurance dicks who sat in his neighbor's bushes daydreaming, as I was about the beach sand on Julie's bikini as she had led me back to her condo earlier that afternoon. While I was playing detective she made a shopping run to stock the comestibles we might need for the rest of the weekend, things like spaghetti and Italian bread and wine.

She was fascinated with my gun. At her insistence I took the bullets out of the cylinder and let her play with it. Most people will grip the stock, wrap an index finger around the trigger and take aim at some distant or imaginary object. Not Julie. She laid it gently on its side in her palm and touched it and stroked it slowly as if it was flesh and blood. She wasn't at all timid with it. I asked her if she had ever fired a gun before, and she said she had shot her father's pistols and rifles out at his hunting camp in Wharton State Forest.

On Saturday evening after we had eaten some of the spaghetti and drank some of the wine, we showered and dressed to go out, but were at each other before we could finish and spent another long night on the bed, exploring, drowsing, talking, drinking wine and making love. I teased her about her expertise in bed, and asked her where she had learned to make love so well, that she must have had a good teacher. She said that she had learned that sex shouldn't interfere with her life, that she could do anything, in bed and out, as long as it wasn't obsessive and that she felt right about it and about herself. She didn't have sex often, but when she felt the urge, she just did it, especially if the attraction to a man was as strong as this one to me. When I asked her when the last time was that she had been this attracted to a man, she answered that she never had. It was flattering, but I was more than ready for some flattery. The brush-off from Grace had made me feel lonely and vulnerable, and I wondered if it amplified in some way my desire for Julie.

She might have been the best lead I had for finding Raymond Stockton, but I decided not to mention him again after Friday night. The immediate coldness that came over her any time I brought up her father was enough to make me put my case on hold for the weekend. On the other hand, she brought Bonnie up a number of times, asking me questions I couldn't or wouldn't answer like: "You think someone murdered her, don't you?"

"I don't know," I would say. "What do you think?"

"Why would someone murder Bonnie?" she would counter.

These little thrusts and parries never went anywhere because we were so distracted physically by one another.

I managed to drag myself away from her Sunday evening as the sun was going down. I was spent, and the wise smile I got from Julie's doorman told me that my clothes looked like they had grown a little too big for me since I had worn them into his lobby Friday night.

By the time I faced the Sooys' knowing grins and got Suzie home, it was almost nine o'clock. I tried to think about why people found speculation about sexual encounters so damned amusing. Maybe it was just that I looked so wiped out. Or maybe they wished they had been there themselves. But I was just too tired to think much about anything. I was hungry too, but tired took precedence, and I crashed, leaving my clothes in a heap beside the bed, but not forgetting to slip the .25 under the extra pillow. I fell asleep thinking about Julie gently caressing it.

18

When I saw the gun again it had followed me into my dreams and was being pressed against my temple by a giant biker with a full black beard who looked suspiciously like Bluto from the Popeye cartoons of my childhood. He pulled the trigger. Click. The gun then somehow became an oversized .357 Magnum whose long barrel looked like a cannon against my tiny head. Bluto laughed and pulled the trigger again. Click. I knew there was a bullet meant for my brain somewhere in the cylinder, and he continued to laugh and pull the trigger. Click, click, click . . .

The insistent click of my security alarm woke me, and I slid my hand quietly under the pillow and wrapped it around a real gun. Warm sunshine streamed over the bed, warm enough that I was sweating under the blanket.

"It's me," Thelma shouted from the porch. "Let me in."

I couldn't find any words in my sleep-dry throat. I fumbled around in the pile of clothes beside the bed and put the gun into the ankle holster and then sat up and pulled on my pants. Suzie started to bark when I stood up. My digital alarm said 8:53. I had slept around the clock. I needed to use the bathroom badly and I was still hungry.

Thelma pounded on the door again, and this time I was able to shout at her to be patient. When I came out of the bathroom I could see just the tip of her nose and her eyes peering through the living room window. She wore a straw hat whose wide brim was crushed against the pane, and when she saw me she darted away toward the front porch again. I shut off the alarm and unlocked the door.

"What are you doing here?" I asked. Suzie danced around her. "Why aren't you at the store?"

"We had a date to go on a picnic."

"Oh, Christ, I forgot."

"Yesterday."

"I'm sorry."

"I was worried about you," she said. She stood on her tiptoes and kissed me on the cheek. "You tell me on Thursday that you got the stuffing beat out of you by angry bikers with guns, and now it's Memorial Day Monday, and you don't return any phone calls, so I came by to see if rigor mortis had set in. And to see if someone was looking after the dog."

"Did you call me this morning?"

"No. I was so sure you were dead, I just got in my car and drove out."

"I didn't check my messages when I got in last night. I was doing surveillance in Ocean City."

"I've been calling for three days."

"I was working on something else too."

"I'll bet you were. What was her name?"

"Julie Stockton."

"Oh, I see. Well now, that is very interesting." She hung her hat on a chair back and sat at the kitchen table while I made a pot of coffee and told her about my weekend with Julie. I left out the biological details, but she didn't seem to care, which was unusual for her. Instead, she pressed me for information about Doc Stockton.

"Her life is entirely separated from her father," I said.

"Stop being defensive," she said, smirking. "Every time you get in the sack with a woman, you come out thinking she needs your protection."

"Thank you, Dr. Ruth. But I don't think I'm being defensive. She hasn't been in touch with her father for several years and has no idea where he is."

"He's still her father. It's a tie you can't break. Even if she doesn't know where he is, she would know where he might be. Where he's been in the past."

"She refused to talk about him."

Thelma knew I was irritated, so she let up a little and said: "All these hours you spent in her apartment, I presume there was time for a little nosiness."

"I searched her mail Friday and Saturday."

"That's all? You didn't go through her closets and her drawers? Dresser drawers, I mean."

"I was never alone in the place. She went grocery shopping once but I was out doing surveillance."

"Go get dressed," she said with mild disgust. "And put your hiking boots on," she said. "We're going to see that bridge."

"What bridge?"

"The one in the photograph."

"I told you I don't have that photo," I said. "I don't even have the other one I took from Rocky. Doc took it when he broke into my office."

"I have that one," she said with a grin and pulled the Xerox copy from a pocket in the folds of her skirt. "How many bridges can there be?"

I took a quick shower, and when I came out hair-wet in fresh clothes, Thelma had found my roll of U.S. Geological Survey quadrangles and spread several of them on the living room floor. She was kneeling over them, a Pall Mall dangling from the corner of her mouth. The maps are large and awkward to view. I poured myself the last of the coffee and cleared off the kitchen table.

"What am I looking for?" she shouted from behind the couch.

"I'll be there in a minute," I said. "Try Atsion quadrangle. That's the one with the Mullica and the Batsto on it."

A cardinal began to sing strong separate notes somewhere near the kitchen window, staking out his space and his right to live in it undisturbed, at least among the other cardinals. The sun was warming the pines, bringing out their sweet scent. I felt a mild urge to read the morning paper, maybe on the front porch, nothing more ambitious than that, and then to watch the river and try to figure out what to do with the rest of the day.

"Where's the name on these things?" the voice behind the couch asked.

In my reverie I had forgotten about her.

"What name?" I said.

"The name of the map."

I took my half-filled cup into the living room and stood over her.

"You are what's called a pain in the ass, Thelma."

"Thank you very much for that compliment," she said, looking up.

"You have it right there," I said, pointing to the Atsion quadrangle that she had spread out in front of her knees.

"That's the Atsion one," she said, pronouncing the name as three syllables.

"Same thing," I said. "The Pineys say 'At-Sign.'"

"How would I know? I'm not a Piney," she said. "I'm a sophisticated Philly girl. Pineys are those people at the beach whose legs are too white and have big red insect bites on them. If anybody's a Piney, you are."

"And you're a shoobie."

"That sounds anti-Semitic."

"It isn't. Shoobie crosses all ethnic and religious lines."

"I'm not a shoobie," she said emphatically.

"My, aren't we sensitive today."

"You're frustrating me. You won't take this seriously."

"I'm sorry," I said. I put my cup on the fireplace mantle and squatted beside her. "Where are we going?" I asked.

"I was hoping you'd tell me."

"Did you bring food?"

"Fried chicken and Beluga caviar."

"Good, then let's just go on a picnic. There's nothing to be learned out there, Thelma. Trust me. But it's a great day. We can get a bottle of wine at the liquor store in Nesco. They open at eight. Gives the boaters a chance to get loaded early."

"I'm sure their selection is excellent."

"Wait'll you see how well Thunderbird goes with caviar."

We turned our attention to the map at her knees. The Geological Survey maps are drawn on a scale of one to twenty-four thousand, or roughly two and one-half inches for each mile, with contour intervals of ten feet. They are very detailed and show every body of water that you can't step over and some that you can. I had collected them over the years from various camping supply stores and from the Rand Mcnally store in midtown Manhattan. I knew the local ones pretty well. I had pored over them when I started to consider moving down here. Now I used them to plan canoe trips and walks in the woods. There were three bridges in the area that would make good picnic sites. There was a bridge over the Wading River on the Chatsworth Road that we could reach by car. There were also two bridges over the Mullica that were on sand roads and could only be reached in a four-wheel drive vehicle. Constable Bridge wasn't far from where I could park, but Quaker Bridge would be almost a ten-mile round-trip, enough to give me a pleasant amount of exercise and enough, I calculated, to discourage Thelma from any further searching today. The bridges were all iron, as I recalled. That raw material was readily available just under the white sand that nurtured the fragrant pines. I pointed these locations out to Thelma. The one over the Wading was on the Jenkins quadrangle.

"Are there any more?" she asked.

"There may be some further north, but I don't know about them," I said.

"Okay, we'll go to these. Take all these maps in the car. We'll check the ones that are easiest to get to first."

I plucked out the Atsion and Jenkins quadrangles from the pile and folded them several times and stuffed them in my pants pocket. The rest I rolled up and handed to her. We decided to go to the bridge on the Chatsworth Road first. She wanted to take her new Buick, but when I told her I always took Suzie on outings in the pines, she changed her mind and let me take the Honda.

We both knew the bridge over the Wading River on the Chatsworth Road was not the place before we got out of the car. We stood at the bridge's railing watching two young men swim below us while Suzie wagged her tail and whined, wanting to join them. When the men noticed us, I asked: "How's the water?"

"Cold," said the one who had come up to stand on the sand bank. He stood dripping at the edge of the dark, swift current. The other was treading water and looking up at us. The one on the bank wore cut-off blue jeans. His legs and torso were still winter pale, and he had several large red insect bites on his legs.

At Batsto I turned up the dirt road on the far side of the lake and stopped after less than a minute at the first canoe landing. There were four cars parked there at a widened spot in the road. Beyond that the road was white sand, rutted with four-wheel drive tracks.

"End of the line," I said to Thelma.

"What do you mean?" she asked.

"I can't take the car any farther," I said. I got out and opened the back door and Suzie bounded out and began running in energetic circles in the parking area.

"You mean we're walking?" she said through her window.

"Unless you want to eat here." I opened the trunk and took out the picnic basket.

She got out reluctantly, clutching the soggy paper bag that held the bottle of white wine we had purchased.

"It's only about a mile to Constable Bridge," I said.

She reached in the car and took the photocopy of the Polaroid off the dash and slammed the door. "Isn't there a cab or something? Why didn't we come in the motorboat?" she asked, sweeping her arm in the direction of the lake.

"Real hard to get it up the dam," I said.

She looked at me curiously for a moment and then snorted a little laugh, and we started up the narrow road. Suzie ranged out ahead of us on the sun-dappled white sand, vanishing and then returning at a lope moments later as if to hurry us on to the good times ahead. As we walked I began to understand the efficacy of Thelma's plan. There were any number of iron bridges in South Jersey that none of us had ever seen that might match the vague description of the one in the photograph. But we were probably headed for the only two that were also located in piney woods and had sand roads leading up to them. Charcoal burning and iron ore mining had both thrived in the nineteenth-century Pine Barrens, and both had needed roads as well as bridges to haul their products out of the wilderness. When the market for charcoal and pig iron died, the roads and bridges remained, and when the automobile arrived, the well-traveled ones were upgraded as county and state routes and maintained, while others that were now obsolete, like the one we had chosen for our hike, were left to revert to those original sand trails, no longer traveled by wagons pulled by mule teams, but by recreational vehicles equipped with high chassis and four-wheel drive.

19

Thelma wore out even quicker than I thought she would. We weren't a hundred yards from the car when she lit her first Pall Mall. She began to complain that I was walking too fast, although I thought I was going at a snail's pace as a favor to her. By the time she was on her second cigarette, she asked me to stop and take a short break. I stood while she sat on a log and smoked, her forehead moist, the dark bags under her eyes sagging even more from her exertion. I knew Quaker Bridge would be out of the question, and I was beginning to wonder if we would even make it the mile to Constable Bridge.

In all fairness to Thelma, we walked much more than the mile that the straight dotted line on the map indicated. We had started beside the Batsto River and were angling northwest to reach the Mullica, whose waters were spanned by Constable Bridge. The double tracks of our route were constantly intersected by trails and other sand roads, running at all angles across ours. Each time there was a fork in our road, I chose the left path thinking this method of navigation would lead us eventually to the Mullica. But twice it drew us down into sandy cul-de-sacs surrounded by cedar swamp, and we had to backtrack a good half-mile to recover the road that led to our bridge. The swamp was fed by the Mullica, and the trail probably crossed it in a very dry season, but it was impassable now in the late spring. The Pine Barrens weren't so far from civilization that you couldn't eventually stumble out of them no matter how lost and panicked you were, but it was a very easy thing to wind up in trackless gloom and spend a very scary and unplanned night on the ground.

I think I was more relieved than Thelma to finally reach the little bridge. The cool morning breeze had stopped. It was almost noon and the sun bore down on us now through the still air. Thelma's breath was coming in short gasps, and I was beginning to wonder if I would have to carry her, as we rounded a bend in the trail and the open space around the bridge came into sight. The river was no more than fifteen-feet wide at this point and ran swiftly under the bridge. The water is dark brown from the iron ore and cedar roots it passes over, but it comes directly from the forest and is pristine and clear, passing through no civilizations and containing only the efflu- via of its own marine life, and of the hawks and white-tailed deer and other animals that inhabit its banks.

We sat on the bulkhead just upriver from the bridge, our feet dangling, while I rummaged through the basket and found the plastic cups. The last time I had visited this spot was in a canoe. While Thelma spread the picnic along the bulkhead, I poured cups of wine and then climbed down and put the bottle in the cold river. Suzie splashed in and tried to retrieve it, and when I called her off, ran up the bank alternately bounding in joyous circles and digging furiously in the sand just for the hell of it. Thelma spread caviar on thin English crackers, and when we had finished the contents of the jar, she lit another cigarette and asked: "Are there any box maples here?"

Both banks were lined with box elders, and I told her so. She stood up and brushed sand from her skirt and took out her photograph. A bass jumped with a heavy splash near some reeds on the other side of the bridge. I watched the ripples spread and vanish and then turned my attention to a leg of fried chicken. The dog sat beside me eyeing the chicken intently, but when I told her to get lost, she turned and trailed Thelma curiously up the bank. I was just taking my second bite out of the fat part of the leg when Thelma called to me excitedly from the top of the bank where the road turned back toward the lake.

"This is it," she shouted. "This has to be it."

She was holding her Xerox copy of the photograph at arm's length and examining a clump of young trees that we had walked past only a few minutes before. I turned to see for myself but made no effort to get up. Box elders tend to grow as a bunch of shoots, competing with each other until one full-grown maple stands alone, and these were no exception. There were five gray-barked trunks, each about three or four inches in diameter and standing about ten feet high.

"If you've seen one box elder, you've seen them all," I said. "Look at them. They're all along the river." I made gestures with my chicken leg.

"But this one matches the photograph," she said, trotting excitedly down the bank to me. "Look," she said, thrusting the paper copy at me. "Look at the broken branch on the left and those pine trees just to the right of it. They're the same."

"Those are cedars on the right," I said.

"Okay, okay," she said. "But it's the same cedars. You have to admit that."

I stood up and hid the half-eaten chicken leg in the picnic basket where Suzie couldn't get at it. I looked around for her but didn't see her. When I reached Thelma I took the photograph from her and examined it while I chewed the mouthful of chicken.

It was the right spot for sure. There were no leaves on the clump of young trees in the winter picture, but it was definitely the location. Maybe Rocky had been the photographer, and they had come up here on dirt bikes or in Julie's Pathfinder. I held the copy of the photograph, pretending to study it, staring at Julie's image, devouring the details of her face and feeling an erotic stirring that was a reminder of the weekend I had just spent with her.

"Well?" Thelma asked excitedly.

"Well what?" I countered.

"This is the place, no?"

"I guess so," I said. I handed the photograph back to her.

"You don't sound too excited," she said. I turned and she followed me back toward our picnic over the river.

"At the risk of dampening your enthusiasm," I said. "So

what?" I sat on the bulkhead again and pulled up the hinged top of the picnic basket.

"But we're right here," she said. "Where Bonnie came with the men who probably killed her."

"And I'm no closer to locating them now than I was when I got up this morning."

"But you have to admit, it was a nice piece of detective work."

"That it was," I said. "Now let's do something relevant. Like drinking the rest of this wine. Then when we get back to the cottage I can turn you loose on a really big case. I'm missing a blue and red argyle sock. I haven't seen it since I did the wash last week."

"It's a good thing I'm not sensitive," she said. She paused and then added: "Like you."

"What does that mean?" I asked.

"It means that if you had found that bridge, you'd be strutting around demanding praise like you were Sherlock Holmes or Angela Lansbury or somebody."

"You're angry," I said.

"No, I'm not," she shouted. She stood above me at the edge of the bulkhead, glaring down at me, her arms folded tightly over her chest.

"Sit down," I said, patting the tablecloth opposite the picnic basket from me. "Eat some chicken. Have some more wine. Relax."

Reluctantly she lowered herself to the bulkhead, dangling her legs over the river. It was remarkable how short her legs were. I thought about commenting on the fact, but wisely decided not to. Instead, I poured her another cup of wine. When she had taken a long, slow sip, she said: "That second picture was taken right here. Right along this bulkhead."

"How do you know that? There is no logical way for you to know that." Now it was my turn to be irritable. "We've never seen that picture. It could have been taken in Utah or Outer Mongolia."

"You told me that the guy who saw it . . . I forget who it was—"

"One of Grace Somers's pit bosses."

". . . that the guy who saw it pretty much described Raymond Stockton and Rocky with Bonnie."

"Well, the mind plays funny tricks. Maybe that's what I heard because that's what I wanted to hear. Maybe it was Robert Redford and Manuel Noriega and Madonna."

"The guy said that the woman specifically said she was looking for Bonnie Arnold."

"Okay, your logic dictates that it wasn't Madonna."

"She must have taken it."

"Who? The woman who showed it to Grace's boss?"

"No, your friend Julie. She's in this one and Rocky isn't. He must have handed her the camera when they got down here to the river, and she took the one with this bridge in the background."

"How do you know it's this bridge? Or that the guy in the picture was even Rocky?"

"Will you please stop it with the devil's advocate bit? You're wearing it out."

"You may not be sensitive today, but you sure are touchy. Let me see that photograph."

I took the Xerox copy from her and unfolded it. It was getting worn from her pocket. I looked at it and then turned and looked at the clump of box elders where it had been taken only a few months before, and I tried to remember what Grace's pit boss had told me about the picture he had been shown.

"It was a Polaroid, right?" Thelma asked.

"The other photograph?"

"Of course, the other photograph."

"I can't remember. I don't even know if he told me that. Or if I thought to ask him."

"Could they have come up here more than once? I mean, and taken another set of pictures? On another day, with another camera? And if they came up here a lot, why would this be such a favorite spot?"

"Okay," I said. "I'll take your little leap of faith. Suppose it was the same day and the other picture was the next one in sequence? Where does that leave us? They came, maybe they ate like we're doing, and they left."

"I agree with you," she said.

"You do?" I feigned astonishment.

"Yes, I do," she said. "So that leaves us with the next logical question. Who was the woman?"

"You just lost me on that one. What woman?"

"The woman who had, or has, the photograph; who showed it to Grace's boss. Who is she?"

"I haven't the foggiest."

"Well, you should find out. Do you know what she looked like?"

"I think he said she was in her forties. Nice build."

"Your kind of detail."

"Some things I remember better than others. She wore glasses too, I think. I have it in my notes at home."

I heard Suzie bark at some distance on the other side of the bridge and upriver. She was deep in the pines and I couldn't see where she was but I was glad to locate her. When her barking continued, I began to worry that she had cornered some animal and might get hurt.

According to the *Atlantic City Press*, rabid raccoons had begun to turn up in the county, and I couldn't remember when Suzie had last been vaccinated.

Thelma started to say something else, but I held my hand up to stop her and warn her that I was going to call to the dog, but when Suzie heard my shouts, the pace of her barking only quickened. I stood up, brushing sand from my pants, and walked across the bridge toward the sound. There was very little undergrowth in the area once you got away from the river. Pitch pines and juniper were mostly what took hold in the dry white sand. Three million years ago, before the Ice Age froze the polar caps, this entire forest had been ocean bottom. Now it held the same sand as the famous beaches of the Jersey Shore. When Suzie began to hear my footsteps, her barking increased in pitch. I couldn't see what she was barking at when I first came on her—all I saw was a lumpy patch of sand that looked like it had been disturbed by digging animals. I was leery of spooking some cornered animal, and when I approached the lumpy area, Suzie bolted away from it and spooked me. At that point I supposed the lumps to be some sort of carrion, but when Suzie came charging back, barking even more feverishly, I realized that I was looking at a sand-covered hand. And somewhere a couple of feet above it, the familiar shape of a human head.

20

I never did get accustomed to seeing corpses. Some people do, like Dr. Shapiro, the A.M.E. who had autopsied Bonnie at Kings County. I spent the second half of my police career as a homicide detective so I became inured to them most of the time, but I hadn't seen one in the flesh in a couple of years, and this one caused my stomach to do that familiar flip-flop and made sweat break out on my forehead. I pulled Suzie away from it by her collar. I had some vague fear that she might dig around the face and scratch the flesh, and I didn't want to see what kind of corruption might appear if she broke the skin.

The body was in a shallow grave, hastily buried. There were an abundance of narrow clawed tracks around the face, left by the raccoons that had dug down and exposed it. He couldn't have been there very long because he hadn't yet begun to rot, although sand clung to the bloated soft flesh of the face as I wiped it with my handkerchief. Even with sand in the dry open eyes, I recognized him.

"Meet Rocky Starza," I said, dropping the sandy handkerchief and turning to Thelma, who had come up behind me and stood frozen, her hands covering her mouth. Flies began to settle on his eyes as soon as I stood up. Unconsciously, I backed away from him several steps and tripped over a protruding pine root. When I lurched to catch my balance, Suzie squealed and darted away from the body. She had been sniffing the site in a timid crouch, and now she ran to a safe distance and began to bark. When I shouted at her to be quiet, she slunk toward it again, her nose twitching, trying to pick up some sense of what we had found, and keeping her weight shifted toward her rear end, ready to retreat again if that sense told her she was in danger.

I tried to remember when I had last seen Rocky. It seemed like it was in the very remote past. Was it Wednesday? He had wanted to shoot me, and he had beaten and kicked me and then tried to drown me. Every time I moved I still felt pain from the beating he had given me. I wanted revenge for that pain, and I was surprised at the regret I felt at finding him dead. I owed him a beating that I would now never be able to give him.

There wasn't any damage to his face or head that I could see that might indicate how he had died. The sand that covered the middle part of his body was a darker color. The raccoons had been digging there too. I got a piece of a pine limb and scratched in the area around his chest and stomach. He was wearing the leather vest he had on the night he had come to the cottage with Hell Knuckles. It didn't take much scratching to determine that the stain was blood, a lot of it, moist and clotted, mixed with the sand.

A surprising wave of pity swept over me. He looked so lonely and far away. Who would tell Loretta? Tell her that her strutting little drug addict, the father of her unborn baby, was moldering into the Pine Barrens sand. He seemed so out of place among the whites and greens of this stark, sunny wilderness. A city kid lost in the woods. For centuries his ancestors had jammed themselves on top of each other in the fetid apartments of Napoli or Palermo. He was at home on the dangerous streets of New York, but put him in a weedy lot and he was lost and terrified. And now he was lifeless and fly-blown in a shallow grave. I thought about just walking away and letting him rot. He was far off any path, and the raccoons and the summer rains would soon make him an integral part of the landscape.

I crouched again and spread the handkerchief over his face as best I could without touching the pallid flesh or the sand-clogged eyes. Silently Thelma handed me rocks, and silently I took them and placed them on the corners of the white cloth.

Standing, I took Suzie by the collar and led her back toward the bridge. When we had crossed to our picnic site, Thelma asked: "Are we going to leave him there?"

She began to pack up the basket with quick nervous movements. "What if they come back?" she added.

"Who?" I countered, my mind elsewhere. I wanted to go back to the site without the dog or Thelma. I couldn't figure out how they got him there. The pines were too thick in there for any sort of vehicle.

"Whoever killed him," she answered. "Do you have a gun?"

"Yes," I said.

"Do you want any more chicken?" she asked, slamming the top of the packed basket before I could reply. "You could smell him," she said.

"I know," I said.

"Let's go." She jerked the basket off the bulkhead and swept up the picnic cloth in a ball and turned away from the river.

"We can't both leave," I said. "Calm down."

"I'll go then. I'll bring the police. If the killers come back, you have your gun."

"Nobody's coming back here," I said. "Put the basket down."

She stopped and half-turned, staring at me like she hadn't heard me.

"It's okay," I said. "Whoever killed him hid him here. They think that's the end of it. They won't be back. Put the basket down, please. It's okay."

Reluctantly she put the basket in the sand at her feet but still clutched the red-and-white checked cloth.

"Let's finish the wine and try to figure out what to do," I said. "Get the glasses out." I took the table cloth from her and looped it under Suzie's collar and knotted it and then tied the other end to one of the supports on the bridge approach. Then I walked down to the river and retrieved the wine bottle. While I was down there my beeper went off, its irritating insistence shattering the stillness of the woods. When I looked down at my belt and saw an Atlantic City exchange on the

LED, it took me a moment to realize it was Julie's number in Ventnor. Then, a pleasant erotic feeling surged through me. I deactivated the beeper so it wouldn't go off again.

There was only a swallow left for each of us but the routine of pouring and drinking it took the momentum out of Thelma's panic and stopped her flight.

"To Rocky Starza," I said, holding my cup aloft. "About to be a father, no longer a drug addict; he tried to kill me twice. I'll miss him like a boil."

Thelma tried to smile. Her mouth turned up but her eyes still darted about in fright. When she finished the little bit of wine and lowered her cup, I noticed that she kept her eyes aloft. I followed her gaze and saw two turkey buzzards gliding in wide circles on the thermal drafts above us.

"They smell it too," I said.

"Will they hurt us?"

"Only if we're dead."

"Can you shoot them?" She looked at me in alarm.

"There'll be plenty more. I don't have enough bullets. And besides, they keep the woods clean."

She leaned down and put her cup in the picnic basket, and said: "Okay, let's go."

"I'm going back," I said.

"Where?"

"To the body."

"Why?"

"Because it's fresh. And I want to get it all in my mind. It'll be different when we come back. And then the police will be tramping all over the place. They might not even let us into the scene again. I don't have any juice with the cops down here like I do in New York. I might even be a suspect."

"Why would you be a suspect?"

"Because they know I'm looking for him. If they don't have anybody else to connect with him, I fill the void."

I took her cup out of the basket and carried both of them down to the water and rinsed them out.

"I see what you mean," she said. "Even though we know it was Ray Stockton."

"You're probably right," I said. "But don't forget that other biker with the tattoos on his knuckles."

"They did it together, obviously. How else would they be able to carry him up there?"

"I think he walked," I said. I put the cups back in the basket and turned toward the bridge. Thelma started after me.

"I want to look at it by myself," I said.

"That's fine by me," she said, keeping pace beside me. "But there's no way I'm going to sit here alone in the open with killers on the loose in the woods and those things up there ready to swoop down on me." There were three vultures now. Occasionally one would tilt from its flat glide to observe the scene below.

"Let's go then," I said. "But you do what I tell you when we get there, and no tramping around the body."

"I can promise you I don't want to go anywhere near it," she said with a look of distaste.

Suzie whined when we started across the bridge, but I shouted at her to be quiet.

"It's so obvious that Stockton took the money and ran," Thelma said as we turned off the road. "Rocky threatened his whole operation, so Rocky had to go. It's always money, always."

"What operation? There's no operation, just a lot of people who want to hurt Rocky and Stockton. Maybe one of them caught up with Rocky."

"What about the piney-Philly-biker drug operation?"

"You be quiet too," I said.

"You treat me like a dog," she said.

She fell behind as we walked and then, near the grave site, she stopped entirely and let me go on ahead.

There wasn't much more to see. There hadn't been any rain in almost a week, and the sand was too dry to hold any good tracks, even in the heavy shade beneath the pines. The one moist spot was around Rocky's middle, and only raccoons had left their markings there. I had scraped away enough sand so that you could see the shape of the top half of him. With the white handkerchief over his face, he looked like a B-movie mummy about to sit up from a two-millennium slumber. If there was anything else to be learned there, it had been brushed away. And not by me. Wide swirling designs led out to the road and in the opposite direction beyond the grave. I followed this swept trail into the woods and found a long-handled spade about thirty feet from the site. If I had to guess, I would have said that Rocky dug his own grave or at least helped Doc do it. But why had he walked in here? Was he driven at gunpoint or did he come voluntarily? I dug a little more around his midsection, enough to assure myself that his life had bled out into the white sand. He had certainly been alive when he got there. Maybe he wasn't conscious, but his heart had pumped a lot of blood before it quit. From what I had heard of Doc, he was certainly strong enough to carry Rocky the hundred yards or so from the road if he was unable to walk. Or Hell Knuckles could have helped him with that chore, although nobody but Rocky himself could have put that rusty brown stain into the sand. And if there were two of them and a spade, why was the grave so shallow? Were they in a hurry? Had someone come along and seen them?

I left the spade, and when I got back to the grave site, Thelma was standing near the corpse.

"I thought you didn't want to get near him?" I asked.

"I'm still afraid they'll come back," she said. "I know they won't, but I was working my way over to be near you. I just can't get past him." She nodded toward the grave.

"He won't hurt you," I said.

"I can smell him," she said. She looked up through the pine boughs in the direction of the soaring vultures and added: "Let's get out of here."

"I don't want to miss anything," I said. I turned back toward Rocky, and she mumbled something I couldn't hear.

"What did you say?" I asked without looking at her.

"I can't move," she said.

"Move where?" I was trying to decide if I should lift the handkerchief and have another look at his face.

"Away."

Something about the way she said it made me turn. In my concentration I hadn't paid any attention to her, and now I realized she was frozen with fear. I was tempted to just pick her up and carry her out. She couldn't have weighed a hundred pounds. But I didn't want to leave any one-way trails to confuse the local cops when they arrived.

"Can't you just walk away?" I asked.

"No, I can't. I just can't." Her eyes were fixed on the body now, watching it as if it might move.

"Well, your mouth doesn't seem to be paralyzed," I said.

"Now is not the time for levity," she said through tense, half-closed lips.

I did pick her up finally, but just by the arms. Then I rotated her so that she was facing in the direction of the road and put her down and took her by the hand and gently urged her forward until she was walking on her own. She glanced back four or five times before we got to the road and also looked up more than once to check the location of the buzzards.

The pine bough that had served Doc as a broom sat near the road when we got out into the sunshine. Thelma lit a Pall Mall, and when she had blown a long relieved cloud of smoke out into the clear piney air, she said: "I guess this is the part of detective work that I don't like."

"You have to take the good with the bad," I said.

There were no discernible tire tracks on the sand road, only the two ruts that were the road. The only foot tracks that I could see were the ones Thelma and I had made, so I had to assume they drove in.

"I like the deduction part. That's sort of like doing the *Times* crossword puzzle," Thelma said as we walked back toward the bridge.

"Hell, anybody can do that part," I said, smiling. "That's why millions of people read crime novels. The hard part is shooting people and getting knocked over the head and digging up rotting corpses. That's the part very few have the stomach for."

"If millions of people can do the deduction part, how come you couldn't?" she shot back. "You wouldn't even have come out here if I didn't insist. And look at what we found. You've been looking for this Rocky for weeks between here and New York, and I found him for you practically in your own backyard."

"You know something, Thelma? I should have left you back there with that corpse reaching up for your ankle."

"What do you mean?" The fear came back into her eyes for a moment and she glanced down at her legs. We had reached our picnic site.

"Two minutes ago you were so scared you were ready to pee your pants. Then you get back to safety and you start rubbing it in about my detective skills again." I reached down and untied the tablecloth from the bridge and from Suzie's collar. Suzie, happy to be free, bounded up and down the riverbank in tight running circles.

"I'm going back," I said.

"Back where?"

"Where do you think?" I balled up the tablecloth and turned away from her. "I'm going to cover him with this, so the buzzards and 'coons stay off until we can get the police back here."

"I'm coming with you."

"Stay with the dog. I'll be right back."

"Yes, Master," she said. "Arf, arf," she added when I turned away from her.

Her clowning was strictly bravado. She and Suzie trailed me up the road when I turned into the woods again. "We'll wait by the road," she said. "I don't want the tablecloth back either."

"I'll buy you a new one."

I'd had a nagging feeling I'd missed something when we walked out, but this time the scene seemed complete. I spread the red-and-white checked cloth over him and found some rocks to hold it down. I had to scrounge for the rocks, which were scarce in the sandy landscape. Suzie came about halfway into the woods and then pranced out beside me to where Thelma was waiting at the road. Thelma looked relieved to see me, but kept eyeing the circling buzzards.

"I thought they only had those birds in cowboy movies," she said.

I ignored her. When we reached the river, I scooped up the picnic basket, and we started down the road toward the ranger

station at Batsto, where there was a telephone. I could feel an
anger rising in my gorge. I kept getting close to Doc Stockton,
and then he would elude me. I hadn't been able to find Rocky
until he was of no further use to anyone, and now for all I
knew, Stockton was on his way to Florida or Mexico. I was
sleeping with his daughter, and I wasn't sure that was a very
good idea either. I knew too much about his drug operation
too, although he was out of business here whether I stayed on
his trail or not. His credit and his credibility were shot all to
hell with the Philly mob and with the law. Rocky knew too
much and had probably been eliminated because I was closing
in on him. Julie was my link to Stockton now, a fact that he
would be all too aware of if he found out about us. But why
would he stick around? He could lose me easily by simply
leaving town. I had no way of finding him and no reason to
look for him except to revenge Bonnie's death, and I wasn't
going to chase him all over the continent even if I had the
resources to do it.

"Slow down," Thelma said.

She had fallen behind and now had stopped to lean against
a tree. I was about thirty yards ahead of her and had not seen
her stop.

"You're not going to smoke a cigarette, are you?" I asked.

"I can't," she wheezed. "I'm too winded."

The route out was not as confusing. Each time there was a
choice of paths, I took the left one, and now through the pines
I could see the water and lily pads of Batsto Lake.

"I'm going on ahead," I said.

"You can't leave me here," she whined.

"I'm not leaving you. I'll drive to the pay phone at park
headquarters and make the call and then come right back and
walk out with you. If you keep moving and keep the lake on
your right, we can't miss each other. I'll be back in five minutes."

"What lake?"

I pointed toward the shining open space beyond the pines.
There were already several holiday canoers on the water.

"What if Stockton comes back?" she asked.

"Subdue him and hold him until the police arrive."

"Very funny. What about the buzzards?" She looked up. "Where did they go?" she asked.

"They stayed with Rocky," I said. "Hold the dog."

Reluctantly she took Suzie by the collar. I turned and began to jog before she could change her mind. The sand was loose and hard to run in, but I was in the parking lot at Ranger headquarters at Batsto in less than ten minutes, hardly enough time to work up a sweat.

I called the township police from a pay phone in the parking lot behind the information center. I knew the state boys would come and pick and poke at everything and then the murder investigation would settle with the county, but Columbia Township was where I lived, and I didn't want any resentments from the police force in my own backyard, so I called them first. I asked for Sergeant McKelvey, but he was off-duty for the holiday. The dispatcher was a woman who acted like bodies turned up in the woods in Columbia Township every day. I hung up and started walking out the park entrance road. I got all the way past the gatehouse before I saw the white township Chevy Caprice turn off 542 into the park. I flagged it down as it approached.

The driver was very young. Without the navy blue uniform, I would have guessed sixteen or seventeen, although he was probably in his early twenties. He couldn't have been shaving yet. His eyes regarded me skeptically from under his peaked cap. No hair showed under the cap except a short blond shadow that I assumed was the lower part of a tight crewcut.

"You the guy that called?" he asked. When I owned that I was, he said: "You found a body in the woods." I nodded and he said "Get in."

"It's up past the lake," I said. "It's all soft sand up there. Maybe we ought to get one of the rangers to take us up in a four-wheel drive."

"Naw, that's okay," he said. "Get in."

I slid in beside him thinking maybe he was a little too young and shy for law enforcement, until he stepped on the gas. He didn't drive like a twelve-year-old at all. He cocked the wheel and fired us around in a reverse spin that shot me forward in the seat before I had even shut the door tightly. With the bubble lights flashing and the siren shrieking, we shot out onto 542 and then up the hard gravel road beside the lake. He didn't slow down when we hit the soft sand above the canoe landing but sped right on ahead, all bounce and roll, firing it over the washboard ripples and through the sand ruts. I realized that he had grown up putting old cars and dirt bikes through their paces on these sand roads. He'd bog now and then when he had to slow down on a turn, but he was always able to plow out of it. Twice he swerved up out of the ruts and crashed through laurel bushes and oak brush to avoid soft spots. Most of this driving he did with one hand, holding his microphone in the other to keep the dispatcher informed of his location.

Thelma must have heard us coming because she was well off the road trying unsuccessfully to hide behind a large pitch pine but, at the same time, curious to see who was coming. She hadn't walked more than a hundred yards from the spot where I'd left her. I pointed to her, and we shot up out of our sand ruts and over the bank and came to a scraping halt in a patch of juniper. I wondered if there was anything left of the Chevy's oil pan.

Our patrolman's name tag said Richards. "Get in," he told Thelma as she hurried up to the car.

Suzie bounded into the back seat with her and we banged back down into the narrow ruts again. I directed him through a series of forks and switchbacks, each of which he reported on his microphone, and as Constable Bridge came into sight, a white Jeep with the township star on it closed the gap behind us and trailed us up the rise of the opposite bank. I spotted the brushed trail easily and both vehicles banged off the road on opposite banks and stopped. We all got out with a lot of door slamming. The guy driving the jeep was Sergeant Jim McKelvey in an off-duty outfit of ragged jeans cut off at midthigh, a green T-shirt and leather boaters. Richards tossed him a quick salute and waited for him while he took a pair of construction boots from the back of the jeep and laced them on, sockless, in place of the boaters.

"Hello, Leeds," he said, crossing the road.

"Hello, Sergeant."

"You the one that found the body?"

"My dog dug it up. I asked for you when I called it in. How'd you get here so fast?"

"I had my police scanner on in my kitchen. Anybody you know?"

"The guy I told you about."

"The one you were looking for? How did you know he was here?"

"I didn't."

His eyes met mine and held them too long. I fought not to break the contact until he turned and bent to examine the swirling trails of brush marks.

"Is this the way we're going?" he asked.

I nodded, and he swept his arm in the direction of the woods, indicating that I should lead the way.

21

When the forensic people started to show up, Sergeant McKelvey told Patrolman Richards to ride us to our car. I asked if I could stay to see Rocky when they got him totally out of the sand, and McKelvey shrugged his consent. Thelma didn't stick around for the viewing. She took the dog with her and walked out and sat in the open back of the Jeep. That's where Richards and I found her. She didn't look so hot. Her face was pale, and I counted four flattened Pall Mall butts around the Jeep. There were a half-dozen men in there at the grave site at that point, taking pictures and sifting through the sand. I had showed them where the spade was. It had prints on it but they were probably all Rocky's. Someone had strung yellow plastic police tape from tree to tree to mark the spot along the sand road.

It looked to me like Rocky had been shot three times, once in the back directly on the spinal column and twice near enough to his heart to cause the massive bleeding that had soaked the sand. They also found a snub-nosed .38 beside him in his grave, fully loaded but unfired, probably the same gun he had held to Grace Somers's temple the week before at my cottage.

Patrolman Richards's driving was much more subdued on the way out. I was tempted to comment on it, but neither he nor Thelma said a word, and I didn't want to break the silence. Thelma continued the mood on our drive to the cottage. I wanted to talk about Rocky and what we had found, but Thelma would only mumble one-word answers to my rambling analysis. When I had left the grave site, Sergeant Mc-Kelvey told me to take Thelma to the cottage and wait for him. Thelma didn't like that at all when I told her.

"I want to go home," she said. "This sort of thing doesn't happen in Longport or Margate."

"You'd be surprised," I said. "Remember the football player who strangled the girl on the beach a couple of summers ago?"

"That was an exception."

"You think these woods are filled with bodies?"

"What does he want to talk to me about?" She ignored my sarcasm.

"He wants to talk to both of us."

"I can understand that he wants to talks to you. But why me? What am I, a suspect?"

"You found the body," I said.

"The dog found it."

"You knew where to take the dog."

"Dumb luck."

I figured McKelvey would focus his questions on her, but I didn't tell her that. I would have done the same thing if it was my investigation. His reasoning would be that I was the professional, so she would be more likely to make a mistake. If we had anything to hide, of course. And if Thelma made mistakes, which she didn't.

When McKelvey arrived, we sat at the kitchen table and he began by asking me a few background questions about Rocky. At first I thought he might be operating under the cop philosophy that the world was a better place without Rocky in it, no matter who did him in. I told him what I knew about the police investigation of Bonnie's death in New York and gave him Conlin's name and precinct. I could tell he didn't believe we had simply stumbled on the body. When he began to zero in on Thelma, she came out of her funk and recanted her dumb luck statement to me, giving a detailed and enthusiastic explanation about the deductive logic that had led her to the location. Her shrill enthusiasm told me she was laboring in the guilt that many witnesses to a crime feel when they think they have become a suspect. McKelvey didn't appreciate her theories much either.

"Tell me again how you knew you'd find Rocky buried near the bridge?" He directed the question to her, and I was glad he did, because I didn't have an answer for it.

"I didn't say that," she countered.

"Didn't say what?"

"That I thought we'd find Rocky."

"What were you doing out there in the woods then?"

"Having a picnic and running down leads."

He glanced at me curiously. "What kind of leads?"

"We have a picture that was taken near the bridge," Thelma said. She pulled the photocopy of the Polaroid from her skirt pocket and slid it across the table to him. "That's the murdered girl," she said, pointing to Bonnie.

"I thought it was a drug overdose," he said, turning to me again.

"It was," I said. "But we have reason to believe she was with Rocky when she died."

"Who are these other people?"

She identified Doc Stockton and Julie. I didn't like the idea of the police dragging Julie into the investigation, but I needed all the help I could get flushing Stockton out, especially if he was in Florida or out of the country.

McKelvey studied the picture again. Finally he asked: "Where's Rocky?"

"He's in another picture."

"Can I see that one?"

"We don't have it."

"Where is it?"

"We don't know."

He stared at her in silence for a moment. "There's no bridge in this picture either," he said.

"I know," she said. "The bridge is in the other picture too, with Rocky and Bonnie and Doc."

"What other picture?"

"The one I just told you about. The one we've never seen."

"If you've never seen it, how did you know what bridge to go to?"

"The box bushes are the same."

He lifted his head and rolled his eyes up briefly. I could tell she had lost him. I wasn't sure if she had done it intentionally or not, but it was effective either way. And she certainly wasn't lost at all.

"Box elders," I explained.

"You went out there to look for box elders?" he asked, astonished. "They're all over the place."

"Not true," Thelma said triumphantly. "They are only near water. Like bridges."

"Oh," McKelvey said. He had given up. He looked briefly out the window at the river and drummed his fingers on the table and then folded the picture and put it in his shirt pocket.

"Someone stole the original of that from my office," I said. "I'll need a copy."

"I'll make one and leave it in the township office for you," he said, standing. "Do me a favor, Leeds. Stay out of this."

I shrugged.

"Don't push it," he said. He smiled nervously at Thelma and then glared at me. "Let us do our work. I know you feel bad about the girl's death. But you've got to stop poking around. You were a cop. You know how it screws things up."

"You have a funny way of saying thank you," I said.

"Who's your client? Her family?"

"Confidential," I answered.

"I'll let that go for now too. But if I need to know and you won't tell me the next time I ask you, I'll lock you up."

"When you need to know, I'll tell you," I said. I was only half lying to him. I didn't have a client anymore, but I intended to report finding Rocky's body to Benjamin Arnold in hopes of finally convincing him that Bonnie had been murdered.

At the door, he turned and asked: "Can you tie Rocky to Bonnie?"

"Not without Stockton," I said.

"Sounds like we're both looking for the same guy," he said.

There were four messages from Julie on my machine but I didn't call her until after Thelma left. It was after five when I put in the call, but Julie didn't answer. I didn't leave a message on her machine. I opened a small jar of marinara sauce and boiled angel hair pasta for supper and ate it with half a loaf of Italian bread and a glass of red wine. After I ate I called Julie again. I was going to leave a message, but at the last minute I hung up on her machine again. There wasn't any baseball on the radio because it was a holiday and all the games had been played that afternoon. I read for a couple of hours, tried Julie again, drank a bottle of beer and then went to sleep.

It was a little after one A.M. when the phone rang. I was sleeping soundly but I awoke with ease, surprised to hear Julie on the line. She seemed just as surprised to hear me.

"I'm so sorry to wake you, Con."

"What's up? Is everything all right?"

"I just got in. I didn't think you'd be there. I was going to leave a message."

"Why didn't you think I'd be here?"

"I thought you told me something about going to New York."

"I don't remember telling you that, but I probably will go."

"I tried to get you all day, and you never returned my call."

"I tried you a couple of times this evening. I felt funny about leaving a message."

"Why?"

"I'm not sure. I think it's because I don't know much about you. I didn't know who else would hear it."

"There's never anybody here but me. Unless you're here."

"I had no way of knowing that. Where were you?"

"Out. I met a friend for dinner in Philadelphia."

"Who's the friend?"

"That's none of your business. Someone I know from school."

"A man?"

"Yes."

"It's after one o'clock. Did you have a date?"

"No, not a date date. He's a friend, a dancer. We got to talking."

"Oh." I was surprised at my reaction, at the dry jealousy swollen in the back of my throat.

"What did you want to say that you didn't want anyone else to hear?" she asked.

"I don't know."

"You can't remember?"

"Yes, I can remember."

"What was it?"

"Well . . . I enjoyed being with you."

"Where? We didn't go anywhere except dinner. Do you mean you enjoyed being in bed with me? Having sex?"

"Yes."

"Do you mean you liked fucking me?"

"Yes."

"Which time?"

"I don't know." I was growing dizzy with lust. I had an erection that felt like the Empire State Building.

"When I sucked you off on the balcony?"

"Yes. Stop it. Why are you talking like this?"

"Why are you shouting? Talking like what?"

"I don't know. So . . . so graphically."

"That's what we did."

"You're angry. Why?"

"I'm not angry." Her voice rose in pitch.

"Yes, you are."

"Where have you been? I called you all day. I even beeped you."

"You are angry."

"Okay, I'm angry, I'm angry, I'm angry," she screamed. "Why didn't you fucking call me?"

It was rage I was hearing, not anger. It surprised me. I told her about Rocky then, and that quieted her. She listened silently, prompting me now and then with a question about detail, particularly when I described the corpse.

"I've never seen a dead person before," she said. "Except in a funeral home. How did you know where to look for him?"

I told her about Thelma and about matching the location to the pictures. "She got lucky," I said.

"Who's Thelma?" she asked.

"My landlady."

"Do you sleep with her?" she asked.

"She's in her sixties."

"So? Is she pretty?"

"No. And she smokes constantly."

"That can be a turn-off. Is Rocky the one who murdered Bonnie?"

"I think so. Your father is involved. He was in the picture too."

She was silent for a minute. I didn't say anything either just to let it sink in.

"Do you think Raymond killed this guy?"

"Yes. You were in the picture too."

More silence. This time I spoke first.

"Do you remember the trip?"

"I don't know. Was it in the winter?"

"Yes. Or maybe early spring. The maples were bare."

"I remember now," she said. "Bonnie and I wanted to go canoeing. Raymond gave us a ride in. And that guy was with him. So, that's the guy Bonnie was seeing. Mr. Secret. He was a little creep. I remember him real well now. He tried to hit on me whenever Raymond and Bonnie couldn't hear him. I couldn't wait for them to leave."

"Did they pick you up too?"

"No. We left our car at the Cedar Bank Marina and canoed down to their dock. And to think that was the guy that Bonnie was sleeping with. I never put that together. He didn't seem interested in her at all that day."

"Was that the day he first met her maybe?"

"Yes, now that you mention it, it probably was. I'd love to see the picture. I can hardly remember what he looked like. It's funny to think of someone you've met as being dead. Why don't you bring it over?"

"What?"

"The picture."

"He's not in it, Rocky."

"Why not?"

"I think he was taking the picture."

"Oh?"

"When should I come over?"

"Now?"

"It would be after two by the time I got to the shore."

"I don't have to leave for work until eight-thirty."

"I don't have the picture," I said. "The cops took it."

She paused and then said: "Do you think they'll contact me because I'm in it?"

"I don't know. Maybe."

"How exciting. Why don't you come over anyway."

"Even without the picture?"

"I don't care about the picture. I want to be in bed with you. I want you inside me. I want you to fuck me. I want to feel your body thrashing when you come. I want you to fuck me and fuck me and fuck me until I scream."

I didn't say anything. I couldn't; my mouth was too dry.

"Well?" she said finally.

"Well what?" I managed to answer.

"Are you coming?"

"Over there?"

"Yes." Her voice was husky. "I'm so turned on just thinking about you. About your body. Your scars."

"I could come tomorrow. We could have dinner when you get home from work."

"Now, goddammit." Her voice was suddenly insistent and angry.

"It's been a long day. I'm so tired that—"

"Now. I need to be with you, Con." Her tone softened. "I need to touch you. To have you inside me."

I paused and then said: "Okay."

I was exhausted, but I found myself saying I would be there within an hour. Certainly lust was driving me. But there was something else. I think I didn't want Julie to be angry. Her anger came so suddenly that I agreed to get up and get dressed and drive for forty-five minutes in the middle of the night just to avoid it.

She greeted me at her door still dressed in the outfit she must have worn to dinner in Philadelphia, a beige skirt and a dark green cashmere V-neck over a white button-down blouse. She wore stockings and sensible brown heels. The clothes were expensive and tasteful and made her look like a tall, elegant doctoral candidate.

Our first kiss was like a train collision. When we finally broke apart she didn't say anything, just pulled the door shut behind me and stepped into the middle of the living room and began to undress. Very slowly. She was wearing some very special things under those conservative clothes. A black half-bra pushed up the bottom of her full breasts. The exposed nipples stuck straight out and had been reddened with rouge or lipstick. The stockings came to the middle of her thighs and were held up by a black lace garter belt. She wore no panties.

When her outer clothes lay in a pile at her feet, she took me by the hand and led me into the bedroom, and without turning out the bedside light, pushed me gently down on the bed and undressed me and made love to me gently and slowly at first and then working herself into a fury of passion, moaning and pulling off me momentarily to shout vulgar and erotic phrases, while I writhed and tried to hold on and then exploded into her, and then slowing and holding me warm and limp inside her.

After a while, I tried to lift my head off the pillow, but it seemed like too much of an effort. She slid up beside me and I held her loosely in the crook of my arm. I tried for a moment to unhook her push-up bra but I didn't have enough strength to make a fist to grip the catch.

I fell asleep like that and when I awoke, she was gone from the bed, but the light was still on. My watch said it was only a quarter after three, but I felt refreshed, like I had slept more than the forty-five minutes or so that I had been out. I wondered what had wakened me, but then I saw her standing on a chair, looking for something on the top shelf of her closet. She was wearing a white silk ankle-length robe, and when she stepped down from the chair and turned toward me, the robe swung open and I saw that she had taken off the black lingerie and was naked underneath the silk. The rouge was gone from her nipples, probably worn away from sliding her body around over mine. As she came toward the bed, she saw that I was awake and watching her, and she modestly pulled the robe together with one hand. In her free hand she held what looked like several bank account passbooks.

I pushed myself up against the headboard and propped a pillow behind my back. I was naked except for my socks and the .25 in the ankle holster, but I've never been the modest type. She dropped the small books to the floor and sat on the edge of the bed and let the robe fall open again revealing the breasts and the rippling muscles of her dancer's stomach. I reached out and stroked the hard stomach, and she pulled the robe open more and leaned toward me so that our naked chests pressed against each other. She kissed me and then slid up into bed beside me.

"Oh, Con," she said, her eyes watching my face as her head snuggled into my chest. "It's so good. I love to be with you."

"I enjoy your company too," I said.

"I love you so much, Con," she said.

I've never known how to respond to that statement. With Mary Ellen I simply used to repeat it. I love you too. And when I said it with Mary Ellen, I meant it. Now I didn't say anything.

She waited for a response and when she realized she wasn't going to get one, said: "It's too soon for you, isn't it?"

I nodded.

"I can live with that," she said and sat up and swung her legs to the floor and pulled the robe together again. She bent over and picked up the little books she had taken from the closet. They were indeed bank account passbooks.

"I thought you might be interested in these," she said. "I found them at the house last week."

There were three books from two different banks, all of them for accounts of Raymond Stockton. All of them had been closed on April 30, including one, a CD that had been penalized for early withdrawal. He had withdrawn a total of forty-two thousand dollars on that day.

"These were in a house?" I asked. "What house?"

"Raymond's house in Linwood."

"He still lives there?" As Thelma would say, sometimes the obvious eludes me. "Is he still there?"

"Of course not. He's probably in Mexico or Florida."

"When were you there?"

"Yesterday."

"Was there any sign that your father has been there?"

"Not that I could tell."

"I want to go there. Can you get me in?"

"Now?"

"No, tomorrow."

"I have to go to work. And then I have a dance group at five in Moorestown. I won't be home until after seven."

"Give me the key."

"Oh, I don't know about that."

"I'll go tomorrow morning."

"But what if Raymond shows up while you're there?"

"Let me worry about that. I hope he does."

"He can be very violent."

"So can I."

I took my socks and holster off then and we made love again, this time at a more leisurely and relaxed pace. She murmured that she loved me again at the end of it, but I couldn't respond. I didn't think we had found out much about being with each other, except in the area of being very good physically with each other. I certainly was in lust. And maybe I could find a way to love her, but that is a very complicated emotion, love. I'm not even sure if it is an emotion. It's more like a situation. Anyway, I was pretty sure I was not in it, at least not then. In fact, talk of it made me want to run away, to put my clothes on and bolt. But her taut athletic body kept me there. For all that lusty telephone prelude, we only made love one and a half times, and very conventionally at that. Instead of staying up ravaging each other all night, we slept soundly in each other's arms and woke to the sound of her alarm at seven-thirty.

I made a grab at her night-warm nakedness as she shut off the alarm, but she was up and flying. She pushed my hands away and promised to come back and make love after she had taken a shower. But I fell asleep again, and the next time I awoke, she was at the door of the bedroom, fully dressed, saying: "There's a half a pot of coffee in the kitchen and some

English muffins. I left the butter out.' The key to the house in Linwood and the address are on the dresser. Be careful. I love you. See you tonight."

I had lost the mood to make love anyway. I waved half-heartedly and rolled over, thinking I would sleep some more, but the silence of the strange surroundings and the smell of the coffee from the kitchen wouldn't let me. I got up and took a shower and didn't even notice that it was raining until I was sitting on the bed tying my shoes.

There was a note in a small envelope on the kitchen table. The envelope said *Cornelius* on it in fancy calligraphy. She had also drawn a heart with an arrow shot through it. The note itself was a profession of love as childish as a high school crush. There were also descriptions of explicit sex that we had done or that she planned to do in the future that made me blush. I read it a couple of times while I drank a cup of coffee and became increasingly aware each time that Julie was too young for me, especially emotionally. The erection that bulged against my fly told me she was just right physically, however.

I poured a second cup of coffee and went into the living room and sat on the couch watching the rain stream down the glass doors to the balcony. The gray of the surging ocean blended with the sky, making it impossible to tell where the horizon was through the blur of the rain-streaked glass. I had the blues. The Ventnor Condo Blues. I had no idea what I was doing there. I didn't belong there. It was the kind of place that I would never create for myself. It didn't look lived in with the minimal furniture and no rugs and four cups and glasses and plates. There were no books except three college textbooks on a small shelf above the television. I wanted to get some news on the radio, but I couldn't find one.

I read the note again and then stuffed it into my pocket. She had said last night that she could live with my inability to love her, that there was plenty of time for that and that she had a lot of patience. This note indicated just the opposite. The plenty of time that she had patience for seemed to run until about seven that evening when she got home from work and we cooked dinner and began our conjugal relationship. The note was very explicit and insistent and made me want to run. It was too early. She was too young. And I still had strong feelings about Grace Somers, hopeless as they seemed to be.

The apartment suddenly seemed too small, and somehow it felt repulsive for me to be there. I stuffed the note in my pocket, along with the address of the Stockton house in Linwood and the key, and I bolted, locking the door behind me. As I stood waiting for the elevator, I had the feeling I had left something behind in the apartment, but I didn't have a key so there was no way to go back to check. I had my gun, I had my wallet and I was fully dressed, so I couldn't have left anything.

I guess I thought I could leave my blues in the apartment, but when I got down to the lobby and slid by the doorman's knowing grin and finally stood out on the rainy side street trying to remember where I'd left my car, I knew I hadn't left my blues behind. I had to go to the cottage to let Suzie out before I went to the house in Linwood but the mild depression I was in led me to the nearest familiar thing, my office in Margate. It was just after nine, and Thelma's boutique was still dark. I hid the car back on Winchester Avenue so Thelma wouldn't see it and come upstairs to visit me, even though it meant walking an extra block and getting soaked. I bought a container of coffee, locked the street door behind me and snuck up to my office. The gray rain didn't do much for the dim light in the office, but I didn't turn a light on. I really didn't want to see Thelma and rehash yesterday's events. I didn't know why I had gone to Julie's apartment. I didn't want to be involved with her. I had every intention of bringing her father to justice for the murder of Bonnie. Or killing him. Whichever opportunity he presented me with first.

I just sat there for a long time looking out the window at the rain. My jacket was wet through, and I began to shiver. Eventually I heard Thelma or one of her girls opening the boutique. I didn't like being so down. I dug out a bottle of Laird's Applejack that I kept in my desk drawer and poured a healthy measure into my container of coffee. That stopped the shivers, but it didn't help my mood any.

I thought maybe I was disappointed that I wasn't making any progress in finding Bonnie's killer, but I had unearthed Rocky less than twenty-four hours earlier, and now I sat with

Doc Stockton's house key burning a hole in my pants pocket. I guess what I didn't want to admit was that on top of everything else I had a simple case of postcoital depression.

A picture that I carried in my head of Rocky's fly-blown body being unearthed by the township police didn't help either. Sand clogged his open mouth while two cops dug carefully around his matted hair and the turkey buzzards circled hopefully overhead.

22

slipped the .25 from my ankle holster and put it in my
jacket pocket before I got out of the Honda. I was parked
on a street in Linwood two houses down from Raymond
Stockton's driveway. It was four o'clock in the afternoon and
the sky was still gray. The rain had stopped but it looked like
it might start again at any minute. There was no pile of newspapers on the front steps or mail spilling out of the metal box
beside the front door, nor any of the other classic signs that no
one had been home for a while. The curtains were pulled back
in all the windows and the shades half-drawn. Even the grass
had been recently cut.

The house was not what I would have imagined for Doc
Stockton. It was a simple single-level rancher with maybe two
or three bedrooms sitting on a fifty by one hundred foot lot
surrounded by a belly high cyclone fence. I had cruised the
place in the morning on my way home from Julie's condo.
There had been only housewives home in the neighborhood
then, but since housewives notice everything, I had decided not
to enter the place until late afternoon when I knew there
would be more distractions and my visit would not stick out
like the event of the day. I had used the free time at home to
work on an insurance report. Thelma called twice, as did Julie
from Philadelphia, but I let the machine handle all my calls.

The Stockton house was sided with dark brown asphalt
shingles. A short driveway led to an attached two-car garage.
Similar houses with different colored shingles sat to the left
and right of it down the length of the block and across the

street. There were tricycles, bicycles and skateboards on other lawns. Kid noises came from all directions, and a dog yapped incessantly in a backyard across the street. It wasn't the kind of neighborhood where I wanted to let a bullet or two fly, but I kept my hand on the cold metal in my jacket pocket anyway as I stepped out of the car and approached the front door.

There were no lights on that I could see, and no curtains fluttered. I pulled the aluminum storm door open and took out the .25, holding it close to my body so the kids who were playing in the street couldn't see it. I stepped in between the doors, laid my ear up against the wooden one and pushed the door bell button. I could hear chimes inside, eight of them, bing-bong, bing-bong, etc., and then the house was silent again. I switched the gun to my left hand and fished the key out of my pocket and put it in the lock. My heart was beating like a drum roll. It occurred to me in a rush that maybe Doc or someone else was in there waiting in ambush, and maybe, just maybe this was the end of the line for this case. If this had been a cop job, I would have gone back to the car and radioed it in and then waited for backup, lots of it. My information had slowly formed a portrait of Doc as a man who, somewhere along the line, had been hurt and hurt badly so that he didn't care what he did now to other people; didn't, in fact, even notice other people if they stood between himself and something he wanted. If I cornered him, there would be no moment of decision or discussion. He would kill me coldly and move on. With that in mind I turned the key and slowly pushed the paneled door open.

There was a knot of kids, maybe seven or eight of them, gathered now at the end of the walk, watching me. I flashed them what I hoped was a reassuring smile and stepped inside and shut the door quietly behind me. I gripped the gun with both hands at shoulder level, wishing now that I had something with a little more stopping power in my hands, like my .45 or the dirty 9mm I'd taken from Rocky.

The house smelled of lemon oil and ammonia like it had been cleaned recently. I stood frozen in the hallway, my gun covering the corridor in front of me. A trickle of sweat broke down my forehead, paused on the bridge of my nose and then veered off down my right cheek. Somewhere in the back of the house I could hear the ticking of a clock.

I slid along the hallway with my back to the wall and turned, bouncing into a crouch, gun preceding me, into the living room. No one. Moving silently I burst into the dining room, angling off against a wall, gun out in front again. Nothing. The same in the kitchen, a bathroom and two bedrooms. The house was larger inside than it had looked from the street. I poked behind doors and opened closets and ducked down to peer beneath the beds. Back in the living room, the thermostat was set at sixty degrees. I turned it up to eighty and when I heard the muffled roar of the furnace come on in the basement, I wondered why it hadn't been shut off for the summer, even though I knew Doc had undoubtedly left in a rush and had probably not been much concerned about saving a little heating oil. I turned it down to sixty again. There was no one in the basement either. A mouse skittered down the side of a drainpipe behind a pair of stationary tubs in the laundry room. Back on the street level I opened a trap door and checked the crawl space between the ceiling and the roof. The garage was empty too. Doc Stockton was definitely not at home.

I went back to the vestibule, locked the front door and started a systematic search of the house. There are two ways to search a place, the neat way and the not-so-neat way. I actually preferred to do it the neat way. Then I can tell where I've been, and I know if I've missed anything. Somehow when I toss a place, I always get to the point where I can't remember what I've seen and what I haven't seen.

I went through his closets and chests first. There were plenty of warm-weather things like bathing suits, shorts and short-sleeve shirts. You couldn't draw a conclusion from that, except that some of the things he left behind were fairly new. A bathing suit and a pair of hiking shorts still had price tags on them, and I carried them out to the front hall and left them on the mail table where I would see them when I left so I'd remember to take them with me. If I could find the store where he purchased them, maybe I could put some time frame on his disappearance and on his movements over the last month. All my information up to now seemed to be just so much smoke.

Nobody on either side, cops or robbers, knew just when this drug deal and rip-off had gone down, and the participants weren't talking, especially Rocky. What I had from most people was just a lot of guessing.

There were guns hidden everywhere in the house. I found six handguns, five semiautomatics and one revolver, plus a nasty sawed-off 12-gauge shotgun in his underwear drawer. There were two more full-barrel shotguns and two rifles stacked in the bedroom closet, and up in the crawl space beneath the roof I found a Thompson M-1 with a loaded 30-shot magazine. A quick check revealed that it had been illegally converted to automatic firing. Ray Stockton did not lack for firepower. He could have overthrown a small third-world country with the arsenal I found. I knew the Linwood police department would love to come calling here if I ever needed them. And if these guns were the ones he left behind, what would he have with him when we finally met? I decided right there to start carrying my .45 from now on, at least when I went looking for Doc.

There were lots of other things that he left behind. In fact, I began to wonder if he even took his toothbrush. I went to the bathroom to check. He hadn't, nor had he taken his razor or a brush and comb set or a leather travel kit to put them all in. Again, this was not unusual.

The highest estimates had him making off with almost a half million dollars in cash. Now that Rocky was dead, he wouldn't have to split anything. Fugitives with that kind of buying power rarely went home for their favorite sweater.

They say that clothes make the man, and the contents of his wardrobe told me plenty about Doc. He had tailored and expensive three-piece suits and Harris Tweed sport coats and wool slacks by the dozens. There were hand-made monogrammed shirts in his drawers and at least a half-dozen cashmere sweaters. I didn't count them, but he must have had a hundred ties, mostly silk designer makes. I did count the shoes. There were twenty pairs in varieties from brogans to tassel loafers. He had wonderful if costly taste in lawyer clothes and the money to indulge it. There were other expensive clothes in the closets too, biker clothes. Leather stuff, black jackets and vests with and without chains, eight pairs of heavy biker and cowboy boots and a collection of helmets, including two spiked Prussian army jobs, one of which he must have been wearing when he clobbered me and fled Andersen's Bus World with Rocky on the back of his bike. Some of the jackets and vests had insignias and patches on them for the Atlantic County chapter of the Pagans motorcycle club, a club I knew about from the press clippings I had read on Stockton's work with them. The *Atlantic City Press* said they were the second-largest motorcycle club in the country after the Hell's Angels. I wondered where the *Press* got their information.

I went out to the garage again and looked more closely at the collection of bikes there. There were three Harleys and a beat-up Bultaco dirt bike parked at a parallel angle along one of the car spaces. The other car space was empty. One of the bikes was the white Police Special I had seen fleeing Andersen's.

I returned to the house and stood in the kitchen. It was an ordinary suburban kitchen, except there was plenty of expensive booze in a cabinet under the sink, including a bunch of single malt Scotches I had never heard of. I found myself a rocks glass in a cabinet over the sink and poured myself one of them. It was sippin' whiskey at its best, smooth and smoky with a taste that went right up your nose into your brain. I leaned against the sink and flipped on a reproduction of an antique radio that sat at the back of the butcher block counter. The Beatles came bouncing out singing "Penny Lane," and with the Scotch in my head, I was in a whorehouse in Saigon for an instant and pleased to be there.

For an instant.

I heard a lot of Beatles songs for the first time in Vietnam. Guys would bring the albums from the states and give them to the girls. I never liked Scotch much but it was the big status drink in those joints. I took another sip and wandered back to the living room. "Penny Lane" ended and the disk jockey identified the station as WOGL, your golden oldie station, twelve-ten on your dial in Philadelphia. Without introduction The Doors started "Light My Fire."

I took another sip and looked around the room as Jim

Morrison stretched the word *fire* into two syllables. I wanted to turn everything off and go home for the night. Nobody much liked The Doors in Nam, especially the black guys. They called Morrison names that questioned his sexual preference and did a lot of speculating on how he would behave if God, by some miracle, saw to it that he was drafted and sent over to join us. I sat on the couch as the song's long, whiny instrumental riff started. I was getting nowhere. It was becoming apparent to me that I was looking for something that didn't exist. Ray Stockton was just your average normal lawyer–civic leader turned biker and drug dealer. He was probably in the country somewhere and not in Mexico or Brazil or Timbuktu like he wanted everyone to believe. I was beginning to suspect that Julie knew his whereabouts, or that he at least was in contact with her when he needed something locally. And if that was true, was she informing him of my movements? I even had my doubts that he had killed Rocky. That job might have been done by the same people that were after him. That neat Pine Barrens burial had Philly mob written all over it. The Pines was their favorite dumping ground. I was on the same merry-go-round I had been riding with Rocky, but unlike that quest, this one had little hope of success because Doc had the means to evade his pursuers for a long time.

I really hadn't learned anything in Doc's neat little suburban house either. He lived alone and bought himself expensive clothes and whiskey. You could say that about a lot of lawyers. His taste in pop music seemed stuck in the sixties. But so was mine. I even had the same oldie station programmed onto my car radio dial. His avocations were motorcycles and recreational drugs. Most of the time that didn't put you over the edge either. He was able to clean out forty-two thousand dollars in bank accounts, and he owned a two-bedroom rancher in Linwood. Still fairly normal. Where was the desperation that put him into drug-dealing and murder? Nothing I had heard about Raymond Stockton seemed to fit this little well-ordered suburban niche. I felt the blue mood of earlier in the day coming over me despite the glow the Scotch had given me. I decided to go out to the kitchen for another sip and then leave. As I pushed myself forward on the couch, I saw a thick photo album on the shelf under the coffee table. I had over-looked it during my search because it couldn't be seen from a standing angle.

I pulled the album out with one hand, and as I stood up to carry it to the kitchen where there was more light, several loose photographs fell to the floor. When I bent to retrieve them, I saw that one of them was the Polaroid snapshot that had been stolen from my office the night of the break-in. I picked it up and stared at Julie and Bonnie, this time in color, and then slipped it into my jacket pocket and carried my empty glass and the album to the formica counter in the kitchen. I intended to look through the album, but I was beginning to feel squirrelly being in the house. Ray Stockton wasn't there, and it didn't look like he had been for some time. There wasn't anything more to learn here. I put my glass in the sink and hefted the opaque green Scotch bottle. It was almost full. I uncorked it and tilted it up to my lips and took a long healthy swallow.

The end of The Doors's song was an impotent scream of rage. This time Morrison made *fire* into three syllables. That had to be a Guinness World Record. What a pant load. I snapped the radio off, annoyed. I never did like The Doors. I scooped up the heavy photo album carefully, corked the bottle and put it in my other jacket pocket and left, pulling the door locked behind myself. I half expected to see a crowd gathered at the end of the walk or even a patrol car waiting for me to come out. But the neighborhood buzzed on toward the dinner hour without taking any notice of me. As I turned the ignition key on the Honda, I remembered I had left Doc's new bathing suit and hiking shorts on the mail table. Two boys rode by on bikes, turning their heads to look at me as they passed. I put the car in first gear and slowly pulled away.

23

The sun had set and the river was deep in twilight by the time I pulled down my bumpy drive. Only a gray line of light lingered above the dark cedars across the river. Inside the cottage, I stood and thumbed impatiently through the album, flipping by family pictures that included a chubby little girl I recognized as Julie and an older boy who must have been her dead brother, Mark. The booze had made me both angry and hungry. I heaved the album onto my couch and put the bottle of Scotch on the dining room table and left. I drove down Landing Road to the Cedar Bank Marina and drank some draft beer and ate a cheeseburger at the bar. There wasn't much of a crowd yet, and there probably wouldn't be, since it was the first night after a holiday weekend. Nobody bothered me. Even Tom, the bartender, who usually wanted to talk with me about the detective novels he was addicted to, spent most of the time I was there around on the other side of the horse-shoe-shaped bar watching the early innings of the Phillies game.

I paid my check and wandered out onto the docks. Only about half the thirty or so boat slips were occupied. They would all be full by the Fourth of July. The air was warm and damp and stirred by a light breeze. The river was at dead low tide, and on an impulse I made my way to the end of the stone bulkhead and down onto the gravel beach. By the time I had descended to river level, my eyes were adjusted to the darkness, and I walked the short distance upriver to my cottage, leaving my car in the marina lot where I could pick it up in the morning. The tide was just right for a river walk, and it was very peaceful and relaxing to be down next to the gentle flow of water. There was just a sliver of a last-quarter moon left but it wasn't hard to find my footing. I had taken this route home enough times to know where the runoffs and cedar stumps and mooring chains were, and somehow I managed to avoid all of them. Near the cottage I saw the silhouettes of some mallards as they slipped into the water, quacking irritably.

My phone was ringing as I unlocked the cottage door. I gave Suzie a good scratch behind the ears while I waited for the caller to leave a message. It was Julie, letting me know that she had just arrived home from her dance group, and I could come over or call her when I got in.

I turned the Phillies game on. It was only the fifth inning, but they were already down by seven runs, so I didn't pay much attention to it, just left it on to keep me company. It was warm enough to have the windows open, and cricket noises came in from the dark night while bugs thudded into the screens. I got a glass, poured myself two fingers of Scotch and opened the album.

Inside was a portrait of a family gone sour, starting with early baby shots of Mark and Julie and their pretty mother, as well as the short-haired and serious young lawyer, Raymond Stockton. The pictures wouldn't have meant a lot to someone who didn't know the family, but from the newspaper clippings I had read about his political career's rise and fall, and from the information Julie had grudgingly given me, I was able to fill in the gaps and finish my own portrait of the man who in less than six years had gone from being a Linwood City Councilman to the demonic president of the Atlantic County chapter of the Pagans. His inauguration to this last post had taken place in a pine-paneled room crowded with celebrating bikers. A red-eyed Doc hugged two burly laughing women, both of whom had hiked their T-shirts to reveal full sagging breasts and bulky waistlines for the camera. Doc laughed too and pointed to a huge red and white button pinned to his leather jacket that said "The Boss."

That pine-paneled room seemed to be the interior of a hunting camp. The same fete that inaugurated Doc had spilled

outside to the porch for a group portrait. Above the revelers
hung a carefully carved wooden sign that identified the place
as the Bogside Rod and Gun Club. Throughout the album
there were more conventional family pictures taken at the
same site, most of them of Mark and his father, including two
with gutted deer strung up from a cross beam in front of the
building. The father and son stood close to these carcasses
with their shotguns cradled proudly in their arms. In the first
one Mark looked to be about twelve. In the second he was a
foot taller and sported a scruffy first-growth of chin whiskers.

The phone rang but I didn't answer it. It was Julie again.
Her message was still civil, but an edge of restraint had crept
into her voice. I poured myself two more fingers of Scotch.

If I didn't learn anything new about Doc from the album,
certainly the rest of the family came into focus for the first
time. Mark seemed to imitate his father, going from crew-cut
little league baseball player to a junior biker with a silver
swastika earring. He had angry good looks and had developed
the hint of a sneer in his smile before the pictures of him
stopped. The few shots of Marcia Stockton were all early ones,
usually holding or touching one of the kids. She always had a
tentative smile on her face, although sometimes a tired exas-
peration showed through the smile. Julie had inherited her
high cheekbones and her delicate nose and mouth.

There were a lot of pictures of Julie throughout the album,
from chubby child to angular and beautiful Princeton graduate
complete with mortarboard and gown. My intimacy with her
over the past few days caused me to examine each one of the
photographs with intense curiosity. She had developed sooner
than her peers, who stood self-consciously with her in some of
the early photos. She seemed quite proud of her newly swollen
breasts, posing in bathing suit profile with a hand behind her
head and a coy over-the-shoulder look. She must have been
about fourteen. The chubbiness vanished in the later high
school pictures when shots of her in dancer's leotards began to
appear. But the really striking good looks didn't start until the
college pictures. There was one photo of her in a plain short
skirt, the muscles of her long legs now well-defined, that
reminded me of the heads that had turned, both male and

female, when we had entered the Crab Pot that first night.

I closed the album and poured a dollop more of Scotch, surprised to see that I had consumed over half the bottle. It was almost eleven o'clock and the Phillies game had ended. They scored three runs in the ninth but it was too little, too late as usual. I listened to the postgame show to get the A's score, but they were at home in Oakland and the game was just starting. The phone had rung three more times, but each time Julie had hung up, if in fact it had been her. I tried to remember the last time it had rung, and realized that I hadn't heard it for over an hour. Suddenly the clicking of my alarm startled me, warning me that a car had turned into my drive-way. I stood up from the table, knocking the chair backwards to the floor with a clatter behind me. Suzie stirred, but I clamped my hand over her nose and gave her the "quiet" com-mand and lurched over to the light switch, surprised at what half a fifth of Scotch had done to my equilibrium. I snapped off the ceiling lamp and stood in the middle of the room, avoiding the glow angling into the room from the yard lamp. I could hear the car crunching gravel now, and a moment later Julie's Pathfinder moved slowly into the circle of yellow light.

She drove tentatively as if she was uncertain she was at the right house, although "C. Leeds" was clearly marked on the mailbox at the beginning of the drive. When she reached the log at the wide spot where the gravel ended, she did a slow K turn, pausing when her headlights fell on the cottage. She kept the wagon in low gear and drove very slowly on the way out too, maybe hoping she would confront me coming home in the Honda.

When I was sure she was gone, I opened the refrigerator and took out a Corona and sat in the darkness sipping it for maybe another fifteen minutes. Then I turned on the light and popped in a tape of a Mozart symphony and sipped another Corona. At exactly midnight, I dialed her number. She answered in the middle of the second ring.

"Where have you been?" she asked angrily.

"Atlantic City," I lied. "I ate a steak at the Knife and Fork and then went for a walk on the Boardwalk. It was a nice night for a walk."

"You could have come up here."

"I played some blackjack."

"I would have joined you."

"You told me you didn't like Atlantic City."

"I like to play blackjack."

"Next time."

"Promise?"

"I wish I'd had you with me. I blew about fifty bucks. The good news is it took me three casinos to do it."

"Why didn't you call me?"

"I just did."

"I'm sorry." She calmed down. "Did you go to Raymond's house?"

"Yes."

"Did you take anything?" I had the feeling she already knew the answer to that question.

"A bottle of Scotch and a photo album."

"What album did you take?"

"The one under the coffee table. Family snapshots. You certainly were a sexy kid."

"You had no right to take that album."

"I'll bring it back."

"Where did you say it was?"

"Under the coffee table. Were you looking for it?"

"No, but I had forgotten about it. There are pictures of me in there that are embarrassing."

I walked to the dining table with the phone and without sitting down, flipped the album open.

"You can't change history," I said. I found the bathing beauty pose. Her breasts seemed too large for the rest of her adolescence, but she was obviously very proud of them.

"But you don't have to see it."

"You're beautiful now," I said, flipping backwards to a photo of her and Mark standing on the front lawn at the hunting lodge. She was maybe six and Mark eight. They both wore the bottoms of bathing suits. Julie's waist rolled over the edges of the suit, and folds of baby fat swelled from her armpits. "What do you care what you used to look like?"

"I didn't want you to see them. I love you."

"It works the other way around," I said, commenting quickly on the first part of her statement and ignoring the second. "I'm so turned on by you that when I see pictures of you, even as a fat kid, it makes me want you even more."

She was silent for a long moment, and then with a stern note in her voice, she said: "I don't like that." And then, her tone shifting to a serious insistence, she asked: "Do you love me?"

"Look, Julie," I said. "Being with you gives me a lot of pleasure. But let me come to the love thing on my own. I just stopped seeing someone else. And I'm having a problem with the age thing."

"I told you that was no big deal."

"Just give me some time. You can't will a person to love you."

She paused again. She was waiting for me and I had the urge to say more, but it would only get me in deeper, so I fought the urge back. Finally, she said: "That's a song. It's very sad."

I kept still, thinking about how young she was. I knew the song.

"Bonnie Raitt," she said. "'I Can't Make You Love Me.'"

We went into more silence.

"Can you come over tonight?" she said after a while.

"No," I said gently, and then because I knew she would pursue the subject, I added quickly: "Your mother was a beautiful woman." I had flipped to a picture of the woman standing beside Mark, who sat astride a pony looking as if he might cry. "You got your looks from her."

"I know," she said. Her voice was very low, almost a whisper. "When I was young, I never thought I could be as pretty as she was."

"You said she was in Oregon."

"Yes."

"Did your father ever go there? Could he be there now?"

"No."

"How can you be so sure?"

"She doesn't want him to know where she is. I'm the only one who knows. She was in Chicago for a while, but he found her and tried to make her come back."

"He wants her back?"

"He needs somebody around to torture."

"How about you?"

"What about me?"

"You're still around. Does he torture you?"

"We don't speak. I told you that."

"Ever?"

"I saw him in Atlantic City last winter. I crossed the street. He didn't see me."

"Who goes to the house?"

"What do you mean?"

"The house is clean. The mail has been taken in. The grass is cut. Who does all that?"

"The cleaning lady has a key. I pay her. He hadn't paid her for two weeks and she called me. I mailed her a check. The same with the guy who cuts the grass. I've been going there twice a week to take the mail in. That's when I found the bank books."

"What were you looking for?"

"Money."

"Would you have taken it if you found any?"

"Of course."

"Aren't you afraid you'll run into him?"

"I'm not afraid of him. And he wouldn't dare come there anyway. Too many people are looking for him who know where he lives."

"Do they get in touch with you too, like the cleaning lady?"

"Yes."

"The police?"

"Yes. Linwood and the State Police. They both told me to call if I ever hear from him."

"Would you?"

"Of course. He should be locked up. He's a danger to society."

"How so?"

"He doesn't know right from wrong."

"Was he always like that?"

"No."

"When did he get like that?"

"I guess after Mark died. He really upped his drug consumption."

"Did you ever hear any talk about him manufacturing drugs?"

"Isn't that why everyone is looking for him?"

"What about the mob? Did they ever contact you?"

"I guess that's who that was."

"What do you mean?"

"Two men were waiting for me outside work in Philly one night. They asked me if I knew where he was."

"How did you know they were gangsters?"

"They were real polite but they were kind of low class. They scared me. I saw one of them in a car coming out of Raymond's street last week when I was driving over there. If he'd asked me, I would have told him Ray wouldn't be there if he was in the area."

"Where would he be?"

"He'd go to the club."

"The hunting club?" I asked. "Some of these pictures were taken there." I couldn't remember the name until I flipped ahead to the biker group shot on the porch. "Bogside," I said.

"That's the place."

"Where is it?"

"Did you ever hear of a town called Forest City?"

"No."

"It's below Chatsworth and west off 563. It's a ghost town now. There used to be some abandoned houses there but they've all fallen down or burned."

"When's the last time you were there?"

"When I was in high school."

"How do I get there?"

"Do you know where Buzby's is in Chatsworth?"

"Is that the general store?"

"Yes. They'll know where it is."

"The camp?"

"No, the town. When you get to Forest City you might not recognize it because there aren't any buildings standing anymore, but there's only one road that goes north. It's a sand road, but it used to be drivable. It's about two miles up that road."

"Who owns the place?"

"Raymond does now. He bought it with some other lawyers from Atlantic City twenty years ago. But they all quit or he bought them out. Are you going there?"

"Yes."

"When?"

"Tomorrow. Do you have a key?"

"No. I wouldn't go there."

"Do you mean I shouldn't go?"

"What if he's there?"

"That's why I want to go there."

"He'll kill you."

"Not if I kill him first."

"Oh God, be careful, Con."

"I will."

"Can I come over there?"

"Where? To my place? Now?"

"Yes."

"It's too late. I'm going to bed."

"I'll join you."

"You'd never find the place," I said, leaving the door open for her to tell me that she'd been here already.

"You could give me directions," she said. "I'll find the place. I'm real smart."

You sure are, I thought.

24

I woke up with a blistering hangover. I didn't really think I drank that much, so I blamed it on the smooth, smoky-tasting Scotch. I tried to sit on the porch with a cup of coffee, but the birds and the bright sunshine bothered me, so I went back inside and moped around until I got the energy up to shower and dress. That ritual made me feel a little better. I was grateful I wasn't dealing with breakfast and Julie and another awkward morning after. In the kitchen I managed to get a little cranberry juice down. I made some whole wheat toast but left it in the toaster.

The prospects of a day in the Pines pleased me, but this time it was an armed business trip and not a romp with Thelma and Suzie. With extreme care and repulsion, I hid the dark green Scotch bottle in a kitchen cabinet, resisting the urge to take a swallow for medicinal purposes. I spread the Geological Survey maps out over the photo album on the dining table and found Forest City right away. Ghost town or not, it had been there when the quadrangle was drawn in 1956. It looked easy enough to find by car, although there was no dotted line running north to indicate the sand road that led to the Bogside Hunting Camp.

The phone rang, and I thought about not answering it. I really didn't want to talk to Julie, but when I picked it up, Sergeant McKelvey was on the other end of the line.

"I just got the ballistics report on the bullets they took out of your friend, Roland Starza," he said.

"He's no friend of mine, Sergeant."

"Call me Jim," he said. He was being too friendly. "They don't match the one I found in your bookcase."

"What about the gun that was buried with Rocky?"

"You're way ahead of me, aren't you?"

"I used to do this for a living, Jim."

"No match there either. That was a thirty-eight."

"It was a snub-nose, right?"

"How'd you know?"

"I saw it the night he jumped me at my house. It was Rocky's own gun."

"So we still don't have the gun that killed Starza."

"What caliber was that one?"

He paused for effect and then said: "A forty-five." Another pause. "Like your Springfield."

"I'll be more than happy to bring it in for ballistic tests," I said.

"Not yet," he said.

"You're wasting your time on me, Jim. I just wanted to beat his brains in. I didn't want to shoot him. I haven't fired that forty-five in a couple of months."

I wanted to tell him about Doc's arsenal in the Linwood house, but I wanted to go through the place one more time, and I knew that if the cops got in there, nothing would be left to find when they finished.

"I just wanted you to know what we have."

"Like I said, Jim, I used to do this for a living. And when I did, I hardly ever called up private citizens to give them information about a case I was working on. Especially if they were P.I.s meddling in my investigation."

"You know, Leeds—"

"Call me Con."

"Con. You've got a big chip on your shoulder. I was trying to be helpful."

"And you're trying to stir something out of me, Jim, and we both know it. You don't believe I gave you all I got."

"I talked to your Lieutenant Conlin in New York City."

"Brooklyn," I corrected.

"I talked to him about the girl." He paused and I could hear him shuffling through papers, looking for the name.

"Bonnie," I said.

"I talked to him about Bonnie."

He paused, but I didn't rise to the bait, so he added: "Conlin said she spent some time at your place."

I was surprised and annoyed at Conlin.

"I was hired to find her and protect her until I could return her to her grandfather, who was my client. She spent two nights at my cottage before they could pick her up. She was a teenager. Conlin spends too much time sitting on his brains."

"Back it up one step, Con. You said her grandfather *was* your client. What's your interest in this matter now?"

"Curiosity."

"Well, we all know what that did to the cat. Lieutenant Conlin also said you were a good guy."

"My mother could have told you that—"

"And that I should cooperate with you when I could."

"But she's dead."

"Who?"

"My mother."

"Is there a next of kin?"

"For my mother?"

"No, for Starza. Conlin didn't have anything on him, except his yellow sheet. County wants to get rid of the body."

"Did they do an autopsy?"

"Of course. Death by bullets. Some traces of methamphetamine in the blood. Nothing else."

"How about his veins?"

"He definitely had them."

"Were there needle tracks?"

"The report didn't mention them."

"He has a pregnant girlfriend."

"I guess it'll have to do. Maybe she knows about his family."

"Can I call her first? She seems like a nice kid."

"You get around, don't you?"

"You married, Jim?"

"Yes."

"You married guys always think us single guys are fucking our brains out."

"Aren't you?"

"I wish," I said, and then I thought of Julie. Thought of her slowly opening her moonlit white thighs.

"Tell her to call me. What's her name?"

"Loretta. I don't have a last name."

"Tell her to call me."

I knew she probably wouldn't, but I didn't tell him that. I hung up. My head was throbbing. I went in the bathroom and took two of the prescription Tylenol. Conlin really pissed me off. I dialed his number but the detective who answered the phone said it was his day off. I just wanted to yell at him. When I hung up, I was glad I didn't get him.

I sat at the table and flipped through the album again, killing time, waiting for the headache to go away, but something about the pictures annoyed me and I realized I was getting angry at the whole damn family, victims and victimizers alike, including a pretty mom in Oregon I didn't even know and a dead son. It was almost noon. I stood up and went into the bedroom and slipped the shoulder holster over my head and opened the floor safe. I popped the clip from the .45 to make sure it was full and took a spare clip from the safe and locked it again. When I slipped the gun into the holster it felt solid and reassuring against my ribs. I took a box of .45 ammunition from my dresser drawer, loaded the spare clip and slipped it into my pocket and carried the box with me. I still had the .25 on my ankle but it was only backup once I was wearing the bigger gun. Suzie tried to push by me as I went out the door, but I yelled at her and she slunk back inside. My hangover had me feeling meaner than a cornered bear.

I got a little meaner too when I got outside and remembered that I had left the Honda at the Marina for the night. I walked down Landing Road this time, the fresh air and the Tylenol taking away some of the headache, but when I got to the parking lot I saw that I had forgotten to close the car windows for the night. It hadn't rained, so there was no damage done, except that the pitch pines are loaded with pollen in late May, and a film of chartreuse dust covered the outside of the car, plus the dashboard and seats as well. When I tossed the roll of maps into the car, a light green cloud exploded from the seat.

I drove out past Weekstown and turned north on 563 down through the cattail marshes to the Green Bank Bridge. The woman who operates that drawbridge was just lowering the barrier, but she held it up until I could drive across. I waved to her and she waved back. There was a forty-foot Bertram rumbling on the upriver side of the bridge waiting to pass. I waved to the pilot who was up on the flying bridge with a woman in a big floppy straw hat. He didn't wave back, but she did. Maybe he was in a mean mood too.

If you blink you can miss Green Bank. There's a small elementary school, a firehouse, a liquor store and a rowdy piney bar called the Green Bank Inn that occupies an old house at the intersection of 563 and 542. It was barely noon on a Tuesday, but there were already a motorcycle and two pickup trucks in the parking lot. For a moment I thought about stopping for a quick one myself just to help the Tylenol chase my hangover. But I had already lost most of my enthusiasm for this wild goose chase, and I knew that if I got my butt up on a bar stool, it would take a whole afternoon to get it down.

A few miles above Green Bank as the land rose away from the river, the pitch pines gave way to tall oaks and these in turn to the open vistas of blueberry farms. Picking season had started, and there were already Mexicans working the early varieties, small groups of men in straw hats among bushes that stretched in orderly rows far back across the white sand. Soon the low dikes and levies of the cranberry farms appeared, mile after mile of man-made bogs and here and there at road level, the low concrete block dormitories that housed the pickers until the last cranberries were floated up out of these bogs in early November.

I turned into the road to Forest City and pulled over to check my maps. The pavement went up a little rise and back into another pitch pine forest, and I saw from the map that it went all the way across the barrens to the town of Tabernacle and State Route 206. No cars or trucks came along while I was stopped there. In the stillness I could hear the warm spring breeze stirring the trees and bushes. It was pleasant to be alone. There was no way anyone could interrupt me out here; no ringing phone that might be Julie. I knew I had lost the angry impulse that I carried with me when I left the cottage. I was pretty sure I wouldn't find Doc today, but I had to run the lead down, even though I was beginning to realize that I didn't want to do this now or ever again. I didn't care about Doc any more. Rocky was enough revenge for me. I wanted to go to New York and talk to Ben Arnold again, and if he wasn't interested in taking this to the end, I'd let the police investigation run its course. It seemed to me that they had enough to tie Bonnie's death to Rocky, even if they closed the book on it with just a negligent homicide against him. Sometime, somewhere, Doc would get his. It was obvious too that Julie knew more than she was telling me. But I wanted to let that go too. Her neediness overwhelmed me, and although I knew that I would climb into my empty bed on many nights to come thinking about her warm young body, I decided I didn't want to see her again. Decisions were easy to make alone in the pines. Keeping to them, especially the next time I saw her, was another matter.

I just wanted to do some insurance work and get on with my life. Bill Harrison had talked Founder's into paying for a chartered helicopter to see if I could get some pictures of my fake paraplegic while he was marlin fishing out in the canyons. I was looking forward to the flight. I just had to make the arrangements. I had never been up over the Jersey Shore before.

I pulled back onto the pavement and was soon in pine forest again with the breeze stirring waves of lime-colored dust out of the dark boughs above me. I had an idea I would call Grace Somers when I got home. She had said several times that she would love to ride to New York with me if she could get her mother to stay with the kids. If we got out of town where no one knew us, maybe she would feel safer being with me. I had the impulse to turn around, but it was about the same distance home in either direction now, so I pressed on toward Tabernacle on the other side.

The road soon leveled off along a ridge of oaks, and the pavement ended, but a good base of gravel and dirt had been added to the sand, and it was graded level and two lanes wide. I kept my speed at about fifty, raising a mighty cloud of dust in my rearview mirror. Forest City had once been a crossroads like Green Bank, and the road entered town and departed almost as quickly as the nineteenth-century prosperity that had built the place. I would have missed it entirely if I hadn't caught sight of a large hole in the ground that I recognized as the foundation of a house. I stopped and backed up and saw that it was stone-lined and half-filled with sand. There were more along the north-south stretch of the crossroads, the other main drag of Forest City, which had become a pair of weedy ruts. I shut the engine off and got out of the car. I could hear the wind again, and see it moving the dune grass around between the foundations. There were ghosts here all right. I could feel them. Ghosts of miners and their families whose dreams had died when the iron ore beneath the sand became too costly to smelt and haul out to the rail lines. Ghosts of charcoal burners whose fuel smelted the iron and whose craft had now been made obsolete by the little petrochemical turds that now cooked America's summer hot dogs and hamburgers.

I walked about fifty yards along each street and decided there wasn't any other way out of town. The road to the Bogside Gunning Club had to be off the north end of the crossroad. I started the car and turned cautiously into this road, grass scraping the undercarriage. For about a mile the track followed a stream that eventually veered off to the right. There was a fork at that point, but the branch that followed the stream was overgrown and did not look like even deer had been on it in some time. My road went straight ahead and was the obvious choice. I tried to drive like Patrolman Richards, but I had learned to maneuver a car on the solid if sometimes dangerous streets of Brooklyn and did not have the flair for sand that the piney cop did. I didn't bog, but I did a lot of bouncing. Richards possessed a rhythm that had kept his patrol car moving smoothly with well-directed spurts of acceleration. My instinct was to try to steer around soft spots or the high center strip that constantly threatened to drag the Honda to a stop, and this kept me fishtailing up over the turf banks of the twin ruts. I crossed three or four other sand tracks angling in from various directions plus two more forks. At both forks the more traveled and straight path always seemed to be to the right. I should have noted my mileage at Forest City because I began to realize that I had driven longer than the four or five miles Julie estimated for the trip in to the camp.

The choice at the next fork seemed to be a left, but that led me in a straight line to the bank of the stream that I could have sworn had been well off to my right somewhere. I followed the stream again until it began to widen into a swamp behind a large and elaborate beaver dam. The road kept cutting a new brushy trail at intervals to avoid this water, but eventually it just gave up and vanished abruptly into the swamp. I sat for a moment cursing silently and looking into a dark maze of white cedars and then backed the car into a tight K-turn, momentarily catching the front bumper over a stump but managing to pull off with a loud crack and thump. I got out to assess the damage, but most of it seemed to be to the stump. I got back in and completed the turn and that's when I bogged down, hopelessly hung up on the undercarriage, my drive wheels spinning deeper and deeper into the sand.

I made a couple of angry attempts to rock the Honda off its reef, but only succeeded in churning more sand out from under the wheels. Finally it wouldn't even rock, and when I got out, I could see that the front wheels had dug themselves clear, and the weight of the car rested on its undercarriage. When I shut the engine off, it got very quiet. Not a peep came from bird or insect. At the cottage, the creatures in my little riverbank community were used to my clatter, but here every living thing was holding its breath, poised to see what would happen. Although the sun was shining through the tops of the trees, it was dark as night in the swamp ahead of me. And ominous. The tangle of deadfall that had accumulated over the centuries made an impenetrable wall rising from the brown water at the base of the crowded trees. I didn't have any choice about direction. I extracted my keys from the Honda's ignition and began to walk back up the twin ruts away from the swamp. As I walked I realized that my little burst of anger was quickly dissipating. It was a pleasant spring day, and I was relieved that the search for Doc Stockton was over. I would

walk out, find a garage or get one of the locals to pull the
Honda free and leave this case behind me forever. My hangover was mostly gone, and I was beginning to feel the first
twinge of hunger. I looked at my watch and was surprised to
see that it was almost two-thirty. I had started late but I didn't
realize the day was going by that quickly. I was thirsty too. I
chose not to try the still water of the swamp, knowing I would
hit the clear running stream again before I reached any
dwellings, probably somewhere above the beaver dam. Each
time there was a choice of tracks, I took the left one, keeping
the edge of the bog as my guide. I had been in the Pines
enough to know how turned around you could get without
some landmark to use as a bearing.

It was three-fifteen when I passed the beaver dam. I slaked
my thirst with a little water from the stream and consciously
chased the rising anxiety I felt by telling myself that I still had
almost five hours of daylight, which was enough time to walk
all the way to Green Bank if I had to.

The road split again soon after the dam. I seemed to
remember coming down to the dam from the fork on the right,
so I took it. It was impossible to recognize the Honda's tracks
in the dry sand. As I often did when I was in the Pines, I began
to wonder who drove out here and why. There was plenty of
evidence of vehicle traffic, but you seldom saw anyone. The
park rangers from Batsto must come up this way occasionally,
although I wasn't sure if this area was part of the state forest. I
had already seen a couple of barrier ditches along the way, so
the fire prevention people were in here too. In the fall there
were hunters, and all year 'round there were people like me
who just liked to come stroll in the woods.

I wasn't being at all cautious when I came on the hunting
club. I had been walking through an area that had been
burned over sometime in the last ten years. Except for an occasional hardy survivor, all the older pitch pines stood black and
dead, while thousands of young shoulder-high trees flourished
around them. The pitch pine thrived on this cycle of burn and
replenish. The heat of a forest fire burst its cones and scattered
the hard seed across the sandy soil.

I was surprised to look up and see a large clearing about

two hundred feet ahead of me across this burn and, in the middle of it, the low whitewashed concrete-block structure of the Bogside Gunning Club. I recognized it right away from the photographs. In my mind I already had the case closed and in the file drawer and was striding along a pleasant path in the Pines making good time toward a paved road. I stopped abruptly and held my breath but didn't hear any sounds. I was reaching inside my windbreaker for the .45 when Hell Knuckles stood up from behind the baby trees at the edge of the clearing directly ahead of me. He had a deer rifle leveled at my chest.

"Don't," he said, and I had no doubt that he meant it.

I froze.

"Take your hand away slowly." I wasn't sure it was him until I heard his voice. He moved toward me, keeping just out of reach of my lunge. The rifle was a thirty-ought-six. The last time I had fired one of those it had been at a thick telephone pole, and the slug had blown a large splintery hole out the back of the pole and looked like it had not even slowed down on the way through. I knew it would go through me, bones and all, like I was warm butter.

"Use the other hand now, nice and easy, and put it on the ground."

I took the .45 out of the holster with two fingers of my left hand and purposely let it drop into the sand. The rifle barrel followed it momentarily, and as I crouched to pick it up, I slipped the .25 from my ankle and shot him once just below the belt buckle and rolled to the right into the young pines. I thought he might get a shot off, but he didn't. It probably wouldn't have hit me anyway because for the split second that it took the .45 to hit the ground, I wasn't covered. I leveled my gun on him through the trees, ready to pop him again, but he had dropped the rifle and was doubled over clutching the little hole I had made in his lower intestine. Then he sat down in the clearing and moaned and looked at the dark blood oozing between his fingers. Then he looked at me and rolled his eyes up in his head and flopped back onto the brown grass and sand.

A strange silence fell over the forest and the clearing again;

no birds, no bugs, just his gasping. He kept his head still, eyes looking straight up at the sky. His body shook with his short, labored breaths. He tried to say something, but it was only a whisper and I couldn't understand it. He seemed to sense that because he drew a deeper breath and coughed and said in a louder voice: "I'm gut shot."

His head rolled around like he was looking for me, but he couldn't lift it. "Why'd you want to do that?" he asked. His voice trailed off again. He didn't want an answer. He was concentrating on his rapid breathing, and I was close enough to see sweat starting to bead up on his forehead.

It seemed best for me to be quiet anyway. I didn't know who else might be in the building, and my little .25 was just a pop gun in this kind of fire fight. My hands had started to shake too, and I knew the six shots I had left wouldn't be very effective. I could see the .45 in the sand about ten feet to my left but I didn't want to move the little pines I was under and draw any fire. All these speculations were suddenly answered by the crack of a rifle from one of the windows of the club.

I flinched, thinking the shot had been fired in my direction, but when I glanced at Hell Knuckles again I could see that he had stopped breathing. It would have been difficult for him to do so anyway since the lower part of his face was now a bloody mess. From the angle that he lay toward the building, it looked like the bullet had entered the top of his skull and exited at the bottom, tearing off most of his jaw. His body had a violent spasm and then lay still. I banged off three shots that took out the glass of the top half of the window and bought me a second to seek better cover. I made my trembly knees work and lurched up into a loping crouch, grabbed the .45 as I passed it and zigzagged back through the little pines to a more substantial tree trunk.

I have been in firefights before, both in New York and in Vietnam. My hands always shake. I can operate my weapon and shoot fairly accurately, but on the reloading I am a spastic disaster. I popped the clip of the .45, and because I was afraid of dropping it in the sand, I sat at the base of my tree so it would fall in my lap if it jumped free from my trembling hands. A burst of fire from an automatic rifle raked the woods

around me. I didn't need to check the clip. It was full. I took a
deep breath to calm myself and jammed the clip back in the
.45 and felt my pocket for the spare. One in the chamber and
two clips of eight plus four in the .25. Twenty-one rounds.
Hardly what you'd call siege materiel. But then again, who
had who trapped? Doc might be confined to the hunting club.
And I was already thinking about ways of flushing him out.
But my position wasn't exactly tenable either. I had my back to
an impenetrable swamp, and I was in unfamiliar and confusing
terrain. I wasn't even sure I could find the goddamn car again.

I stood up, careful to keep the blackened pine trunk
between myself and the building. The clearing where the clubhouse stood was on slightly higher ground, and behind me
down a gentle slope were the cedars that marked the edges of
the dark swamp. I tried to remember what I had seen in my
brief glimpse of the building. It was a long one-story concrete-
block structure with seven or eight windows and a small porch
sheltering a back door. I couldn't remember any parked vehicles or an approach road. They had to be on the other side of
the building. There was no way I could get past the club by
following the swamp, because the young pines provided only
scant cover on that side. I could go back and make a wide
berth around it and walk out. But in assessing my options I
began to realize I didn't want to leave. I knew I would never be
this close to Doc again. This might be my last shot, and I had
to figure out some way to take him before he took me. If he
had anyone else with him, he could easily outflank me, but
who would obey his order to go out into the field now, after
seeing what he had done to Hell Knuckles?

All these questions were zipping around in my hungover
brain when I heard a motorcycle fire up on the other side of
the building. My impulse was to charge the building to try to
catch him before he got away, or at least to throw a few shots
at him, but I didn't get through thirteen months in the jungles
of Southeast Asia and twenty years of police work in Manhattan and Brooklyn by acting on impulses like that. The bike
took off with the throttle laid open in a high-pitched whine.
After a few moments of receding whine, the woods quieted
again and returned to bird noises. I looked at my watch and

made myself wait ten minutes before I loped in a running crouch down the slope toward the swamp.

I took a careful fifteen minutes to circle uphill around the camp, keeping to cover and expecting a potshot every time I moved my position. There was a motorcycle lying on its side in the sandy parking lot, and the front door was ajar but not enough to see into the dark interior. I scanned the windows carefully and then took a deep breath and sprinted across the sunlit white sand.

When I got inside I found the Thompson M-1 from Doc's Linwood attic beneath the window I had shot out. It was obviously what had been used to finish off Hell Knuckles. I didn't touch it or anything else once I got inside except to kick some doors open to make sure I was alone. I didn't want the cops to find my prints on the M-1 when there was already a slug from my .25 in the body outside.

You could have missed the drug lab if you'd never seen one before. I had been in much more elaborate ones in Alphabet City apartments on the Lower East Side of Manhattan. This one consisted of two ten-cup Pyrex measuring beakers plus some saucepans and mixing bowls just like the ones grandma used for mixing the biscuits. There was also a small pill press and some gallon wine jugs with adhesive tape labels marked with names like "Juice" and "Stuff." In one of the pantry closets I found a stack of blotters wrapped in plastic and a heavy-duty manual paper cutter. The whole setup wasn't much more elaborate than a rig to make home-brewed beer. Two of the jugs were labeled P/P, otherwise I might have missed the whole thing. P/P had to be short for phenylacetone, or P2P, the necessary ingredient for concocting methamphetamine, the poor man's cocaine. What I had found was a cute little acid and speed kitchen that could turn out dope for the maker and his friends, but was far from a high-capacity chemical plant that could supply the greater Philly area and the Jersey Shore.

Once I was sure no one else was in the building, I went out the back door and walked across the clearing and squatted beside the body of Hell Knuckles. Why had he been killed? He obviously knew something Doc wanted to silence, but what? I didn't want to touch him, but my curiosity got the best of me and I turned his left hand over to see what was on the other set of knuckles. M-O-M was scratched across his index, middle and ring fingers. The pinky had an arrow-pierced heart on it. The motorcycle out front was the white Police Special. I had thoughts about riding it out to a phone, but the spark plug was smashed and the gas line cut. I went back inside and stripped one of the bunks and brought the blankets out to cover the body until someone got back here.

It took me a long time to walk out. I got turned around a couple of times, but after dark I oriented myself by the pink haze above Philly to the west. The fact that there was no moon made it impossible to see anything at ground level except the vague ribbons of white sand that ran this way and that. I recognized Forest City when I plodded through it, but I couldn't see the foundations and could only sense the clearings on either side of the road. I don't know how people in the Pines got around before electric lights. I guess they just stayed home at night. The clear night sky, on the other hand, was very busy with air traffic coming and going from Philly and New York, moving lights and vague roars up in the stars above the ground-level blackness. The Jersey Devil was afoot for sure. I hoped to see him. Being an ancestor of mine, maybe he would give me a piggyback ride to the nearest telephone. But he never showed up.

Two Pineys in a pickup who were out drinking beer and jacking deer stopped for me when I got out to 563. They dropped me at a Wawa store a little before ten o'clock. Wawa is where it's at after dark in the Pines, a beacon in the lonely night. There were two cars in the parking lot, a green Pinto and a Columbia Township patrol car. Inside I found Patrolman Richards drinking a Pepsi and talking to the night clerk, a freckled-faced redhead who looked too young for the gold wedding band she wore. That saved me a quarter calling the shooting in, and Richards soon had us back at the hunting club. It was even more of an adventure riding with him on the sand roads after dark. I was showing him the body of Hell Knuckles when Sergeant McKelvey arrived. I walked them both through the site, and then when the forensic crew arrived and McKelvey was busy with them, Richards and I drove down to my car and towed it out of the soft sand. When we got back, I gave a statement to a county detective named Battaglia while we waited for the county medical examiner who was apparently lost somewhere out in the sand maze like I had been. I wanted to leave but McKelvey asked me to stick around. The rifle was wiped clean, and I think he thought I had wiped it, because I could see him looking for a reaction when he told me about it. I wasn't being arrested or detained, he told me. He just wanted me around when he thought of what he wanted to ask me. I was bushed from my long walk, but I stayed and catnapped on the front seat of the Honda. There was a little breeze to keep the mosquitoes away, and around midnight it got chilly enough to roll up the windows.

It was almost three A.M. when they finally let me go, and when I got home, the Baron was on my machine. He had been arrested that afternoon by the Atlantic County prosecutor's office for the shooting death of Rocky. It annoyed me that nobody had told me that when we were out at the hunting camp, and it also told me that they were still trying to figure me into the equation somehow.

I reached the Baron on his car phone. He was on his way home. "If you killed him, don't tell me," he said. "But if you did, I love you, baby. And the world is a better place with that motherfucker out of it. And I owe you. Now get me out of this. Irene and the kids need me."

It was a bullshit arrest, and I think everybody involved knew it. The county had no evidence to build a case on, only the Baron's continuing threats of revenge against Rocky. Bail had been set low because the judge didn't think much of the arrest either, and the Baron's lawyer had gotten it lowered even further and sprung him. Barbay was angry about the arrest, although still happy as hell that Rocky was dead.

I spent most of the next day, Thursday, with state and county investigators and Sergeant McKelvey. I had been trying to get the law interested in Bonnie's death for two weeks, even if it was just on a negligent homicide charge. Now they were tripping over each other to investigate Rocky's death instead.

They were much more interested in proving that Winston Barbay killed Rocky because that was premeditated and therefore Murder One.

In mid-morning, after another round of questioning in McKelvey's office, I had led county detectives and state and local police to the Linwood house, and that seemed to divert them from their case against the Baron. They spent four hours going over the house, hauling out all the guns, padlocking the doors and sealing the place off with yellow tape. I had some slim hope that they would find the gun that killed Rocky, and that find would get the Baron off the hook, but there was no .45 among the weapons they brought out. I had the only .45 in the crowd that day strapped under my left arm, and when McKelvey showed me the handguns they had confiscated, I caught him looking at the bulge in my sport coat the way a schoolboy looks at the bulges in his teacher's sweater. That gun was still with Doc or he had ditched it somewhere, maybe when he shot Rocky.

There were local reporters and a camera crew from Channel 6 in Philadelphia outside when the police finished. One of the detectives from county, a guy named Bolan, who seemed to be in charge of the investigation, gave a little statement about looking for Stockton because they thought he could provide information about the killing at his hunting club and also about the body found near Batsto on Monday. He didn't say Doc was a suspect, but he didn't have to. Connecting those two killings for the press made a sensational story. All the elements were there. The biker, lawyer, community leader and drug merchant now wanted for murder. The might of the media was now unleashed on Doc.

This case was closed for me. I could put Bonnie in the sequence even if they didn't want to right now. They soon would. My individual capacity for manhunts was limited to the range of the Honda and a lot of luck. The police had now captured and sealed off both of Stockton's bases of operations, his home and his club, initiated an intensive search for him and given a story to the press that would be in every daily newspaper on the East Coast on Friday and on most television stations by eleven P.M. It was time for me to go back to my insurance work.

When I got home in mid-afternoon, Julie was on my answering machine three times, the Baron twice and Thelma once. I got Thelma's machine when I returned her call, and the Baron's too. McKelvey's educated guess had been that the charges against him would be dropped by the weekend. I told his machine that and hung up.

Julie answered on the first ring. She was furious that I had let the police in with the key she had given me. I explained to her that they had a warrant, and that if I hadn't unlocked the door, they would have kicked it down. She had been visited for an extensive interview by two county investigators. She said she was frightened. She didn't want to have anything to do with her father and repeated a statement I had heard her make many times that she wasn't responsible for his actions. She said she was afraid he would come to her for help. I pointed out that some of the rumors had her father making as much as four or five hundred thousand dollars on his drug schemes, and that if they were even partially true, he would hardly need her help. I was starting to have my doubts about the magnitude of his operation though after seeing his pathetic little pharmaceutical plant in the Pines, but I didn't tell her that. She asked me to ride over and stay with her, but I told her I was going to New York. Doc wouldn't come near her now anyway. He had been around the law long enough, and on both sides, to know that all kinds of cops would be watching his daughter's movements now, waiting for him to turn up. She said that didn't make her feel much better, because cops were just bikers who got paid for it, and then she slammed the phone down. I dropped the dog off at the Sooys' and headed north on 206.

25

By early evening I was sitting at the bar in the River Cafe sipping a big wide Tanqueray martini and watching the light show across the river in Lower Manhattan. The River Cafe is an elegant restaurant on a barge anchored on the Brooklyn side of the East River between Pier One and the massive stone columns of the Brooklyn Bridge. A red sunset was dying behind the skyscrapers of Wall Street. The office lights were getting brighter and beginning to join the festive lights of the South Street Seaport in casting their reflections on the dark water of the river. The air was pleasantly warm, and most of the tables outside on the deck were full. A red tugboat pushed a barge filled with gray sludge down river, scattering the lights on the water like a shower of sparks. A moment later a party boat passed headed north under the Brooklyn Bridge with maybe sixty or seventy well-dressed people leaning against the starboard railings holding drinks in their hands. A lot of them waved to the people on the deck of the River Cafe, but no one out there waved back.

The flash of Cynthia Arnold's long legs caught my eye in the bar mirror. I turned to see her striding down the ramp onto the barge and getting a lot of attention from the maître d'. I had called her when I got to the city, and she had agreed to meet me for drinks. Ben was going to join us later for dinner. She wore a dark blue double-breasted suit without lapels and a white silk blouse whose ruffled décolletage only hinted at the swelling beneath it. The clothes were simple. It was the woman wearing them who attracted the attention. Beyond her the doorman and the parking valets followed her progress with interest and admiration. The cocktail-hour crowd of mostly men parted for her, and when she reached me I realized I had forgotten how tall she was. I stood and we shook hands, and when she leaned over to graze my cheek with hers, our shoulders were almost level.

"How nice to see you again," she said, meeting my eyes with a steady curious gaze.

"Would you like to sit outside?" I asked.

"This is fine," she said, sliding up on my bar stool and riveting the attention of both men working behind the bar.

"What a wonderful view," she said. "I don't get here often enough. And I only live just up the hill."

A Hatteras Motor Yacht cruised silently by, heading upriver, eighty or ninety feet of teak and brass and gleaming white on the dark water. An elderly couple sat on the afterdeck under bright hurricane lanterns looking up at the Brooklyn Bridge looming high above them. There were a lot of places this luxury pleasure boat would have looked out of place, but not here. Nothing looked out of place in New York.

The closer bartender had put a napkin on the bar in front of Cynthia, and both men were waiting for her request even though there were several customers along the bar who were impatient to have their drinks replenished.

"White wine spritzer," she said. The closer bartender dove for a glass, and the room relaxed again and went about its business.

"You look tired, Con," she said, turning to me.

"I went to bed late and got up early," I said.

"But compared to the first time I saw you, almost anything would be an improvement." She laughed. I laughed too.

"No black eye this time," I said.

"No junkie glint in there either. Ben was so sure you were one of the drug addicts. I dearly love the man, but he tends to see everything as a conspiracy. Like that little man who's running for president."

"Perot?"

"Yes. Maybe that's how they both got so rich."

I drained my martini, and gave the glass to the bartender

for a refill as he put Cynthia's pale spritzer in front of her.

"I do have a couple of sore ribs this time," I said. "I got them from the same guy. Bonnie's old boyfriend."

"Did you catch him this time?"

"He's dead," I said.

"Did you kill him?" She frowned but managed to look at me expectantly at the same time.

"I wanted to," I said. "But I didn't."

The bar had continued to fill up until people were now standing three-deep. I left out my relations with Julie as I recounted the details of my investigation to Cynthia. I don't know why. Well, actually I do know why. In my scheme of things, Cynthia was semi-eligible. She was big and sexy and flirty, and I liked to be with her and hoped to be again. Not in bed. She had a husband for that. But maybe dinner or drinks again the next time I was in the city. And somehow I sensed that if I told her I was having an obsessive affair with the twenty-six-year-old daughter of the man who seemed to be ultimately responsible for Bonnie's death, her opinion of me might be a little tarnished.

The Arnolds had arrived back in New York just the night before from a week in Switzerland, Cynthia told me. Ben had business in Europe and then she had joined him and they had managed to get in some spring skiing. She told me that Ben Jr. and Dan Pickering had left before Memorial Day for the Arnold summer house on the coast of Maine, but that Ben Jr. had been taken ill shortly after they arrived. He was now in a hospital in Portland and not expected to come out alive. She and Ben had cut their stay in Switzerland short and would be flying to Maine late Friday night. While we were on that sad note, one of the bartenders came over to Cynthia and asked if she was Mrs. Arnold. She nodded that she was, and he put a telephone in front of her and plugged it in under the bar.

"How did you know I was Mrs. Arnold?" she asked him as he handed her the receiver.

"He described you," he said, nodding toward the phone and then meeting her stare.

She flashed him a smile. I love women who know how to

take compliments about their looks. Even if it's a slightly lech-
erous one.

She intoned a series of yeses into the phone, then said:
"That's too bad" and, after a pause: "I'll tell him," and hung
up the phone.

"Ben's stuck in a meeting," she said. "He wants us to eat
and he'll try to catch up with us later on."

"With Bonnie gone, you'll become Ben's heir when Ben Jr.
dies, won't you?" I blurted it out. It was a question I had
intended to ask Ben, but now he might not come.

She stared at me for a minute. Then she said: "Do you
want to continue in that vein here at the bar, or do you want
to get a table and discuss it over dinner?"

I tossed a twenty on the bar, but the bartender didn't move
a muscle, and that made me look at the tab. I fished out
another twenty and put it on top of the first one and turned
and motioned to the maître d'. Although there were a lot of
people outside on the deck, the dining room was still only
about half full. Cynthia asked for a window table and got it.
When he had seated us, I held a ten out and he made it disappear and did a little bow, looked down Cynthia's blouse and
left.

We ordered more drinks. She switched to Pellegrino water
and I had a third martini. We smiled at each other and
admired the view until our waiter had put the drinks down
and left. Then Cynthia said: "If I'm a suspect, I hope it's on the
long list, not the short one."

"I'm sorry for being so tactless," I said. "When there's a
murder . . . and when people gain from it, sometimes you can't
help but wonder at their good fortune."

"Would it make you feel any better about me if I told you
that I really do love Ben?"

"I feel fine about you already."

"Even if I stand to become a multimillionairess when Ben
dies?"

"It depends on how soon he dies."

She let out a short burst of laughter and then turned suddenly serious and said: "The problem with a May-December
marriage in other people's eyes is that May always seems to

have some motive that is detrimental to December's health."
This time I laughed, and she continued: "Yes, I will inherit
Ben's money if I outlive his son, which seems pretty likely. Or
rather I'll share it with Williams College. But there's enough
for both of us. Or at least I know there's more than enough for
me. And yes, I'll get the house. So you can see that this job certainly pays better than hospital work. When I was a nurse, I
took care of a lot of people I didn't know and I just barely met
my bills and obligations each month, and now I have only one
patient, a slightly irritable older man who also happens to be
very, very rich. And the pay is so much better. And I happen to
love him too. But don't get me started on definitions of love."

She smiled a sweet but sarcastic smile. "I've even figured it
out," she said. "If Ben lives to be ninety, it will come out to
about eighty-five dollars an hour. And that's on a twenty-four-
hour, seven-days-a-week basis. I'll be fifty-five and raring to
go. Don't forget to leave me your phone number. You'll probably need a nurse by then yourself."

We both laughed, and I said: "If it's any comfort, you were
never a suspect. It's only a matter of time before the police
turn up Julie's father and nail him for the murder of his partner. When that happens we'll probably get the details of what
happened to Bonnie."

She took a sip of her water and began to look over her
menu.

"That's the second time I've seen a little dark cloud cross
your eyes when I mentioned Julie," I said.

"You're very observant," she said. "Let's order. Let's get a
bottle of wine too."

She ordered grilled swordfish. I liked the sound of it, so I
ordered it too and then suggested we start with chilled oysters.
She picked a bottle of Chablis, and when the waiter left, she
looked up and said: "Now you're going to ask me about
Juliana."

"You're observant too," I said. It was odd to hear Julie's
full name used.

"She seems to be a lovely woman," she said. "But I had
the sense that she was never very good for Bonnie."

"I had a chat with your housekeeper this afternoon. She

said something like that too." The Arnold house had been my first stop when I arrived in New York.

"Ben told me on the phone just now that you had talked with her."

"Didn't she tell you?"

"She reports to Ben."

"I hope I didn't get her in trouble."

"You can't. She's a fixture. Blind loyalty to Ben. Just the kind he needs. The Scots are like that."

The wine arrived and then the oysters. I let Cynthia do the wine tasting. She approved and the waiter poured us each a glass.

"Aren't you loyal too?" I asked.

"Believe it or not, I am. But not blindly loyal. If Ben screws up, I don't accept it. With Peg, he can do no wrong."

"She said Bonnie—she called her 'poor Bonnie'—she said she was a follower and that a portion of her was empty and she was always looking for someone or something to fill it up."

"I'd say that was a fairly accurate appraisal. She'd been with Bonnie from birth. What else did she tell you?"

"Not much more. She clammed up like she was keeping some dark family secret."

"She was."

"What secret was that?"

"Con, Bonnie is . . . " She hesitated and looked out the window and bit her lower lip. It was night in the city now. "Bonnie was . . . an incest survivor."

The term threw me a little bit. I had never heard it before. It sounded like support group jargon. I knew survivors of Vietnamese prison camps, Holocaust survivors, cancer survivors. It was a serious word. *Survivor.* Incest survivor. My mind raced to recall any brothers, male cousins. Cynthia anticipated my next question.

"Her father," she said. After a pause she added: "It's quite often an adjunct to alcoholic or addictive behavior. That plus physical and verbal abuse." She kept her eyes on the wine glass that she had half-raised to her lips. When she sipped the wine, her eyes met mine looking for my reaction. I put my glass

down. I didn't want to drink any more or eat my oysters. I
wasn't sick; I just didn't want anything more.

"I don't know how to react to things like that," I finally
said.

"Most people don't."

"How old was she?"

"It's not really important."

"Could he have infected her with AIDS?"

"None of her tests were ever positive. But it was a concern. A worry. I think that worry fed her drug addiction. Like
her guilt did."

"And what does this have to do with Julie?" I asked.

She looked back into her wine glass. "They knew each
other from a group," she said.

"Julie wasn't involved in AA or NA. She hardly even
drinks."

She met my eyes again. "It was a survivors' group. Incest
survivors."

Now it was my turn to watch my wine.

"You mustn't think less of Juliana," she said.

"Why not? You do."

"I don't think she was a good influence on Bonnie, no. It
was difficult to be around Bonnie and not take advantage of
her. Bonnie was a classic victim. She worked at it. Subcon-
sciously she wanted people to hurt her. Then she didn't have to
feel her own pain. Or be responsible for it."

"You sound more like a shrink than a nurse."

"If I ever go back to work in a hospital, it won't be as a
nurse. I'm studying clinical psychology at NYU. I'll have a
master's degree by December. Are you sleeping with Juliana?"

"That's not for publication," I said. "Does Mrs. Abraham
know about Bonnie and her father?"

"Of course. Bonnie brought it to Peg first when she was
fourteen. But Peg would never tell you. She doesn't even know
that I know. Her advice to Bonnie was to kill him."

"Who? Ben Junior?"

"Yes. Fortunately, Bonnie then told Ben, and he inter-
vened."

"When you finished talking to Ben, you said: 'I'll tell him.' Is that what you were supposed to tell me?"

"Yes."

"And how do you feel about it?"

"Julie brought Bonnie into that circle."

"She encouraged her to go to NA meetings."

"That was the good part. The bad part was that she met Rocky at those meetings. She began a relationship with him too early in her recovery. She was still too vulnerable. If Juliana's father is directly or even indirectly responsible for Bonnie's death, then Juliana bears that responsibility too."

"Blood for blood," I said.

"My mother was Italian," she said as our grilled swordfish arrived.

Ben Arnold never made it to the River Cafe. I walked Cynthia up the hill to Columbia Heights and gave her a sisterly kiss on the cheek at the foot of her stoop at about ten-thirty. I walked to my basement apartment from there, detouring down to the promenade from Pierrepont Park to Remsen Street. Most of the office lights across the river were out by this time, but the view across the harbor of the island of Manhattan was still breathtaking. When I got home, there was a message from Ben apologizing for missing our dinner and telling me to meet him in his office at eight the next morning.

26

Ben Arnold's investment firm, Arnold, Kuhn, Fertig and Bradshaw, occupied the thirty-third through the thirty-sixth floors of a building just off Madison Avenue in the low fifties. Ben's office, along with Mr. Fertig's, was on the thirty-sixth floor, which was as far as the elevators went. I didn't see any separate listings for Messrs. Kuhn and Bradshaw.

Riding up, I glanced at my watch and noticed that not only was I punctual for the appointment, but that I was five minutes early. On the way home from dinner I had avoided walking by Clark Street Station and the gin mills on Montague Street. I had told myself that I deserved a nightcap, but I was dog tired from two days of police questioning and the drive to the city, so I passed it up. I had consumed the lion's share of the Chablis anyway, and the walk home felt like it was all uphill. I slept like a baby in my basement apartment that night.

The receptionist was already at her desk when I stepped off the elevator. She looked to be about my age, her dark hair pulled into a bun. Huge glasses and minimal make-up didn't quite obscure her trim good looks. She wore an expensive gray suit with padded shoulders. There were leather couches and leather-topped coffee and end tables. The magazines were expensive ones about architecture, business and yachting, and the paintings on the wall were French and American Impressionists and real. A bronze Degas dancer stood on a plain round pedestal between two of the couches, highlighted by a single spot from the ceiling. There were two mahogany doors, one on the left wall and one on the right.

"Good morning, Mr. Leeds," she said. "Mr. Arnold will be ready for you in a moment."

"Aren't you the early bird," I said to her.

"I'm here at seven each weekday morning," she said.

"Blind loyalty, no doubt," I said, thinking of Mrs. Abraham.

She looked up at me and smiled very sweetly. "Huge salary, outrageous benefits," she said.

A tiny red light began to flash on the panel of her telephone instrument.

"Mr. Arnold is in there," she said, nodding toward the door on my right. "He'll see you now."

At first I couldn't find Ben Arnold when I stepped into his office. The room was massive, large enough to house a light manufacturing industry or a roller-skating rink. The east and south walls were lined with tall windows that provided a panoramic view of the lower half of Manhattan all the way to Wall Street and enough of Queens and Brooklyn across the river to see how they formed the western tip of Long Island. I finally located Ben standing in front of a large fireplace with a carved marble mantle. We shook hands and then sat in leather chairs on either side of the fireplace.

"Thanks for coming so early," he said. "I'm trying to get some tasks out of the way so I can leave for Maine. Cynthia said she told you about my son."

I only nodded. I wasn't sure what he meant that Cynthia had told me. He sensed my confusion and added: "His doctor says he's dying. Sad commentary on my life that I have things to do before I can get away for that event, isn't it? Outliving a child is one of life's worst tragedies. Unfortunately, he had to experience that too with his own child."

I knew right then that we weren't going to be talking about incest. I didn't want to anyway.

His hand went inside the lapel of his suit coat and came out with an envelope that he handed to me. I cracked it enough to see that there were hundred-dollar bills inside, maybe twenty-five or thirty of them.

"What's this for?" I asked. I didn't try to refuse it.

"The fact that you continued the investigation of Bonnie's

death without remuneration has not gone unnoticed, Mr. Leeds. I'm sure you understand that I couldn't have you telling people that you were working for me in any way. In any retributive sense that is."

"Don't worry, I would have denied it. You fooled me too." I laughed briefly to tip him that I was joking. He turned the corners of his mouth down slightly to let me know that he still disapproved of my sarcasm.

"You've done an excellent job, nevertheless," he said. After he handed me the envelope, he had folded his hands in his lap and they remained there, unmoving, a sign of his calmness and total control. For a moment I wondered if he thought I had shot Rocky, but finally I realized that he didn't care. I had been on Rocky's case, hounding him and shaking him loose. Rocky was now dead. He didn't want to hear any more. But I had more I wanted to say.

"Please understand that I didn't come here to ask for money," I said. He waved his hand, a signal that what I said was unnecessary, but I continued: "I came here to tell you that I'm finished with this case and that I'm satisfied with it. I don't have the resources, or want them, to trail Raymond Stockton around the hemisphere. I don't have all the explanations but I think I have a good idea what happened to Bonnie. And I think Stockton is ultimately responsible."

"Raymond Stockton is Juliana Stockton's father?"

"Yes. I don't know if she is implicated in any way, either by commission or omission."

"Why don't you let the police handle it from here?" He couched it as a question, but I knew it was an order. Nobody ever hands you money without wanting something for it.

"The police aren't much interested in Bonnie's death," I said.

"That's just as well," he said. "I've wanted it that way, and it has worked out for the best. Publicity, especially the adverse sort, can be devastating in my business."

"A friend of mine has been accused of killing Bonnie's boyfriend. And I'm not sure the police aren't trying to tie me into it too."

"That's the electrical contractor?"

"What electrical contractor?"

He reached inside his coat again and this time extracted a wallet-sized electronic notebook, opened the hinged cover and used his index finger to punch up information.

"Walter Barber, Escort Electric, Pleasantville," he read.

I knew he was talking about the Baron, but his information confused me.

"I think his name is Barbay," I said.

"Perhaps," he said. "My information is from the police report. Spelling has never been a strong law enforcement skill."

"Could I see the report?"

"Certainly," he said. He apparently gave some signal to the receptionist that I didn't see, because she appeared at the door.

"Please bring a copy of the fax that came yesterday concerning my granddaughter," he said.

We waited for it silently. She came right back and handed him some copied pages, maybe six or seven. He looked them over briefly while I watched her depart. I noticed she wasn't wearing a wedding ring. She had great legs.

When he handed me the pages, I saw that they were copies of the arrest report by one of the county investigators. It didn't much matter to me what kind of information the Baron had given them, but I was surprised to see that there was no yellow sheet attached to it. Maybe they had run his record later and didn't bother to send it along. I was going to see Conlin in the afternoon, and I would get him to run it.

I scanned the sheets. They called him Walter Barber all right. I memorized his social security number. The address for his house in Pleasantville was correct. I handed the report back to him. He got up and walked to his desk, a giant slab of marble with nothing on it but a phone and the sunlight that streamed through the eastern windows. He put the report on it and stood silhouetted by the windows.

"My recollection is that this man Barber's wife was helping Bonnie in her narcotics recovery program," he said thoughtfully.

"That's correct," I said. "Her name is Irene."

"Is there any reason to believe that he had anything to do with the people who caused Bonnie's death?"

"No."

"Cynthia thought he might need some help with his defense."

"It won't go that far," I said. "The charges should be dropped by early next week. They have no case at all; no weapon and nothing to tie him to Rocky except his threats of revenge. It would help if somebody, myself included, could turn up the real murderer, or the weapon. It was a gun, a forty-five."

"The real murderer, in your opinion, is the same man you mentioned before."

"Stockton."

"Yes. Raymond Stockton."

He pulled a pen from his shirt pocket and noted the name on his report and looked up at me.

"I have a very blunt question to ask you," he said. "In retrospect, I'm sure you'll understand the reason for it. And I hope you won't be too offended by it now."

"Fire away," I said. It was difficult for him to apologize, and I wasn't sure that was what he had just done.

"Were you intimate with my granddaughter?"

"You mean sexually?" I asked. I knew what he meant, but I wanted him to say it. We held eye contact. His nostrils flared.

He nodded. It was a tense moment.

"No," I said.

"Did she ask you to?"

"To sleep with her?"

"Yes."

"Never," I lied, knowing there wasn't anyone alive who would contradict me.

He turned to look out at the sunny cityscape below him, and I could see the lines of sadness in his face. As if anticipating my thoughts, he said: "Bonnie's death has been very difficult for me. My son will be dead before the summer is over. It all seems so hopeless. All this . . . " He swung his arms to include the room and the view. In doing so, he turned his back on me, and I saw his shoulders twitch. I stood up. The interview was over.

27

I took the F train back to Brooklyn. On the way to Manhattan it had been crowded with rush-hour commuters, but now I had a seat and could notice how much cleaner and less threatening the subway seemed from the way I remembered it. I bought all three New York daily papers at an underground kiosk, but only the *Post* had any mention of the case. A single half-page column on page eight was headed: "South Jersey Politico Sought in Killings." It was an inaccurate story about the shooting at the hunting club and mentioned Rocky's killing only very briefly at the end.

I called McKelvey when I got to the apartment. His dispatcher said he was on another phone call and asked me if I wanted to hold. I said no and hung up. Let Columbia Township pay for the call. It had been too late for me to call him when I got home from dinner with Cynthia. He hadn't really wanted me to leave, but when I insisted, he had asked me to check in with him each day that I was out of town.

I was looking through the *Daily News* a second time to make sure I hadn't missed the story when he called back.

"The New York papers make it sound like you can't tie Rocky's killing to Doc," I said to him. I didn't tell him it was just the *Post*. I figured he'd be flattered.

"You should know better than to believe what you read in the newspapers," he said. "You were a cop. Newspapers are the same size every day, regardless of how much news there is. If they don't have enough news, they make it up. If they have too much, they leave some out."

"Have the charges against Barbay been dropped?"

"Barber," he corrected.

"What's this Barber crap? That's the second time I heard that."

"That's his name. I thought he was your friend."

"He is."

"His name is Barber, in case he didn't tell you."

"And the charges?"

"They'll stand until we come up with something better."

"The hell they will. You know you don't have a case. His lawyer's going to the NAACP and the Feds if you don't leave him alone."

"Come on, Con. This is South Jersey, not New York. We don't have a lot of police brutality or civil rights suits down here."

"Yeah, the men are men, and the women are proud of it. Especially if they're white."

"I'd watch that kind of talk around the county boys if I were you. That's just a friendly warning. They're dying to bring you into this too."

"How do I fit in?"

"They think you might have put those forty-fives into Rocky. They were here checking your permits yesterday."

"I told you I'd be glad to bring that gun in for a ballistic test."

"You might have to. You don't have a nine millimeter laying around anywhere, do you? Don't answer that, because if you do, it should be registered here and it isn't. I know you don't, but just in case you do, I'd lose it real quick."

"What else?"

"You mean besides the fact that they don't like New Yorkers?"

"Nobody likes New Yorkers."

"They don't like my report about how that slug got through your door and into your bookcase."

"What's that mean?"

"Well, the good news is that they probably will come out and pay you a visit."

"And the bad news?"

"They may already be doing it."

"You mean they could get a warrant to go through my house?"

"Wouldn't be hard, since one of the decedents fired a shot at you. Not that they always go through channels. After all, you are two hours away right now. Did you always have a warrant when you went through a door up in New York?"

"If I had a good case and I wanted the evidence to stand, the answer is yes. If I was fishing, that's when I had the occasional unauthorized peek. What are they looking for?"

"You could have killed Rocky that night he put you in the hospital. You obviously had a disagreement."

"Is that what they think?"

"They don't like your version on either of these killings."

"Do they have better ones?"

"Sometimes an investigation is like putting out a newspaper. You fill it up if it's empty."

"Why are you telling me all this?"

"I'm the closest thing you've got to a friend down here right now, Con. Maybe you'll have a chance to turn something up while you're in New York. You should work real hard at it while you're up there."

"What about Philly? Did anyone ever connect there?"

"Lots of dead ends there. There was supposed to be a drug deal and a rip-off but nobody seems to know anything about it. The state police talked to some bikers who said Stockton was basically a small-time player, an asshole, a confused junkie. One day he was trying to buy eighty thousand dollars worth of cocaine and the next day he wanted to sell home-made speed and acid. Nobody took him very seriously. He was doped up most of the time. If the trail goes anywhere, it goes to New York. Rocky had connections up there."

"I know. I still have to get in touch with his girlfriend."

"Bernadette?"

"Loretta."

"I was hoping to hear from her, but I wasn't holding my breath. What are you waiting for?"

"I'm not crazy about having to give her the good news. The baby she's about to have doesn't have a daddy anymore."

"Sometimes no daddy at all is better than the daddy you get."

"You got that right."

"Can I ask you a personal question, Con?"

"Sure. You may not get an answer, but go ahead."

"Are you an alcoholic? Or a drug addict? I don't mean a lush or a junkie. I mean someone who goes to those meetings."

"No. Why?"

"The county boys make you with that crowd."

"When I was looking for the girl—"

"Bonnie? The one who bought it in New York?"

"You have a good memory. When I was looking for her, I bumped into some of those people. Alkies, drug fiends. They call themselves things like that. Barbay and his wife belong."

"Barber."

"How come you're not doing this investigation, Jim? You seem so interested, and you seem to be on the right line."

"I've got my sixty square miles of Columbia Township to worry about, Con. Those killings happened here, so I stay in touch with the cases, but when they get out of county or out of state, I go back to my tool thefts and DWIs. We had a tractor vanish the other day. With the disk harrow still attached. Quite a mystery, let me tell you. And I was able to put a lid on it. Turned out the owner's brother-in-law had borrowed it, sort of permanently, because he owed him money. That kind of thing. That's what I do."

"It's a nasty job, but somebody's got to do it."

"That's the idea. Now those county boys, they're a cut above that kind of work. They got a fancy crime lab and a prosecutor on their ass all the time, and they don't like any retired cops from New York City nosing around in their space, telling them how to do their job."

"Somebody's got to do that one too."

"That's not how they see it."

"How's that?"

"You really want to know?"

"I'm not sensitive. I just look like I am."

"They say that if you were any good, you'd still be on the job."

"Ouch."

"There's more."

"What's that?"

"One of them. One of these guys with eyes the color of ice that nobody has ever seen smile. The kind of cop who brings in a high percentage of his suspects in rubber bags. He wanted to know what ribs the bikers busted."

"Why? So he could bust the other side?"

"No. So he could bust the same ones again."

"I can't wait to meet him."

I read the *New York Times* and then walked up to Court Street and ate hummus and a plate of stuffed grape leaves from the lunch menu at a Yemen restaurant. The owner was a neighbor of mine on Warren Street. He came out of the kitchen to say hello, and after the meal, he brought me a cup of thick, sweet Arabic coffee.

After I ate, I strolled south on Court Street into Carroll Gardens. I had an appointment to see Conlin at his station house when he came on at four o'clock, so I had a couple of hours to kill. There was a "Be Right Back" sign hanging in the glass panel of the door at what had now become Mola Bus Charters and Travel Agency—Tax Returns Prepared, *Se Habla Español*. I was hoping I wouldn't find Loretta. Then I wouldn't have to give her the bad news about Rocky face to face. I could call her and say I walked down to see her but she wasn't in. I stopped in a little bakery and had a cup of cappuccino and three pignoli cookies and came out of the place wired from all the strong coffee I had been drinking. New York is an eater's paradise. I never have to watch my weight in the Pines, but the minute I get out of the car in Brooklyn, I can feel the pounds start to mount up. Loretta was inside typing a letter when I came back past the agency. She was a very slow typist and had to concentrate on her hunt-and-peck style. She didn't look up until I got to her desk, but when she did, she jumped up and gave me a big hug, as much as was possible with her giant hard stomach between us.

"You owe me dinner," she said.

"I do?"

"The last time I saw you, you said we'd have dinner the next time you came to New York."

"I remember a lunch promise. But I don't remember owing it to you."

"Whatever you say. How about tonight? It might be the last chance I'll get to go out before I have the baby."

There is something exquisite on the face of a pregnant woman. A contented introspection. They seem to be pleased as hell with what is going on inside themselves. They glow. I thought about not telling her about Rocky. I had done a lot of death notification as a cop. You never get used to it or find an easy way to do it. And you always debate with yourself about how you can get out of doing it.

"You'd better sit down," I said, backing away from her arms.

"Oh, shit," she said. Her mouth stayed open and she felt behind herself for her chair without taking her eyes off my face. When she was down I told her.

She didn't blubber or shriek. In fact, her expression didn't change at all. But something went out of her eyes. Joy, maybe. Or hope. She stood up and hung her arms around my neck again.

"I'm glad you're here," she said.

"So am I," I said.

I don't know why I had ever wanted to tell her over the telephone. She held on but she kept her eyes on my face. I could see a single tear make its way down each cheek. The phone rang, but she didn't answer it, and when it stopped, she put the answering machine on. We closed the place and put the "Be Right Back" sign in the window again and went to a luncheonette and sat in a booth in the back. It was two-thirty by then, and the place was empty.

I told her everything I knew about Rocky's death. At least everything I thought she should hear. She wanted to know what he looked like when they dug him up, and I told her he looked fine. She told me he had some relatives on Staten Island, and she gave me their names and addresses. I told her I thought Atlantic County still had the body, but I wasn't sure how long they kept them, and that I would put the appropriate county people in touch with the relatives about the body when I got back tomorrow.

She told me two NYPD detectives had paid her a visit the day before yesterday asking questions about Rocky and where he might be. She said she had been angry with me briefly for giving them her name, and I realized Conlin had put them on to her.

The last contact she'd had with Rocky was on the Thursday before Memorial Day weekend. He'd phoned her for the first time in over a week and chatted with her like he'd never left. He needed money and was trying to get her to ask Mr. Russo to loan him a thousand dollars so he could go to Florida. He had told her he had to go dig something that day or move something. She mentioned it because he had always hated physical work, although he didn't consider driving a bus physical work, except he couldn't do that for Mr. Russo right now because there were people looking for him. And she had confirmed that there certainly were.

"So if this drug deal was big like he had said," she asked. "Why did he need money again so soon?"

"He was a drug addict," I said. "They always need money. Or maybe his partner took it all."

"I guess you're right. As much as I wanted him to come back, I was beginning to realize that I was afraid he would."

I walked her back to her agency. The sign was down and the door was open when we got there. She asked me if I wanted to come in and talk to Russo, but I declined. My mind was elsewhere. What had Rocky been digging? Had they cached the money at Constable Bridge? Is that what made Rocky dig his own grave? And, was there any money? There were a lot of different opinions on that last matter, the money.

We stood on the sidewalk in front of the agency, and I heard her making dinner plans for us that evening. I vaguely agreed to pick her up at her apartment at seven-thirty, but when I got back to my house I realized that I hadn't written down her address or telephone number.

I packed quickly and then called the agency. A man

answered with a simple gruff "hello." I assumed it was Russo. When I asked for Loretta, he said she had left for the day.

"Could you give me her home phone number?" I asked.

"I can't do that," he said. "Who is this?"

I told him.

"You're her detective that's looking for Rocky, aren't you?"

I owned that I was.

"You still can't have her number," he said. "She's had a lot of trouble. I don't know you from Adam. You might be part of the trouble. I can call her and have her call you though, if you want."

"I was supposed to have dinner with her tonight," I said. "Just tell her I had to leave for Jersey, and I'll call her when I get a chance."

"That's why she went home early, to get ready to go out with you. She ain't gonna like this."

"Tell her I think I figured out what happened to Rocky," I said and hung up.

At four-thirty I pulled into a Roy Rogers on the New Jersey Turnpike and dialed Conlin's office from a pay phone. I had decided I would get a cellular telephone installed in the Honda when I got back. Ben Arnold's wad of hundreds sitting snugly in my pocket made that decision a lot easier. When I got Conlin on the phone, he was annoyed, but that was his usual state.

"I came to the precinct specially to meet you," he said. "I had some field work to do, and I didn't need to be here until six or so."

"We're meeting right now," I said. "What golf course were you on? Dyker Beach or Marine Park?"

"Marine Park."

I was glad I hadn't gone to his office. I didn't think he had any new information. I just wanted to yell at him. And on the telephone, that was all we could do, yell; not roll on the floor with each other like we might have done if we started our yelling face to face.

"You had Barbay arrested, didn't you?" I asked.

"Who?"

"Winston Barbay."

"The drug counselor and his wife?"

"They're not drug counselors. They're friends."

"You told me they were drug counselors."

"No way."

"It doesn't matter. I talked to someone down there about them too."

"Who? Atlantic County?"

"No, a local guy. Said he knew you."

"McKelvey?"

"That's him."

"Goddammit, Jack. I gave you those names in confidence," I shouted.

A fat guy in baggy shorts walking by the bank of phones gave me a startled look and hurried into the safety of the food line in Roy Rogers.

"I thought I could help him make his case," he said. "He told me they had Barbay tied to a stiff down there. Said it was the guy you were looking for."

"What did you tell him about me?"

"Nothing, Con."

"Nothing," I screamed. "You gave him a fucking report on me." People streaming in from both the north- and southbound parking lots were now all giving me a wide berth.

"I didn't send him any reports on you."

"You answered his questions. That's a report."

"Look, Con. I've got a dead white girl in my precinct. People are still calling me about her. I get dead black people on a daily basis. Lots of them. I hardly ever get more than one or two calls about any of them. And on most of them I don't get any."

"You got a log on those calls?"

"Of course."

"Fax it to me."

"No problem, Con. I'm glad you calmed down. I—"

"You got a yellow sheet on Barbay?"

"No."

"Get one. His name might be Walter Barber and his wife's name is Irene." I gave him the Baron's social security number and my fax number.

There was a pause while he wrote things down, and then he said: "Do you think he killed the girl?"

"No way. He saved her life."

"Did he kill the guinea? That's the one they're trying to pin on him, right?"

"He didn't kill anyone. He's my client. I'm just curious about him."

"Listen, Con. I'm sorry about tying you to something. I had no idea. That guy McKelvey is a slick bastard."

"They like to close all the files down there in South Jersey. They expect nice neat answers for everything."

"Those hicks should all have to work in the city for a month or two. It would do them good. Here, when you close one file, three more open up. I thought you were involved with the girl. It was out of concern for you. Honest to God."

"I told you I wasn't."

"I didn't believe you."

"Did you see the *Post* today?"

"This morning I did. Why?"

"There's an article about another killing down there. The guy was one of the bikers who stomped me. It's inside near the front."

"I'll look it up."

"They say I had a motive for that one."

"I'd say you did too."

"Fuck you. You got anything for me?"

"Like what?"

"Don't get cute, Jack. Like any more of Rocky's movements when he was in New York."

"Yeah, a little. A friend of mine in your old precinct down on the East Side, you don't know him, a detective named Melendez. He said one of his snitches told him Rocky came to the Hell's Angels clubhouse and tried to interest some people in angel dust and speed."

"When was this?"

"I don't know. Maybe a month ago."

I waited for the rest of it. He paused for a moment and then said: "There was a girl in the car. Nobody got a good look at her, but it had to be your Bonnie."

"What happened?"

"Nothing. They told him to go fuck himself. Nobody liked the smell of it at all. They don't need to buy from strangers."

"Anything else?"

"It's a miracle I got that much, Con. This is one thin jacket on this girl. And the case is pretty much closed now anyway."

"Down here they want to get cases off their desk with neat solutions. In the city we just wanted to get the shit off our desks. Any way we could."

"You got that right. There's a lot going on up here. We could always use you back here, Con. You wouldn't be the first retiree to re-up."

"South Jersey needs me, Jack. I got to help keep the fish population down. Thanks for everything."

"Always a pleasure, Con," he said sarcastically. I hung up and got back out on the turnpike with the eighteen-wheelers.

28

Julie reached under the hard lobster membrane with her index and middle fingers and pushed the slippery meat out the end of the tail. Using the tiny two-tine fork, she dipped the long chunk in her glass of drawn butter and lifted it to her mouth. She watched me over the bite, waiting until she had my attention, and then slowly began to suck the snowy meat in past her red lips. Her eyes stared at me, amused and teasing, and when she had half the fat cylinder in her mouth, she bit strongly and precisely, severing the buttered end and chewing it energetically. I used my nutcracker to smash the shell on one of my claws.

We were eating in the Harbor View Restaurant at Trump Castle in the Inlet. There had been a light crowd when we arrived and plenty of tables. The restaurant wraps around half the front of the casino on the second floor so there are mostly window tables with an elevated view of the marina backed by the towers of the Boardwalk casinos and hotels. It was Friday night and the place was filling up fast with players.

Julie was wearing a navy cotton-knit dress that clung to her and turned heads from the moment the parking valet opened the Honda door. A man two tables away stared at her repeatedly while he carried on a distracted conversation with the other three people at his table. She and I were also having a hard time sustaining a conversation. She hadn't wanted to come to a casino or anywhere else in Atlantic City, but when I called her, I told her I had the urge to play blackjack and I would buy her dinner if she would come along. She had been sullen at first because I wouldn't stay and have sex with her before we left her apartment, but a couple of Rob Roys before our lobsters had cheered her up. I was telling her about the Baron, but I had the feeling she was only pretending to listen.

The Baron or Winston Barbay, as I knew him, had been born Walter Barber forty years ago in Atlantic City. The information was all in Conlin's fax, which had been waiting for me when I had arrived at the cottage late in the afternoon. It confirmed the arrest report that I already had. Walter Barber had spent four years in the Navy after high school and had a couple of arrests for assault afterward. He had done six months in Jamesburg for possession of narcotics during the winter of 1977–78. Otherwise he was clean. No dope peddling, no larceny, no prostitutes. I had called the Baron, amused, after I read the sheet. I told him he was under suspicion of being very middle class.

"Well don't tell nobody," he had said. "My reputation down here would be ruined."

"You're an electrician?" I asked.

"I learned it in the service," he said. "Then I got sober in prison. That changed my life."

"You have a contracting business in Absecon."

"I have a partner too. He takes care of the office, and I supervise the field work. We have contracts with four of the casinos and another one with Atlantic City."

"I distinctly remember you telling me that you worked girls out of some motels in Egg Harbor Township."

"I didn't know you very well then. I was just trying to keep up the legend."

"So at night you're really checking for burned out bulbs, even if you're dressed like James Brown at the Palladium."

"Something like that," he said. "I like the action. And the mystique. So do my customers. Who you expect takes care of all those lights anyway? Some honky in a Toyota truck with 'Skip' sewed above the pocket of his overalls?"

"Actually, I never thought about it. But if I did, a man in a pickup would be what came to mind."

Julie laughed at the story. Her interest had perked up when we got to the prostitution part. She had met the Baron once with Bonnie and had been taken in by the stereotype too. We skipped dessert and wandered into the casino. When I asked Julie if she wanted to play, she told me that she would just cheer for me, so when I saw an empty seat at one of the ten-dollar tables, I took it. There were other tables with seats, but that particular one was the one I wanted. It was Grace Somers's table.

Every player was bust, except one Chinese guy, as I slid into my seat. Grace sat with a nine and an eight and dealt the guy a ten. He totaled out at twenty and she paid him and then glared at me as I put two of Ben Arnold's hundred-dollar bills on the table. For a moment, I thought she was going to ask me to leave. She had the right to do that with the approval of her pit boss. She put two stacks of chips in front of me and took the bills. The pit boss had the stubby arms that very short men have. He also had a weight lifter's oversized chest that bulged out the lapels of his suit, and I wondered if he was the guy I had talked to on the phone when I had been looking for Bonnie. Grace wore a white shirt and gold and black brocade vest with tuxedo lapels, the standard for this casino. I was a lot more pleased to see her than she was me. She had a very pretty face even when she was angry. I saw her eyes travel over my shoulder and rest on Julie, and then she began to deal.

She won my two hundred in less than fifteen minutes. She wasn't cheating, but she played against me with a vengeance. At one point, she dealt to a sixteen without asking me. The card was a queen and busted the hand, and several of the players looked at me expecting me to squawk, but I didn't. When the last chip was gone, I put two more hundreds on the table and offered my seat to Julie.

"I don't know how to play," she said. She had just finished a Drambuie on the rocks and was putting it on the waitress's tray and taking a fresh one.

"I'll teach you," I said, putting my hands on her waist and lifting her onto the stool.

Grace glared at me again and put down two more stacks of chips.

Julie learned well and had a lot of beginner's luck. After

half an hour of play, she had about three hundred dollars in front of her. When she finished the second Drambuie, she circled an arm around my neck and whispered in my ear: "I want to go. I'm getting turned on just brushing up against you."

I didn't argue with her. I picked up her chips and separated three of them and moved them forward on the felt as a tip to Grace. She held them out in front of her for the Eye in the Sky and the pit boss to see, and then slipped them into her clear plexiglass tip box. I didn't look back as we walked away, but I could feel her eyes boring into my skull until we got out of the room. Julie clung to me on the sidewalk while we waited for the car, pressing her legs against my hip and swaying slightly so that each of her thighs slid back and forth across the side of mine. The doorman pretended not to notice. She tongued my ear as we drove out Brigantine Boulevard, and at the first red light, pulled my head sideways into a smothering kiss that didn't end until the cars behind me began to honk when the light turned green.

I kept her off me after that, and when we finished the short drive up the island and were sitting outside her condo, I told her that I was going home because I had an early morning helicopter surveillance job. This was just a little lie. I had chartered the helicopter before I left for New York and she knew it, but what she didn't know was that I had canceled the flight by telephone before I left New York that day.

"You could leave from my apartment," she said. "Tomorrow is the first day of my summer dance group in Moorestown, so I have to leave early too. In the afternoon I have to go to Philly and order textbooks. What airport are you flying out of?"

"Pomona," I lied.

"You told me Bader Field before," she said.

"They switched it. If you knew, why did you ask?" I said with an exaggerated snarl. "Don't you believe me?"

"I don't really give a shit," she said, opening the door and getting out. "You're not here tonight anyway. You're too distracted." She leaned back into the car and said: "Do you have something going with that blackjack dealer?"

"No," I lied. "What makes you think that?"

She stared at me levelly for a moment and then said: "Fuck you!" and slammed the car door.

I thought about staking her out and following her the next day, because by now I was pretty sure she knew where Doc was, but I had other fish to fry and she probably did run a dance class and have books to buy tomorrow.

When I got home, there was a message from Grace on the answering machine. She was no longer angry or even puzzled.

"I need to talk to you about the girl you brought to my table tonight," she said. "I'll call again on my ten o'clock break. If I miss you, I'll call you in the morning."

It was 9:35 by the kitchen clock. I took a cold Corona from the refrigerator and turned on the Phillies game.

The phone rang promptly at ten.

"Why haven't you called me?" Grace asked right off the top. I realized it had been premature of me to think she wasn't angry.

"You told me you didn't want to see me," I said.

"That's right," she said. "But I never said I didn't want to talk to you."

"I was going to call soon, but—"

"But you decided to come visit me instead. And bring your blonde friend along and teach her how to play blackjack."

"She wasn't my friend."

"I'm being sarcastic."

"I was afraid of that."

"Do you know who that was?" she asked.

When I didn't answer, she said: "I think it was the same woman who was showing Bonnie's picture around the casino earlier in the month."

"You're sure of that?"

"Fairly positive. Rick said so too. She must have had a wig on then. Her make-up and glasses made her look a lot older, but it's hard to miss that figure. What's going on?"

"I don't have all the pieces yet, but when I do, I'll let you know."

"Will you? Call me, I mean, and let me know."

"I promise."

"How have you been, Con?"

"Busy. How about you?"

"Same old stuff."

"Kids okay?"

"Great."

"I think about you."

"Me too."

"I'm going to run. I have to go back to Atlantic City."

"Tonight? What for?"

"I think I know who busted my head open a few weeks back," I said.

"When? That night we went to your cottage?"

"No, before that. I think it was her, the woman I brought to your table tonight."

"Are you going to find her?"

"No, I'm going to see if I can find a guy who might have seen her at the motel. I'll call you tomorrow."

"Be careful. I'll talk to you then."

Cruising through the dark piney night moments later, I began to sing. It wasn't a conscious choice, the singing. One minute I was noticing the wisps of fog trailing up out of the blackness of Egg Harbor Lake, and the next minute I realized I was belting out "I Just Called to Say I Love You" along with Stevie Wonder coming from WMID-FM in Pleasantville.

It took me less than half an hour to get to Andersen's Bus World. The parking lot was crowded with buses just like it was in the daytime. Atlantic City shimmered in spotlight tones of ruby and beige down across the dark expanse of marshes and waterways. Green laser beams shooting up into the night sky swung back and forth over one of the casinos. The gate bar to the lot was down, and a heavy man with greasy black hair sat in the security booth.

"What can I do for you?" he said. He was eating a sandwich, but he put it down when I pulled up to his window. I could tell I made him nervous. I wondered if he was armed down below the window where I couldn't see his hands.

"I'm looking for the guy who works in this booth during the day."

"Which one? There's four of them."

"Little black guy. Lots of gray hair. Maybe in his late sixties."

"That'd be Gene."

"Gene what?"

"You got a card or something? I'll leave a message for him to call you."

I took out a twenty and folded it in half lengthwise and held it over the edge of my open window.

"I need to get in touch with him tonight," I said. "Can you give me his telephone number?"

"His last name's Cunningham. He doesn't have a telephone."

"Can you tell me where he lives?"

"Sure," he said. He took the twenty and stuffed it in the breast pocket of his uniform jacket. "He lives in the Inlet."

"You got the address?" I asked.

"Of course," he said. "I wouldn't have said I knew where he lives if I didn't. You got another twenty?"

For a moment it seemed like a good idea to get out of the car and rip his throat out, but that probably wouldn't have made him any more inclined to tell me. And besides, he still had that one hand out of sight. I put another twenty up, and he took it with the hand that I could see and told me an address on Tennessee Avenue and then put the gate up so I could turn around in the lot behind the booth.

The address on Tennessee Avenue was easy to find. The building was a rooming house with a big wide porch running around the second floor, up where it could catch the ocean breeze. It had probably never been a very classy Atlantic City address even in the city's heyday, and it was a lot shabbier now. The block consisted of weedy lots, partially vacant buildings and a burned-out shell. I counted only four houses with lights on in the whole block plus a small well-lit grocery store on the corner with a hand-painted sign. A group of young black men stood in front of the store talking animatedly. They all had scarves tied around their heads or baseball caps turned backwards or both. It was a pleasant spring evening but there were no other people on the street. I could see the young men stop talking abruptly when I pulled on the Honda's emergency brake. They stared at me as I crossed the sidewalk and mounted the steps to the porch.

I had to strike a match to see the names on the buzzers. There were twelve buzzers, but only eight had labels. I leaned on the one that said E. Cunningham. It was almost eleven o'clock but there were plenty of lights on in the three stories above the porch. I waited a few moments and then pressed the button again. I was about to start pressing other buttons when I heard a voice say: "Who's down there?"

"Where are you?" I asked, looking up into the darkness.

"Come to the edge of the porch," the voice said.

I walked back the way I had come and descended three steps and looked up. There were four windows along the story above the porch. They were all open and in the far left one a slight black man leaned out. He was wearing a white T-shirt, but I couldn't make out the features of his face.

"Is your name Gene?" I said.

"Who wants to know?" he asked. There was no contempt in the question, just a simple request.

"My name is Leeds. I'm an investigator. I was at the bus motel about three weeks ago. I got into a fight with a driver from Brooklyn named Rocky. He ran away with another guy on a motorcycle."

He was silent for a long time. I was afraid he might go inside and shut the window, but finally he said: "I read about them finding his body in the paper. He clobbered you that day. You had a big shiner. You was tryin' to hide it on the way out, but I seen it. I remember you. You gave me a twenty-dollar bill on the way in."

"That's right," I said. "Did you get a good look at the driver of the motorcycle?"

"No," he said.

"You couldn't give me a description?"

"Not hardly. She buzzed right around the gate on the way in. And then I never did get a look at her on the way out."

"So it was a woman?"

"You bet. You hardly ever see one driving a motorcycle."

He pronounced it moto-sickle. "I figured that's what you two was fightin' about. You see a woman and two guys who look like they been fighting, that tell you the whole damn story."

He laughed, and I began to back down the steps.

"I hope you got a car," he said.

I pointed to the Honda.

"That's good," he said. "This is no place to be walking around at night."

I got in the car and started it. He was still in the window when I pulled away, but he was looking toward the young men on the corner so I didn't wave. Everyone on the corner pretended they didn't notice me when I drove by.

29

I got home Friday at midnight and immediately crashed into bed. The dog had been fed by the time I picked her up at the Sooys' that afternoon so I didn't have any chores to do and could strip to my underwear and slide between the sheets. I was out in a wink and a heartbeat.

It had been a jam-packed week, starting with the discovery of Rocky's body on Monday and ending with the drive to New York and back. I was bushed. Taking Julie to Grace's black-jack table had been a stroke of genius, but finding out that the helmet on the Harley had been a woman, that one was pure luck. It was a lot like my days as a cop. Whenever I had some good luck on a case, it always seemed to come at the end of a great deal of hard work.

Normally, I'll sit up and drink a beer and listen to the radio or read before I turn in, but before I knew what hit me, Suzie was bouncing around my bed while my alarm buzzed in the long morning light of six A.M. I had slept like the dead and, aside from being a little stiff from lying in the same position for six hours, I felt like a million bucks.

I put a pot of coffee on while I washed up and took a cup with me in the car, along with the dog and a shovel. When we got to Batsto Lake, Suzie bolted into the woods as soon as I opened the car door, happy to be on another adventure into the pines. She soon came back to my side and stayed close as I followed the river upstream from the north end of the lake. It was a warm spring morning and there were already several canoes in the water.

Most of the yellow police tape surrounding Rocky's grave was on the ground or tangled in the briars and juniper nearby. Suzie cautiously sniffed at the edges of the pit the police had left behind. I wasn't sure what I was looking for. Maybe the missing .45, the gun that had killed Rocky, or the drug money, which probably never existed. I knew I was out of options at that point. I had a pretty good idea that Stockton and Julie were linked in more ways than I knew, and if there was anything the police hadn't found at this site, father or daughter had plenty of chances to return to get it.

When I stepped into the shallow pit I noticed that there were fresh raccoon tracks down there. The 'coons had scratched a good-sized hole in the center of the pit, and had left a frenzy of prints around the edges. The scent of Rocky's blood leached into the sand must have brought them back to the site in crowds since Monday. I began to lift out shovels full of the stained sand from the center area. I worked slowly and distractedly, thinking about how I could prevent Julie from bolting like her father. I wasn't equipped or financed to zoom all over the world looking for these people. Once they got out of the Bos-Wash Corridor they were gone—good-bye for me, and it was time to move on to the next case. About all I had left in the way of tactics for finding Doc at this point was to follow Julie or confront her with the information I had gathered and make her tell me where her father was. And it seemed unlikely that she would come across with that information since she refused even to talk about him when I mentioned him.

But something had drawn Rocky back here, something that was important enough to trick him into digging his own grave. That's what I hoped to find as I turned out a growing pile of white sand. I stopped to catch my breath and then moved forward a couple of steps and continued digging, expanding the area of my excavation. After a few minutes, the shovel struck something that felt like a pine root. As I squatted to push the sand away from it, a shadow passed over my eyes and skimmed across the white sand. I looked up and saw two turkey buzzards soaring in wide circles above me, and at almost the same instant I became aware of the stench of death in my nostrils. Suddenly I could see that the sand-coated pine root was actually the top of a human head.

I jumped from the pit like I had been bitten by a snake.

Suzie began to bark and dart around in circles thinking I had initiated some chasing game, but when she saw that I was only standing silently over the pit, she came back and peered in with me. She whined quietly when the scent reached her and then looked up at me as if to ask what we were going to do now.

I slid back into the pit and began carefully to scrape away sand with the point of the shovel. The eye sockets were all clotted with sand, and I made no attempt to clean them out, but there was still enough facial flesh clinging to the skull to allow me to recognize Raymond Stockton, politician, father, biker, lover, petty dealer of drugs and user of same. He had been buried deeply, and the police excavation had missed him.

I began quickly to shovel the pile of white sand back into the pit, and when I had covered the putrid face enough to keep the buzzards away, I stood leaning on the shovel, sweating and out of breath.

Forty-five minutes later I was in Julie's condo. I had stopped at the cottage for my little kit of burglary tools, but she had not locked the dead bolt on the top part of her door, and I was able to slip the knob latch with a credit card. The doorman had told me she wasn't home when I came through the lobby, but I gave him a wink and told him I had a key. He recognized me and smiled knowingly.

I had been alone in the apartment before and had nosed around in an orderly way but had found nothing suspicious. This time I tossed the place thoroughly, sifting through every inch of space. I made a mess, but I didn't care. I was hoping to turn up the missing .45. I knew that it would tie her to Rocky's murder. But I would take anything I could get, especially anything that might connect her to Bonnie's death.

I dumped her plants and inspected the soil. I scattered the contents of her spice jars on the kitchen counters. I turned her mattress on edge and cut it open with a butcher knife from the kitchen. At the bottom of her underwear drawer I found the picture that she had showed to Grace's pit boss. In this one

Bonnie was sandwiched between Stockton and Rocky. It had been taken in the same Pines location and was a match to the one I had found in Rocky's travel bag. Julie must have taken it either before or after Rocky had snapped her with Doc and Bonnie. Under the box spring I found a safe deposit box key taped securely to the wooden frame. I slipped it in my pocket along with the picture. On the desk with some of her text-books was a small pile of bills. Her most recent telephone bill was among them and, in addition to some long distance calls to Brooklyn and Philadelphia, I recognized my own number repeated frequently on the list. I went through the rest of the bills and was opening the drawers of her desk when something began to nag at me about that phone bill. When I opened it again, I saw that all the calls to my cottage at the other end of the county were clustered from May 22 onward. There were thirty-two of them from that date to the end of the billing period on May 26, a testament to the obsession that had been our brief affair.

But there were also two calls made on May 9 and May 11. I didn't know Julie then. I hadn't even met her until I drove up to New York a week later. A calendar in the kitchen showed me that May 11 was a Monday. That made it the final night that Bonnie had stayed at my cottage, the night I had gone out with Grace and come home to find Bonnie agitated and hiding in the woods. What could Julie have said over the phone to agitate her? Was it Julie or was it someone else who had called from this phone?

I found the .45 as I was coming out of the kitchen. Julie was standing in the middle of the living room pointing it at my chest.

"What are you doing here?" she asked angrily.

I fought back the urge to put my hands up. I didn't want them to be that far away from my own .45, which was nestled under my armpit.

Keeping the gun leveled at me, she took in the mess in the living room and then edged toward the bedroom door and looked briefly in there. She was wearing cut-off jeans and a red blouse with the front tails tied up in a knot to expose her flat brown stomach. Her legs were tanned too.

"I'm glad you're finally home, Julie," I said. "Someone broke in. The place was a shambles when I got here."

"Fuck you," she shouted. "What are you doing here?"

"Would you put that gun down, Julie? Please."

"How did you get in here?" Her eyes were narrow and suspicious.

"The doorman let me in."

"Bullshit. He said you told him you had a key."

"I thought you had a dance class in Moorestown."

"The gym was locked. We couldn't find the custodian. I finally came home."

"Do you carry that gun around with you all the time?"

"No, but I took it with me today."

"Why?"

"I thought maybe I could get you to meet me in Philly later in the afternoon for a drink."

"And the gun?" I asked, but I already knew the answer.

"I was going to kill you and leave you in the street."

"Look like a robbery?"

"Exactly."

"And now?"

"I'm just going to kill you."

"Here?"

"You're burglarizing my apartment."

"It's over, Julie. I dug Doc up this morning at Constable Bridge."

She looked startled and even backed up a step.

"And I just called that detective from Columbia Township, McKelvey," I said. "I told him everything. He knows I'm here."

"You're full of shit."

"He's on his way over here," I said. She took several steps backwards and slipped the chain lock on the door without taking her eyes off me. I had never looked down the business end of a hostile .45 before. It seemed much bigger from that angle. I didn't know if she would kill me or not. Her eyes were empty of emotion, but I had seen them fill quickly with hate before.

"Where's the money?" I asked.

"What money?"

"Your father's money."

"Raymond didn't have any money."

"What about the drug deal?"

"The drug deal was all air," she said. "Rocky set it up to scam Raymond out of his savings." As she said this she moved across the living room to the balcony doors to make sure they were locked. Morning sunlight fell across her strawberry blonde hair.

"So he withdrew forty-two thousand dollars to make the buy?" I asked.

"Nosy little bastard, aren't you? Looking around and looking around. I shouldn't have given you the key to the house in Linwood. I only wanted you to think he took that money for his getaway. I thought you were interested in me; that we had something going. Otherwise I wouldn't have given you that key."

"We did have something going," I lied. "We still could."

She moved out of the sunlight and smirked at me.

"It's too late," she said. "The money's in my safe deposit box. It's mine now, and I deserve every penny of it."

"Why?"

"For the shit I put up with from him," she said angrily.

"What kind of shit?"

"Don't you worry about it."

"Did you kill him?"

"Who?"

"Doc."

"No, Rocky did. I told him to."

"Why?"

"Because I told him to," she repeated loudly. "Rocky would have done anything for me. And, the forty-two thousand dollars was a lot of money to him."

"Why did you tell him to kill Doc?"

"Because I wanted him dead. I've wanted him dead for a long time. A long time."

"Why?"

"Because I did. That's all you need to know. You're going to die anyway, so that's all you need to know." Her voice rose in anger again.

"How did Rocky kill him?"

"He shot him. We took the canoe up the river. They were doing coke and drinking Jack Daniels. Raymond was untying the canoe. Rocky shot him."

"Just shot him. For no reason."

"They were arguing."

"What about? Bonnie?"

"You're very perceptive."

"That's usually what men argue about. Women."

"She egged him on. He just couldn't keep his hands off her. She was a little slut."

"Did he kill her?"

"She was a slut. She slept with Raymond. Can you believe that?" She chuckled. "She fell for that sanctimonious bullshit he used on all the newcomers."

"What newcomers?"

"In his addiction programs. He used twelve-step programs to find vulnerable women. The thirteenth step. AA was like his orchard."

"Did he kill Bonnie?"

"Who?"

"Your father."

"He was already dead by the time Bonnie died. I knew she'd tell someone eventually. I thought she told you, but after you and I spent that weekend here, I knew that she didn't."

"Why did you kill Rocky?"

"Because you were on to him. And I knew you'd find him. He was getting too far into heroin and I kept having to give him money. And then he said he was going back to that girl who was going to have his baby. And get into a methadone program or a drug rehab. He was the last link. I told him we had to move Raymond's body because I was afraid animals would dig it up and hikers would find it. As long as everyone believed Raymond was on the run from bikers and the mob and the police, no one even suspected he was dead."

"And they could blame everything on him."

"That was the plan."

"So you went back to Doc's grave and Rocky started to dig and—"

"And when I thought the hole was deep enough, I shot him."

"And you thought that was the end of it."

"It was. Even if they found Rocky, Raymond was still missing and I knew they would say he killed Rocky."

"You were right."

"Except for you. You just kept coming. Even when the police were finished."

"Why didn't you kill me?"

"I thought I could scare you off. But you don't scare."

"That's why you sent Rocky and that other goon to my cottage."

"That other goon was the guy you killed at the hunting camp. His name was Marbles, possibly because he didn't have all of his own, and he was totally devoted to Raymond. He thought Raymond was alive and well in Florida and calling me with orders. We were going to kill you and plant you at the hunting camp. Let Raymond take the rap. But you came from the wrong direction and got the jump on him."

"I got lost."

"I was going to push you off the balcony here one night too. But they would have tied it to me and it would have opened a can of worms. One night I even drove out to your cottage to shoot you, but you weren't home."

"I was there. I saw you from the window. My car was at the marina."

"You're a lucky bastard . . . until now. It's a shame I have to kill you here. You'll make a mess. I don't suppose I could persuade you to jump off the balcony."

"I don't think so," I said.

"It's better to shoot you as an intruder anyway. You know I had everything under control. Bonnie was an accidental overdose. And Raymond would get blamed for killing Rocky. And they would never find Raymond. Case closed. But you kept coming."

"I was convinced Doc killed Rocky too until a blackjack dealer at the Castle identified you."

"You son of a bitch. That's why you took me there."

"The guard at Andersen's made you too. The day you

came in on Doc's motorcycle. It's all around you now, Julie. You can't get out of it. The police know. They'll be here any minute. Why don't you give me the gun?"

A little smile crossed her face and she didn't answer me. Keeping the gun leveled at me, she slipped her thumb into her shorts and popped the button at the top of the fly. The jeans were very tight and sprang open exposing more of her flat stomach and the top of her red panties.

"If I give you the gun, will you make love to me?"

"How did you kill Bonnie?"

"Will you get on your knees and kiss me and lick me and put your fingers in me until I come?"

"Tell me how you killed Bonnie."

She had a dreamy look on her face. "With drugs," she said.

"What kind of drugs?"

"Dilaudid. Morphine. Heroin. Fentanyl."

She hooked her thumb into the waist of the shorts and wiggled them down over her hips until they dropped with a soft thud at her ankles.

"Did Rocky help you?"

"Rocky never did anything. He bought the drugs, but all he wanted to do was get high. He couldn't get it up half the time. He was useless."

"Not so useless that he couldn't kill your father."

"He didn't kill Raymond. I did." She had a crazy triumphant smile on her face.

"You just told me Rocky killed him."

"I lied."

She laughed but her eyes bounced around nervously. She was suddenly very agitated, and I worried about her finger on the trigger of the .45.

"Actually, it was sort of like Rocky did it," she continued. "He was the one who was supposed to do it. He was going to do it that night. He agreed to. Doc had just taken the money out of the bank."

"How did you kill him?"

She hesitated and I didn't think she was going to tell me. She was looking around the room like she was trying to find a way to leave. Suddenly she met my eyes and said defiantly: "I shot him."

"Where?"

"At Linwood. I just shot him once, but he bled like a stuck pig. Fortunately he was in the bath tub."

"Why did you kill him?"

"Bonnie was there. I had been looking for her for three days. She was staying there with him. I caught them taking a bath together. When I ran into you at Rocky's motel, it had just happened. I was coming to get Rocky to help me get the body out of the house."

"Did Bonnie help you too?"

"No, she was scared to death. She couldn't stop crying."

"Why didn't you kill her then?"

"She wasn't there when we got back. Besides, she was my friend. I didn't think I needed to. But Rocky got me worked up about her later. He said she would tell people."

"You called her at my cottage. How did you know she was there?"

"I got lucky. After I got Rocky away from you at the motel, he told me your name, and I looked you up in the phone book. I called that night and got your machine. I tried it two nights later and Bonnie answered."

"Whatever you said scared her. She left the next day."

"I told her that if she stayed in Jersey, she was going to get hurt. I'm sorry if I messed up your sex life."

"I wasn't sleeping with her."

"Why not? Everyone else was."

"Not my type."

"Am I your type?" she asked.

I didn't answer her. She smiled and hooked a thumb under the elastic waistband of her bikini panties and pulled them down over the thin line of white flesh on one brown hip. Keeping me covered, she reached across herself and slid them down over the other hip. They whispered to her ankles with the shorts, and she stepped away from the pile. The faint odor of her musk hit my nostrils, tangy, exciting. I could feel a stirring in my crotch. It was the first time in my life I had ever had an erection with a .45 pointed at my heart.

"Why don't you put the gun down and come over here?" I said.

For an answer she began to unbutton the red blouse. After the second button, I could see that there was no bra under it.

"How did you kill Bonnie?" I asked. She had the blouse unbuttoned but didn't take it off.

"Rocky and I drove to New York, and I called her," she said. "She agreed to meet me for lunch," she said. "We went to a Thai place in Brooklyn Heights. I put Dilaudid in her curry."

"What's Dilaudid?"

"It's a synthetic morphine. Pharmaceutical. Very expensive on the street. Very powerful. She was nodding out by the time we left the restaurant. She went to sleep in my car, and I shot her up with heroin and brought her back to Jersey."

"Where did you keep her?"

"At the hunting club."

"Was Rocky with you?"

"Of course. He bought the drugs in New York. I didn't know how to get that stuff."

"Who kept shooting her up?"

"Me."

"Just you? Not Rocky too? The pathologist who autopsied her body said it was done by an expert."

"I've had plenty of practice."

"On yourself?"

"No, I never used drugs. Raymond used to make me shoot him up."

"When? Recently?"

"No, when I was a kid. I wouldn't do it now. Are you crazy?"

"How old were you?"

"The first time I did it, I was eleven."

It was difficult to think of anything to say with that image in my mind's eye.

"He told me it was medicine," she said, wanting to finish the confession.

"Did your mother know?"

"She didn't even know he was a drug addict until right

before she left him. She was incredibly naive. I think it scared her and she didn't want to know. So she pretended she didn't see it. When she found out, she just left. "

"How did she find out?"

"She caught us. She didn't pack anything. Just put her coat on and left. I'll never forget the look on her face. He scared her. It was long overdue, her leaving him. I went out to Oregon two years ago and tried to see her. She wouldn't return any of my phone calls from the motel and when I went to her house, she wouldn't answer the door. She'll be glad he's dead."

She started to say something else but bit it off and glared at me.

"You just keep pushing and pushing, don't you?" she said angrily.

Again I couldn't think of anything to say. I was sure she was going to shoot me. Her body began to tremble and her breasts shook inside the red blouse.

"How old were you when she caught you?" I blurted it out.

"Shut up," she screamed. Tears welled up in her eyes and spilled down her cheeks.

"Julie, I—"

"Shut up." She screamed it again, her face distorted with pain and anger.

I extended my arms and took a step toward her.

"Get back." Her voice exploded. I froze again.

"You think you have some rights, don't you? Some rights in this matter. You think you can comfort me. You actually think you can make me feel better; fix me. But you can't. I don't need you. Don't you see that? I don't need you or any other man to like me, to approve of me. Why do you think I need you? Because I slept with you? You think you can help me? Or save me? What a joke.

"It was classic. He used to make me feel like it was my idea that we had sex. The child abuser always makes his victim feel that there is some consent on her part. I won't tell Mommy if you don't. He did the same thing with drugs. We smoked pot and had a lot of giggles and a couple of times we even sniffed heroin until I refused to do that any more.

"When I fucked you . . . " She gagged but didn't take her eyes off me.

"When I fucked you or any other man, it was like I was washing him away. Do you understand that? Like I was cleansing myself of his presence, of ever having him inside my body, in my mouth. He used to make me blow him. That's how we started. In a shower at a campground when I was eleven. He used to come into my room to kiss me good night, and one kiss led to another. I was eleven years old. It didn't stop until I was a freshman in college."

She sobbed and I moved quickly to her and took the gun away. She gave it up easily. I reached down and separated her shorts from the pile on the floor and handed them to her. She slipped into them and zipped the fly and buttoned the waist button. She had to tilt her head to the side to see what she was doing through her tears. I led her over to the couch, and she sat down numbly without looking at me.

After a long while, I asked: "How did you get Bonnie into that park?"

"She walked in." She said it almost in a whisper.

"Walked?"

"She was loaded with heroin. We let her out of the car at about four in the morning and told her to go sit on the bench. She was a good little zombie by then and did what she was told. I had just popped her in the butt with enough street fentanyl to kill King Kong and wiped the needle down and handed it to her. We didn't really care what she did. We knew she'd be dead in an hour, or maybe twenty minutes if we were lucky. She walked in and sat down and we took off. The rest is history."

I tried not to think about Bonnie. And about Marcy Park in the dead of night in a dead-end neighborhood in a Brooklyn ghetto. It made me feel lonely and far away.

I put Julie's gun in my pants pocket and took my own .45 out of the holster and pulled the slide back to throw a bullet into the chamber. I didn't point it at her, just kept it ready in case she got her nerve back and tried something. Then I dialed 911 and told the woman who answered where we were and what was going on.

EPILOGUE

I was sitting on one of the stools Thelma keeps at the little wallet and perfume counter in the back of her boutique while Grace Somers browsed a rack of cotton summer cardigans nearby. It was six-thirty and Thelma was at the front of the store locking up. Grace put on a navy blue sweater and walked to a three-panel mirror beside the rack to get a rearview of the sweater's length. She turned her head over her shoulder and stretched up on her toes, a move that exaggerated the curve and fold of muscles in her calves. She glanced at me and caught me admiring those calves and the rest of the length of her and she smiled. I smiled back. We had reservations for dinner at seven-thirty at the Longport Inn. I had told her I would take her anywhere except the Crab Pot, the restaurant Julie and I had gone to on our first date.

Thelma had just let Bay-ling Kravitz out, and I could hear her telling a persistent customer out on the sidewalk that the store was now closed. When she came back to the counter, she was a little perturbed.

"The summer is here," she said, sliding up on the other stool. "Obnoxious shoobies, God bless them. That woman wanted to come in and browse while I closed the register. She even promised not to buy anything so it wouldn't mess up my count."

"Those obnoxious shoobies give you a lot of business, don't they?" I asked.

"We take in seventy-five percent of the year's gross between the Fourth of July and Labor Day."

Grace hung the blue sweater up carefully and joined us,

and when she did, Thelma slid off her stool. "Let's go back to my office and have a drink," she said. "If we stay out here, they'll see us and knock on the door."

"Maybe you should stay open longer."

"I'll be open until ten starting tomorrow. I have two new college girls coming to work in the morning." She smirked lecherously at me, hiding her face from Grace.

Her office was air-conditioned and chilly. The blinds were half-closed against the setting sun, the slats casting a striped shadow pattern on the far wall. It was a nice office, nicer than mine upstairs. It was actually a suite. The business area had a huge mahogany desk, computer, filing cabinets and book-shelves. Another separate area contained throw rugs, a couch and two easy chairs and a small kitchenette. Grace asked for club soda, and Thelma poured herself and me three fingers of Johnnie Walker Black, neat.

"Want to join us for dinner?" I asked. "Our reservations are for seven-thirty."

She finished handing our drinks out and plopped down in one of the chairs. "I can't," she said. "I get together with a bunch of ladies one night a month. We're mostly widows, six to eight of us, sometimes nine."

"Mah-jongg?" I asked.

"It's a very serious poker game, wise guy. So serious, you couldn't afford it."

Grace laughed.

"Actually, I'd love to be with you," Thelma said. "But it's my turn to play host, so I can't back out. So you've got about forty-five minutes to give me all the gory details."

"I don't know where to start," I said.

"How about at the beginning. Or better yet, the end. Where is Julie now?"

"There are a lot of jurisdictions involved, including New York City, so I think the state police have her somewhere, probably Trenton. The last time I talked to McKelvey, he'd had a call from the FBI too."

"What will happen to her?"

"With murders in two states, I think she'll be away for a long time."

"What about your friend, the pimp?"

"The Baron?" I said. "He's not a pimp. He's a lighting contractor."

"He dresses like a pimp."

"I know. He told me I dressed like a preppie. Charges against him were dropped two days ago. They never had a case."

"Julie created a lot of confusion, didn't she? She was a clever girl. It was really a perfect set-up for her, wasn't it? She would have gotten away with it if you hadn't been so persistent."

"You give me too much credit, Thelma. It was unraveling on her, and she knew it. That's why she broke into my office upstairs. To see if she could find out what I knew. She took that Polaroid and the computer-sorted phone list you had made. She knew I would suspect her because of that material, so she began to zero in on me."

"That was her that came over the roof? What a desperado."

"It certainly wasn't Doc like I first thought. He was dead already. I think somebody else would have found those bodies eventually."

"But the police wouldn't have identified them," she said. "Julie had every angle covered. It was supposed to look like a mob hit. The wiseguys from Philly do a lot of that sort of planting in the Pines."

"How do you know that?"

"I read the papers. Deer hunters and berry pickers are always coming across buried corpses way back in there. But when? So they came across Rocky and Doc two years from now; they'd just be another bag of bones. Two bags."

"Anyway," I continued, "the mob, or rather the people in Philadelphia and New York who might have participated in something like this, didn't know about it and didn't care. Nobody stole any drugs or money from them. The only victim was Doc and his savings. They even drove his car to Philly and left it on the street without the plates to make sure it got stripped. The rest was Rocky's smoke screen with a little help from Russo, his employer, in New York. Russo would tell people that the mob was looking for Rocky, but Russo's secretary never saw any of it.

"They were dopes, screwups, especially Doc. The potential to run a profitable lab from the hunting camp was there, but he used too much of his own product and it never got off the ground. Even criminal activities take some work and management. Rocky was a small-time hustler, and light on brains. He wanted to be a criminal, but he couldn't figure out how to be, so he drove a bus to supplement his income, sort of like an actor who works as a waiter.

"The only one who wasn't a screwup was Julie. She saw, in Rocky's friendship with her father and their dumb shady ambitions, an opportunity to do her father in. And when she dangled it in front of Rocky, he saw it as an opportunity to take more from Doc than he could ever make as his partner. I don't think Rocky realized he was Julie's dupe until the first slug hit him after he had dug his own grave out there at Constable Bridge. Unfortunately, Bonnie got caught up in this whirlpool."

"Where did they meet?" Grace asked. Thelma and I glanced at each other. I was a little leery about giving Grace all the lurid details. She had already walked away from me once because some bikers had frightened her.

"They met at a support group."

"What kind of support group?" She wasn't going to let me be vague.

"For incest survivors."

We avoided each other's eyes, and there was a long silence in the room. I knew Grace was shocked. Finally she said: "They were both so respectable on the surface. One from a wealthy family, the other from a professional background. It's the kind of thing you'd expect out in the Pines; inbreeding, I mean . . . "

She stopped, embarrassed, and I jumped in and hurried on.

"Bonnie had a drug and alcohol problem and Julie got her to start going to NA and AA meetings. That's where she met Rocky, and through him, Doc."

"So Julie took Rocky away from Bonnie, right?" Thelma asked, and I nodded. "She could get any man she wanted," she continued, her eyes locking for a moment on mine. I became aware of a sinking feeling in my stomach that bringing Grace there wasn't really a good idea.

"But she had such contempt for men in general, and a deep-seated hatred of her father, that men meant little to her except as she could use them for her own gain. Women meant little to her too, especially if they got in her way. Bonnie may have been an incest survivor, but she was definitely not a Julie survivor."

I finished the last of my Scotch and looked at my watch. It wasn't quite seven and the restaurant was only five minutes away. I was thinking of a way to end the conversation and leave, but Thelma wasn't about to let me get away. She brought the bottle over and poured me another healthy splash.

"I don't understand why they took her back to New York," Grace said. "They had made up their minds to kill her. Why not bury her in the woods too?"

Thelma smiled because she knew the answer to that one.

"They didn't want any connections made to Doc's killing," I said. "Even though they didn't plan on his body being found, Julie was bright enough to know that if they planted Bonnie near where she had disappeared in Brooklyn, no connection would ever be made to anything that happened in South Jersey. In fact, while we were waiting for the police yesterday at her apartment, she told me that Rocky and she had argued about it, and that he hadn't wanted to bother taking Bonnie's body back to the city. It gave Julie a fairly good alibi too. She went to work the next day as if she'd spent the night at home, although from midnight to five A.M. she'd been on the road with Rocky disposing of Bonnie."

"When you went up to the funeral—" Thelma said.

"Memorial service," I corrected.

"When you went to the memorial service, did you suspect her then? She was there, right?"

"I suspected everyone at the service. It's the way I was trained. But she couldn't have put Bonnie in that park by herself, even if Bonnie did walk in. Until I began to connect her to Rocky, she was way down on my list. Everyone else close to

Bonnie had a better motive. Julie never really fit any scheme . . . until the moment I realized I was digging up Doc's body from that spot where we found Rocky."

"She came very close to succeeding, didn't she?" Thelma said. "You were the last obstacle. If she could have killed you and blamed it on a chance street crime or on the fugitive Doc, she would have been free."

"She had it pretty well cleaned up, I guess."

"She needed to draw you into a vulnerable spot and pop you."

"But she didn't." I frowned at Thelma. I wanted her off the subject of Julie and myself.

Thelma took the hint and asked: "Why was Bonnie's I.D. in her underwear?"

"Julie wanted people to know who she was. She didn't want the body lost forever in some city morgue. Her identity created the scenario Julie needed to divert the police from a serious investigation. Rich girl junky overdoses in needle park. The police bought it and shelved the case right away, especially with Ben Arnold's pressure to put a lid on it."

"Is he pleased? Or does the publicity bother him?"

"No, he's pleased. The media now have Bonnie painted as the innocent victim. They don't have all the sticky details, so they put a nice neat label on her as sweet, put-upon thing, earnest student-artist victim etcetera, which keeps the Arnold family nose clean, at least in the public eye. What's left of the family, that is."

"Sad," Thelma said.

"Not that sad. He sent me a check for five thousand dollars today."

"Whoopee. You owe me a dinner."

"Why?" I teased.

"For helping you find Rocky's body."

"When you saw that corpse, I thought you would die too. And then I'd have had two bodies on my hands. You were more trouble than help that day."

"Well then, for all the deductive work I did on this case up there in your office."

"Send me a bill," I said. I stood up and Grace followed my lead. "How about tomorrow around five-ish?" I asked. "I'm going to the Baron and Irene's for a barbecue."

"Love to," she said. "We can drink some more Scotch and talk about murder and mayhem all night."

"They don't drink."

"Can we bring our own?"

"I'll find out."

"I wish I could go tonight," Thelma said.

"Do you want to go tomorrow night?" I asked, turning to Grace.

"I thought we were taking this one date at a time," she said. "I have to work tomorrow night anyway."

I looked at Thelma and smiled and shrugged.

"I'll see you tomorrow," I said.

I took Grace's elbow and steered her to the front door and turned the bolt and let us out. Thelma locked the door behind us and waved as we walked down Ventnor Avenue toward the Honda. The sun sat blood red over the marshes and bay, and the air was still and warm, like the prelude to a pleasant mid-summer night. Grace's eyes met mine when I opened the car door for her. She smiled and slid into the passenger seat, and I returned the smile and shut the door.